Those
Who Favor
Fire

To my family

Those Who Favor Fire

Those
Who Favor
Fire

A Novel

Lauren Wolk

RANDOM HOUSE

NEW YORK

Grateful acknowledgment is made to the following for permission to reprint previously published material:

EDNA ST. VINCENT MILLAY SOCIETY: "Dirge Without Music" from *Collected Poems* by Edna St. Vincent Millay (HarperCollins). Copyright © 1928, 1955 by Edna St. Vincent Millay and Norma Millay Ellis. All rights reserved. Reprinted by permission of Elizabeth Barnett, Literary Executor.

FAMOUS MUSIC CORPORATION: Excerpt from "Moon River" by Johnny Mercer and Henry Mancini. Copyright © 1961 by Famous Music Corporation. Copyright renewed 1989 by Famous Music Corporation. Reprinted by permission of Famous Music Corporation.

HENRY HOLT AND COMPANY, INC., AND JONATHAN CAPE, A DIVISION OF RANDOM HOUSE UK: "Fire and Ice," the final stanza of "Reluctance," and title usage of one line from "Fire and Ice" from *The Poetry of Robert Frost,* edited by Edward Connery Lathem. Copyright © 1951, 1962 by Robert Frost. Copyright © 1923, 1934, 1969 by Henry Holt and Company, Inc. Rights throughout the British Commonwealth are controlled by Jonathan Cape, a division of Random House UK. Reprinted by permission of Henry Holt and Company, Inc., and Jonathan Cape, a division of Random House UK.

POLYGRAM MUSIC PUBLISHING: Excerpt from "Midnight Train to Georgia" by James D. Weatherly. Copyright © 1971 by Polygram International Publishing, Inc. All rights reserved. Reprinted by permission of Polygram Music Publishing.

Library of Congress Cataloging-in-Publication Data
Wolk, Lauren.
Those who favor fire: a novel / Lauren Wolk.
p.   cm.
ISBN 978-0-812-99240-3
I. Title.
PS3573.05652T48   1998
813'.54—dc21   97-39827

Random House website address: www.randomhouse.com
Printed in the United States of America on acid-free paper

BVG 01

BOOK DESIGN BY BARBARA M. BACHMAN

146484122

Book
One

When a spider plunges from a fixed point

to its consequences, it always sees before

it an empty space where it can never set foot,

no matter how it wriggles.

— SØREN KIERKEGAARD, *from* Either/Or

Chapter 1

Halloween was hellish in Belle Haven. It hadn't always been that way, except in the minds of its small children, who could not imagine that the world had been any different—that there had even *been* a world—before their own momentous arrival in it. But the year that Mary Beth Sanderson died, Halloween was, at best, impure, corrupted by its cavalier association with the dead and dying both. Less than a week had passed since the earth had opened up and taken Mary Beth, and the town was still in mourning. But Halloween was Halloween, and the people of Belle Haven went about the whole thing with the last of their resolve.

It was as if they couldn't pass up the chance to polish Belle Haven's silver lining, to flash it one last time in the cool light of an indulgent moon. Despite misgivings, those who had not yet left Belle Haven carved their jack-o'-lanterns with exceptional precision, decorated their trees with elaborate ghouls, and chose their candies with care. Then they entrusted their children to the uncertain dusk, warning them to beware not of child snatchers or rapists or bullies but of the very ground they walked on.

Living on top of a fire makes people cautious. It makes them wonder whether a flaming tentacle is at this moment winding its way toward the root cellar. It makes them walk softly and sniff the air for sulfur like a species of strange, two-legged deer. It makes them fight amongst themselves when the conversation turns to the tired old question, now nearly moot, of whether they should pack their bags and leave or stay and, quite possibly, die.

• • •

Rachel Hearn had listened to such arguments for a long time now—in the grocery store, at the post office, on the radio, in the street. She understood the urge to go as well as the resolve to stay. She even understood the really stubborn ones who saw the boreholes spouting their plumes of yellow smoke, who watched litter turn to ash as it blew across the hot ground, who had known Mary Beth Sanderson for every one of her thirteen years and still refused to take the fire at its word.

"It'll never get us," they'd say. "The fire's nowhere near my house." But they all owned canaries and kept one eye on the ground.

Rachel Hearn thought there were simply too many pianos.

"What the hell are you talking about?" asked Joe. Most people knew him by this name alone. Just Joe. "What in blazes have pianos got to do with the fire?" (Fire puns, intended or not, were an accepted and rarely acknowledged part of conversation in Belle Haven.)

Joe was sitting on a tree stump this Halloween night, dressed as a troll, eating a huge, tight-skinned MacIntosh and watching a handful of children sneak slowly down the street toward him. To cross the old and narrow bridge that took Maple Street over Raccoon Creek, the children had to first pass close to the stump where Joe sat, collecting his toll. Rachel, done up as a witch, perched on the rail of the bridge, swung her feet in their tall boots, and absently stabbed her own palms with her sharp witch's nails.

She said, "I once heard someone say that the reason more Jews didn't try to escape Nazi Germany before it was too late was because they couldn't bear to leave their pianos behind." In the face of Joe's silence, she hunched inside her tattered gown and closed her eyes, lulled by the language of the water passing under the bridge. "Too many roots," she explained, "that went too deep."

Joe had a different theory. *They're paralyzed,* he said to himself, wiping the apple juice from his chin. *Paralyzed.* He said it with gentle contempt, exasperation, and great fondness.

Whenever people asked Joe whether he was going to stay or leave, he'd say, "Why the hell do you care what I do? What in hell is the point of even asking?" But everyone knew that he would leave only when Rachel did, perhaps with her, perhaps alone.

Hell was a word heard often in Belle Haven. The reporters who had been coming into town lately never failed to ask, in the rare interviews they were granted, "Do you think of this fire as a sort of hell?" Then, glancing casually at their notes, they'd drop names from Dante and paraphrase the Bible, all the while wielding their microphones like weapons.

None of them expected much from Joe. Most passed him by altogether. His clothes were threadbare, his hands were thick with calluses, and the expression on his face was meant to discourage their intrusions. But a few, hoping to add color to their copy, laid their analogies carefully before him, smiled with impatience, pronounced him illiterate with their judge-and-jury eyes. Joe invariably backed away down the street, saying, as he walked, in a slow and thoughtful way,

> *Some say the world will end in fire,*
> *Some say in ice.*
> *From what I've tasted of desire*
> *I hold with those who favor fire.*
> *But if it had to perish twice,*
> *I think I know enough of hate*
> *To say that for destruction ice*
> *Is also great*
> *And would suffice.*

"I'm sorry," he would say over his shoulder. " 'Fire and Ice.' Robert Frost. Not mine, although I, too, favor fire."

Now, from his lookout on the tree stump, Joe watched the trick-or-treaters inch toward him, giggling with fear. Nearly at his feet, wary of his big troll hands, they stopped, reached into their candy sacks, and pulled out the apples they'd been given by the few old ladies who still refused to leave Belle Haven to its fire. The children placed the apples carefully into the bushel basket that Joe used to collect his toll each year.

"Pass," he growled, waggling his horns at them. At this, even the older children trotted across the bridge, laughing like goats, all real fears forgotten.

The children gone, Joe polished up their grubby apples, made adjustments to his costume, and studied the stars. "How's business been this year?" Rachel asked him, and her voice, in this lull, sounded too loud, too old.

"Terrible," he said and, shrugging, managed to look endearing despite the tufts of green hair that sprouted wildly from his ears.

"I ran into Anne Schifflebien at the Superette last week," Rachel said, easing down off the rail to take up a new spot beside him where she could see his face and he could see hers if he chose to. "She seems to think there's something not quite right about a grown man extorting apples from children."

"I'm the troll," Joe replied, tilting his head back for a better look at the Seven Sisters. "It's my job."

"She said you've forced her into giving Cracker Jacks this year."

"I'm evil, I am," Joe said. He picked out an apple and offered it to Rachel.

Rachel returned to the rail for a while, eating her apple, and watched the occasional children pass, but she soon began to feel that she was spoiling the whole thing, despite her witch's rig. The bridge was Joe's domain this night, not hers. She'd already taken her basket of candies down to the huge willow tree in the park by the school where the children knew they'd find her, a tigress one year, an octopus the next, crouching or coiled among the branches, waiting to drop treats into their gaping bags. They had liked her as a witch, they said, because of the glow-in-the-dark spiral that climbed up her wonderfully pointed hat.

"I'll eat you up, my little pretties," she had cackled in reply and showered them with chocolate kisses wrapped in foil.

But that was all done with, and Rachel could not think of a way to make the night begin again. So she gained her feet, thanked Joe for the apple, and walked off down the street, her long black gown trailing behind her, a distant portion of red, smouldering horizon catching her in silhouette. *My, my,* thought Joe. *What a beautiful witch she makes.*

Rachel Hearn was twenty-three years old. The fire that burned under Belle Haven had started shortly after her tenth birthday. Garbage dumped for years in an old mine pit two miles from her house had somehow caught fire, and the flames had crept hungrily underground. They had followed shafts rich in timber straight down to the tunnels, to a feast of unmined coal, and had fed on coal veins ever since—slowly, quietly, but without pause. The government had sent experts in to track the fire, measure its girth, forecast its activity, predict its demise. Some said it would burn for a thousand years.

If not for the violence of its repercussions, this deliberate, nearly placid progression might have seemed more bovine than anything else. But, like the anaconda, it tended to creep up on its victims. Most easily, perhaps, on the swiftest among them, those most certain of their chances of escape.

There were now several places in Belle Haven where the ground had caved in without warning, where the heat coming up from below was 500 degrees Fahrenheit. And although boreholes had been drilled throughout the town to vent the fire's hideous, sulfurous fumes, every basement was equipped with a monitor that sniffed the air filtering up through the ground and sounded an alarm at the scent of poison coming quietly in.

Rachel often wondered about the canaries imprisoned throughout the town. Would someone deeply asleep, full of meat loaf and parsley potatoes and lemon chiffon pie, be awakened by the death throes of a small, yellow bird grown tired and dispirited from a life behind bars?

She had once considered equipping herself with a canary or two and had even gone so far as to visit the pet shop over in Randall. BUDGIE BLOWOUT said the sign in the window. BUY ONE, GET ONE FREE. Inside, she had followed the bird sounds to the cages at the back of the shop.

Some were awhirl with parakeets: lime green, purple, yellow, spring sky blue. They had black-and-white wings, small white faces, black eyes. The bigger parrots, spotting Rachel at their cages, stuck out their tough little tongues. One had zebra stripes around his eyes, white, leathery cheeks, and a long, blue, lady's-hat tail. Another had a white cowlick and a blue-rimmed eye, his partner a green cap and a black beard. The canaries were a feeble yellow. The jungle-colored lovebirds in the cage next to them looked as if they were dying.

The last cage Rachel came to held two Mollucan cockatoos. They were big birds, white with bright yellow underwings. They were cleaning each other and ignored her as she stepped before their cage. They didn't seem to notice the din around them. It was as if they were sitting in a clean and wonderfully distant rain-forest. The sign on their cage said they'd been marked down from $799.00 to $699.99. Rachel left the store without a canary. She would never have a bird for a pet. That much she knew.

Instead, Rachel had dozens of spider plants, which had grown plump and juicy on their diet of tainted air. At least as many spiders roamed unchallenged through her house, kept the plants free of pests, and, said Rachel, brought her luck.

"Never kill a spider unless it's as big as a Buick," she had once told Ed, the mailman, when he arrived on her front porch to find her rescuing a sack of baby spiders from her mailbox, just in time.

She felt equally protective about all of the more vulnerable creatures with whom she shared her patch of ground. After a heavy rain she'd don slicker and rain boots, grab her worm spatula, and head for her front walk. She'd scoop up the half-drowned worms that were dragging themselves raw across her walkway and put them in a nice, dry, loamy place in the lee of her compost heap. Rachel Hearn had the richest compost in Belle Haven. In the springtime, when young frogs filled the twilight with their unearthly song and insisted on crossing the roads, cars notwithstanding, Rachel never drove on country lanes after sundown. And in the summer, loath to spill poison into the ground or spew it into the air, she relied on ladybugs to keep the aphids from her roses.

For only seven dollars and fifty cents, Rachel had once ordered a thousand ladybugs from a catalogue. When they'd arrived, stunned and angry, Rachel had sat down and cried over her complicity. A thousand ladybugs packed into a mesh bag, folded up into a cardboard carton, and sent tumbling through the postal system had been delivered into her hands, and she was nearly sure that she could hear them weeping. She had waited until the cool of the evening and then set the open package among her roses, but when she returned in the morning she found that the box was still nearly full of ladybugs. It took hours of careful prodding before they began to leave of their own accord, and then the exodus began in earnest. They stumbled out in their endearing way, so perfect, the kind of bugs Disney might have invented, and took refuge in her incredible garden.

If they were confused by the fact that every single plant in this garden—from tulip to lilac—was cradled in its own spectacular pot, they never let on. Perhaps they were charmed by the pots, which Rachel made with her hands, her wheel, and her kiln. Most were wrapped in brilliant ribbons of color, glazed to gleam in all kinds of weather, and fashioned with such care that they never toppled, not even in storms. Rachel had been told that the hill on which her house stood was relatively safe, for there were no mine tunnels directly below her, no coal to speak of, not that anyone knew of, right close by. But Rachel had come to be a skeptic of sorts and was loath to plant her flowers where the fire might, on a whim, bake them black.

"And what do you plan to do if things heat up too much around here?" Joe had once asked her as she filled the back of a huge ceramic turtle with nasturtiums. "Those pots will turn right into ovens, Rachel."

"That day may never come," she had replied, her eyes on her work, "so why think about it now?"

In much the same way, Rachel had never liked to think about the monitor in her cellar, the changing configuration of the fire, the parents who bundled up their pallid babies and put Belle Haven behind them, sorrow and resignation clear in every step they took away from town. But eventually the fire had given her no other choice but to look straight into its face and admit the very things she had fought so hard to deny.

As she climbed the front steps of her hilltop house this Halloween night, Rachel turned to gaze for a moment at the cauldrons that had laid claim across the northern fields. Whenever the fire climbed close to the crusty skin of the earth, whenever it broke through, it made an angry sore that oozed and bubbled and pulsed. Rachel forced herself to stay a while longer, to watch the fire burning until her eyes began to ache. Then, chilled by the sight and by the impartial autumn air, Rachel went inside her beloved house, trembling with prayers, searching for but not finding a way to stop this night from its progression.

By the time Rachel had made her way to her bedroom, Joe had found his way slowly through the woods behind her house, covered his apples with a bit of canvas to keep off the frost, and climbed the ladder to his house. He'd built it in a mighty walnut tree on land he didn't own, with wood he'd salvaged from fallen barns near and far, with nails others had given him outright, with his own potent sweat.

He would never again sleep in this refuge. The fire had come, winter was close behind it, and much as he loved this place, he would not die for it. But on this Halloween night he was content, unafraid, wrapped in worn but mended blankets, and could see the stars without even opening his eyes.

Chapter 2

It was easy for the people of Belle Haven to remember the day when the fire began. Most of them had been at the Fourth of July parade, in itself quite memorable and as perfect a companion for a fire's genesis as anyone could want. When Rachel thought about that day she often wondered how much of her memory was authentic, pure, and how much had been garnered from more than a decade of conversations, of all the things said and written about the fire, of scrapbooks and church sermons and the songs children made up when they skipped rope. In a way it didn't matter. Whether her memory of that day was purely her own or a blending of things she'd encountered since, Rachel knew that it was in many ways her most important recollection, one that was somehow linked to all the rest, even those from much further back into childhood. For her, as for most people in Belle Haven, the fire was a landmark against which nearly all events were measured. Things had happened either before or after the fire took root: births, deaths, marriages, divorces, catastrophes, celebrations. There were other ways to recount their history but none more familiar.

The Fourth, that year, had been too hot, too dry, too hard. The farmers walked around with their heads tipped back, watching for clouds, feeling the air with their skins, aware of the dust. The children were all tired out before the morning had waned. The smaller ones sat in the shade, panting like cats, their hair wringing with sweat, waiting for the sound of the band. The air was white with heat. Cicadas screamed. The tar on the street was so hot that the smell of it hurt Rachel's nose as she sat atop the mailbox outside Paula's Beauty Salon waiting for the parade. She'd imagined that the mailbox would be a clean, comfortable perch. She had not counted on it being so hot. Her thighs stuck to the metal.

"You all right there, Rachel?"

"Great," she said, sliding her arm through her father's. "But maybe I'll get down now. I'm too big for this sort of thing." She seemed too mature for many such things, now that she was ten.

When she slid down off the mailbox, her skin stuck, came away from the metal all at once, and would have sent her sprawling if her father had not held her by the arm.

"You're about as graceful as I am." Her mother laughed. She had on a blue-and-white gingham dress with a red belt. Rachel was wearing a pair of red shorts, a white blouse with blue stripes on it, and a red ribbon in her hair. She had painted red and blue stars on her Keds. Her father, who was an electrician, wore what he nearly always wore in the summertime—dull green work pants with a short-sleeved, Perma-Prest, one-pocket shirt, leather belt and boots, a plain cap. For the Fourth, he always flew a flag up at the house and, when the Belle Haven veterans marched by, saluted theirs.

"I hear the tubas," Rachel said. The children came running from under the trees and sat along the hot curb. Rachel's mother stepped back and slapped the flat of her hand against the beauty-shop door. "Band's coming, Paula," she called through the screen. Paula carried a half dozen hair clips on the collar of her blouse and a pair of scissors in her hand when she came through the door. Cora Ball, completely unabashed, swept out behind her in strange array, a pink sheet draped around her shoulders and dusted with bits of her gray hair, half her head glinting with clips.

"Who's gonna be lookin' at me . . . and who cares anyway?" Cora laughed, and Rachel found herself filled with admiration.

Before the sound of the band became much louder, the parade leaders turned onto Maple Street and down toward the crowd. Teenage boys with painted faces and homemade tricornes popped wheelies on their bikes. Three antique cars puttered by, their horns off-key. Kids with soapbox cars. The veterans, hot and breathless in their tight, old uniforms. A horse-drawn hay wagon done up like a float with a papier-mâché Statue of Liberty that everyone said looked just like

Molly, who worked at the checkout over at the A&P. A girl in white boots and flag colors, twirling a baton. Then the school band: small, ragtag, magnificent.

Finally came the polished fire engine and the volunteers who manned it, sweaty and exhausted in their gear. It was, for many of the children, the most wonderful part of the parade, for as the truck trundled slowly past they were permitted to run alongside, step up on its running boards, run their fingers along its hoses, smell the gleaming smell of it, feel its engine rumble. Rachel was just wondering whether she was now too old for this when the radio inside the cab began to chatter.

The firemen shooed the children back. The siren burped, the big truck swung slowly off Maple onto a side street, the firemen all waved their arms for people to stand clear, and then the truck was away, siren going, lights spinning, dust rising in its wake.

Nobody knew where it was headed. It wasn't until much later, at the picnic out by the Methodist church, when they'd all had their fill of chicken and potato salad, baked beans, corn bread, five-bean salad, red Jell-O mold with white marshmallows and blue gumdrops on top, lemonade and punch, and sparklers nearly invisible in the afternoon glare, that they heard about the fire in the mine pit.

"But it's out now. Took no time hardly at all to put it out." George Spade, one of the volunteers, was the first of them to shower and come looking for his lunch. Rachel was watching his paper plate to see what would happen when George put it down on his knee. There was so much food on it that beans were falling off the side. "But there's such a mess of garbage in that pit that we had to give it a good soaking, you know. It's been so dry we didn't want to leave any stray sparks behind." He nodded, satisfied. Everybody was watching for the other firemen to arrive so they could be fed, settled in the shade, applauded.

It was not until a good week later that someone noticed smoke spilling from an old mine shaft out by the pit and figured that the Fourth of July fire had not been put out after all. Nobody figured that it would still be burning thirteen years later.

For the first few years the fire seemed little more than a nuisance. Even when the contractors who were sent in to contain it botched the job, even after the fire began to wander down along the mine tunnels out under the fields around Belle Haven, everybody decided that it was a distant threat at best. There were maybe a dozen houses and a church scattered out along the western edge of the town, directly above the tunnels that ran north more than a mile before they hit the fire. Nobody living out there seemed too worried.

Most of them agreed with Henry Buck, who had a three-bedroom on an acre right smack above a tunnel. "I say, come on in. Cut my heating bill in half, I bet. Maybe cure Sandra's rheumatiz." He shook his head, took off his cap, fingered a seam. "What's it gonna do, come right up through all that dirt and singe my butt?" He had a laugh like an old car, all wheeze and hiccup.

To Rachel, too, the fire seemed at worst a minor threat. She had begun to learn the truth about the world, to recognize its many perils: all manner of holocausts, crimes beyond comprehension, extinction, plague, anonymity. In comparison, the fire seemed little cause for concern. Like others her age, Rachel also felt somewhat invulnerable. If, at night, she thought of missiles arcing up over the pole, by day she felt as if she would live to do great things, accomplish all of her dreams, survive any disaster.

And because she approached adolescence in the safety of a small, close-knit, law-abiding, sweet and peaceful town—where there was no real poverty or menace to distract her—Rachel surrendered to an irresistible preoccupation with which no distant fire could compete. She spent a great deal of time thinking about herself. She thought about the kind of person she was and how she might evolve.

Without a brother or sister to loosen her hold on her parents and theirs on her, Rachel had spent her earliest years thinking that there was nothing in the universe to compare with their lives together. Keeping house with her mother, marching down the hill to do the marketing, spending long hours in the garden, popping the jaws of obliging snapdragons while her father tended their tomatoes . . . for Rachel these were labors of love, proof that her parents were better off with her than without.

If her mother became upset with her—for smearing her clothes with egg yolk, breaking something forbidden, talking back—Rachel would simply drag her down by the hand, grab her around the neck, and kiss her. Bring her a glass of water. Brush her hair. "Sorry, sorry, sorry," she would say. Her mother would smile and hold her, hum with pleasure as Rachel brushed out her long hair, and play Rachel's favorite games, even though she was really too busy and might easily have said so.

Rachel thought that she had won her mother over with her penance and her charm. She didn't know that, even had she been endlessly difficult, rebellious, and vain, her mother would not have loved her less.

When her mother suddenly collapsed one morning to lie gasping in the garden, it was six-year-old Rachel who ran to a neighbor for help, who told her father how the blood had spread across her mother's old gardening slacks, who stayed near her mother for many days, until she was finally back on her feet again. The following week, when she saw her weeping mother unravel a tiny yellow sweater, Rachel crept off to the kitchen, made her own lunch, and did not ask for a single thing that whole day. She had seen enough of patience and kindness to practice them, and so she did.

In those early years, no one thought twice about Rachel's eagerness to please, to be whatever she thought her parents wanted her to be. But as she matured, it became obvious to everyone, and to Rachel herself, that she was far less prone than her friends to the mild rebellion that all parents expect from even the sweetest of their daughters.

When her friends began to wear makeup—too much, and poorly— she joined them with great misgivings.

"Ah," her mother sighed when Rachel came home from her friend Estelle's house one day, her lashes clotted with bottled tar, cheeks as red as friction burns. "So soon." She shook her head. "I was just as anxious, when I was your age, to grow up. What a shame."

Other mothers, Estelle's among them, scrubbed their daughters clean, forbade such experiments. But Rachel's mother simply sighed, turned back to her sewing, and let the thump of her foot on the floor pedal, the angle of her spine, speak her disapproval.

After that, Rachel, alone among her friends, left her face bare.

At fourteen, just when Rachel was becoming accustomed to her alarming breasts and the messy, painful periods that some of her friends celebrated and others cursed, she discovered that although they were all tied together in these physical ways, they were also taking the first steps along separate courses that could keep them squarely apart, maybe even for life.

"Have you ever been finger-fucked?" The flashlight in her face made Rachel blink, which hid some of her shock, gave her a moment to decide whether to tell the truth or take the dare.

She was surrounded by a half dozen girls in sleeping bags. They looked, to Rachel, like giant, moulting insects. To admit to them not only that she had never been finger-fucked but that she did not even know what this meant was too much. So she smiled and said, "I'll take the dare." Try as she might, she would never be able to forget having to stand in front of her companions and lift her nightgown, ease her underpants to her knees, and show them the shadow of hair that had begun to grow. They had giggled. One or two had actually joined her. To compare, they said.

When she learned that another sleepover party was to be held in the loft of a barn and that boys had been told, Rachel said, Sure. Of course she would go. But a few hours beforehand she went into the bathroom and stuck her fingers down her throat.

"You missed a great party," Estelle said. "Stupid time to get sick."

"Figures," Rachel said, shrugging. But in the years to come she learned other tricks that saw her through all kinds of tight spots: how to drink slowly and by sips; how to kiss a boy without granting him further license; how to blow smoke through her nose without inhaling; how to lie to her parents without argument or repercussion.

As she came of age, Rachel watched her friends closely, as if they were birds. She was careful not to stare or to interrogate, but she was always aware of how they conducted themselves and how they chose their words. This was how Rachel looked at the world: she kept vigils, spied, tempered her instincts with all kinds of reasonable reactions to what she saw.

She came to realize, by comparison with schoolmates and by scrutinizing the way people treated her, that she preferred to be as she was, a peacemaker and a good daughter. In the struggle to define herself, to name the things that made her unique without relinquishing her ties to those around her, Rachel isolated this facet of her character, held it up to the light, and pronounced it beautiful. With great deliberation, she practiced diplomacy, tact, and kindness. A strange curriculum for a girl her age, but one she relished. It was hard work to avoid trouble, but it made her feel good. And that was enough.

Having convinced herself that her life was the best anyone could hope for, Rachel became convinced, too, in terms that she herself could not articulate, that to doubt her blessings in any way was to risk them, and certainly to dishonor them.

It did not occur to her that counting herself as a daughter first and a separate and independent person second had so colored her view of the world that she could not see herself clearly in it.

Rachel was content with her choices. She might even have been truly happy if her behavior had been less deliberate. If she had been more herself and less the way she thought she ought to be. If she had only had a guitar.

That was all Rachel wanted for Christmas the year she turned fifteen. Nothing but a guitar. She had long since investigated the cost of a piano and found it too high. Something she simply could not ask for. Something she would have to do without. But a guitar was different. Expensive, too, but not out of her grasp. Not entirely.

It was only a week past Thanksgiving, but Maple Street was already rigged with ropes of tinsel and colored lights, there were plastic reindeer in several front yards, and all the mannequins in the Sears window display wore red velvet elf caps on their sculpted heads.

"What do you think I ought to get Dad for Christmas?" Rachel whispered. She and her mother were sitting at the kitchen table after supper, paring apples. Her father was watching a Steelers game. The radio in the kitchen, turned on low, played Bing Crosby singing "White Christmas."

"A bottle of cornhuskers lotion and a pound of dried apricots, same as always."

"Yeah, but what else? Something different. Something that *I* actually go out and buy for him." She sliced the last bit of skin from her apple, halved it, quartered it, cored it, sliced the quarters into an enormous bowl.

"Why don't you make him something? He loves everything you've ever made him."

Rachel picked up another apple. "Like what?"

"How about you embroider a couple of hankies for him?"

"I already did that."

"Knit him a scarf."

"I could do that." Rachel rested her forearms on the table. Her wrists were getting sore. They needed enough apples for seven pies. Her mother had orders for fourteen apple, two pecan, two coconut-cream, three pumpkin, and one banana-cream. For tomorrow, noon. The cream pies and half of the apple were cooling on the counter.

"Or maybe just give him a head rub every night Christmas week and clean up his bike. I don't know a single thing he'd like more than that."

That sounded good to Rachel, something she did well. Something her father would love.

"What about you?" She looked across the table at her mother and picked up a fresh apple. "Not something you need. Something you *want.*"

Rachel had expected protests, reluctant talk of hand cream and hairpins, but was surprised with the answer she got.

"Something I want," her mother mused. "Well, actually, there is something." She shook her head. "And I'm not trying to let you off the hook either. It's something you could do for me that would be hard for me to do myself, in all kinds of ways." She got up from the table and carried the big bowl of sliced apples over to the sink, began to mix them with brown sugar, white sugar, and cinnamon.

"You know my grandmother's house?" she said.

It was an old house, way out past the tunnels, boarded up. Too old now to be any good to anyone. Part of a farm that no one farmed anymore, bought up by the coal company but never mined. "They're going to be tearing it down any day now," Rachel's mother said. "Or burning it, maybe. So I called up and asked if anyone would mind if I went back to look for a memento of some kind." When she turned the apples over with her big spoon, a lazy cloud of cinnamon dust lifted and settled above the bowl. "My mother never took anything with her when she married. Her parents—my grandparents—were terribly upset with her for getting married so young, I suppose for leaving them all alone, and so abruptly, to marry a man they barely knew and didn't much like." She began to roll out pie dough with a fat pin. "Anyway, I spent quite a lot of time there when I was a kid. Usually without my parents along. It was a long walk for me, but I didn't care. I loved going over there. I loved the house. I loved the garden. My grandparents were wonderful to me. And then they died when I was still little. And then my own parents died before you were born. And I haven't been inside that house for thirty years—it's been empty for the last five anyway—but, I don't know, maybe a scrap of wallpaper, or one of the old porcelain sinks. I used to play at the kitchen sink all the time, got all wet, went home wrinkled. Take your father over there, Rachel, and bring me back something. That's what I want for Christmas."

And Rachel sat there at the table, paring apples, aghast. For she had begun the conversation with only one thing on her mind—the guitar she had seen on their last trip to Randall. For herself. For Christmas. It was the thing she had planned to name when the conversation came back her way, when her mother finally said, "And so what do *you* want this year, Rachel?"

But the conversation never turned, and here was her mother with tears in her eyes and a whole peck of apples still to peel.

A week later, when Rachel and her father arrived at the house where her great-grandparents had lived, they found the ground around it so overgrown with frozen vines that they could barely reach the front door. The windows were all boarded up. The doors were nailed shut. The window boxes had long since fallen off and apart. There were chimney bricks lying about, but they seemed an inadequate keepsake, the daffodils bottled up underground too fragile to move, the cornerstone simply impossible. But then, while her father waited, Rachel took a screwdriver and, from the heavy front door, removed the old, weathered handle and a knocker that someone had fashioned from the head of an ancient hammer. In the grass around back of the house she found a cast-iron ring on a hinge welded to a small iron plate, for tying up a horse, perhaps, or pulling open some sort of hatch.

The cold metal made her hands hurt as she carried these treasures away, but she thought of all the other hands that had touched them over the decades and promised herself they would not be neglected again.

On Christmas morning, when Rachel heard her mother on the stairs, she lay in her bed, listening. Heard her mother go into the kitchen, saw a bit of light in the hallway when her mother switched on the kitchen light, heard the water running for coffee, the radio softly giving the weather, the scrape of a chair. Rachel hugged herself beneath her quilt, smiling, until she heard her mother open a cupboard, shut it, turn on the tap once again, and then nothing. Silence. And then feet on the stairs again, quickly, and her mother in her doorway, at her bed.

"I'm up," Rachel said, and her mother was next to her in an instant, grabbing her in her arms. "I had forgotten," she was saying. "I had forgotten all about that old thing, and I never even thought to tell you where to look for it, but you found it. And it's absolutely worthless, but, oh, Rachel, my grandfather made that hitch for me. It was on the wall right next to the back door. I used to tie up Sam there, my dog, when I was inside having lunch, so he wouldn't run off. And now it's down in my kitchen with a dish towel hanging on it, and I just couldn't be happier."

And then Rachel had taken her mother's hand and led her to the front door, opened it, and was right there when her mother saw the handle and the knocker, all cleaned up and really quite nice. She would never forget how she felt standing there on the front step in the December cold, watching her mother's face.

She had made a scroll for her father. *Head rubs all week,* it read, *upon demand.*

"You'll put me into a coma," he said, smiling. "You know me too well, Rachel. Couldn't have picked a better gift."

"And your bike's ready for spring," she said. "Oiled, polished, with a new seat and new reflectors, front and back. I replaced that missing spoke and the one grip on the handlebar."

"This I gotta see," he said, on his feet, so that she had to wait until he'd returned from the cellar before it was her turn to open her gift.

She had been careful not to look for it under the tree. She did not want to see a telltale shape, feel for weight or texture, guess at all. For a month she'd been dropping hints, doodling guitars in the blank margins of the funny papers, strumming the air with her hands. But the box that her parents put into her lap was too small. When she opened it, she found a beautifully bound copy of *Little Women* by Louisa May Alcott and a new pair of knitted gloves.

Rachel loved books, especially good ones, and hated how cold her hands could become on the walk to school. But she had wanted a guitar so very badly. Her parents hadn't known that, of course. And if they had? Guitars weren't cheap. And, regardless of the expense, her parents had always believed that if Rachel paid for her whims, she would learn discipline and good sense. If she wanted a guitar, she'd just have to buy it herself, much as she'd had to pay to have her ears pierced. ("It's barbaric," her mother had said, "to put holes in your ears." And Rachel, after a week, agreeing, had let the holes close over like wounds.)

"Thank you," she said, lifting her face into the light of the Christmas tree, smiling, nested in torn wrapping, her lap bright with ribbon. "It's the most beautiful book I've ever seen. The gloves are great, too." And she had meant every word, from her heart.

When Rachel told Estelle what she'd got for Christmas, Estelle was appalled. "That's even worse than this," she said, pulling a lime green turtleneck out of a box on her bed. "I told them I wanted a pink angora sweater. That's all. Pink angora or nothing. So they get me this." She flipped it back into the box. "I got the sales slip from my mom, but she told me I'd have to go on my own to exchange it. Which is her stupid way of getting even."

Rachel sat on Estelle's bed and stared. She was filled with awe, disdain, and raw envy. She disliked herself for wanting the chance to indulge herself the way Estelle had done, to open the floodgates and let things pour out, unchecked. But she knew that she would not do so. She knew that it would take far more than a disappointing Christmas to make her lose control and risk losing, too, the things that mattered most to her. Rachel planned never to show her parents any sort of discontent, for she did not want them to doubt at all the way she loved them, loved Belle Haven, loved things just the way they were and the way she hoped they would always be.

What Rachel did not realize was that her parents knew her right down to the bone.

"She's something, that girl," her father said. He was sitting in his favorite chair with a cup of coffee and a seed catalogue. It was not yet New Year's, but he had already begun to anticipate the spring.

"Hmmm." Her mother settled next to him on the wide arm of the chair, plucked the catalogue out of his hands, and flipped quickly from lima beans to hollyhocks. "What did she do?"

"Hey. Gimme that."

"Hang on a sec. Here. Look at this. No, this one. The old-fashioned kind with the single petals."

"Good. We'll plant some by the corner of the porch."

They looked over the marigolds together. "So what did Rachel do?"

"She never said a word about that guitar."

"What guitar?"

"The one she wanted for Christmas."

Suzanne Hearn closed the catalogue on her thumb. "Rachel wanted a guitar for Christmas?"

"Yes, I think so."

"She never said anything to me. And neither did you." She smacked his arm with the catalogue. "That was mean."

"You know we can't afford a guitar. And who would teach her to play it? Guitar lessons cost money. Besides," he said, "I'm not convinced she'd stick with it. Let her borrow one and give it a try, then we'll see."

"I wish I'd known. I might have worked something out. A used one, maybe."

"No sense in worrying about it. She's up there reading that book as we speak. She's not upset. Why should you be?"

"Hmmm. I'm not so sure."

"About what?" He took the seed catalogue out of her hands, flipped back to beans.

"You know Rachel. When's the last time she seemed upset about anything? Sometimes I can tell that she's worried, but she seems quite up to sorting things out by herself, so I usually let her."

"Good."

"Not good. She's just a kid. Maybe we ought to . . ." Suzanne closed her lips, shook her head.

"Ought to what?"

"*I* don't know. Give her some of what she wants without making her ask for it. 'Cause she won't, most of the time. She ought to be doing what kids her age are *supposed* to do, for God's sake. Like every other kid in Belle Haven. This all seems too easy on us."

"You want to buy her a pack of cigarettes? Put her on the Pill?"

"Don't be an ass, Fred." She leaned against him so that he was squashed into a corner of the chair.

"Then don't you be." He pushed her back up, fondly. "Rachel wants to behave herself. Let her. She's all right."

"I don't know. They say the straightest arrows are the ones that end up causing the biggest fuss in the end."

"Who's they?"

"*They.* People."

"*I'm* people. I say let her be."

As was their wont, Suzanne and Frederick Hearn agreed that Rachel's small struggles would strengthen her, that her self-absorption would help her to know herself well, to understand her choices, to make the right ones. And if their happiness was Rachel's greatest concern, so be it. They could lead her, direct her, with little fuss, away from the things that might harm her. Toward the things that would make *her* happiest in the end.

They laid their plans carefully. Rachel followed them in lockstep, unprotesting, happy to oblige. And if any of the three of them had ever witnessed the catastrophe of good intentions gone bad, they had forgotten. Or decided to look the other way.

Chapter 3

Eight years later, sometime between the rise and fall of the Halloween moon, the man who called himself just Joe lay in his tree house, christened with dew, and dreamed an old, familiar dream.

It was a long, absorbing dream that pulsed and murmured with a red, pervasive tide and the endless beating of a heart. In his dream, he drifted along with the hazy tide, bumping gently against soft, engorged walls, and finally became wedged in a hot cranny, wrapped in a web of capillaries, as safe as he would ever be.

As he took hold of his mother, and as her body embraced him, he rocked with her gentle gait, thrived on her warmth, began to be her son. All was well. He trembled with tremendous growth.

And then someone else arrived.

Instinct told him that this arrival was in some ways unnatural. A mistake. A second passenger where only one belonged. Not a twin: a follower. But a sister nonetheless.

Through the long, hypnotic dream, he shared the womb with this second child, meted out whatever nutrients he could spare, made adjustments to grant her room. But long before she was ready for the world, he kicked out with his perfect heel in a moment of fetal selfishness as natural to him as sleep and left a furrow in the soft bone of his sister's face. And there was nothing that either of them could ever do to change that.

Joe awoke. For a moment he lay completely still, not sure where or even who he was. Then he saw, through the window by his bed, the branches of the walnut tree, black against the milky sky, and he began to breathe again. He could feel the dream receding, and he knew he would soon be unable to remember any of it. He would wake again in the morning, his face stiff with cold, unsettled by a vague memory of the moon shining on his face, the dream gone.

Before it left him he clung to it as he always did, for it reminded him that life can be perilous, full of random repercussions, even for the innocent and the well-intentioned. But the only alternative was not to live, and not to love. He had to remind himself of this, for Rachel's sake as well as for his own.

Just Joe was born Christopher Barrows. Healthy. Content. His sister, Holly, swept from the womb four weeks early, was smaller than her brother, bald and spindly, her face misshapen and her reactions slow.

"The male was conceived first," the doctor explained to his gaggle of interns, "the female a month later when a hormonal irregularity permitted a maverick egg to ripen, become fertilized, and implant itself as a secondary embryo in a womb already inhabited." The doctors were unforgivably excited about the baby's combined ailments.

Chad Barrows, looking into the incubator at his infant daughter, was glad that her face was turned away. "What can you do for her?" he asked the doctors.

"She'll need some special care," one replied, "but she's in no real danger."

"Her face," Chad said through his teeth. "What can you do about her face?"

The doctors looked at one another. "Nothing," one said. "Perhaps when she is older, plastic surgery. Every year we are able to do more and more. But there's nothing we can do for her right now."

Though the doctors were right, Chad was unconvinced. He was very wealthy. There was nothing he had ever been unable to buy. But after hearing the same prognosis from the best specialists in New England, Chad finally relented. He had his son, after all.

The baby boy was perfect: healthy, happy, handsome. Wonderful to look at. Eventually, Chad even took to putting his open hand on his son's warm, downy, pulsing skull, holding it there as if to convey by osmosis his own brand of wisdom.

"There's no reason either of them should ever know what really happened," he said to his wife, Kay. "He's not to blame. He didn't mean to hurt her." Just as Chad, lowering himself onto his newly pregnant wife, had not meant to conceive an irregular child. "I'll not have him feeling guilty later on, or her resentful. We'll make something up. Tell them you fell down the stairs. They never need to know." Chad was good at keeping secrets. He was a careful man who made sure that his wishes would be carried out. It was therefore a long time before his daughter found out what her innocent brother had done.

Nicknames were traditional in the Barrows family. In keeping with this tradition, Charles Barrows was known exclusively as Chad (never Charlie) and his wife, Katherine, as Kay. It seemed natural to them, then, to select nicknames for their children first, and more formal ones almost as an afterthought. The name they gave their daughter, Holly, reminded them of young girls in plaid frocks and ponytails, armed with hockey sticks, sweeping down a green field. (The formal name they put on her birth papers, Harriet Caldwell Barrows, was for her maternal grandmother, long dead, and Kay's own maiden name, long relinquished.) And from the day he was born, their son, Christopher James, was known by all as Kit.

"It's one of those names," Chad mused as he watched his infant son waking. "Like something out of a book. It suits him."

Kay Barrows lay curled in her hospital bed, suffering, joyful. "It's the kind of name given to handsome boys. Kit. Clean. Sharp. Neat. Unforgettable. Girls are going to fall in love with him."

When he saw his wife, later, nursing their daughter, Chad parted the small, sucking lips with his finger and pulled the blanket over his wife's breast. "The doctor said she wouldn't be able to nurse. Her mouth is askew, Kay. She won't be able to suck properly."

"But she can. She's doing fine."

"Who nurses anyway? The stuff they make in tins is better for the baby. Everyone says so. And this will ruin you." He flipped a hand toward the blanket. "But if you're going to nurse, nurse Kit. Nothing wrong with him."

"She's the one who needs me more." Kay pulled the blanket away and helped her baby to begin again. "And I have enough milk for both of them. Plenty. He'll get his share."

But before she had finished nursing Holly, Chad had sent a nurse for a bottle of warm formula, settled himself in a rocking chair by the window, and was teasing his son's lips with drops of milk.

Watching them from her bed, Kay was struck by a familiar onslaught of panic, heightened by the discomforts of her recent ordeal. Where had this man come from? How was it that they had children now? When had all of this happened? She wondered, suddenly, if there was any sort of honorable retreat, or if she was bound to these people for her lifetime. And then she looked at her husband again, and she realized that he was hers and she his and the children, now, theirs. She breathed out a long breath, felt her womb contract, and said, "I think we're very lucky."

"I suppose we are," he said, his eyes on his son. It was three days before he held his daughter for the first time.

Kit was six years old when his mother went sailing one evening and died in a storm. By the time he was ten he remembered very little about her except that she smelled like oranges.

Holly also remembered her dead mother. But she remembered more. She remembered her mother coming into her room each morning, gathering her up into soft arms, and carrying her down to the warm kitchen. It was where Holly spent her waking moments, watching her mother halve a dozen fragrant, heavy oranges, squeeze their frothy juice into a tall, iced glass, and place it on the table for her husband. It did not seem to bother Kay when Chad failed to comment on her thoughtfulness or even scolded her under the solemn gaze of their cook. "Just look at your hands," he'd say, not touching them. "You look like a grocer."

As long as her mother was alive, Holly knew she was much loved. She was not old enough to understand or fret about her disfigurement. When she looked in the mirror, she smiled and babbled and made faces like other children. When her mother tucked her into bed at night, Holly offered her cheek, usually the damaged one, for a kiss just like any other child. And when other children asked her how she'd come to have such a face, she was as unabashed as her brother was when asked how he'd purpled his thumbnail.

"It happened before I was born," she always said, then went on to more important things.

It was Holly's mother who taught her to love her crooked face, her smallness, her weakness, her vulnerability. Her mother even managed to make Holly's frequent illnesses enviable. She'd prepare elaborate picnics and carry them up to Holly's bedroom, read her dozens of books, sing her hundreds of songs, lie next to her in bed and tell her about the hours before she and Kit had been born.

"There was lightning but no rain," Kay remembered, "and at one point a full moon. And in the morning there was fog."

Holly did not speak to anyone except Kit for weeks after her mother was killed. She was only six, but she suspected that her father didn't like her very much. And although she had always adored her brother and thought that he loved her just as much (for he had always been a willing playmate, always been where she could find him, always called her "jolly Holly"), the weeks following their mother's death had changed him, reordered him into a smaller version of their father, so that she felt she had lost her brother, too.

What Holly didn't know about was the cruelty of strangers. Grade school taught her that. Had Kit been with her, things might have been different. But shortly after her mother died, her father sent her off to a boarding school for girls while Kit stayed home with his father and the people who were paid to tend them.

His mother and sister gone, Kit was lonely for the first time in his life. The huge house seemed to have become ugly, and the toys he had played with for years suddenly had the feel of dead things. But then his father took him to the Orient, Africa, the capitals of Europe, to islands of luxury bordered as much by starvation as by the sea. From his father, Kit learned that the world would never be the same for him as it was for most of its other billions. They would die far earlier than he would. They would be hungry, sick, unhappy, afraid. He would be fed, tended, indulged. "That doesn't seem fair," he said one day, shortly after he'd turned nine.

"Fair?" replied his father. "Who said anything about fair?"

When Kit was ten years old, he, too, was sent away to boarding school, where a hundred other boys all wore the same blinders with which he had been fitted and where the lessons his father had taught him were reflected in every eye.

It was here that Kit learned boredom, impatience, disrespect. Over the years, he learned how to threaten, how to charm, how, on rare occasions, to retreat. And when, home for his sixteenth birthday, Kit opened the door to his new forty-thousand-dollar sports car to find a five-hundred-dollar prostitute inside, he learned yet another lesson about privilege and power: that there is little in this world that cannot be purchased.

By nearly any definition, Kit was a spoiled boy. But his attitudes were studied. They were something he practiced constantly and displayed openly, but they had not altogether penetrated the border of his skin. Under the watchful eye of his father, he learned how to do what was expected of him and to hide at all cost the reluctance—at odd times the rebellion—that fought to keep a fingerhold on his heart. He carried his vices like weapons, separate and apart. Not reluctantly, but not without misgivings.

It was therefore with a certain dread that he approached his father the day after his sixteenth birthday, alarmed at what he and the prostitute had done the night before and unsure of what to tell his father. Should he thank him? Should he slap him on the back? He often felt that he knew his father very well, but it was at times like this that his father, their lives, the very clothes they wore seemed indescribably alien.

"Father," he said, sitting down to blueberry muffins and coffee. "Good morning."

"Hmmm," said his father with his cup to his mouth, a newspaper folded in his free hand, his eyes busy with finance. After a moment he glanced over at Kit, who gave him a careful, generic smile. "Is that all you're having for breakfast?" Chad asked.

"I'm not very hungry," Kit said.

This time, "Huh." A sort of surprised grunt. A small leer. The closest Chad Barrows ever came to complicity or an admission that he had delivered up his son to a whore.

By the last days of May 1980 Kit had finished his junior year at Yale and thought he'd learned most of the things his father could teach him. He knew about finance—everything to do with money and how to make it. He knew about politics. He knew how to have things done, quickly and with little fuss, and how to make the world work to his advantage. He had accompanied his father often enough, listened to him always, watched him, copied him, come to know his colleagues and what they had to teach a young man just starting out. He had worked alongside his father, been scolded and, nearly as often, praised. Together they had planned his future, imagined it, looked forward to it. Everything, for Kit, rolled smoothly along. Every promise, his father said, would come to pass. But then Kit arrived home a day early from college and found that the senior Barrows had been holding out on him.

It was actually Holly who taught Kit this lesson. He had been with her little since their childhood, for they were only at home together during holidays and summer months, which Holly spent in as much seclusion as she could manage. At eighteen, she had insisted on living, during her time at home, in the apartment over the carriage house in which they stored their automobiles, and Kit had taken care never to violate her privacy. And when Holly visited the main house for meals or rare conversation, Kit found her so changed from the small girl he'd known that he had little to say to her. She had become so withdrawn, so serious, so separate from everything that he considered important. While he spent his summers as his father's apprentice, she spent her days sailing, or wandering in the woods, squandering her hours, scribbling in blank books, keeping her distance. While he welcomed every chance to ally himself with his father's colleagues and to make for himself the beginnings of a name, she seemed content with her autonomy and her solitude. The occasions when she sought him out were usually as awkward as they were rare, and they always left Kit with the disturbing impression that he had somehow done her wrong.

She had seemed, as a child, such a good and eager companion that Kit sometimes wondered what had happened to change her so radically. But most of the time he did not think about her at all.

On the night of May 20, 1980, Kit arrived home from Yale for the summer, set to present his father with a 3.2 average and a brace of Maine lobsters. When he drove his car into the carriage house, he was surprised to find a strange car parked there. And when he pulled in alongside it and switched off the quiet engine, he was startled to hear music coming from the apartment overhead and then the uncommon sound of his sister laughing. He imagined that Holly had invited a friend to visit and was relieved to discover that she had one.

Feeling better and better, Kit gathered up his lobsters, and, leaving his luggage for others to negotiate, headed for the house.

A cluster of magnolias adorned the stretch of lawn between the carriage house and the main residence, and as their blossoms moved in the breeze, the trees anointed the night air. They reminded him, suddenly, of his mother, who had planted them. This unsolicited memory unsettled him. It made him feel that closed doors should remain not simply closed, but locked.

Kit nearly walked right into his father.

"Good God, you startled me," Kit said, offering his hand. "What are you doing out here? I meant to surprise you, and now you've spoiled it. Did you hear the car?"

"Kit," said his father, leaning close. "Welcome home." His eyes were not fully open. He stank of whiskey and filthy hair, and his hand in Kit's was shaking. With overwhelming revulsion, Kit realized that the grass at his father's feet was glazed with vomit. He was then astonished to see his father sit down in the wet grass and settle himself with a phlegmy sigh. Kit stepped carefully out of the soiled grass and crouched down next to his father.

"What are you doing out here?" he whispered. When Chad did not answer, Kit turned and looked where his father looked.

At first he saw nothing extraordinary. The night was quiet but for the waxy chafing of magnolia petals overhead and the lobsters who scrabbled mildly inside their bag. Then Kit looked up toward the widow's walk that adorned the carriage-house roof. Holly stood there, drenched in lantern light. She was with a man. As he watched, they embraced each other.

For the rest of his life, Kit would remember the sight of his small, imperfect sister leaning tenderly against this man, both of them plain and harmless against the huge sky. But try as he might, he could not ever recall dropping the bag of lobsters, one part of him glad, another tempted to call out some objection to what he was witnessing. He could not remember saying anything, but he must have spoken, for his father suddenly turned to him and said, "Shut up, Kit. It's none of our business."

And suddenly Kit became truly alarmed, not because of the scene that was playing itself out on the carriage-house roof but because his father had chosen to watch it from the cover of the magnolia grove, drunk to the point of sickness, to the point of scolding him as if he were a child.

Kit didn't understand what was happening. Only minutes before he'd been in his tiny car, hair flying, the air cool against his face, and everything had been as it should be.

"I'm going up to the house," he said, but was again, momentarily, disoriented when he discovered the escape of his lobsters and realized that his father had gained his feet and was staggering off toward the carriage house.

"This way," he said, grabbing his father's arm and steering him toward the house, leaving the lobsters behind.

When they cleared the trees, Kit looked up at the night sky and saw the sugary, reddish fog that heralded fine weather. It brought the sky too near and made the vague, hidden shape of the moon look like a fresh bruise. And he did not breathe freely again until he had coaxed his father into the house, where everything was much as it had always been, and shut the door behind him.

Chapter 4

When seventeen-year-old Rachel Hearn was voted prom queen at the end of her senior year of high school, a few of her more enthusiastic neighbors began to call her the Belle Haven Belle.

"Don't," she said to her father when he repeated this, laughing, his sleeves cuffed with garden dirt and peat. "It's awful. Next person who calls me that is going to be sorry."

"Oh, sure. Mr. Maxwell says, 'Well, hey there, Rachel. How's our Belle Haven Belle?' You say, 'Suck eggs,' and kick his cane out from under him." He chuckled at her.

"How would you like it?" She pressed the heels of her hands into the soft dirt around a young tomato plant.

"You're going to kill that plant, Rachel."

She dug her fingers down either side and gently lifted the dirt a bit. "You'd hate it," she said.

"You're a pretty girl." He reached into a tray, gently combed apart the tangled roots of the seedlings.

"Thanks," she said. "But I don't like all that business. I don't like to feel dumb, and that's how I feel."

"Nobody who knows you thinks you're dumb, Rachel." He set out the last of the tomatoes and started on the peppers. "You've got to re- member that some people around here are getting a little bit worried about the fire. They feel like they're living with a tiger. So they have a tendency, you see, to celebrate any lambs they come across. Anything good and certain. Presto!" He threw his hands into the air. "The Belle Haven Belle is born."

Rachel tossed a clot of dirt at her father, which made him laugh some more. They planted seedlings for a while.

At the end of a row, Rachel's father pushed himself up off his knees and stretched the cramp out of his back. "I've been meaning to talk to you about going away in the fall."

She looked up at him from under her hand, but he was backlit by sun and hard to see.

"Your mother and I are glad you're going to college, and we know that you're clever and you've got a lot of common sense and you'll be just fine by yourself." He picked up a watering can and gave the seedlings something to drink. "But you've never really been away from here, Rachel. We want you to be careful. You get into any sort of trouble, you just call us. Never be afraid to call us. No matter what's gone wrong."

Rachel's throat hurt. "I won't," she said, coming to her feet, trampling a pepper plant on her way to him. His shirt against her face was hot with sun and work, and she was sure that she would remember the smell of it for the rest of her life.

Suzanne and Frederick Hearn knew that with a single word they could keep their daughter with them. "Stay," they could say, and she would. She was happy enough with the chance to go to college and smart enough to see the need, but they knew she would choose them if they let her. They had therefore been the ones to insist that she leave.

"Nothing's going to threaten your education," her father had told her. "Not some boy, not your feelings for this town, not the fire, not us."

Rachel's parents were as smart as she was. With their combined decades of experience, smarter still. But their formal education was incomplete and their knowledge of the world secondhand. When they read their child's verse, heard her stories, witnessed her grasp of mathematics and science, they were frightened by their limits and by their mortality. In their prayers they insisted that they not outlast her. But to see her come of age, to see her come into her own . . . that was their other wish, and at times they felt consumed by it. They asked themselves how they could possibly send her away. But to their daughter they said, "You can always come back. A few years away won't hurt."

So Rachel went off to a small New England college that could afford to pay her expenses and did so with a hefty scholarship. Among the brightest students, she excelled. Her professors knew her name. She made plenty of friends, learned to live with another girl in a room three yards by five, chose to live alone once she had earned the privilege. "It's always easier to find company," her mother had once told her, "than solitude."

For two years she was happy at school, happy back home for the summers, the fire coiled in the near distance. She had Hemingway, Freud, Copernicus, Jefferson, Eliot. She had Angela, who ran the only coffee shop in Belle Haven and could not be matched for pure wit, wisdom, and gritty charm. Rachel had the finest of parents. She was fit. Most of the time, she felt as if she were on the verge of bursting from her skin.

If anything, it was only romance that she missed. College boys, as a breed, had proven uninteresting or, on the whole, more trouble than they were worth. They had flocked to her, attracted by how she looked, by the way her body swept, riverlike, from one smooth curve into the next. But they had not seemed to listen to her when she spoke. And they rarely said anything that she had not heard a dozen times before.

Holding out for something better, she had watched her friends suffer disappointments, cry into their hands as one after another they were awakened to the reality that many young men—whether they meant to or not—broke hearts. And she had waited more than once, among the magazines and the ashtrays, while down the hall a friend lifted her feet into a set of cold stirrups and lived through the sound of a vacuum sucking her dry.

If a boy did manage to stir Rachel, so that she found herself quickening or shy, she ordinarily drew back. She was not at all cynical, not worldly, certainly not wise in matters of the heart: when it came to such things she was simply cautious. Not in the way that victims are cautious. She had never been assaulted or in any way misused, and the boys in Belle Haven had wooed her in a safe and simple way that had never caused her alarm. She had as much as told them what kinds of lines she drew and where.

It was not fear that made Rachel reluctant. It was longing.

She had seen the way her parents treasured each other. She had studied their affection. They had never seemed embarrassed by it. Rachel had often seen them become quietly aroused, had watched them tangling like young bears, harmlessly rough, affectionate, and so absorbed with each other that at times she felt forgotten.

She had once asked her mother, "How does it feel to be in love?" Her mother was kneeling in the grass with a knife in one hand, a pot of warm beeswax in the other. She was grafting a strong, juicy twig of pear tree to an adoptive stump. She had made a clean cut in the stump, eased the transplant into the cleft, and was now binding them together with wax. It was something that took practice and care.

"Oh, I don't know," her mother finally said. "The feeling changes over time. In the beginning it's almost like a sickness. It takes you over and it eats you up, and if you're loved back, it thrills you. It absolutely thrills you. And then, later on, if it lasts, it settles down a bit. It comes back at you often enough, that feeling of complete joy." She worked the wax with her knife. "I'll be brushing my teeth and I'll hear your father yawning and fumbling around for his robe and suddenly I can barely stand up, I feel so good. Sometimes it's a long time between the moments when I'm aware that I still love him that way. You get busy with everything else. There are other people to love. You, for instance. Things change. Things stay the same." She smoothed the cast of wax once more with her blade. "I have a lot of things to feel lucky about. Your father is one of them, and by now I know he always will be." She sighed when she saw the look in her daughter's eyes. "You'll know what it feels like when you feel it," she said. "Isn't that what mothers are supposed to say?"

Then she smiled at Rachel, put the lid on the pot of wax, and surrendered the tree to its fate.

When Rachel left home, for the first time free and on her own, she remembered these things and allowed her expectations to rise. Whenever she met a boy, she could not help but measure him, perhaps more severely than he deserved. Fair or not, Rachel's hopes were as ingrained as her resolve to satisfy them. And so Rachel waited. And then came Harry.

The professors called him Henry, for that was the name they were given by the registrar—Henry Gallagher—but everyone knew him as Harry. He had joined Rachel's class as a junior, having transferred from another school, and so it came as a complete surprise when Rachel first saw him one day as she sat in the refectory having a bad lunch of ham loaf and macaroni salad.

"Have you ever read *Charlotte's Web?*" she said to Paul, the best of her school friends.

He shook his head, daydreaming.

"Read it," she said, peering at her macaroni. "The pig in it, Wilbur, gets fed all this luscious slop. Scraps of this and that, soup labels, potato peelings. Somehow it all sounds just great. I'd trade this slop for that any day." She threw down her fork. "What I wouldn't give for some five-bean salad." And that's when she looked around and saw Harry, three tables down.

He was quite a lovely man, as a painting is lovely, or a meadow, and looking at him made Rachel feel hungry in a completely physical sense.

Paul pushed his own plate into the middle of the table. "Key lime pie," he said. "Or maybe a proper hot dog." He laced his fingers behind his head. "Let's have dinner off campus." He turned to look at Rachel, then over toward Harry. "Oh, hell," he said.

"What."

Paul shook his head. "Another one bites the dust."

"What?" She turned to look at him, her eyes slow to focus.

"Never mind," he said. Then, "Come on. Russian lit in fifteen minutes."

And from then on, for the rest of her life, Rachel would not be able to eat ham loaf without thinking of Harry Gallagher.

Three weeks later, when she discovered that Harry had joined Paul's fraternity, Rachel wasted no time. There was to be a party at the house Saturday night. She hated frat parties. She had been to a few, for reasons she could no longer fathom, and had gone home feeling soiled and frightened. That Paul belonged to a fraternity confused her, for he was her friend and, in her experience, a decent person. But, since she found most young men confusing in one way or another, Rachel gave Paul the benefit of the doubt and believed him when he said that they were not all wild and amoral. She trusted Paul. So it was to him that she turned for help.

"I want you to introduce us, casually, if we run into him. Don't embarrass me. Don't make a big deal out of it. I've seen him a lot lately. We even danced a dance the other night in the Blue Room. But it was so noisy that we didn't say anything, really. Just danced. I want to meet him properly, that's all."

It was one of the last warm nights for months to come, and they were sitting on the statue of Walt Whitman that pegged the campus green. Paul wore a pair of crumpled red boxer shorts, dirty white sneakers without any laces, a backward ball cap, and a pair of sunglasses. No shirt. His chest was peeling from too much sun. He had a plain face, pale eyes, no accent, hair the color of mud. He was whip thin. He often wished he'd been born a more colorful, robust boy. But he was a good sport with a quirky sense of humor, and Rachel had never felt threatened by him in any way.

"I'm surprised at you," Paul said.

"What's so surprising? Why shouldn't I want to meet him?"

Paul didn't answer her right away. For the thousandth time, he studied the way her hair matched her eyes, as if a painter had trailed his brush through a loamy brown, auburn, and ginger and used the same rich skein to color them both.

"You're right," he finally said. "What's it to me if you end up with some brain-dead jock? See if I care."

They didn't talk for a while. Rachel watched the stars and thought briefly about Belle Haven. Paul watched Rachel and slowly became convinced that it was time to take back his heart.

Then, "All right." He sighed. "I'll introduce you if that's what you want, but I think you're being foolish."

"I thought you liked Harry."

"I do," he said mildly.

"You just called him a brain-dead jock."

"That doesn't mean I don't like him. Some of my best friends are brain-dead jocks." He squinted at the stars. "But he's not right for you."

"And if I decide to prove you wrong?"

He shook his head. "Don't come crying to me."

"I wouldn't do that. If you're right about Harry, he'll be my mistake."

"I am," Paul said quietly. "He will. Mark my words."

The night that Rachel Hearn met Harry Gallagher began well enough. True, the party was stupidly crowded, as such parties are. The floor was awash with beer from a leaky keg, the bathrooms unspeakable, the music hurtful, the boys predatory, the girls undone by the humiliating hope that they might be the ones to save these boys from each other and from themselves.

But it was hard to see such things from their midst. Excitement has a way of gilding filth. And there was, in truth, an element of purity even at the evening's lowest ebb, for many of the people in the fraternity house that night were there almost against their will and had no intention of pursuing or becoming prey.

"It looks like *The Rape of the Sabine Women*," Rachel said to Paul as they sat at the top of the stairs and watched the crowd boil below.

"No horses," he pointed out.

"True, though there is a cow tethered out front. I've been trying to figure out why—beyond the obvious link between livestock and frat boys—but I think I give up."

"It's White Russian night," he replied.

"I see. And that's the czar out there tied to a tree?"

"Cream," he said impatiently. "Vodka, Kahlúa, and cream. White Russians."

"Ah," Rachel said, shaking her head. "Frat humor. I might have known."

For a while she and Paul sat on the steps, watching halfheartedly for Harry Gallagher, and chided each other gently. They drank their White Russians too quickly, linked their arms and told secrets, and finally decided to call it a night.

"I feel like a lamb escaping the slaughter," she said, laughing as Paul walked her back to her dorm. It was one of those cold and clear October nights, fancy with stars and plumes of chimney smoke. The cold cleared Rachel's head a bit, but her lips and cheeks were still numb from the vodka and she felt sleepy as a child. She let her feet shuffle through the dying leaves that lay upon the sidewalk and gave little thought to the dangers of walking abroad so late at night, regardless of escort. Even the sudden appearance of Harry Gallagher at the curb ahead, splendid in his trademark Camaro, failed to alarm her.

What will be will be, she thought lazily. And gave herself up to fate.

It might have been the ice cream, drowned in banana liqueur, that Harry fed her when the three of them reached his apartment. Or perhaps the shock of having so many unexpected things happen to her, one after the next, for hours on end. Whatever the cause, Rachel kept only a few remembrances of that night, and these made her recoil even after many years had passed.

"Come over to my place for ice cream," Harry had said on the cold, star-ceilinged street where they'd met. Nothing had seemed so wrong with that.

"You can't eat ice cream without a splash of liqueur," he'd said in his sloppy apartment. And Rachel had felt her muscles contract in anticipation.

"I'll take you home in a minute," he'd promised. "Finish your drink."

But then she and Harry had watched an old *I Love Lucy* rerun, side by side on the derelict couch, sipping from the same glass of syrupy booze, while Paul glared and muttered in a corner. Everything Rachel was doing astonished her, but she felt certain that nothing bad could happen while Paul was with her. And even when she glanced over and noticed that his chair was empty, she knew that he would not have left her there alone. The liqueur had made her drunk very quickly. She was not even aware that her head had fallen onto Harry's shoulder. But when he turned her into his lap and began to move against her, she knew it. She felt as if she had left her body and was watching from above, shocked and amused at the sight of flesh below. Her sense of time was so confused that it could have been minutes or hours before she felt all in one piece again.

"Where's Paul?" she finally mumbled, pushing her hair from her eyes and wondering how she'd burned her mouth. It was sticky and raw. Her breasts, she realized, had been bared. Harry was taking off her shoes. He pointed toward the kitchen.

"He's in there," Harry said as he placed her shoes quietly on the floor. "He can take care of himself."

One part of Rachel knew precisely what was happening and reluctantly welcomed her impending metamorphosis. Twenty-year-old virgins were as rare as comets, and Rachel had long since decided that her virginity was too distracting. Besides, she was curious about sex and had difficulty imagining what it would be like. It was therefore with a somewhat scientific attitude that she approached the whole experience, watchfully open to possibility.

Another part of her looked at matters differently. This boy was, really, a stranger. Rachel knew only that something about the arrangement of his eyes, the grain of his hair, the contours of his hands shocked her senses into a new state: she had never before been attracted to anyone as she was to Harry Gallagher. Disarmed, she was inclined to think the best of him, to anticipate the discovery of a fine and honorable boy inside the lovely skin. What Paul had said about him, what she had heard here and there from disappointed girls, did not matter to Rachel. She felt almost virtuous as she made her decision to judge him according to what he said, what he did, and nothing else.

Sober, Rachel might have allowed her indecision to escalate and, eventually, to lead her safely home. As drunk as she was, she simply declared a stalemate, put her concerns aside for the moment, and concentrated on keeping her feet as Harry took her by the hand and led her to his bedroom.

She did not say a word as he shut the door and pushed her gently onto the mattress. When he knelt over her and began to unfasten her pants, Rachel closed her eyes and allowed herself to drift, to recall the absolutely safe and satisfying feeling of her mother's hands putting her to bed when she was very small, perhaps drowsy with fever, removing her socks, lifting her compliant limbs, arranging the blankets over her, moving quietly about the room.

Harry removed the last of Rachel's clothing, tugged her from the edge of the bed, all without a word. He paid her no compliments, made no inquiries, offered her no protection. He addressed himself not to her but to her flesh. Through it all, Rachel kept her silence and, with it, a degree of distance.

The weight of his body on her changed things. It yanked her into the here and now, purged her memories of home and comfort, so that she opened her eyes and suddenly felt as if she had a great deal to say. But it was as her lassitude left her that she felt herself tear. She hissed like an animal, bit right into her lip, and, through the rest of it, coached herself gently, silent and removed.

This is inevitable. It happens to everyone. I should never have waited so long. Maybe it's like chicken pox: much worse the older you get. God, this is awful. After tonight I won't have to worry about this anymore. I'll be through with this part of it. I'll know what it's like. I won't ever let it be like this again. They say the first time is awful. Thank God they told me. There is no pleasure in this. Not for me, anyway. Is this what men are after? They must know something. Or maybe they just set their sights lower. Or maybe they just don't know any better. Isn't he through yet? He's not even looking at me. I'll have to ask Paul about this. He's a man. He must know something about it. There must be more to it than this, even for them.

When Harry rolled over onto his side and straight into a deep sleep, Rachel waited until her insides had slowly rocked to a standstill and then, floundering against the tangled sheet, threw up in her naked lap. She would have laughed at this whole astounding turn of events, but she was concentrating fiercely on containing her nausea and cleaning herself. When she dragged the soiled sheet into the bathroom with her—feeling vaguely like a giant snake shedding its skin—she found the cloth streaked with blood. She tried to assess her wounds, but bending over made her feel sick again, and faint. So she climbed carefully into the bathtub, blinking at its brightness, and pulled the linen in after her. The hot spray of the shower stung her cheeks, inflamed by Harry's whiskers, and scorched her swollen breasts. It took all of Rachel's strength to stay on her feet, to stay awake, and to tamp down the invasive impression that she had made a terrible mistake.

It wasn't the sex that alarmed her. It wasn't the blood or the sickness or even the way she'd surrendered herself so completely, so quickly, so knowingly.

It was the distance he'd put between them in that ill-made bed, the back he'd turned to her, the realization that he had never once called her by name.

Chapter 5

On his first morning home from Yale, Kit Barrows woke early, showered, shaved, dressed carefully, and crept past his father's bedroom door, down the stairs, and into the kitchen. While he waited at the table, the cook made him a pan of bacon, a stack of toast, and a pot of black coffee. She knew what he wanted without asking, and she knew him well enough to keep quiet. There were mornings when he was friendly and talkative, but this was not one of them.

When he had finished eating, he picked up the phone, dialed the carriage house, and asked Holly to join him in the garden as soon as she could. He did not apologize for waking her. Nor did he ask her if she was alone. The thought of her asleep in her bed did not even enter his mind.

There was an old gazebo in the garden where Kay Barrows and her children had feasted on strawberries and read stories through the hottest part of many summer days. As Kit sat there, waiting for his sister, he passed the time by thinking about business school, Wall Street, and wealth. Such daydreams never failed to fill him with anticipation. They did not fail him now. When he saw Holly making her way slowly through the tulips, he stood up reluctantly and put his hands into his pockets.

"Hello, Holly."

"Hello yourself," she said. When they sat down, they kept a yard of bench between them. "What's so important that it can't wait past the crack of dawn?" But as she looked up from her tennis shoes, she for-gave him with a modest smile. It made him uncomfortable to see the way her face worked. The way her skin stretched taut over her bones. He did not see how it could be anything but painful.

"I'm worried about Dad. I wanted to talk to you before I saw him again."

"He's not up yet?" Their father had always been an early riser, as if to sleep in daylight was to miss an opportunity.

"No. He was . . . he had too much to drink last night." To which Holly showed no surprise at all. "I found him outside when I got home. In the magnolias. He must have been drinking for some time by then. He was sick." Kit worried a loose button on his shirt. "It was awful. I don't understand what he was doing out there, acting like that."

He looked at Holly, hoping she'd be the one to say, Maybe it had something to do with the man I was with last night. But she didn't. She simply blinked slowly, sleepily, and looked out at the tulips in their beds. She seemed to have lost interest in what he was saying. "You don't seem too concerned," he said.

"I'm not," she said to the tulips. "Why should I be?"

Despite the way Holly had distanced herself from their father, Kit had expected more than this. "Because it's so unlike him," he said. "I would have been less surprised to find him playing bingo."

Which got him another ghost of a smile.

"How do you know what's like or unlike him?" she said, the smile receding.

"How do I know? No one knows him better than I do."

Holly looked at him for a long moment. "Of the two of us," she fi-nally said, "I know him better."

Although Kit suspected that Holly's tryst on the carriage-house roof was linked to his father's strange behavior, and although he was often easily annoyed by things she said and did, Kit had not called her out here for a scolding. Now, however, in the face of this claim, he felt himself become angry.

"That's ridiculous, Holly. You've done everything possible to avoid Dad for as long as I can remember. What makes you think you know him better than I do?"

Holly had become accustomed, over the years, to being repri-manded by her brother and her father. She had learned to expect little from either of them. Certainly not much in the way of affection or respect. But she had also grown tired of holding her tongue, keeping her own counsel, and on this invigorating spring morning she was for once unwilling to hold herself in check.

"What do you want from me?" she asked him. "You call me out here, tell me a sad story about Dad drinking, remind me that the two of you are great pals. What for?"

She was right. It didn't make a lot of sense. But none of what he'd seen since coming home made much sense to Kit. "I guess I was curious to see if you knew what was bothering him. If it had anything to do with your visitor last night."

"My visitor." Holly looked out at the tulips again. They were dependable flowers. Tough. Lovely, even in their last days. "Yes, it had everything to do with my visitor." She pushed her hair back away from her face with both hands. "But I don't really think that's any of your business, Kit. And since you know Dad so goddamned well, figure him out for yourself." She pushed herself up off the bench and straightened her clothes, slipped her hands into her pockets, and took a step away from him. "I'm sorry you had such a lousy homecoming," she said. "But I'm sure things will be much better from now on, if you put last night out of your mind."

As she turned to leave, Kit's inclination was to let her go, take her advice, and start over fresh when he saw his sober and predictable father back at the house. But there was much here that he didn't understand. And it bothered him to think that Holly might know something too important to be left in her hands.

"I don't want to put it out of my mind," he said, although he did. "I want to know what's going on in my own house."

She turned back and stood thoughtfully, considered what he was asking of her, weighed his words carefully. She said, "Be careful, Kit."

But he didn't know what he had to be careful about. "For God's sake, Holly, if there's something going on, I want to know what it is. I'm sorry, too, if I walked in on a problem between you and Dad, but I did. And I'd like to know what it is. I might be able to help."

For the first time Holly became upset. Her chin trembled as she looked at him. She bent a little at the waist as if standing up straight were too difficult. "I don't think you can," she said after a moment. "And I'm certain that you're going to wish you'd left well enough alone." But she didn't leave. Instead, she returned to the bench and sat down again, waited quietly, gave him one last chance to go his own way, much as he had done for more than a decade now.

"Tell me," he said, more gently than anything he'd said to her in a long time. "Tell me what's wrong." He sat patiently next to her and gave her some time. And the minutes that she took to collect herself and to consider her words were the last moments of the life he'd always led and had thought he always would.

"I guess it's wrong to think you could leave well enough alone," she murmured, more to herself than to him. "Nothing about this is well enough. But I've been handling it, getting pretty good at it, since I was eleven years old." She looked at him, as if she hoped that he would interrupt her, change his mind, opt to prolong the silence they'd honored between them for years. But he did nothing. Said nothing. Simply waited.

"When I was eleven years old," she continued, looking away from Kit, "he . . . Dad . . . began to . . . to bother me, whenever I was home from school." She kept her face turned away from him, and as he listened he wondered if he were hearing her correctly. "At first it was little things," she said, the words coming faster now. "Some of them he'd been doing for years, but I never really thought about them. Like coming up behind me when I was at the piano, standing very close to me so he was pressed up against my back. He never hugged me when I was little, or kissed me, and I used to love it when he'd stand like that behind me. I thought it was something any father would do. I'm sure it *is* what most fathers do, in a very different way. For very different reasons."

And all at once Kit did not want to hear another word. He was terribly afraid of the things Holly was saying. She was slowly turning the knob of a door he'd never expected to find in the house at his back, and if such a door existed, if she pulled it open all the way, he knew that he would not want to look through it, to see what waited on the other side. He stood up and began to walk away from her, down the steps of the gazebo, shaking his head. "No, no, no, no," he said. "You're not going to do this to me."

But she had given him his chance, and he had lost it. "Do this to *you*!" she called after him, scrambling to her feet. "To *you*. No one has ever done anything to *you* in your whole goddamned life. You come back here and sit down and listen to me until *I* decide to stop. *I* did not start this. *I* did not call *you* out here. *I* did not badger *you* into talking about the wreck he's made of *my* life. All I've ever asked of you is a little privacy, which you've insisted on denying me. But if you think you have the right to summon me out here, interrogate me like this, then I certainly have the right to answer you the way *I choose* to answer you."

She was shouting, her neck webbed with tendons, her arms so stiff at her sides, her hands clenched so tightly they looked like clubs. "All right," he hissed, holding his palms out toward her, both afraid and half hoping that his father would hear Holly and come striding out to silence her. Kit climbed the steps of the gazebo as if he never expected to leave it again and stood as far from her as he could, his back against a pillar. "All right. Get it over with. Tell me how he's wrecked your life." But he was afraid to his bones that he already knew.

"You won't believe me," Holly said. All the anger had gone out of her. She seemed tired and almost as if she, too, wanted nothing less than to talk about her life. "But I meant what I said before. Now that I've started I'm going to tell you everything I've got to tell. And then I want you to leave me alone. I don't ever want you to bring it up again."

Kit felt as if he ought to be the one saying these things, for it was precisely how he felt. He wanted her to get it all over with and then put it to rest. If it was something she had lived with, then it was certainly something he could live with, too. It had to be.

But as it turned out, it wasn't.

Holly's father had never raped her. He had stopped short of that. She never said the word *incest* or *abuse* as she told Kit the story, although she might have. Her father had been more subtle than that, at least in the beginning, when Holly was only eleven, and on top of that small for her age. He had often walked in on her in the bathroom, as if by accident, especially when she had just stepped out of the shower. She had sometimes woken up in the night to find him sitting on the edge of her bed, his hands resting on her hips or her legs, but before she'd come fully awake he would walk out of her room without saying a word and in the morning she would wonder if she had dreamed the whole thing. And then she would feel unclean for dreaming such a dream.

For years she had felt nervous and confused around him, for no matter how hard she tried to stay out of his way, to do nothing that would draw his attention, he always found a way to cross her path, to stand too close, to collide with her and then reach out as if to save her from a fall, grabbing her around the middle one time, by the shoulders the next. "Clumsy girl," he would say, and then as she left he would touch her with his eyes. If anything, it was this impalpable touch that left bruises.

Much as she had hated boarding school in the beginning—still small, her mother newly dead—Holly had eventually come to love her exile and to dread the approach of every holiday, every summer home. Over time, she became more self-assured and was strengthened by her association with a stern, resourceful headmistress, the daughters of other important people, and the world at large. And by her fifteenth birthday she had outgrown the insecurity and confusion that had prevented her from knowing how to behave in the face of her father's strange interest—whether to be alarmed, how to deflect his advances. She expected her father to notice the change in her, when she went home again: to look at the way she kept her head up, her shoulders back, and her eyes steady, and be intimidated. She expected him to see, in her, a challenge. But she did not expect him to take it.

When he did, when he walked straight into her bedroom the first night she was home again, a day earlier than Kit, when he shut the door behind him and stood glaring at her as she lay absolutely still in her bed, when he suddenly rushed toward her and pulled away the covers and opened his robe, Holly knew that she was completely alone. There was no one to hear her scream. There was no one to protect her. There was no one to stop her father from wrenching away her nightgown and pinning her with all his weight in the bed where her mother had once brought her picnics and read her books and polished her heart until it shone.

Chad Barrows would have raped his fifteen-year-old daughter that night, and he did try. But, whether he had drunk too much or failed to completely disarm his conscience, he was unable to do what he'd intended. His body seemed to have greater scruples than his soul.

After that, Holly went home only when she had to. Christmas, Easter, summer vacations were all spent in odd maneuvers. Because Kit was usually home, too, Chad was more careful, but Holly still made sure never to be caught alone. She locked all doors behind her. She accepted every invitation to spend time away from home. And, when her father approached her one morning in the woods behind their house, she stood her ground and said, as loudly as she could without screaming, "If you touch me, I will tell Kit."

Had she known how effective this threat would be, she would have issued it much sooner. Her father's eyes had widened with fury and alarm. He panted like a wild man. He took one more step toward her and stopped, his hands slowly clenching, and said, "If you tell him, I will break your fucking face."

"My face!" She had actually laughed. "Go ahead! Maybe you'll improve it."

This time, the strength she'd gained from years of unhappiness made some impression on him. Either that, or he felt he had no choice but to let her be. Whatever the reason, Chad backed off. Although he still watched her and seemed always to be holding himself in check, he never touched her again. He did not try to stop her when she eventually moved her things into the carriage house. And when she finally brought a man home with her for the first time, her father stood among the magnolia trees with a bottle of whiskey in his hand and showed her that she was even stronger than she'd thought.

Kit sat in the gazebo beside his sister and felt that a large part of him had slipped free of its bones and now hovered somewhere nearby, listening, waiting for the remaining parts of him to rise and follow. He felt light-headed and was sure that if he stood up too quickly, he would collapse, maybe die. He could only imagine one cure for what he was feeling, and that was to prove Holly wrong.

"If all this is true," he began, "I would think you'd have told me a long time ago."

Holly looked at him curiously. *"If all this is true,"* she said. "Didn't I say you wouldn't want to believe it? I don't blame you." She laced her fingers behind her neck and worked her head cautiously from side to side. "You were only a kid when all of this was happening. What could you have done?"

Kit tried to remember what it was like to be that young. "You were just a kid, too," he said. "I can't believe you thought you could handle a problem like that by yourself. There must have been another reason why you didn't tell me." *It never really happened,* he thought. *That's why you never told me.*

"You're right," she said, dropping her hands and straightening her shoulders. "The truth is, I didn't tell you because you're a bastard. That's why."

Kit leaned away from her. He wished he were sitting on her other side, where he could not see the ruined part of her face. "What did I do to deserve that?"

"It's not so much what you've *done*. It's what you *are*, Kit. What you've become. What's been happening to you ever since Mom died."

When Holly looked at Kit's face, saw how carefully he was breathing, how pale he had become, she realized that she was asking too much of him, that she had to lead him through this one step at a time if she hoped to reach him in the end. "For God's sake, Kit, we've behaved like strangers for years now. We barely spoke to each other back then. What would you have done if I'd come to you and said, 'Dad keeps touching me'?"

Kit had no answer. He might have laughed at her. He might have told her not to be a fool. He might not have listened in the first place. He did not know what he would have done. "I don't know," he said.

Holly sat back and looked at him in silence. "Thank you," she said after a moment. "That's the only answer I would have accepted."

They sat for a while. Then, "What about later on?" Kit said, the questions he'd assembled refusing to be dismissed. "When things got worse? If he really did what you say he did, why didn't you come to me then? Or leave altogether?"

"You see? You say things like that, you call me a liar, and you wonder why I didn't come to you."

"Oh, please, Holly. Did you really expect me to accept this story without any doubts? He's my *father*. I've never known him to do anything like what you're claiming he's done. Why should I believe you? Why should I disbelieve him?"

Holly put her hand on Kit's arm. It was the first time either of them had touched the other in many months. "All right," she said. "That's fair. It's natural for you to deny what I've told you. I denied it myself, for years, so I can't blame you for doing the same thing. Which answers your question. I didn't come to you when things got worse because I knew that if it came to a choice between him and me, you'd choose him. In fact, you did choose him, a long time ago. Why such a choice was necessary, I don't know. I suppose it's because of the kind of man he is. The more distance I put between him and me, the less chance I had of keeping you."

Kit was ready with his next question. He knew that he had another choice to make and that he would not be able to make it until he had asked every last question, weighed every last answer, and hopefully found a way to walk out of this gazebo a whole and healthy man.

But before he had a chance to ask anything else of her, Holly said, "I also think that the only way to learn the really important things in life is to live them. People learn things best on their own, in their own good time. Which is another reason I never told you. I kept hoping you'd grow out of his shadow. He's a bad man, Kit. I know that's a childish word. It makes him sound like a little boy. But that's what he is . . . bad. Maybe it's not all his fault. Maybe the seeds were in his blood or in his upbringing, but he fed them, let them put down roots. Like you're doing." The tulips, Kit noticed, appeared to be nodding. He suddenly felt outnumbered. "But I think there's still a chance for you," Holly said. "That's why I've told you all this. What he's really like."

Kit suddenly found it difficult to remember what he had meant to ask Holly. Nothing came to mind but a memory of sitting in this same gazebo with his mother at his side.

"It's impossible," he said slowly, turning the memory around until it showed him another way to defend both his father and himself. "It doesn't make any sense. You can't say things like this about Dad without questioning everything you know about her."

"About who?" And for the first time Holly too looked afraid.

"Mom. You can't honestly think she'd have married a monster. She was smart. She would have seen signs. She would have known if he was capable of such things, long before he ever did them. She never would have stayed with such a man. *You* may not remember her, but—"

"Not *remember* her! Christ! Shut up! Don't you talk about her!" And suddenly Holly was swinging her arms at him, her hair flying in her face, the tears she must have been saving for years streaming down her cheeks. He grabbed her arms and held her against him, wanting to silence her, wanting to hurl her into the garden, and yet wanting to mend everything about her that was broken, wanting everything to be all right and not knowing how to make it so.

"I'm sorry," he said, trying to quiet her. "I'm sorry."

But something had come loose inside Holly, and although she no longer struck out at him she now threw back her head and bared her teeth and said, before she could stop herself for the millionth time,

"She sailed those waters her whole life, but she headed straight into a storm, Kit. Alone. She *chose* to do that. She *died* because she did that. But if we didn't have her body to prove it, I'd be sure that she was alive somewhere as far from him as she could get."

Holly clawed her hair back and dried her face with her hands. She was spent. She sagged against the wooden rail at her back. "I'm sorry," she said. She sounded as if she'd run a hundred miles. "I didn't mean to say anything about that. I'm probably wrong. It had to have been an accident."

"It was an accident," Kit said through his teeth. He couldn't look at his sister. His heart had stopped beating. How he continued to live he did not know. He could not move. He had no strength left at all. "It was an accident. It was an accident."

"It was. I'm sure you're right." Holly could see that her brother had to believe this absolutely. "I was upset. I shouldn't have said that."

Kit's heart began to beat again. Slowly. Like an old man's. And as it did, one last question slipped up out of the place that had flourished in the half-light of his father's shadow. "If all this is true," he said once again, "not the part about . . . about her . . . but the rest of it. If all of that is true, why didn't you leave? How could you have stayed here?"

Holly sighed. A part of her, too, wished that she had never come out to this garden, never said any of the things she'd forced herself to say. "At first I was too young, and what he'd done was fairly innocuous. Not in hindsight, but at the time—more confusing than anything. And later, I was too afraid of him to tell anyone. And too embarrassed. If he'd raped me, yes. I know I would have gone for help. Or if he'd tried a second time, I would have told someone. Maybe even you. I don't know. If he had, maybe I would have gone off on my own. But he didn't. I was unhappy and scared, but I wasn't home that often. And once I'd moved into the carriage house, things were better." She'd spent years scrutinizing her own behavior, coming to understand why she had done what she'd done, and it should have been easy to explain herself to Kit. But it wasn't.

"Besides, think about what you're suggesting, Kit. How would I leave? Dad gives you money, but I have none of my own. Certainly not enough to live on. Dad bought you a car, but not me. I suppose I could go out, try to find a job where looks aren't important, and never come back here again. I suppose I could do that. But why should I? I want to write. That's all I want to do. I don't want to have to struggle to make a living. Which sounds spoiled, I know, but I'm not asking for anything more than I've been led to expect. So I'm biding my time, Kit. In a few months, we turn twenty-one. Our trust funds will be ours. And then I will go."

Kit nodded. He was almost through. "I can understand all that, I guess. But you have to forgive me for having my doubts." He saw her face harden. "Come on, Holly, put yourself in my shoes. Every time I open a newspaper these days I read about some woman making terrible accusations against her father. It's become the fashion to blame every problem on something that happened in childhood. Except half the time it's an incident that's remembered in a dream or in hypnosis or at the hands of a very persuasive therapist. Who's to say what's a real memory and what's not? How is a father supposed to defend himself in a situation like that? I'm sorry, Holly. Too many of these accusations turn out to be false, which is not to say that the women involved don't honestly believe their own lies. I'm sure some of them do. But that doesn't change the fact that they're lying."

Holly took a deep breath. Her hands clutched each other in her lap as if they belonged to two different people. "I don't know why I thought you would believe me," she said. "I should have known better."

"You yourself said it was natural to believe in my own father, Holly. You yourself said it would be hard for me to accept what you've told me."

"But you saw him!" she cried. "Crawling around in the dark. Spying on me. If you don't believe my explanation, then give me a better one."

"For Christ's sake, Holly, there are a thousand explanations. I won't know why until I ask him."

Holly flinched as if her bones had turned to blades. She began to shake her head. "You can't talk to him about this," she said. She was trembling.

She doesn't want to get caught, he said to himself, and a part of him bloomed with satisfaction. *She's been lying.*

"Why not?" he said. "Doesn't he deserve a chance to defend himself?"

"He'll kill me," she said, and although he did not believe this, it was clear that she did.

"Don't be ridiculous. Granted, if he's guilty of doing what you claim, then I admit he's cruel or sick or both. But to exaggerate the problem isn't going to help matters."

"I'm not exaggerating anything, Kit. But I know him. I know that he's capable of far more than he's actually done. Let me ask you this." She turned on the bench so she faced him straight on. "What if I'd told you that he did rape me that night, that I became pregnant, and that he forced me to have an abortion. Would you consider all that worse than *trying* to rape me?"

Kit went cold inside. "Of course I would."

"But why? *He* didn't stop himself from raping me. His *body* did, thank God. But if he'd been able to, he would have raped me, and I might have become pregnant, and we both know I would have had an abortion. I've made the mistake in the past of underestimating him. I don't make that mistake anymore."

"All right," Kit said, working his way back to the place where he'd found his best footing. "But I still can't believe what you've told me—that my father is some kind of monster—without hearing his side of the story. Surely you realize that he has the right to defend himself. But if he can't . . . if it turns out that you're telling the truth, I'll help you. And if you're not, we'll both help you."

"You'll both help me?" And then, understanding, "You think I'm crazy," she whispered. "You're going to go to Dad and he's going to tell you some fairy tale, and once again I'm the one who's going to pay for something someone else has done."

Kit didn't like what was happening. He hadn't set out to say anything of the sort. Lying she might be, but crazy, no. And yet, why would a sane person make up such a terrible story? Again, he felt himself go cold inside. No matter what he believed, no matter which choice he made, he would be facing something awful.

"You can't tell him," she said again, with great urgency. "You can't do that to me."

"Then convince me," he said, not really thinking about what he was asking of her or bringing on his own head. "Convince me you're telling the truth. Convince me he's a liar."

He did not think that she could, but he was wrong.

Holly stood abruptly and began to pace in circles around the gazebo. As she walked she snatched at the vines that draped down to claim the pillars, wrapping them in blossoms and bees. At one point she stopped to bury her face in their leaves, to breathe in their scent, not caring if she was stung. She seemed strengthened by them. And when she turned to face Kit, she seemed to have reached some sort of decision.

Holly sat down. She shook out her hands, crossed her arms, and looked at Kit's face for a long minute. She loved his face, despite how he had turned it away from her over the years. He looked much as he had as a young child, his eyes the same evening blue, his hair still the color of thumbed gold, his face sharper now, and stronger, but not so that it had lost the sweet shape of his boyhood.

Seen from one side, they looked alike. But not from the other.

"This is the hardest part," she finally said. "This is the part I swore I'd never tell you." At the look in his eyes, she said, "Not because it's so terrible. It isn't. In fact, it's one of the kindest things Dad has ever done. And it's something that doesn't matter. Not in the least. When I found out, I was startled by it, and it made me think about a lot of things in a different way, but it never bothered me, and it shouldn't bother you."

Kit made a gesture with his hands to hurry her. He had already heard more than he had bargained for, and he had no desire to open any more doors, but he wanted more than anything else to get it all over with.

"Just after Christmas," Holly continued, "my freshman year at Bryn Mawr, I went skating. I fell. I hit my jaw." She touched the damaged side of her face. "The next day I woke up with a horrible toothache. It was the first time I'd ever needed to see a dentist while I was away from home. Dad always insisted that I see Dr. Bennett during my vacations. But I was in a lot of pain, and I wasn't about to come all the way home. So I went to a good dentist near campus. When he looked at my teeth, he asked me what had happened to my face. I told him that Mom had fallen down the stairs during her pregnancy and that my face had been damaged before you and I were born. I told him about you and me, how you were conceived first. He looked at me in this really peculiar way. I thought he was crazy. Then he took an X ray and examined it for a long time. Then he looked at my face again, and at my teeth, and then at the X ray again. Then he asked me to tell him more about Mom's accident and about you. How many weeks older you were. How much bigger you were at birth. Whether you'd been hurt when Mom fell. He was acting the way people do when they know the answer to a question but they want to see how much *you* know. I told him what I could, which wasn't much.

"That's when he showed me the X ray and explained what must really have happened. He didn't get it completely right, but he was close. Later, when I confronted Dad, he tried to bluster his way out of it. But he eventually told me. In fact, he seemed to enjoy telling me."

Kit began to feel sick. He began to think of ways to leave, now, before she said another word, for he believed that he could not bear anything more and he dreaded to his soul what she might say next.

"It's strange," she said, tears trembling in her eyes, "how we don't question things we're told in childhood, even when we're old enough and smart enough to know better. Mom used to tell me that eating bread crusts would make my hair curly." She almost smiled then. "I was eighteen before I gave that one a second thought. It was the same with my face. I never stopped to think that it might have happened any other way. And even if I had, why would I have ever thought they'd lie to us about it?"

Kit put his head into his hands so that all he could see through his fingers were small, manageable bits of the world. "What happened, Holly? Please just tell me what happened."

"I really don't want to hurt you, Kit. I can remember when we were little and I loved you so much. You were always so much bigger than I was. And I was always sick. I still am sick a lot. I'm not put together all that well." She paused. "And I'm almost grateful for your disgraceful perspective on things: it's probably kept you from feeling guilty about getting the lion's share of everything from the minute you were conceived. I don't want you to feel guilty. I don't want you to feel responsible for something you did before you were born. Something completely innocent. But I do want you to know that Dad is capable of lying in a deep and sustained way. That he's capable of forcing people—doctors and dentists and maybe even our own mother—to back him up. If not to lie, then at least to keep quiet about the truth.

"The fact is, Kit, that I was not hurt when Mom fell down the stairs. That never even happened. I was hurt when you kicked me in the face, Kit. Long before we were born. You were four weeks older, much stronger than I was, your bones much harder than mine. And this time, you have to believe me. Because I can prove it. But also because it will give you something to hold on to. It will remind you that even though he is a terrible liar and a terrible father and in many ways a terrible man, our father has spent the past twenty years protecting you. He was right to keep this secret, I suppose. What you did was entirely innocent." Holly put her arms around Kit and held him as he had not been held since his mother had gone so suddenly to her death. "He didn't want you to bear any blame," she said gently. "And neither do I."

For a long while after Holly left him, Kit sat in the gazebo and listened to the harvest of the bees. He watched a tiny, auburn ant slowly drag the corpse of a paper wasp across the gazebo floor. He followed the patient course of the shadows in the sun-baked garden. He tasted the breeze on his tongue and for the first time in his life noticed his own salt and a subtle, coppery flavor and a trace of the nectar with which the flowers scented the sky. He felt the breeze lift the small hairs on his forearms. He ran his hand over the old wood of the bench where he sat.

He was afraid that if he moved too quickly, the panic that had filled him up would spill over and wash him away, as if he'd never been. He thought about everything Holly had told him, pondered the myth his father had forged, and wondered whether he possessed a tool strong enough to break the bonds of heredity and tradition.

For the first time in years, he remembered his mother in such tremendous detail and dimension that she seemed not to have died after all. He could smell her, feel the texture of her hair, the warmth of her skin. They were on the beach, and he was helping her rig her skiff, hoist its sail, splash it clean of sand. He meant to go out with her, but she said no. Not today. It was too windy. Too late. Nearly time for his supper. She intended to sail out to the first bell, maybe beyond.

Kit remembered how he became furious, threw himself into the sand. How his mother patiently lifted him up and drew him into her lap so that they nestled together in the sand like shore birds. She scolded him gently and kissed him, ran her fingers through his salty hair, told him that he was the best boy she had ever known. Which made him so proud that he wiped his tears with sandy hands, leaving trails along his cheeks, and kissed her good-bye.

"Go on up for your supper," she told him, dragging the skiff into the shallows and climbing carefully aboard. "And look after your sister while I'm gone."

He turned and walked away up the beach toward the sloping lawn. As he reached the grass, he thought he heard her call to him and turned back in time to see her wave and blow him a kiss. She called out again, but he could not tell what she was saying, and so he simply waved back, smiling belatedly, as she turned her attention once again to the sea.

Kit remembered waiting for his mother to return, watching his father go out into the night, going to bed with the knowledge that his mother was missing, waking to the news that she was dead.

He and Holly huddled together in their playroom that awful morning, among their wooden horses and their puppets, until someone brought them breakfast on a tray. But they would not eat and instead clung to each other, dry-eyed, serious as young monkeys.

When their father finally came to see them, they were shocked by his whiskers and his sooty eyes. When they both ran to him, still disbelieving, he grabbed Kit in his arms and walked around the room with slow, giant, random steps. Kit hung straight and limp from his father's emphatic embrace while Holly stood where they had left her and followed them with her eyes.

Kit looked over his father's shoulder and saw his sister watching them. He missed his mother fiercely and began to cry for her. And although he knew that Holly's loss was somehow greater than his own, perhaps *because* he knew this, he was comforted by the knowledge that he was the child his father preferred. He turned his face into his father's chest, wrapped his arms around his father's neck, and was only momentarily distracted when he heard his sister open the playroom door.

Kit was startled to find himself sitting alone in the gazebo, surrounded by tulips. But this was nothing compared with the shock he felt when he realized that until now he had completely forgotten the morning when he lost his mother and his sister both.

Before his father could stumble upon him out here in the open, where he could neither hide nor take a proper stand, where he was still mired in confusion and filled, from one moment to the next, with anger, fear, sorrow, and a surprising strain of relief, Kit rose to his feet and made his way back to the house. The day felt old, but Kit had spent only an hour with Holly, and his father had not yet come downstairs. Still in bed, perhaps. Kit was grateful for the reprieve.

While he still could, he shut himself up in his bedroom and thought about what he ought to do. He believed everything Holly had told him. And yet, he felt so numb and in some ways so removed from what had happened to her that he could not decide on a course of action. Everything of importance had happened years ago. And none of it had been nearly as bad as it might have been. *If it happened at all,* a small part of him murmured, refusing to be gagged.

It would be easy, he realized, to do what he had intended, spend the summer as his father's apprentice, play golf, do the things he'd always done. But it would also be terribly hard.

Kit decided, in the end, to give himself the day. He would spend it with his father, watching him, studying him, looking for an explanation. Perhaps a solution would present itself. Perhaps by the end of the day Kit would know what he ought to do.

And then, if he chose well, perhaps he would be rewarded that night with a dream that would take him back for a second glimpse of the things he had forgotten.

All that day, Kit watched his father carefully. He did not know exactly what he was looking for, but he imagined making the most awful kinds of discoveries: noticing, all at once, that the skin of his father's face was lifting away at the edges and that a moldy skull peeked out from underneath. It was easier now to acknowledge that the time they spent together had often seemed to require rehearsal. Kit realized that he had always planned what he would say and how he would behave around his father, but he found himself too deeply confused to understand why this might be so.

He was furious with his father and afraid for himself. Whenever he thought about his sister, pinned in her bed, he wanted to rip the drapes from their rods and pull the paintings from their frames. At times he wanted to get back in his car and drive away somewhere. But he had only just come home, eager to be with his father again, and a part of him was still looking for a reason to stay.

He found himself acting toward his father as a young boy might toward an older brother: following him around yet having nothing to say, nothing to offer, feeling like an intruder and yet unable to be anywhere in the entire house without wondering where his father was, what he was doing, how he looked when he thought no one was watching.

He knew that he could not confront his father, not without betraying Holly's trust. She had begged him to wait a few more months, until they turned twenty-one and she could run. "I've kept quiet for a long time now, Kit," she'd said. "You can do it for a while." But he wasn't sure that he could do it for a single day.

"What's on your mind, Kit?" His father was sitting in the living room with a scotch and, inevitably, a newspaper. Kit had come in quietly to lean up against the wall, his hands behind his back, like an odd stick of furniture. It was almost evening, almost time for them to sit down to a meal together, and Kit couldn't imagine looking across the table at his father as he'd done thousands of times before, breaking bread with this man, without asking him even one of the questions that were again squeezing into every cranny of his skull.

"Nothing, Dad," he said. "I guess I'm still getting used to being home. It takes me a while, after exams, to unwind. That's all."

"You make me nervous, lurking around the house. You should be out, at the club, chasing girls. Playing some golf while you can. I'm putting you to work in another week."

"Yes, I know."

"Get yourself a new suit. Two. Can't have you at the office dressed like that."

"Give me some credit, Dad." Kit pushed himself away from the wall.

"When it's due," his father said, raised an eyebrow at his son, swallowed some scotch. "Looking forward to having you aboard again, Kit."

"Likewise." He was saying the words first inside his head, so that when they left his mouth they sounded to him like an echo. "I learn more from you over the summer than I do at Yale all year."

"Hmmm. Not sure I like the sound of that. Not sure I don't."

And with that, Chad Barrows gathered up his paper and walked straight out of the room, and it was all Kit could do not to follow him.

And so it went. From one hour to the next, Kit did not know what to think or how to feel. Home for only a day, he felt as if he had been stranded on this plot of land for years, completely out of touch with the world beyond. He wanted to be away, gone, if only for a while, but when he pondered destinations, none seemed to suit. He balked, too, at the idea of explaining such a trip to his father. He could think of no acceptable reason for leaving home now—not even for a day or two—after he'd just come back. His work would begin soon. His father would never sanction an irrational retreat. And Kit could not reveal his motives without putting his sister at risk.

Still, he longed to take some sort of action, some sort of stand, to grant himself a brief reprieve and somehow—and this was the thing he wanted most—somehow to make things right with his sister. He simply could not leave Holly behind.

That night, after his father had gone up to bed, Kit wandered into his father's study, hoping to lose himself in a book, and found instead a way to free himself and Holly both.

He stared at the window behind his father's spectacular desk for several minutes, scarcely moving, and then ran up to his room. To do this thing would force him to leave, at least for a while, perhaps a long while, but he was glad to feel that he had no other choice. So he collected his shaving kit, some clothes, spare shoes, scrounged a paper bag from under the kitchen sink, and carried everything back to his father's study.

Dropping his gear by the door, he walked to the far side of the desk. He first opened the window and then examined the sill for a moment, took up his father's sterling letter opener, and scraped the paint from two small hinges on the far edge of the sill. He loosened each hinge with a sharp rap—paused for a moment, listening for sounds from his father's bedroom overhead, waiting to be sure his father had not heard, would not be storming down to face him—and then, with a bit of coaxing, tipped the sill back on its hinges to reveal a hollow space inside the wall. From this narrow compartment, Kit lifted a locked firebox.

The sight of it after a dozen years filled Kit with satisfaction and, despite himself, pride. "This is between us men, eh?" his father had told him with a conspiratorial wink. "For emergencies, understand? You are never"—and he had become stern for a moment—"never to open this unless you absolutely must. And never in front of anyone else. Don't even go near the window unless you're alone. I'm trusting you to keep this a secret." And Kit had promised that he would.

"But why not have a real safe?" he had asked.

"If you want to make sure something escapes notice," his father had intoned, "don't put a lock on it."

On the wall beside the window was a watercolor of several small and spotless sailboats tacking through a narrow, rocky channel. "Four skiffs tacking to starboard," Kit murmured as he spun the dial on the firebox to the right and stopped at four. "Two prams tacking to port," he continued, turning the dial left to the two. "Eight girls sailing the lot of them," right to eight. "And one lighthouse on the shore." Kit could not remember any nursery rhymes but this one.

As he opened the box, Kit once again marveled at a man who could look at a painting so full of color and light and see in it a way to grant a little boy access to a fortune.

Inside the box Kit found five bundles of one-hundred-dollar bills, three ten-ounce bars of gold bullion and half a dozen gleaming Krugerrands, a small velvet bag that held his mother's rings, and a second bag he'd never seen before. When he turned it upside down, Kit was only mildly surprised at the spectrum of gems, cut but unset, that tumbled across the blotter on his father's desk. He automatically admired their brilliance and calculated their worth but did not consider taking them. He had enough money of his own.

As he poured them back into their velvet pouch, however, he paused over a fiery opal the size of a robin's egg and, without thinking twice, slipped it into his pocket.

Then he locked the gems in the firebox, put the currency, the gold, and his mother's rings into the paper sack he'd brought with him, replaced the firebox in the wall, and closed the windowsill. He knew that his father would notice the intrusion when next in his study, for he liked to stand at the window, his hands resting on the paint-locked sill, and admire his rhododendron. Kit decided not to think about this until later.

Holly was still awake when Kit arrived at the carriage house. "I won't stay long," he promised when she invited him in.

"Don't be ridiculous. You haven't been up here in years. Have a seat."

Kit sat down heavily. Holly looked at the paper bag in his lap. "You want something to drink?" she asked. "Are you hungry?"

"No, no, I'm fine." He looked at his hands. Seemed not to know where to begin. But Holly was a patient person. He had waited for her that morning. She would wait for him now.

He began to speak several times, but each time he stopped after a word or two.

"It's all right, Kit," she finally said. "Believe me, I understand how hard it is to talk about it. You don't have to get it perfect. Just say it."

He looked at her and nodded. "I know," he said. "It's just that I feel so many things. One thing contradicts another. Maybe in a week or a month or a year I'll know how I feel, but right now I'm absolutely flummoxed." He cleared his throat, plunged ahead. "But I've spent the day thinking about everything you told me this morning, and I believe you. I believe all of it. All but one thing.

"You seem to think that Dad was being kind when he lied about how you were hurt . . . about how I hurt you. But I think you give him too much credit. He's spent his entire life perfecting the art of escaping blame. Everything is always someone else's fault, never his. And when he absolved me of my guilt—Christ, before I was even remotely qualified for any kind of absolution—he made me his conspirator. Twenty years ago, he lied so that I would not be blamed. Last night, when I came home and found him under the magnolias, he lied again, said that you and your life were none of my business or his. He's always been good at deflecting accusations, creating scapegoats, saving his own skin at all cost."

Kit put a hand to his throat. His voice had grown hoarse and whiskery. "I'm just like him," he croaked. "You said so yourself." It was as if he had only just noticed that his fingers were webbed or his pupils square.

Holly did not say anything. She looked sad and sorry but not very sympathetic. He had spent years ignoring his own sister, and he was not surprised at the distance that remained between them.

"I'm going away for a few days," he told her. "I'm not sure where. Anywhere but here."

Holly sighed and looked at him impatiently. "Have a heart, Kit," she said. "Don't tell me about your plans to go off soul-searching. I've already found my soul, and I'm dying to take it away from here."

"So what's stopping you?" Kit said. He placed the heavy paper sack in his sister's lap.

"What's this?" she asked cautiously. When he didn't answer, she opened the bag and dumped its contents onto the coffee table.

"The money should see you through to our birthday," Kit said. "And the gold ought to make a nice nest egg. Open the small bag." He watched with real pleasure as she poured their mother's rings into her small palm.

Holly cried for a while after that. She put the rings on her fingers, put her face into her jeweled hands, and cried. Kit smiled at her now and then, when she wasn't looking, and eventually got up and ran his hand over her smooth hair.

He was pleased at her reaction, although he realized that he could not possibly understand the enormity of her relief. He had not suffered as Holly had, though he was beginning to think that his father's influence would give him much to regret. Nor had he ever looked at money the way Holly had. She had known for years that to live in a mansion means nothing if you can't afford to leave it. But Kit had credit cards, bank accounts, plenty of everything. His father had always paid his debts when he came up short and had attended to the nuts and bolts of everyday life so that Kit himself had never had to pay a bill, stick to a budget, make ends meet. High finance Kit understood. But he'd never known what a gallon of milk cost . . . or cared. Nor had he ever learned to take care of himself. There was always someone else to do that, to wash his clothes, cook his meals, clean up after him. Holly had never made her own living, or held even a summer job for that matter, and the money that was allowing her to leave was not money she herself had earned, but she knew how to take care of herself in other ways, was far more self-reliant than her brother, and he both envied and respected her for it.

"I'm afraid you won't have time to pack much," Kit said. "I should have given you a couple of days notice before I"—he nodded at the trove on the coffee table. "I'm obviously not thinking too clearly."

"That's where you're wrong," Holly said, wiping her face with her sleeves. "You're thinking very clearly. Besides, I don't need much time to pack. An hour, tops. There's not a lot I want to take with me. And I don't need to make any plans. I've spent years imagining what I'd do when I had money of my own. All I have to do is throw some things in a suitcase."

"I'll help you," Kit offered.

He followed her around the apartment for a while, bumping into her and getting underfoot, until she finally handed him the phone book and asked him to call a travel agent. "Find out about flights to San Francisco for tomorrow morning," she said, "and book me a room for tonight somewhere near the airport. Somewhere nice."

While he made the calls, Holly finished packing, tucked her riches into a fat leather bag, and carried her things down to Kit's car.

She was gone for such an oddly long time that Kit was on the point of going after her, afraid suddenly that their father might have found them out, when she returned. She was a bit breathless and looked as if she might have been crying.

"Are you all right?" he asked.

"Fine. I'm a little overwhelmed, I guess. It's finally beginning to sink in." She took a quick look in the fridge and, after a moment, reluctantly poured a quart of milk down the kitchen sink. "I hope you won't mind giving me a ride to the hotel."

"Of course not," he said, glad that they would be leaving together.

"Oh, here," she said, fetching a postcard from her desk, writing out a name and a telephone number, handing it to him. "I'll write to you at Yale in the fall to let you know where I am, but I don't think I'd better try to reach you here. If you need me before then, call the Corrigans. Emily Corrigan's my best friend. She's been my roommate at Bryn Mawr for the past two years. When I go back to school in the fall, I'm sure it will be somewhere else, but I'll still be in touch with Emily. She'll know where I am."

Kit was ashamed to realize that he had not known about an Emily, that he had never bothered to ask Holly about the man she'd been with the night before, who had unintentionally played such a pivotal role in their lives. But he believed that there would be time to learn about Holly's life, and he looked forward to meeting her again on neutral ground where the only shadows would be their own.

On their way to the hotel, Kit and Holly Barrows said their good-byes in roundabout ways amid long silences that struck them as less odd than the sound of their two voices together. When they arrived at the hotel, Kit waved away the doorman and helped Holly carry her luggage into the lobby. He said good-bye to her then, held her head against his shoulder for a moment, and drove away without giving a single thought to where he might go. It just didn't seem important at the time.

Chapter 6

When Rachel woke up in Harry's bed, it took her a full minute to remember where she was and why she felt so ill. It was a long and frightening minute, measured by a parade of sensations that compounded her bewilderment, one by one. The clenching of her stomach, the sour film on her tongue, the pasty lethargy of her eyelids, the sticky ache where her thighs met, the sting of her abraded cheeks.

"Thank God," Rachel whispered when she realized she was alone. She lay in the bed for a while, listening, but finally climbed unsteadily to her feet, hoping that Harry would not return before she'd had a chance to dress and compose herself. When she could not find her sweater, she gingerly searched through the clothes that were draped over chair backs and radiators, lampshades and bedposts, across the neglected room. The green chamois shirt she chose was fairly clean, worn just enough to smell vaguely of Harry.

Once in the bathroom, Rachel locked the door and began to clean herself carefully and thoroughly. She ran Harry's toothbrush under very hot water, both before and after scrubbing every part of her mouth, including, especially, her lips.

It didn't surprise her when the cloth she used to wash herself came away red, for she ached and throbbed as if a piece of glass were trying to work its way out of an old abscess. She looked around the bathroom, found a small mirror in the medicine cabinet, and by perching gently on the edge of the tub was able to look down at the reflection of her genitals.

Where her flesh had before been smooth and pink, it was now jagged and empurpled and the point of each tear bore a hard, black knob. Everything seemed to have congealed or clotted in a business-like way, however, so Rachel simply dressed herself again, brushed out her hair, and smoothed her cheeks with white, shaking hands.

She had no idea what she would say to Harry when she encountered him. Part of her was appalled and suspicious, so sure she'd made a mistake that humiliation had already begun to set in. Another part of her set aside the indistinct memory of Harry, grunting and grinning as he detected and quickly dismantled her virginity and then later, when they had rocked to an abrupt halt, turning his back. It was so tempting to think of Harry instead as he had been before last night and as he might be from here on in—a promising boy for whom she longed.

As she left the bathroom, Rachel smelled coffee and heard the sound of the television turned low. She was so nervous that she found it difficult to smile. But only Paul was there to see her enter the room, pale and hesitant. He sat up, shoved a ratty blanket off the couch so she could sit down.

"Don't talk," he said. "Save your strength." He poured her a cup of coffee, built a nest of cushions around her, and opened a window so that the cold October air flowed through the stale indoors like surf.

He told Rachel that Harry had gone out and wouldn't be back until much later in the day. She felt herself slip, then, into a posture of resignation and recognized the beginnings of remorse. But a part of her was unconvinced, well stocked with explanations and pardons. A part of her wanted very badly to believe that her infatuation with Harry would not leave her scarred.

She changed into her sweater and then sat with Paul for a while, sipping coffee and nibbling plain toast, until they felt equal to the long walk back to campus. They went slowly, stopping often, for they were both in several types of pain and had no reason to hurry. It made them feel better to walk and to be together. They talked, laughed from time to time, and singly wondered why it was taking them so long to get down to the business of sharing their secrets. As they crossed the campus green, Rachel finally led Paul to an empty bench in the sun and told him what had happened.

"No kidding, Rachel? Really? Golly. And I thought you two were playing cribbage all night. Well, I'll be damned. Just when you think you know somebody, something like this—"

"Shut up, you ass, and let me finish." Rachel picked up a red maple leaf from the grass and slowly dissected it. "You think you know me so well, but you didn't know I was a virgin, did you?" She had expected surprise, even shock, but she was instantly dismayed to see the effect that this had on Paul. He sat back as if he'd been sucker-punched, put a hand to his mouth like a woman. But he didn't say anything. He simply looked at her.

"I know you told me not to come crying to you if things went wrong with Harry," she sighed. "And I won't. But I want you to tell me honestly whether I would be foolish to expect him to . . . I don't know . . . phone me later. Or come looking for me."

Paul took his hand away from his mouth. "I told you that I'd introduce you to Harry but nothing more. No matchmaking and no hand-holding. If I tell you that you were a one-night stand, you'll deny it. You'll even be angry with me for saying so. And if I tell you that Harry will call, I'll hate myself for postponing the inevitable. Because Harry won't call, Rachel." He got angrily to his feet. "He'll walk right past you in class tomorrow. If you corner him, he'll be civil and smug and call you by the wrong name. But don't take my word for it. See for yourself."

As Rachel watched Paul walk away, she wondered why he was so angry. Perhaps he was feeling some vicarious strains of her own doubt, fear, hope, and confusion. It wasn't until two weeks later that Rachel finally understood the extent of Paul's involvement in her encounter with Harry Gallagher.

Harry had not called, of course. And so she, after a week of wondering and agonizing, had finally convinced herself that it would be all right to call him.

"Hello, Harry?" she said, when a man answered. She could barely hold the phone. Her hand felt as if it were broken. She wished she'd never done this, after all.

"No," he said. "Harry's gone out. You want me to give him a message?" He had a slight British accent, which Rachel thought quite lovely. She had not known of a roommate.

"I don't know," she said. "I guess you could tell him that I called. It's Rachel. I'm a . . . friend of his."

"Oh, Rachel," he said, with a great deal of emphasis on the first part of her name, as if he were saying, Oh, *that* friend. "Yeah, Harry mentioned a Rachel." She listened carefully for clues but was not sure what Harry might have said about her. "This is Skip," he said. "Harry's apartment mate."

"Hello," Rachel said, feeling foolish.

"Listen," Skip said. "Harry will be back soon. You can try him again in a bit. Better yet, come over and wait for him. I know he'll be glad to see you."

Rachel began to smile. She swung her foot.

"I guess I will," she said. "If you're sure it's okay."

"I'm sure," Skip said.

Rachel changed clothes, and then again, then stripped and quickly showered, dressed, and was on her way to Harry's before she realized that her AmCiv discussion group was about to begin without her. She had spent three hours the night before preparing for group. She felt unlike herself, suddenly, and was both elated and alarmed by the sensation. But, as she had on the night that had ended in Harry's bed, Rachel gave herself up to fate and possibility and the hope that there would always be an exception to every rule.

"You don't mind if I eat something, do you?" Skip said. "I'm starved." He offered her white bread, pink bologna, emphatically yellow mustard, and a knife. *Still Life,* she thought. *I haven't eaten bologna in years.*

"Thanks," she said, "but I'm really not hungry."

"Beer?" It was one-fifteen in the afternoon.

"No. Thanks."

Skip took a bottle for himself, pulled out two chairs at the wobbly kitchen table, one for him, one around the corner for her. He ate his sandwich in immense bites. It was gone quickly. His lips were vaguely yellow, and the beer made him belch.

"Sorry," he said. "We've sort of let our manners lapse around here."

Rachel glanced at the clock above his head. She listened for the door. And then, because she couldn't help herself, "You said Harry mentioned me?" she said, and could have ripped out her tongue. She looked down at the tabletop and saw her finger scratching a furrow in the sticky brown skin it wore. She put her hands into her lap.

"Indeed he did," Skip said, smiling. "He had to, really. I do the laundry around here." He grinned, leaning back in his chair.

For a moment, Rachel could make no sense of this. And then,

remembering the bedsheets, she understood. She let her breath out slowly and looked right at him.

"What did Harry say?"

"Well," Skip said. "I have to whisper this." He moved his chair next to hers.

Rachel began to know that this was not what she had been hoping for, but she wasn't sure. She had only just met Skip. Perhaps he was simply eccentric. She had met so many eccentric people here at school. They had, in the beginning, astounded her, but after a time she had found them to be far more trustworthy and predictable than many of the more ordinary people she had encountered since leaving home. And so she gave Skip the benefit of the doubt and reluctantly, her shoulders hunched, offered her ear.

"Harry said," Skip whispered, at the same time sliding his hand around her arm, "that the two of you were a perfect fit." He drew back for a moment, then again into her ear said, "Nice and tight."

By the time she realized what he was saying, he had put his tongue into her ear and was reaching for her with his other hand.

Rachel knocked her chair over backward as she gained her feet and ran to the door. She ran for blocks before she lost her breath. She had left her jacket behind, but there was no way she was going back for it. She had her wallet and her keys. And she now knew everything she needed to know.

Two days later, when Rachel finally found herself face-to-face with Harry, jostled together on their way into class, he had not spoken to her, had shown not the slightest recognition. She had not been surprised but, nonetheless, felt unspeakably sad and embarrassed, especially when she noticed the other boys from his fraternity looking at her in a way that made her want to gouge out their eyes with a spoon.

Even so, even after everything had gone wrong, she had not gone crying to Paul. He had come crying to her.

"I have something to tell you," he said without preamble when she found him waiting outside her room on Friday evening. He was sitting on the floor, drinking a bottle of beer and working a crossword puzzle. Seeing him like this, Rachel was not at all prepared for the confession he had come to deliver. "Come on in," she said, unlocking the door and turning on the lights.

Once inside, he immediately said, "I know you're feeling awful about Harry," but she interrupted with a wave of her hand.

"Oh, please, Paul. It's over and done with, and I don't want to talk about it."

"Well, I do. I like being your friend. It's one of the things I like best in my life. Certainly better than that goddamned fraternity. But I can't even look at you now without feeling terrible. I don't want to be around you. I don't want to think about you. I don't want to talk to you. When you look at me I feel sick. So I have to put things right with you, Rachel." He ran both hands through his hair. "Although putting things right will probably get me kicked out the door, but I'll take my chances."

By this time Rachel was more impatient than alarmed. "For heaven's sake, Paul, tell me what's wrong."

So he sat down on Rachel's bed next to her and, after a moment, began to tell her why he had been so sure about Harry Gallagher.

"Do you remember when Harry sent you out to the kitchen to get the ice cream?" Rachel nodded. "Well, as soon as you left the room he tried to convince me to leave so he could get you to bed, only I wouldn't go. So then he said I could stay as long as I kept out of his way. He said he'd give a signal when it was time for me to get lost."

Paul looked away. Cleared his throat. "There's a code we use," he said. "All of us. It's something we're taught during Hell Week. Part of our initiation. I'll bet you could walk into any boardroom in this country and ask for the signal for 'okay, boys, this one's ready,' and a bunch of hands would go up." He tried to chuckle but couldn't quite manage it. Took a deep breath and blew it out loudly. "I live with a bunch of people who can be pretty vulgar, Rachel, and I guess when I'm with them I can too. I've seen a lot of disgusting stuff, and I've heard some things that I hope to God are lies. But I've never seen anyone act quite like he did that night. He was practically drooling. I don't know, maybe he just seemed worse to me because you're my friend." He looked at her for a moment. "I know I should have intervened, but I was angry with you. For involving me. For making me an accomplice to something I had warned you to avoid. Besides, at that point you weren't very drunk and I figured you could take care of yourself, make up your own mind. I didn't know how . . . inexperienced you were. If I'd had more time, maybe I would have decided to get you away from him, but then you came back in with the ice cream, and Harry spent the next hour plying you with banana liqueur and *I Love Lucy,* for God's sake. And I sat there and watched him putting his hands on you and watched you let him and didn't know whether I should stay or leave or haul you out of there. And then suddenly Harry gave me the signal from behind your head while he was reaching up your sweater with his other hand and he wasn't even looking at me. He was looking at where your pants had come unsnapped, and I went into the hallway and watched you until I felt like I was watching a movie. I almost left, but I couldn't just leave you altogether. And then he took you off, out of my sight, and it was out of my hands." Paul rubbed a knuckle against his lower lip and looked away from Rachel, who was squinting with distaste and eager for him to be gone.

After a while, she went out the door and down the hall to the bathroom. She was gone for a long time. When she returned, she took a small suitcase out of her closet. "Give me your car keys, Paul," she said as she folded up her nightgown.

"My car keys? Why?"

"Because I want to go somewhere for a couple of days and I don't have a car. Is there a problem?"

"No. No problem. Where are you going?" He pictured Rachel driving his old, beloved, bottom-heavy Impala and felt sick to his stomach.

"I really haven't decided," she said impatiently. "Somewhere that isn't here."

Once in the car, however, she knew exactly where she wanted to go. Cape Cod was only a couple of hours away. She could be there by ten. It had been three years since her parents had taken her to New England to look at colleges and to see the Atlantic for the first time, but she felt sure that she'd be able to find the little inn on the Cape where they had stayed for a day. The rooms had been plain and clean with wooden floors and white curtains. Sheets that smelled like wind, and a view of sea and sky.

Crossing the canal was like crossing a border somehow. The air changed, grew sugary with fog, then clear and chill, then foggy again. The trees became stunted and bent. The road was dark, and the headlights of the Impala made the eyes of every meandering raccoon into minute beacons. She encountered few other cars, heard little but the wind, felt her hair thicken with salt, and was glad she had come.

By the time she reached the inn it looked as if everyone had gone to bed. For a moment she was even afraid that they might have closed up for the season. But after parking the car in the small gravel lot, she heard through the still air the sound of voices and of music softly playing. She followed the sound to a lighted window and an un-latched side door. With rising anticipation, she opened the screen door and gave the heavy inner door a shove.

Rachel did not know it, but she had stumbled upon one of those rare places that have managed to keep their secrets. A lot of people knew about the inn's summertime bar with its old wooden tables and its wraparound porch, but few knew about the tiny, off-season bar that was tucked behind the lilacs on the other side of the old, rambling building. The couple that ran the inn opened this winter pub only when they felt like company. If passersby saw a light in the window, they would often stop for a brandy and a chat before strolling on home. Strangers were scarce at this time of year in so small a town, and the chances of one finding the secret bar—and finding it open—were slim. Rachel was one of the lucky ones.

"Hi," she said to the man behind the bar. He wore a navy blue blazer, pants of white sailcloth, and boating shoes. He was an old man with brown, lined skin and little hair, but his eyes were clear and curious as he looked Rachel over.

"Good evening," he said gently. "I'm afraid we're not really open tonight, miss, but as it's chilly I'll pour you one drink if you can show me some identification."

"Actually, I'm looking for a room," she said, afraid now that she should have called first or gone to the kind of town with all-night clerks and swimming pools. "I guess I should have made a reservation."

The old man looked past Rachel toward the two women playing backgammon in front of a small fireplace. "Are we open for guests, Fiona?" he asked reluctantly.

"No, we're not," she said. She wore a housecoat with pink rosebuds on it. Blue veins burrowed like worms along the tops of her feet, swollen in satin mules, and her shoulders were padded with fat. Rachel recognized her immediately, for there were dozens like her in Belle Haven, and knew that this was the woman who hung the sheets out in the sunshine, polished the wooden floors, and made sure that the windowpanes gleamed. When the woman looked up and saw who was asking, she put down the dice and sighed. "I'm sorry, honey, but I just wasn't expecting anybody. I haven't got a single room ready, and it's already so cold upstairs. We only heat up the rooms if we know someone's coming."

"Oh," Rachel said, "I understand," for she usually accepted what she was dealt, even when she knew that a bit of persuasion might turn things her way. "Thanks anyway." She turned toward the door. But after the long, hopeful drive she had no stomach for a night in an infested motel or, worse, in the Impala. She wanted badly to sleep in the room upstairs where she had slept before, next door to the room where her parents had stayed, to look out the window the next morning to find the irreproachable sea waiting there for her. She wanted to be by herself in a safe and sheltered place where people would ask nothing of her and she need not ask much of them.

It was therefore with a certain anxious determination that she turned back from the door, walked up to the tired woman, and said, "I don't need sheets, or towels, or even a pillow. Just a blanket and some soap. Please. And I'll leave everything tidy." She realized that she sounded a bit unhinged, so she smiled and added, "My name is Rachel Hearn. I stayed here with my parents when I was seventeen, and I haven't been back to the Cape since. I'm not sure where to go."

"You college kids are all alike," the woman sighed, pushed herself out of the chair. But she smiled as she said it. "Take my place, Jack," she instructed her husband as she led Rachel out of the bar and down a dim hallway, "but don't drink my brandy. I'll be right back."

The two women stopped at a vast linen closet and then climbed a narrow staircase to the rooms above. "Would it be all right if I stayed in the room with the painting of the rumrunner?" Rachel asked.

"Of course . . . Rachel, is it? I'm Fiona." She led Rachel down the hallway, her old eyes fumbling in the poor light. "This is the room," she said, handing Rachel a bundle of cold, smooth linen so she could open the door, switch on the light, and make sure all was as it should be.

Although Rachel protested, Fiona helped her make up the bed and even tracked down a hot-water bottle for her feet. She was generous with blankets and towels, unwrapped a bar of soap, opened the window for a moment to freshen the air, and then said good night. "I've forgotten your key," she remembered as she was leaving, "but you can collect it at the desk when you go out in the morning. The heat will be up before long. Sweet dreams." And then she was gone.

Since there wasn't yet any heat to hoard, Rachel turned out the light, opened the window wide, and leaned into the night. She could see the light from the bar below her tinting the bare branches of the lilacs and could hear the faint sound of voices. It was that quiet. She felt much as she had as a little girl, comforted by the knowledge that her large, capable, strong parents were in the house with her.

Although she could not see it, Rachel knew that the ocean was very close by. She felt herself thriving on its kaleidoscopic smell, on the sounds of fledgling waves and of the rigging of sailboats at their moorings, beautiful as bells.

She felt so removed from Harry and Paul, from her friends, and from everything that had become important to her in recent years. She felt so near to her parents, the old, ramshackle house she'd grown up in, and all the people whose faces she would still recognize decades from now because they were a part of Belle Haven, as she was.

As she lay in bed that night, shivering and alone, she felt a peculiar joy. It was something akin to the feeling she always had at the end of each semester when it was time for her to go home. It made her smile and hug her knees to her chest, counting the weeks until Christmas break and remembering the taste of Belle Haven snow.

As Rachel drove Paul's Impala back to school on Sunday afternoon, she vowed to keep her sojourn a secret. The little town on Cape Cod with its one-of-a-kind inn, its clean, deserted coves, its trademark skiffs and oysters was a place she hoped to return to again and again throughout her life. She had no intention of sharing it.

Rachel was not yet sure what she wanted to do with her life, what sort of work might best suit her. She had not really defined her dreams. She was not even entirely sure what sort of person she wanted to be and, so soon after Harry, was having trouble imagining herself with another man. But this time away from school had restored her equilibrium and left her hungry for trustworthy people who had good manners and things to teach her that she wanted to learn. She had already lived in one such place, was now leaving another, and was sure there must be many such secrets kept out of sight, around the bend, on the other side of a thousand bridges. She had made up her mind to find them.

Rachel felt rested and relaxed as she opened the door to her room and turned on the lights. No one had warned her that every kind of pain is worse when you go toward it unprepared.

"You had an emergency call from home. Call Dean Franklin immediately." Someone had pushed the note under her door. It had her name on it and the dean's telephone number. She stood there and looked down at it. Then she looked around her room, saw the books and the potted plants, blinked at the colors in the curtains her mother had sewn for her, and wondered who had left a beer bottle on her windowsill.

Several of her neighbors arrived then, having heard her return, and told her that her phone had been ringing, off and on, for more than a day. They had heard people knocking at her door several times, seen Dean Franklin come and go, and knew something was wrong. But no one knew what. Call us if you need anything, they said, and left her alone.

When Rachel phoned the dean, he told her that he'd be right over to see her, but she shrieked at him to tell her what was wrong. So he told her that her parents had been killed in an automobile accident. They had died instantly, he said. Without pain. But Rachel knew of nothing on earth that could promise her this was true. As if to blunt what he said, the dean kept talking. And Rachel continued to listen, holding the phone like a gun to her ear, as if letting go of it meant making a choice to go on with her life.

Her parents, said the dean, had been on their way to have their few, peerless apples pressed into cider. Rachel loved apple cider, and it had always been their tradition, at Thanksgiving, to indulge her minor passion. They had not known, she suddenly realized, of her decision to spend this Thanksgiving at school, with friends. They had not known, either, that she had lately discovered a liking for wine, that she had not given a thought to the cider she would be missing back home. She realized, as she spoke with the dean, that her parents had died while she sat on a small, white beach, wrapped in wind. She was horrified that both of them had left without her. She ached with gratitude that they had left together.

It wasn't until she was on her way to Belle Haven on the bus that night that she felt the keys to the Impala in her pocket—they were like teeth against her thigh—and remembered that she had once known a boy named Harry Gallagher.

Chapter 7

During his first hours of flight, Kit allowed the road to lead him. He simply didn't care where he was going or when he would get there. As he drove, he found nothing entertaining in the moving mosaic beyond his windshield. Nothing from the outside world vexed him. Nothing alarmed him. There was enough boiling inside him to occupy every sense he had. He simply drove.

When he grew hungry, he stopped at an all-night diner where everything tasted of the same rancid grease, was later violently sick in a musky pine forest, and eventually parked in the corner of a deserted rest area and slept until dawn.

Kit woke early the next morning, cold, cramped, and disoriented, unable to see through the car's foggy windows and unsure what he might find beyond them. With his palm he cleared enough of the glass to see that he was parked near a brick building. He was in a rest area. The thought of fresh water made him sit up straight. Water was one of many things he had not thought to bring with him.

Armed with his overnight bag, Kit hurried into the rest house, put on a fresh shirt, brushed his teeth at a rusty sink, splashed cold water on his face, did his best to restore himself. He was exhausted. He was not sure where he was. As clean as he could manage, he returned to the lobby of the rest house and found a map mounted in a Plexiglas case. On it was a small arrow and the words YOU ARE HERE.

Western Massachusetts. The Berkshires. He turned away from the map and made his way out into the open air. Blinking at the morning sky, Kit was astonished to find himself among mountains. He hadn't noticed them in the dark, nor had he felt the lift and fall of the land beneath him. But there they were, all around him, so heavily wooded that they appeared to be furred. They rose up abruptly, sudden as a shout, making him feel smaller than he'd ever felt.

He didn't mind the feeling. To be dwarfed by something as magnificent as these mountains did not diminish him. He felt himself to be in the best sort of company as he climbed into his car and headed back out onto the road.

For every mile Kit put between himself and his father, his perspective evolved a shade. During the night he had been filled, in turns, by loathing, fear, sorrow, and a sort of desperate optimism, each overlaid with irrepressible images of Holly's lopsided face and of his father lurking in the magnolia grove. But as he made his way through the mountains, their peaks softened by countless storms and seasons, their forests gilded by the rising sun, he eventually calmed.

Crossing the border into New York, Kit turned onto a deserted parkway and dawdled south. The trees alongside the road were heavy with new leaves. The grass was so plump and green and bright that Kit yearned to lie in it. He tipped his face into the wind and felt it pull tears from his eyes. And as he began to awaken to the world around him, the part of him that had been fretting about his father and what might be happening at home grew curiously numb and finally became disinterested, as if his life until now had been a job that no longer suited him.

The mountains helped. Compared with these mountains, a man's life seemed as brief as the flick of a bird's tail.

At Route 84 Kit turned west and headed for the Hudson. He'd felt the tug of the big city that waited a bit farther to the south, as if it were an enormous magnet and he a sliver of iron, but he felt a far greater attraction to the mountains and the stretches of pastureland that led him west.

At midday he reached the Pennsylvania border and decided to try a two-lane road that meandered southward along the bank of the Delaware River. He was hungry, hungrier than he could ever remember being, so he stopped after a while at a small restaurant whose crowded parking lot suggested that the food might be worth eating.

At a table no bigger than a stop sign, Kit ordered a bowl of chicken soup and a club sandwich. All the other tables were taken. The waitresses raced among them like quail among cats.

"Are you always this crowded?" he asked the one who returned with his soup.

"It's the Gap," she explained, hurrying away.

Which meant nothing to Kit until he began to see signs for the Delaware Water Gap a couple of miles down the road. He was not tempted when presented with the choice of following the river south to the Gap or turning west at Route 80. The Gap would always be there, but not everything worth seeing could make such a claim. Kit wasn't sure what he was looking for, but he suspected that it would be something easy to miss, something most people overlooked. He had no intention of spending his time on anything that drew crowds.

With this in mind, Kit soon left the interstate in favor of country roads, relying on the sun and his nose to guide him. It was possible to go for miles now without encountering another car. When he came to a gas station, he filled his tank, anticipating the need and wary of wandering through strange country without knowing its resources. For the same reason, he stopped an hour later at a place called the Short Stop Inn. It was still early enough in the day for more travel, but Kit was tired of driving and wanted nothing more than a quiet room and a comfortable bed.

The Short Stop Inn was a big white house covered in asbestos shingles that looked like fish scales. The innkeeper was, predictably, watching a ball game in the tiny bar off the front entrance. Autographed baseball bats were mounted on the walls above the liquor shelves, decals hemmed the mirror behind the bar, from the ceiling a long string of pennants pointed at the floor like a clown's collar, and ball caps hung everywhere from nails, as if this might be the flip side of a hunter's trophy room.

"What can I do ya for?" the innkeeper asked when he spotted Kit in the mirror. He was old enough to be retired, with enough time and energy on his hands to take a lifelong passion and make it his life. Kit suspected that once Christmas had come and gone the man would pack his bags and head south to be ready and waiting when spring training began.

"I'd like a room," Kit replied. "Just me. For one night."

"Well," said the innkeeper, turned on his stool for a better look. "I like a man who answers all my questions before I've gotten around to asking 'em."

Kit waited patiently. He wasn't here to make friends. He wanted a place to sleep, that was all.

"Okay, then," the man finally said, sliding off his stool. "One room, one man, one night. Sounds easy enough."

He led Kit to a tiny office opposite the bar. "I am James Fiester," he said firmly, as if starting in on a campaign speech. "That's with an *ie*, although I get a lot of ribbing at Thanksgiving on account of it sounds like *Feaster.*"

Kit stood quietly, waiting for his key.

"I see you've no luggage," Mr. Fiester said, peering at the floor around Kit's feet.

"I have a bag in the car."

Mr Fiester poked a finger through the venetian blinds at the window and took a peek. "Nice car," he said, as if Kit might not have noticed. "I was going to ask you to pay for the room up front, but it don't look like you're short of cash. I'll settle with you in the A.M."

"Now's fine," Kit said, taking out his wallet. "I might want to get an early start."

"Oh. Okay, then. With tax, that'll be twenty dollars for the night."

Kit had expected more.

"I don't ask much," Mr. Fiester said, as if he'd read Kit's mind, "but the rooms are pretty basic, you know. All I get around here are fishermen, and all they want's a place to drink a few beers, watch some ball, and get some sack time. Out at sunup, that gang. Crazy bunch, if you ask me."

But Kit hadn't asked him, and by now Mr. Fiester was beginning to get the idea that all Kit wanted was to be pointed in the right direction.

"Up the stairs, second door on your left," he said, handing Kit a key. "Local calls only. Bathroom's at the end of the hall. One towel per customer."

First, Kit took a long, hot shower. Lacking soap (for he had never known a hotel that did not supply it), Kit washed all over with shampoo, which took so long to rinse off that the water began to run cold. Then, wrapped in a skimpy towel, he crept back to his room and climbed straight into bed. Although it was still light out, he had no trouble falling asleep, but when he woke in the middle of the night, in the strange room, he had no idea where he was.

"What?" he shouted out, sitting straight up in bed, clutching the blankets. There wasn't a sound but his own breathing. Then it came back to him, where he was and why.

He'd had enough sleep, but he was terribly hungry again. It seemed as if he'd embarked on a painful cycle. Half the time he was tired, the other half hungry. In either state, he seemed prone to a great sensitivity. Everything was accentuated. His problems, when he allowed himself to ponder them, seemed acute. And because their edges were so sharp, he could not bear to consider any of them for very long but instead took them in turns, one after the other, through the rest of the long night.

At times Kit felt afraid, for he did not know himself as he thought he should, as he had once thought he had. Too much had happened too quickly, and he found himself wondering if leaving home had been the right thing to do. At other times he felt a vast relief and did not care why he had left, only that he had.

Toward morning, Kit began to consider destinations. None seemed right. He did not want to stay with friends. He did not want to go back to Yale to exchange work for a stifling dorm room and a hundred days of canned food. He did not want to drive endlessly, aimlessly. Already, he was tired of being forever on his way to somewhere else.

I'll make up my mind today, he promised himself as he gathered up his few belongings. To do what, he didn't know. But he had a feeling that before the day was done he'd have chosen a course, if not a destination.

After eating a huge breakfast at the first coffee shop he encountered, Kit made his way southwest, occasionally crossing a highway but never leaving the country roads he'd come to prefer. The sight of cows and horses in their meadows soothed him. Old barns made him wish for a grandfather, one who knew something about the land. At one point, an inviting meadow so enticed him that he stopped by the side of the road and spent an hour walking its borders, listening to birdsong, and wishing that he knew the names of wildflowers. He'd never paid any attention to birds or flowers before. Not wild ones.

At noon he stopped again to eat a hot beef sandwich and a dish of coleslaw in a German restaurant where the waitresses all wore white bonnets and the menu boasted four kinds of sausage.

Kit had been back on the road for only a few miles when he reached another of those little towns that slowed him to a crawl and clotted the traffic. It was here that he spotted something that appealed to him in surprising ways, and he smiled for the first time since saying good-bye to his sister.

"I want to make a trade," Kit said, waving impatiently at his Jaguar. Big Al, of Big Al's Used Cars and Trucks (WE ON-ER FAIR OFF-ERS), walked over to the Jaguar, ran his hand along its unmarked hide, glanced through the driver's window, and shook his head.

"For what?" he snorted. "The whole lot?" Behind him, a row of aging cars and pickups slowly surrendered to rust and gravity.

"That one," Kit said. He pointed at a huge, elderly motor home with a flat face and dusty windowpanes. Above its twin windshields, large, slanted letters spelled out the name ROAD SCHOONER. A long, red-and-white striped awning was furled above the side door, which stood halfway between bow and stern, and the undented white hull was trimmed with narrow bars of silver. The tires were plump. A long bumper sticker read, GONE FISHIN'.

"For a Jag?" As hard as he tried, Big Al just couldn't manage to hide his excitement.

"For a Jag." Kit nodded. He knew it was a ridiculous trade, but the Jag was tainted now—it had come from his father and had not quite lost its strings—and the thought of driving the old caravan instead, lounging under its candy-cane awning, perhaps even taking it back to Yale with him in the fall, was tempting.

Seeing the shock on Big Al's face, Kit decided to check out the Schooner more thoroughly. If anything, the interior only made him more determined to make the trade. Here was a whole new home: two beds, a kitchenette, cupboards, carpets, and a bathroom with shower. He would need propane, gasoline, some linens, groceries, books, not much else. He drove the Schooner around a roomy K mart parking lot across the street and realized, then, that it was more roadworthy than he had hoped for. And if, somewhere down the road, the old Schooner stopped, so would he. There were other ways to get home.

While Kit looked the other way, Big Al took the Jaguar through a few figure eights and then gleefully pronounced the sleek car fit. "I think I'll drive it for a while myself," he chortled, his big lips bouncing. But when he saw Kit blanch and move, unblinking, toward the car that was still his, he hollered, "I'll throw in a tank of gas and a month's propane," and pocketed the keys. Then he did Kit a bigger favor than either of them realized at the time: he insisted that Kit clean out the Jag, bumper to bumper, before leaving it behind. "You never know what you might turn up," he said wisely.

So Kit emptied the glove compartment, checked the trunk, tipped the visors, glanced in the ashtray, and at the last minute peered under the seats. The string-bound box he found under the driver's seat puzzled him. It was about the size of a Bible and inordinately heavy. He thought that it must belong to Holly, must have slipped out of her luggage, out of sight, been forgotten. But with Big Al waiting impatiently to close the deal, Kit simply added the box to the maps and flashlight he'd retrieved from the Jaguar and stashed the lot in a handsome wooden trunk bolted to the floor next to the Schooner's driver's seat. Then he went into Al's cluttered office and made everything legal.

Halfway into his cringing chair, Big Al suddenly froze. "Got the title with you? Can't do the deal otherwise," he said, looking as if he might well cry.

"Oddly enough, I do," Kit said, and he too looked close to tears. He'd been delighted when, upon turning eighteen, he'd been able to transfer the car into his own name. His father had encouraged the exchange, convinced that it would teach his son to be responsible about his possessions, but Kit knew that it would enrage his father to realize how easy he had made it for his son to take flight.

"Shouldn't keep the title in the car, you know," Al said, lowering himself all the way into his chair, which whined a bit before surrendering. "Makes it easy for thieves—present company excepted, of course," he added, braying.

With his pen poised, Kit looked up. "I don't suppose you'd rent it to me for a couple of weeks?"

"Don't rent," said Big Al. "Never have. Never will, Buy, sell, or get out of the way. That's the business I'm in."

"Well, I guess I've come this far. Might as well go all the way." But his hand shook a little as he penned his name.

"The owner's manual is in the glove compartment, but I'd better warn you right up front," said Al, now that the deal was done. "You'll have to learn a few tricks to keep this baby on an even keel. Watch your corners, even more important, watch your overhead clearance, watch your gas gauge—this thing is a truck, you know. Burns gas like nothin'. But 'cause it's a truck it'll take you anywhere you want to go. Fields, dirt roads, snow. No problem. Trust me. Oh," and here he stopped, pursed his lips and made a face. "You'll have to figure out your own method of waste disposal. Depends where you are, of course. Lots of campgrounds have dumping facilities. Some gas stations even. Laws vary, state to state. The Schooner's equipped with a tank you can drain with a hose into any toilet. Or you can get a portable thing and just flush the stuff, or dig a deep hole, or burn it, I suppose. I don't mean to go on about it, but nothin'll put you off motoring faster than a stench. But you'll figure out what suits you, soon enough."

As he had before, Kit suddenly felt as if he had lost all control and were in someone else's hands entirely. *What in God's name am I doing?* he wondered, more frantically than before and with a measure of anguish brought on by the sight of his Jag basking outside Al's office window. The thought of attending to toilets and the like horrified him. He had begun to feel excited, however, about this adventure. So he said good-bye to Big Al, shook his pudgy hand, boarded the Schooner, and set sail.

Rarely in his life had Kit felt foolish. He'd never been a foolish boy and had not evolved into a foolish young man. At least he'd never thought so. But for the first fifty miles after leaving Big Al's Used Cars and Trucks, Kit made up for lost time, to the disgust of his fellow travelers. For mile after agonizing mile, he struggled to master the combined arts of steering the thirty-eight-foot Schooner along the winding country roads, urging it up the rolling hills, bringing its unwieldy tonnage to a stop in a dozen small towns, negotiating their corners, and changing lanes. After nearly wrecking his new home when he misjudged a left-hand turn in the middle of a congested town—and forcing eight cars behind him to back up into oncoming traffic so that he could extricate himself—Kit pulled into a church parking lot, switched off the engine, and laid his head gently on the Schooner's big steering wheel. He stayed that way for a while, tired, terrified, and ashamed of his incompetence, while the traffic hustled by him. He wondered if his father had ever had moments like this. He tried to picture him afraid, undone, but could not. He tried to picture him as a boy, dirty with play, laughing, curious about the world. But he could not do this either.

He realized then how little he knew about his father. He had seen photographs of his grandparents, long dead, and heard some stories about their lives. More about them than about his own father. He was sorry about this, and it was suddenly important that he dig deeper when he returned.

With time to spare and sudden resolve, Kit began to search for some paper, but there was none to be found. Ahead, on the shoulder of the road, there was litter. It would have to do.

He climbed from the Schooner and fetched a paper bag that had become caught in a fence rail. It was dry, not too dirty, but would nonetheless shock his father more, perhaps, than anything Kit chose to write on it.

He took it back to the Schooner, smoothed it out on the top of the wooden trunk that was bolted next to the driver's seat, and, kneeling down, took his pen from his pocket and began to write. *Dear Father,* he began, for *Dad* was somehow not quite right.

> *You'll think I'm a coward and I suppose you're right. But I could not have stood in front of you and explained why I was leaving. Some things are very clear to me, but you already know about them: that you have always been unkind to Holly; that you have mistreated her, abused her, in fact; that I have been a terrible brother; that you lied to us about Holly's disfigurement; that we both, you and I, ought to be ashamed. Then there are plenty of things that aren't so clear. Why isn't there a single picture of my mother in our entire house? Why have I always been satisfied with knowing so little about anything—anything—except what you have thought important?*
>
> *You can see why I did not wait to speak with you before leaving. Everything is very unclear to me. One minute I think I know what's going on, and the next minute I'm lost. Giving Holly the money she needed to go her own way was the right thing to do. I'm sure about that. (In a way, you must be relieved that she's gone.) But since then I've done other things that amaze me. I feel as if I've been crossed with someone else, as if we—this other someone and I—have merged. You've never been able to put yourself in anyone else's shoes, but surely you know what it feels like to be torn in two directions. The things you've done prove how troubled you are. So I'm hoping you'll be able to imagine my own confusion.*

Considering everything, though, I know there's a good chance you're furious with me. That you feel we've betrayed you, Holly in one way and I in another. Perhaps I would feel that way too, in your shoes. But that's the whole point. I am no longer in your shoes and am now certain that I don't ever want to be. Because of Holly? I can hear you. I can actually hear you saying this. Yes, because of Holly. A few days ago I was so content with myself. Now I am not. Not at all. I need a bit of time and distance. When I've sorted things out, I'll come home.

It's true that I couldn't stay in that house after hearing how you've treated Holly, but it's also true that I want to help you. While I'm gone, I hope you'll face the fact that you need help. And when I come home maybe you'll let me see that you get it.

He signed it *Kit,* folded it up as neatly as he could, and stuck it in the visor, ready for an envelope. He would have to remember to find a stamp too, and a mailbox, first thing. Feeling better now, he started up the Schooner and carefully got back under way.

Kit didn't know, in the early days after leaving home, that these were to be among the most important miles he would ever travel. He didn't yet know much about humility, though he was quickly learning, and never imagined that he'd come to value so pedestrian an attitude as that. He had never before felt the world curve ahead as it did for him then, urging him down its imperceptible slope with nameless promises and endless possibilities. He had never had a home so entirely his own, and he looked forward to inaugurating it soon with a meal and a long night's sleep.

As twilight approached, Kit decided to moor the Schooner at the next likely spot that presented itself. Somewhere near a gas station, he hoped, for he still felt some trepidation about the Schooner's own facilities and furthermore had not yet filled its water tank. Somewhere near a grocery store, too, since the only food he had on board was a half-eaten Snickers bar and a six-pack of ginger ale he'd bought at a gas station that morning. Somewhere civilized, although he wasn't sure what that meant anymore. Perhaps somewhere quiet and lovely, ringed with pastures, where people wouldn't mind giving him some advice and a place to park.

Maybe I'll stop in this next town, he said to himself as he passed Belle Haven's outer limits. But before he'd gone much farther down the road, he came upon a sign mounted on a sawhorse straddling a wide, deserted intersection. DETOUR WEST TO RANDALL, it commanded in orange and black. LOCAL TRAFFIC ONLY. In smaller letters painted by hand underneath was the cryptic message: *New borehole at the Spring Run Extension. As of 5/14, migrating hot spot SE of Jackson's silo. Stay on the road. Pass at your own risk.*

Kit idled at the intersection, pondering the sign, the only man-made thing in sight save the road itself and the furrows in the fields. The last town he'd passed had been as charmless as any he'd yet seen. Randall could turn out to be even worse. And he liked the name Belle Haven. It sounded like a place that won hearts easily and would never turn anyone away. Stronger than anything, however, was the lure of the sign up ahead. As he drove slowly on along the empty road toward Belle Haven, he was filled with curiosity and anticipation, both of which were soon rewarded.

Chapter 8

As Kit was following the road into Belle Haven, Rachel was making a salad for her supper and looking back down the gray months that stretched behind her like a leash, to the time before her parents had died.

She hated chopping, slicing, or paring—could not imagine choosing to be a butcher, or a lumberjack, or anyone who wielded a blade for a living—but she loved salads and no longer had anyone to make them for her. Only one thing made the task easier, and that was her anger.

Rachel stood at the kitchen counter, a gleaming knife in her hand, and fashioned a hundred neat coins of celery while she pictured Harry, working his sly choreography, and Paul, weak-kneed, complying.

The image of the drunken truck driver who had obliterated her parents took the ache from her fingers as she washed the lettuce in frigid water. The police officers who had pried the man from his truck had said he could not keep his feet, had vomited on the road, reeking of alcohol. But somehow his carefully siphoned blood had been misplaced, and so there was no proof, later, of his guilt. He had been convicted of nothing more than reckless driving. And Rachel had been left with the task of identifying the broken bodies of her parents, looking into their torn faces, and, unwisely, touching them. That had been the worst of all—the feel of them.

She dried the lettuce and ripped it into pieces, scrubbed a trio of scallions. At the thought of the state official from Community Affairs who had tried to tell her how, when, and where she could bury her parents' remains, she eviscerated a green pepper with one well-executed twist of its stem.

"We like to keep tabs on where everyone's buried around here," he had told her shortly after she'd arrived home. "Anywhere near the fire, we might have to move the remains at some point. It's a touchy matter. Best to cooperate so things don't get messy later on, Miss Hearn."

"Go away," she'd said, and slammed the door in his face.

Most of the people who lived in Belle Haven were old-fashioned. While they had permitted progress to take its course—in the shape of a better fire engine, new and sometimes alarming books for the library, a free clinic, and a recycling depot—they stubbornly refused to fool with their more deeply rooted traditions. Their grief over the deaths of Frederick and Suzanne Hearn had therefore been shot through with disapproval at the manner of their burial. Rachel had simply refused to consign her parents to the graveyard of the church they had attended all their lives. It was a lovely church that sat out at the edge of town, graced with unfarmed fields, with a graveyard once known for its lilacs. But far below the church was a mine tunnel full of fire, and the graveyard was now surprisingly hot.

It disturbed people to think of the bodies interred there becoming brittle and crisp as they baked. And it frightened them to think of the ground giving way, taking the bodies with it or, worse yet, exposing them to the air. Still, the churchyard was holy ground and people continued to bury their dead in its dusty soil. Folks took the Bible fairly literally in Belle Haven: ashes to ashes, dust to dust. Rachel even more so.

"I want them cremated and buried here, on the hill," she had insisted. But at the last minute, Rachel had changed her mind.

While a hundred mourners plodded up the hill to the Hearn house and quietly gathered in the windy yard, Rachel took the heavy urn that held her parents' ashes and hurried up to her bedroom. She stood in the middle of the room, clutching the urn to her chest, and looked frantically around until she caught sight of a lopsided crock she'd made in the eighth grade. She'd made it big enough to hold cattails or hollyhocks. It would be big enough to hold the remnants of both her parents.

After dusting it out with the hem of her black dress, Rachel filled the crock with the ashes from the urn. They were uglier than she had supposed they'd be, with hard chunks among the soot. She poured them as gently as she could, but even so a cloud of fine ash billowed above the mouth of the crock, and Rachel was left with the taste of the ash on her tongue and a film of it on her eyes. Then she opened the window and with her bare hands pried chunks of cold soil from the vacant window box. She left the window open, cold air flooding the room. Then she crumbled the soil into the urn, stopped it up again, and went down to join the others.

She found her kitchen full of women. There was an astounding assortment of food on the big harvest table, plates and flatware on the countertop. The women were all wearing aprons. Rachel wondered whether they ever went anywhere without them. The scorn she suddenly felt was diluted, well hidden, but nonetheless shocking, and it took Rachel a moment to collect herself, to remind herself that these were the friends of a lifetime, and to remember what she had come to say.

"If you all don't mind, I think I'm ready now." They had not noticed her in the doorway and looked, all of them, ashamed of their chatter, the precision of their cookie trays, the thought that maybe they looked nice, even in black.

"Oh, you poor darlin'," somebody said. Rachel wasn't sure who it was. She was looking down at the urn in her hands, thinking of the crock upstairs and its irregular cargo.

Rachel waited for the women to fetch their coats and then led them out and around to the side of the house, past a stand of lilac trees, past the garden going to rot, almost to the edge of her parents' land, where no one had any reason to go—except, perhaps, her.

She had cleared a spot under an old, twisted apple tree. If she wanted to, she could let the violets come back and cover everything over. She hadn't decided yet.

There were a lot of people on the hill. Those who had not come would be by sooner or later to say how very sorry they were. The thought filled Rachel with dread.

She knelt down and put the urn full of soil into the hole she had prepared. She stayed there, on her knees, while the minister read the service. Then, unconcerned with tradition, she pushed dirt in on top of the urn and tamped it down with hands that had become red and chapped from neglect.

"I would like to recite a poem," she said, calling back a few mourners who had thought the funeral over. "It is called 'Dirge Without Music.' Edna St. Vincent Millay wrote it." And without another word she began.

*I am not resigned to the shutting away of loving hearts in the
    hard ground.
So it is, and so it will be, for so it has been, time out of mind:
Into the darkness they go, the wise and the lovely. Crowned
With lilies and with laurel they go; but I am not resigned.*

*Lovers and thinkers, into the earth with you.
Be one with the dull, the indiscriminate dust.
A fragment of what you felt, of what you knew,
A formula, a phrase remains, — but the best is lost.*

*The answers quick and keen, the honest look, the laughter, the
    love, —
They are gone. They are gone to feed the roses. Elegant and
    curled
Is the blossom. Fragrant is the blossom. I know. But I do not
    approve.
More precious was the light in your eyes than all the roses in
    the world.*

*Down, down, down into the darkness of the grave
Gently they go, the beautiful, the tender, the kind;
Quietly they go, the intelligent, the witty, the brave.
I know. But I do not approve. And I am not resigned.*

Unsure, now, what might come next, those assembled on the hill
stood and watched Rachel as she took one long, last look around.
Then, without further hesitation or the smallest misstep, she started
back toward the house, her chin held high, eyes dry.

Once inside, Rachel washed the dirt from her hands and found herself a vacant chair. From this chair she did not move. Not for food:
someone brought her a plate of meats and cheeses and the inevitable
deviled egg. Not for drink: there was cider from somewhere, but
Rachel could not drink it. Not for comfort: as if she were a queen or,
perhaps, a recumbent bride, the mourners came to her, one by one,
and bent or bowed or even knelt to share with her their sorrow.

"Your parents were lovely people, Rachel," said one of her neighbors, and Rachel was astounded that she could not remember his name.

"Thank you," she said. "They were." She was having trouble with
her voice. It was coming out all wrong. And although she could move

them, she suddenly had no feeling in her legs. These were the people she loved and cherished, but there was nothing Rachel wanted so much as to have her house empty again.

When it was, finally, she moved the chairs back where they had been and went to bed in the middle of the afternoon.

Late that night she took the crock containing her parents' remains down the hill and along Maple Street to Raccoon Creek. She left her shoes balancing on the railing of the bridge—toes hanging out over the water as if inclined to jump—and stepped carefully down the embankment with slippery feet, the poor crock tucked into the harbor of her arm. The shallow creek was icy, and for a moment she became dizzy as she felt the water racing against her ankles. Shivering, she walked down the center of the stream to where it abruptly curved away and broadened, leaving a tiny island of slick pebbles. A stubborn old willow tree reached out from the bank to canopy the island, and a few dormant weeds gave it a degree of permanence.

One of Rachel's earliest memories was of time spent on this island, watching the crayfish spar in the shadow of the willow's branches, cupping the sunstruck water in her hands, and imagining that the twigs she launched on the ceaseless current would somehow find their way to the sea. Her parents, watching from the bank, their arms locked, had not discouraged this notion. As she poured their ashes carefully onto the black water, she imagined that they would follow a similar course.

When she got home not long before first light, she made herself some scalding coffee, wrapped herself up in blankets, and went out onto her front porch to think about how she would spend the months ahead. But, faced with this prospect, she could no longer ignore what she had discovered that morning before the funeral. Exhausted with the drama and the details of her parents' death, Rachel had thought that today of all days she would be spared any further need to make arrangements or heed advice. But she was wrong.

"It won't take but a few minutes," said Mr. Murdock, the lawyer from Randall who had called her out of the blue at eight o'clock that morning and insisted that they meet right away. "I'll come over to Belle Haven. I can be there in half an hour. It's important, Miss Hearn, that we discuss the provisions your parents made for you in their will."

She had agreed because it took too much energy to do anything else. Already long out of her bed, Rachel dressed quickly and then went downstairs to wait for Mr. Murdock, a man she'd never met, never even known her parents had hired. She knew that they had owned the house outright and had never allowed their debts to mount. She knew they had been thrifty and smart with what money they had. But she also knew there was not much to begin with and assumed that there could not now be much to disperse. Certainly not after their deaths were taxed, their cremation paid for, and Mr. Murdock himself duly compensated. For the second time that morning, she was wrong.

"Did you know that your parents had each taken out a life-insurance policy just a few days after you were born?" Mr. Murdock sat across the kitchen table from Rachel with coffee at his elbow and a sheaf of papers in his hands.

"No, I didn't," she replied. She had never heard them speak about such things.

"Well, they did, Miss Hearn. The types of policies that don't mature. In other words, your parents could never have cashed them in." He looked down at the table. "And, if your parents had died of natural causes, the policies would not have paid all that much. But your parents wanted you to be in good shape if they died suddenly, accidentally, as they in fact did." After a moment he looked up at her, clearly uncomfortable with everything he had said but just as clearly anticipating her reaction to his next words.

"In a nutshell, Miss Hearn, each policy stipulated that, in case of the accidental death of the insured party, the beneficiary would be awarded one hundred fifty thousand dollars. And in both cases, the beneficiary is you and you alone."

Which meant that Rachel Hearn was not only a twenty-year-old orphan but a relatively wealthy one as well.

The news of her inheritance had so startled Rachel that she'd found it easier not to think about it at the time. She had thanked Mr. Murdock and said she'd be in touch, shown him to the door, told him that she had to get ready for the funeral. He nodded, disappointed with her reaction, and went away. When he returned later that afternoon to pay his respects, he had the grace to keep his peace, certain that in time she would want to hear more about her inheritance and to claim it.

As Rachel sat on her porch, her feet aching from the cold creek water, waiting out the night, her unsought windfall still seemed so unreal that it didn't bear close scrutiny. She thought instead about what she was going to do now that she was on her own.

No matter how hard she tried, Rachel couldn't feel any kind of kinship with the good, clean girl she'd been only days before. Until Sunday afternoon, she had been a thoughtful daughter. A good friend. Well-groomed, upright, and honest. She had worried about the welfare of others, concerned herself with their happiness, and thought herself fulfilled along with them. She had been touched by everyone and everything in her immediate world. She had anticipated the needs of others, the repercussions of her every action, the consequences of her words, her deeds, even her thoughts.

My God, she thought. *What a waste of time.*

She remembered one day when she was maybe ten or eleven and her parents had taken her to a fair over on the far side of Randall. She had wanted a second hot dog and been willing to wait in a long, unruly line to get it while her parents sat on a bench, resting. When she finally reached the hot dog stand she found herself wedged between far bigger people. The hot dog vendor was running with sweat. His hands looked like meat from reaching into the steam after hot dogs. The smell of mustard was so strong it made Rachel's eyes water. One after another, people who came up beside her reached for the hot dog that was meant for her, took it, paid, twisted away, and were gone.

She could have pushed right back. Summoned her parents. Made a fuss. But for many long minutes she simply stood there, mute, holding up her hand now and then as if she were in school, feeling oddly virtuous. She would not make things harder for the hot dog man. She would not—she would *not*—be rude. That these other people had no manners was no reason she should abandon hers.

A man who had squeezed past Rachel and dressed his hot dog now said to her, as he turned to leave, "You'll never get anywhere in life if you don't learn to speak up, girl."

Rachel remembered feeling torn, then, between the urge to follow his advice (and start by speaking up to *him*) and her long-held conviction that being a good and patient girl was worth its price.

Sitting on her porch, Rachel thought about this decision. It was one she had made over and over and over again: to be the way she had always been. Even as an adolescent, curious and impatient, she had changed little, for she had really had no choice: everyone knew her as a certain kind of girl, and there was simply no way she could disappoint them. No worthy opportunity arose. No reason seemed good enough. And, in truth, she seldom felt the need to challenge the rituals she had practiced for so long. Until now. Somehow, the boys she'd known at college, and the death of her parents, and every other mean thing that had ever touched her life became twisted together and made it easy for Rachel to strip herself down and start all over again.

Her neighbors had noticed the change in Rachel as soon as she stepped off the bus early that Monday morning. She had not been rude or unkind in any way. But she had not reacted to them as they had expected she would. She had not cried on their shoulders. She had not bravely smiled. She had sought neither solace nor advice. She had been unmoved by the casseroles that they had tucked away in her fridge. She had been entirely too reserved for their liking.

What a waste of time, she thought again, sitting on her porch, her parents on their way to the sea. *And energy. Who has the energy to keep all that up for long? Better to say what you think, mean what you say, do what you think is right, live how you want to live. No need to be cruel,* she amended. *Say the cruel parts to yourself. Or don't say them at all. Do the cruel things in your head. Or keep still. Be disciplined.*

It was a start. An anchor of sorts. One she carried with her back to school after she'd dealt with her parents' remains and the tangled business of surviving them. When she arrived back on the familiar campus, she found that it took some effort to avoid backsliding into the rabbit girl she had been before, but clinging to this anchor, Rachel held her ground. Old friends, thinking she was still grieving, made allowances for her lack of social graces. Paul kept his distance and she hers. She made no new friends. Every now and then she went alone to the movies, consumed a sack of M&M's, and wondered where her parents were.

At one point, on a beautiful spring morning when everything seemed suddenly to have changed for the better, Rachel did slip, although at first it felt so good to relax her guard that she did nothing to resurrect it.

Forsaking the library for the campus green, she chose a spot under a maple tree and began to read the sonnets that had seemed such perfect work for a morning like this one. But the breeze and the smell of new grass plucked at her attention, and finally she shut the book and set it aside. The sun felt wonderful on her bare arms. The grass was soft. She closed her eyes.

"Rachel."

She opened her eyes. Adam Greenway, her history professor, had come up quietly and was crouching next to her. "I didn't want to startle you," he said, smiling.

"You didn't," she said. "How are you, Professor?"

"Just fine. You?"

"Okay. I'm afraid I shouldn't have come out here to study though. It's too hard to concentrate."

"Which is why I no longer allow my teaching assistants to hold discussion groups outside, under the trees. It's hard to pay attention when you've got spring fever. My students were writing exams without much meat to them. They were just giving me back what I'd dished out during lecture or what they memorized from the reading assignments. Not much original perspective. Disappointing."

Rachel nodded, bemused. This was unlike Professor Greenway. He had never said so much to her outside of class before. He was watching her intently.

"Rachel, do you remember much about your midterm exam last semester, the one you wrote for me?"

"I'm not sure what you mean," she said slowly. "Do I remember the questions?"

"Your responses. Do you remember what you wrote about U.S. foreign policy during Turkey's '74 invasion of Cyprus?"

"I remember, more or less."

"Do you remember quoting Henry Kissinger?"

"Yes, briefly." The sun behind him made Rachel squint. "But it seems strange that *you* remember. There were over a hundred kids in that class, and we took that exam almost six months ago."

Professor Greenway sat down next to Rachel. "Of a hundred and forty-two students, seven wrote similar exams. Disturbingly so. They all presented the same information, all within the same basic structure and, to a limited extent, even used the same wording. Your exam was a bit different—the structure of your essay was unique, but the information was basically the same and all eight of you quoted Kissinger in exactly the same way. Or almost: you punctuated the quote differently, but the other seven were identical. No one else in the entire class quoted Kissinger. Just the eight of you."

"Are you accusing me of cheating?" Rachel said, blinking with surprise. "On an essay exam? In a class I loved and studied for until my eyes nearly blew out of my head?"

He put up a hand. "I know, Rachel," he said. "I'm not accusing you of anything. I've waited six months to bring this up because I wanted to investigate all other possibilities. But the same thing happened when I gave the *final* exam for that class. All seven exams were nearly the same."

"The same as mine?"

"No. Not at all like yours."

"So you realized I wasn't cheating, even if they were."

"I never thought that you had cheated, Rachel." He smiled at her, as if to prove it. "But I'm sure that you were somehow involved for a while last semester, without your knowledge."

They were both silent for a time. Then, "That was a long time ago, Professor," Rachel said. "What made you decide to bring this up now?"

"Four of those seven students are in my class this semester, too. All four of their midterms were too much alike. So were two other exams written by students I've never had before. But I'm still not sure what's going on, and I was hoping you could give this some thought." He stood up and brushed off his pants. "Let me know if you come up with any ideas."

"It would help if I knew who the other students were," she said.

He thought about that one for a moment. Then he told her. All nine suspects were boys. One of them was Paul.

Rachel had been in such a wonderful mood that morning, felt the first bit of joy since her parents had died. If Paul had been the one to approach her as she sat under the maple tree, drowsing, she might have forgiven him, found a way to patch things up between them. She had begun to feel, recently, as if she had judged Paul too harshly. When she tried to put herself in his shoes, to feel the sort of pressure exerted by his peers, she did not entirely succeed, but this new willingness to see things through his eyes had made Rachel vulnerable to the sight of him walking across the campus green or sitting in one of her classes, intentionally removed. Lately, she had reminded herself of Paul's warnings, admitted that he been right about Harry all along. She began, as well, to miss having a best friend, as Paul had been right from the start.

They had met before classes had even begun, their first year, during orientation week, when herds of freshman had been rounded up,

driven down to their dormitory lounges, and forced to play the kinds
of parlor games that make more ice than they break. Paired by a ruth-
less upperclassman, Paul and Rachel had been told to get acquainted
and then, when it was their turn, to introduce each other to the rest
of the group. "You have five minutes," he said.

All around them, paired strangers were looking at each other in
horror. But Paul looked at Rachel, Rachel at Paul, and with the kind
of minute, flickering signals known to timber wolves and deaf-mutes,
they made up their minds to escape. It was easy, really. The escalating
panic of their classmates made good cover. And within moments the
two of them were running along the corridor outside, twisted with
laughter, free. They had gone for pizza, survived the inevitable, occasional awkwardness of strangers, and become fast friends. Living in
the same dorm that year had made it easier for them to be together at
all hours, studying, escaping the relentless companionship of roommates who would never be friends, laughing at anything and everything, eventually baring portions of their souls.

Even after they had spent a summer apart, even after Paul had
joined his fraternity and breathed its medieval air, even after Rachel
had made other friends and found other diversions, the things that
tied them to each other had not frayed. But much had happened since
then. Everything had changed. And the things that Professor Greenway had told her that morning stiffened the softening regions of
Rachel's heart and sent her off in search of Paul for the first time since
November, grim and suspicious.

She found him sitting on the concrete porch of the fraternity house
with several other boys, an aluminum washtub stocked with ice and
beer, an enormous can of tomato juice, and a few mangled lemons.
They all wore crumpled shorts and sunglasses, nothing else. Behind
her, on the grassy plot enclosed by the fraternity houses, other boys
were playing breakball, taking turns batting a baseball at windows.
Whoever broke the most windows won the game. The losing team
paid to replace them. The game had always struck Rachel as senseless
and inane. Today it seemed to her nearly criminal. She stood at the
bottom of the porch steps and glared at Paul.

"Rachel," he gasped, as if she had come back from the dead. He
didn't seem able to say anything more.

"Hi, Paul. I need to talk to you for a minute."

"Sure, sure," he said. The others watched silently. Paul worked his mug into the ice and grabbed his shirt from the back of his chair. "You want to come up here, have a red-eye?"

"No, thank you. Could you just come with me for a few minutes?"

"Sure," he said, buttoning up his shirt. He looked around for some shoes but found none. There were millions of shards of broken beer bottles and window glass on the sidewalk that looped through the quadrangle. "You sure you don't want a red-eye?" he said, smiling. At which Rachel turned and walked away.

Paul caught up with her before she'd left the quad. "Okay, okay," he said. "Slow down." She stopped but did not turn around. "My car's right up the street. We can talk there."

The sight of the Impala made Rachel's heart hurt, but she opened the passenger door and slipped inside.

"I didn't think you'd ever speak to me again," Paul said, his hands on the steering wheel.

"I didn't either," she said. "Now I'm not sure how I feel. But I need to know something, Paul."

"Anything," he said, as if she should have known this.

"How did you do on the history midterm last semester?" she asked.

"How did I what?"

"You borrowed all my notes, remember? You said you'd lost your notebook somewhere. So I gave you everything I had. Notes from lecture, from section, from the reading. Everything."

"Of course I remember. You saved my life."

"Did you make photocopies?"

"Yes. It would have taken me forever to copy everything by hand."

"Who else saw my notes?"

Paul opened the car door and put one foot into the gutter. "What gives, Rachel? Why all the questions?"

Rachel turned in her seat so that she faced him. "I want to know how it is that you and six of your friends all wrote midterms that were identical to mine. At least in some respects. And close enough in other ways to make it look like I was cheating."

"Oh my God, Rachel, did Greenway say something to you?"

"Look," she said. "I already know that you guys cheated, but I want to know how."

"Are you nuts?" Paul snorted. "If I say one word, those guys will kill me. I'll be out of the fraternity, probably out of school." He looked at her and could not quite keep the smirk off his face. "There's no way in the world that anyone can prove we cheated."

It had taken Rachel a mere ten minutes to find Paul, but in those ten minutes she had come up against the truth. "Somehow, one of you guys got your hands on the exam questions last fall. And then, before the exam, you all prepared your answers. And you helped each other, of course. Shared your notes. Shared *my* notes." Paul refused to look at her again. "But you were all too stupid to make sure you varied your answers. They were so much alike—especially with the Kissinger quote from my notes—that Greenway was immediately suspicious. And then you did the same thing during the final, only without my help. Didn't you?"

Paul said nothing. Rachel waited. Then, suddenly, shocking her, "Get out of my car," he said. "Every time I have anything to do with you I end up sorry."

"So do I," Rachel said when she was able. She suddenly found herself so tired of the whole thing, so weary, that she was barely able to open the door of the old car that had once given her a moment of freedom. It was the last time she ever spoke to Paul.

By the time she walked into Professor Greenway's office the next day, Rachel had realized her mistake.

She told the professor about lending her notes to one of the seven, though she did not name Paul. She had decided to let him hang himself, as he had done before.

"So there's the link to you," the professor said, pleased.

She went on to suggest that the others had stolen the exam questions, although she did not know how they might have done so. And then she told him about her mistake, and theirs.

"At first I thought that they had memorized their answers, but then I remembered how similar all seven were. Nearly identical, you said. Especially the Kissinger quote, which they got from my notes. It didn't seem possible that they could have produced several nearly identical answers purely from memory." The professor watched her and did not interrupt. "They had to have collaborated on the answers and then actually written them out before the exam. Using my notes."

"But how could they have prepared the answers ahead of time? Those exam booklets come in five colors, and nobody knows what color is going to be used until they take the exam."

"They bought all five colors," Rachel said. "You can get them at the bookstore. And then they wrote out their answers in all five book-lets and snuck them into the exam. And then, when they saw which color you were handing out, they just took out the right one and switched it with the blank booklet you'd given them. And spent an hour doodling. I can't believe it. If they had spent all that effort studying, they wouldn't have needed to cheat."

"Sounds pretty far-fetched, but I suppose it's possible. It would be easy to do something like that, trade booklets I mean, if they sat in the back. It's a big class." Professor Greenway sighed. "Any idea how they got their hands on the exam in the first place?"

No, Rachel said. She didn't know how they'd stolen the questions. And that, Rachel thought, was that. She thought she'd heard the last of it.

For the next few weeks Rachel did little more than study. With savage determination, she fueled her mind, distinguished herself in the process, wrote an impeccable set of final exams, and began to pack her things.

On the day of her departure for Belle Haven, set to catch an after-noon bus, Rachel went to the refectory for a final lunch. She was meeting some of the friends she'd barely seen since the fall. She missed them, as if they had gone away somewhere, or as if she had. They were waiting for her when she arrived.

She had sat here with these people hundreds of times before, mak-ing jokes about the food, agonizing over deadlines and syllabi, gos-siping, passing the time before class. Today Rachel just wanted to be away. She had always thought of these friends as people she would re-member fondly once she'd graduated and gone her own way, but looking at their faces around the table, Rachel felt as if she were al-ready remembering them, as if they were locked in her past and could not join her in the place she now inhabited. She tried to think of a way to explain this to them, to excuse herself from their chatter and find her way to the bus station, but then she looked across the table and saw her old friend Colleen pick up a shaker and pour salt all over the bowl of ice cream she had only begun to eat. It was a habit of Colleen's, a wealthy girl from Connecticut, to break her perpetual diet with a forbidden sweet and then, before any real damage had been done, to thwart herself with a dose of salt.

Since Harry, since her parents' death, since Professor Greenway had found her under the maple tree, Rachel had noticed a lot of things she'd missed before, or chosen to ignore. She had come to realize that far too many of the students on this campus—these friends among them—had an extremely rigid view of the world beyond, one that was rarely based on actual experience or sincere investigation, and that they were comfortable with their assumptions. She had come to feel like a stranger here, more an outsider than she had felt on her very first day of school nearly three years before. But it was the sight of her old friend ruining her food that finally made Rachel scramble to her feet and shock them with the brevity of her good-byes.

She met Professor Greenway on the sidewalk outside the refectory.

"I'm glad I ran into you like this," he said, leading her to a bench in the shade.

"I only have a minute, Professor. I'm going home this afternoon."

"I won't keep you long. I just wanted to say good-bye. I hope I'll see you in one of my classes in the fall."

"I'm sure you will," she said.

"And I also wanted to tell you," he said, as Rachel began to draw away, "that we finally found out how those boys were getting their hands on my exam questions. Stupid, really. We made things far too easy for them. But once we figured it out, it was just as easy to catch them."

"Was it your secretary?"

Professor Greenway looked at her sharply. "She didn't knowingly participate, any more than I did, or you either for that matter. We all made the mistake of being too trusting, too naïve. I've always left my exam questions in Nora's in basket, and she's always left a set of typed copies in my pigeonhole, both places right out in the open where anyone could watch for the chance to help himself. But this time we did up a second exam, on the sly. I used the second one. Which all six boys flunked. And you were right about them preparing their questions in advance. One of the six was so lazy that he didn't even look at the exam. He simply handed in the blue book he'd brought with him. The right answers to the wrong questions. Such a waste. None of those boys bothered to study at all, probably didn't go to lecture or read a thing all semester. We'll be more careful in the future."

"So will I," she said.

And, once again, Rachel thought that was that. An end to things. And this time she was right, for she left town that afternoon just as she'd planned, with all of her things in one battered trunk and not a single loose thread to trip her up.

• • •

One week later Rachel stood in her kitchen, thinking of these things, while she prepared her supper. When she noticed the big bowl of salad sitting on the counter at her elbow she was surprised, for she could not remember making it. She felt oddly refreshed, purged, and intensely hungry.

Rachel wiped her hands on a clean dish towel, filled a hollowed-out green pepper with cold water from a jug in the fridge, and drank it down in one long swallow. The water was so cold that she felt it in her jawbone. Then she bit off a chunk of pepper, chopped the rest into bits, and threw them in the bowl. She tossed the salad and ate it much as an animal might: to sustain herself, without fanfare, nothing more.

After the salad she was still hungry, so she grabbed a mug of milk and a pan of brownies she had baked at three o'clock that morning and headed out the back door.

It was a beautiful May evening. The trees were finally in full leaf and the lilac in bloom. The sky was a shade of blue that winter cannot achieve: soft, deep, and variegated, like the eggs of some birds.

Rachel dragged a little cast-iron table over to her tree-slung hammock and arranged the milk and brownies where she could reach them.

"Ahhh," she sighed as she sank back into the ropes. She heard her neighbors down the hill calling their children in for supper. She heard the infrequent passage of cars along Maple Street at the bottom of the hill. She heard the faint but invigorating clamor of geese, far above, straining northward. And, as she swallowed the last of a brownie and reached for another, she heard a screech of metal, a yelp of brakes, and, after a moment, a shout of consternation. Someone unfamiliar with Belle Haven had tried to drive something large over the narrow bridge that crossed Raccoon Creek. Rachel knew she would hear all about it the next morning when Ed delivered her mail. She grinned shamelessly up at the darkening sky, made a pillow out of her arm, and felt glad all over again to be back where she belonged.

Chapter 9

Rachel woke up early the next morning with the irrepressible notion that something unusual would happen before long. To her. Something she might not really notice or fully appreciate. Like a seed, something that would lead to a blossom of sorts, or a fruit. She felt strangely hollow and profoundly hungry. Her skin felt hot and flawless beneath the early-summer blanket. Although it was barely light outside, she was completely awake and felt so competent, so primed, that she craved conversation as much as food. So she sprang from her bed, threw herself into a cool shower, dressed in clothes she'd just laundered—every stitch—and strode out the door with omelets on her mind.

Angela's Kitchen served the best breakfast in Belle Haven. It was clean, and its big ovens sent fragrant drifts clear out to the sidewalk. It was run by a woman who knew how to cook, how to feed people, and how to get along without a husband who was never coming back. Her nine-year-old son, Rusty, made her as happy as she had ever hoped to be. Every time she found a quarter lurking in the shadow of a coffee cup, she tossed it into the shiny metal bucket that sat beside the coffeemaker. So far she had emptied the bucket fifty times. No one ever stiffed Angela. Everyone in town knew she was saving the money for Rusty's education.

"I don't really care whether he gets it in a school or on the road," Angela always said. "As long as he gets it."

When Rachel walked into the coffee shop at seven o'clock that morning, Angela had just pulled eight dozen cinnamon rolls from her great oven and the air was thick with yeasty steam. The smell of fresh coffee, cinnamon, and bacon made Rachel feel almost dangerously hungry, as if she would fight for her food if necessary.

"Well, bless my soul, if it isn't ravishing Rachel." Angela glanced at her watch, lit a cigarette, and waved the match at an empty stool. "Get your ass over here and tell me what has driven you from your bed at such an ungodly hour."

"What ever happened to 'Good morning'?" Rachel said, settling herself at the Formica counter. "I'm hungry, that's all. And I'm out of bread and eggs. And your cinnamon rolls just happen to be slightly better than mine. *Slightly.*" She held up a thumb and forefinger so they were almost touching. "Now fetch me some coffee, please, before I lose my mind."

A couple of workingmen sat at a corner table by the window, nursing their coffees and silently contemplating the sun. Otherwise, the shop was empty. Angela had already been working for hours, getting everything ready for the breakfast crowd, which would be on its way soon. She was a young but perpetually tired woman who looked too much like her mother and not enough like her son.

"You're getting skinny, Angie," Rachel said, wondering again what it would be like to have a sister. "Tell me you're not on a diet."

"Not on purpose. Actually, I think I'm onto something big. A new diet for mothers. It's gonna make me famous, if I can get on *Donahue* or something." She poured Rachel's coffee, gave her some cream, and came around the counter to take a seat beside her. "I call it the Leftover Diet. You eat only what your kid leaves on his plate. It's perfect if you've got a kid who eats all the fattening stuff, leaves bread crusts, vegetables, stuff like that. An inch of warm milk, crumbs in the bottom. Perfect. The only problem is that the longer I'm on it, the more I cook for Rusty. Last night I gave him this huge slab of meat loaf, scads of mashed potatoes and butter, a pile of lima beans. I ate so much I couldn't move for an hour. Plus, if you've got three or four kids, the stuff they leave on their plates can really add up. But the idea's spot-on. It's gonna make me famous." She put out her cigarette, drained her cup, stood up with a groan. "I'm so hungry I could eat a horse."

Which made Rachel laugh. Angela walked behind the counter and faced her from the far side, changed in subtle ways. "What'll it be?" she asked.

All at once Rachel felt near tears. She longed for her mother. She was so very hungry. The coffee seemed to splash in her empty stomach. "I want your apron," she said.

"My what?"

"Your apron," Rachel repeated impatiently. "Your apron." Angela didn't hesitate. She had witnessed the changes in Rachel much as she might have watched a volcano rumbling toward eruption. She untied her apron and lifted its harness over her head as Rachel came around the counter and stood waiting. Angela silently fitted the apron on her friend. "It's all yours, my dear," she said, reclaimed her stool, and lit another cigarette.

Rachel went straight to the big fridge. She assembled three eggs, a dollop of cream cheese, and a ripe tomato. Found a frying pan. Diced a small onion. Collected a bowl, a whisk, a spatula, salt and pepper. She cracked the eggs into the bowl, whipped them into a lather. Cut a disc of butter and set it to sizzle. Swirled the onion in the butter. Poured the eggs into the hot skillet. Added the cream cheese in small chunks, a few cubes of tomato, salt and pepper. "This is my favorite omelet," she said over her shoulder. Angela watched in silence, enjoying her cigarette and the sight of Rachel as she cooked. None of her patrons had ever made breakfast in her kitchen before.

While the omelet swelled, Rachel made brown toast and spread it with butter and jam. She put ice in a tall glass and poured orange juice into it from such a height that the juice immediately frothed up, instantly cold, and the ice cubes whirled. She poured fresh coffee into a clean cup, slid the omelet onto a hot white plate, added the thick, sweet toast, and wiped her hands clean. When she turned to the counter with her breakfast in her hands, she saw Angela smoking another cigarette and noticed the flour that had collected in the lines around her eyes. She saw the tiny pits in her earlobes where jewelry had once hung. She saw pale hair scraped back into a knot, fingernails dulled by detergent, cut to the quick.

"Put out that vile thing, Angela, and here"—she set the orange juice on the counter—"cleanse your palate." She put down the steaming omelet, returned for the coffee, and on her way back to the counter, grabbed knife, fork, cream, and sugar. "Eat," she said.

Their eyes met for a moment, no more, before Angela picked up a fork and began to eat. The two men in the corner stood up, put on their hats, and called out good-byes without comment as they walked into the sunshine.

"Want a job?" Angela asked, omelet in her mouth.

"Maybe someday." Rachel cleaned up the mess she'd made and warmed her coffee. Then she lifted a cake cover off a plate of fresh cinnamon rolls and picked the biggest one she could find. The first gooey, buttery bite nearly dissolved in her mouth. "God, that's good." She groaned.

"Better than sex, when they're fresh. Last longer, too."

"I'll take your word for it," Rachel said, licking wet brown sugar off her wrist as she carried the roll back around the counter and took her seat at Angela's side.

"Hear anything about the doorknob who got stuck on the bridge yesterday?"

"Didn't hear *about* him, but I did hear him," Rachel said, her mouth full. "All the way up in my backyard."

"I got the skinny from Ed just before you got here, and he's a pretty reliable source," Angela said, wiping her plate clean with a corner of toast, "but there's a lot that doesn't quite add up. For instance," she said, reaching for her coffee, "here we have a young man, about your age, give or take, dressed up like a Harvard snot, looks like an ad for L.L. Bean (though, according to Ed, he coulda' used a shave and a shower), talks like he's got a plum in his mouth, driving, get this, a motor home that's half as old as I am. Which, I grant you, is not all that old. But still. Doesn't quite fit his image. Plus"—and here she leaned forward and rested her hand on Rachel's forearm—"he knows absolutely nothing about this thing he's driving. Has no water, doesn't know how to work the pump, the heater. He couldn't even find the gas tank. When it comes time to pay Frank for the gas, he hands over an American Express Gold Card. Looks real nervous the whole time. Turns out the card's no good. So this kid pays with a fifty."

"This clinches it. I always had my suspicions about Ed, but now I'm sure. He's an android. Gotta be. A man gets stuck on a bridge, and within twelve hours Ed could write his biography."

"Shut up and let me finish before this place gets busy."

"You want your apron back?" Rachel asked as Angela slid off her stool.

"Nah. Keep it on," she replied. "Suits you."

Rachel smiled all the way through a second cinnamon roll while Angela, mixing pancake batter in a huge bowl, told her the story of Belle Haven's newest arrival.

"Just Joe. Frank doesn't remember the name on the card. The kid cut it up and threw it out, and Frank can't be persuaded to troll his Dumpster for a second look. Old bastard. Anyway, the boy says his name is Joe, just Joe, but if there's one thing he's not, it's a Joe."

"This according to Ed."

"Right. But Ed's got very good judgment."

"Absolutely," Rachel said, still smiling. She couldn't remember when she'd enjoyed a breakfast more.

"After Frank hauled him off the bridge and gassed him up, he sent him out to Ian Spalding's place. Haven't been any campers out there for months 'cause the hot spots make them nervous, but he's still got hookups and privies on a real nice piece of ground near the crick."

Angela heard the bell on her door jangle and turned to take a look. "Well, speak of the devil," she muttered.

Rachel saw Joe for the first time in the polished side of a ten-slice toaster and therefore spent the next few minutes thinking he was fat. Out of the corner of her eye, she watched Angela hand him a menu and pour him a cup of coffee. She was afraid that if she looked at either of them she'd burst out laughing. So she leaned over the counter, hooked a dishcloth with her fingernail, and began to wipe down the countertop. She polished a pair of salt and pepper shakers, decided to top them up, but Angela, suspicious of her motives, reached over and took them out of her hands.

"Thank you, Rachel," she said. "I must've missed this pair." But Rachel was not to be so easily put off.

"May I take your order now?" she said, turning, and looked straight into the eyes of the man who called himself Joe.

He had had better nights. Once he'd arrived at Spalding's defunct campground he had managed to find the spot that Mr. Spalding had assigned him and had then unpacked the groceries he'd bought at the Belle Haven A&P, filling his sink with ice and perishables until his tiny fridge was up and running. Bolstered by a cheese sandwich and a tepid beer, he filled his water tank, got his generator going, and, having finally read the owner's manual cover to cover, unlocked the mysteries of on-the-road hygiene. The toilet and all its attendant complexities still gave him pause, however, so he thrashed his way through the impressive collection of spiderwebs that seemed to be doing as much as nails to hold the nearest privy together and speedily took the first steps toward relieving himself.

It was damp and gloomy in the privy, though, and he simply could not force himself to sit down on the moldy seat below which untold horrors lurked. Even more appalling was the thought of shining his flashlight into the unspeakable pit. So he set it down, clambered up onto the wooden bench, and carefully, carefully stood up—all the while terrified that the old and soggy wood would suddenly give way and he would plunge down into the noisome depths. Standing so that he was straddling the despicable toilet seat, he was unknowingly veiled with the cobwebs gracing the rafters, only vaguely aware of something clinging lightly to the helixes of his ears.

As he lowered his pants, he felt an almost overwhelming need to talk to himself aloud. To say things like, "What in hell am I doing in a privy—a *privy*—in the middle of this godforsaken wilderness?" But he took pains to keep silent. He had never yet talked to himself. He would not start now.

Slowly, he crouched above the toilet seat, lowering his pants to his ankles in order to free up his legs. Almost immediately, he heard the approaching drone of a mosquito and knew, when it abruptly ceased, that it had landed on him somewhere. It wasn't until he felt an astonishingly painful jab in his left buttock that he realized where. As he reached awkwardly back to defend himself, he was yanked off balance by the pants that hobbled him. With a purely involuntary scream, he pitched forward, knocking the flashlight over and slamming into the privy door with his head and shoulder. The door flew open like a torpedo hatch, and he landed on the mossy ground, bounced once, and skidded into a tangle of thorny bushes. The bounce, which had knocked the breath out of him, left him heaving and gasping, tucked up like a fetus, his pants still down around his ankles.

Ian Spalding was getting old, and his eyesight wasn't what it had once been. But he knew his way around his land. Glasses were a pain in the ass, he thought as he headed out to check on his new and only tenant. It was warm and still, and he was enjoying the feel of the night as he walked down the grassy lane that cut through the woods to the campsite. He stopped now and then to listen for the whisper of bats, to refresh himself with the sight of stars. As he approached the campsite, he almost turned back: it was one of his favorite indulgences to lie full-length in his unmown yard with nothing between

him and the star-spangled sky, a pipe warming his palm, and sometimes the sound of owls, waking from their dreams.

This Joe who had come to him so suddenly was a nothing sort of
boy. Handsome, yes, but that wasn't something he had earned. Arrogant, the way he had come straight out of the blue, saying I want this
and I want that with every other breath. Hardly worth his trouble.
But everyone deserves a place to sleep, water for his thirst, warmth
when it's cold, fire, food, safety. So he'd allotted the little prick a
campsite, helped him sort things out, and felt it only right to look in
on him before bed. Now, despite the lure of the stars, he continued on
through the trees—and broke into a run when he heard a muffled
scream up ahead.

Something white was thrashing around in the bushes near Joe's
campsite, but without his glasses Ian couldn't make out what it was
exactly. He paused at the edge of the woods to arm himself with a
long and spiky branch, then went on more slowly. Skunks were fairly
common around these parts. Rabid ones less so, but not entirely out
of the question and dangerous as all hell. He warily crept toward the
thing, sniffing the air, wondering where Joe was. Whether he'd heard
the scream. Whether he'd done the screaming. Maybe the boy was
lying there in the bushes while this possibly rabid skunk gnawed his
head off.

Closer now, Ian admitted to himself that whatever it was, it appeared to be much larger than any skunk he'd ever seen, rabid or
not . . . about two, maybe three feet long, with a big, moon-shaped
head on it, bucking and doubling up on itself like it was in pain,
which made Ian think again about the scream he'd heard. What in
the hell is it, Ian wondered, taking another step closer and belatedly
unclipping his flashlight from his belt. As he fumbled with the
switch, the thing in the bushes begin to wheeze and splutter . . . and
to roll slowly toward him. His adrenaline pumping, Ian lifted his
club high over his head and shined the light directly at the creature's
round, white head.

Even without his glasses, Ian knew a rump when he saw one. He
quickly lowered his flashlight. "That you, Joe?" he said. His heart
was still beating like a jackrabbit. Okay, so it wasn't a three-foot-long
rabid skunk, but it still looked to be some pretty weird stuff. "That
you, Joe?" he repeated, club in hand, wondering if maybe he shouldn't
just scamper on back home and let the boy get on with whatever it
was he was doing out here in the bushes with his ass hanging out.

"Oh, God," the thing whimpered, and Ian knew.

"Tell you what, son," he stammered. "I'll just wait on your doorstep. I'll be right there if you need me." And he hurried away.

As Spalding rounded the end of the Schooner, Joe struggled to his feet. It took a moment for him to realize that his pants were still down around his ankles. The feeling of illness that engulfed him then made his lips tremble. He wanted so badly to be away from this place that he turned to look into the woods and to consider quite seriously whether he could walk through them and so, eventually, back where he belonged. But the thought of his father—like his sister's stories and the useless credit card—made him feel a much worse sort of fool than a narrow bridge, an elusive gas tank, or, now, an unflattering posture ever could. With a sigh, he wiped the dirt from his face and hands, returned to the privy, and sat squarely on the cold seat of the toilet he'd so disdained.

Spalding was still waiting for him when he returned to the Schooner, so Joe asked him if he'd like to come inside for a beer. "All right," his landlord said a shade too loudly. After a pause, he left his club outside and followed Joe in.

For an hour or so, Ian and Joe explored the Schooner, learning its secrets and applauding past owners who had added the sorts of things that make even small homes comfortable: an extra-high table in the kitchen booth granted more room for long legs and crossed knees; strips of padding tacked to the sharp edges of counters and cupboards testified to the amount of head-banging that can go on in tight places; buckled straps looped along the edge of the ceiling suggested fishing poles, paddles, and other gear awkward to store. Joe had noticed none of these things until Ian pointed them out.

Ian then helped Joe unpack the assortment of goods he'd selected from the tiny Sears in town: sheets and towels, a can opener, laundry line and clothespins, a lawn chair, a washtub, matches, a coffeepot, Scotch tape, pencils, a pad of paper, dishes, a pot with a lid, a skillet, hangers, a broom and dustpan, and various and sundry other things no young man on his own should be without.

All of this had taken a good deal of time and more energy than Joe had thought he had left. It seemed beyond possibility that he had first laid eyes on his Schooner only a dozen hours before: that in those few hours he had learned to drive a motor home, nearly wrecked it several times, partially wrecked it once, shopped in stores he'd never before in his life contemplated entering, talked to people who said things like "yup," eaten cold beans from a can (and been pleased with the function of his new can opener), fallen headfirst from a rotting outhouse, inadvertently exposed himself to another man, and then astonished himself by offering this same man a drink.

By the time he said good night to Ian and crawled into his store-scented bunk, Joe was so exhausted that he began to understand the habitual haggardness of young mothers. But there was a certain gladness, too, that came from his management of things he'd always before left to others both more menial and more capable than he. Gladness, too, from the way Ian had laughed when he had learned the reason for Joe's unusual behavior at the privy's door. Laughter so innocent and so consuming that it had made Joe laugh, too, for the first time in days.

He lay in his bunk and thought about the hot spot he'd passed on the way to Ian's place. People in town had warned him that he would pass one, but it had not looked all that threatening, really. Not from the window of his substantial Schooner. Not from a football field away. But it apparently had an erratic sort of temper, flaring up one moment and then subsiding the next. It had frightened him, intrigued him, made him decide to have a closer look. Some other day.

As he lay in his bunk, the night half gone, he felt as if he had lost himself to outlandish circumstance. He knew why he had left home: that much still made sense to him. But how had he ended up in a motor home, in such an unlikely place? And how to explain his renaming, his unrehearsed selection of the simple Joe, there among the pumps at Frank's Gas 'n' Go, surrounded by the men who'd helped him extricate and become better acquainted with his Schooner. Joe. A mechanic's name, stitched above a pocket hung with a greasy pen. Not even Joseph, which was not in any real way related to Joe. Just Joe.

He felt unsettled, jumpy. His brand of self-confidence had always been fueled not by trustworthy instincts, intuition, or even the fundamental senses that most people rely on for survival, but instead by trappings: good looks, good grammar, wealth in the form of cars, clothes, and the like. His confidence was therefore shaken by his new trappings, by the trades he had recently made: the Schooner for the Jag, beans for lobster, Sears for Saks. All easy enough to change back again, he thought, pulling his virgin blankets closer to his chin. But it was the image of his sister locking doors behind her that made him ache and mutter, chastised with dreams, until the crows announced the morning.

With a wonderful feeling of reprieve, he slipped quietly from his bed, wrapped himself in a blanket warmed by his body, and went outside. As he wandered around his campsite, looking out across the fields, then toward the woods that framed them, Joe was surprised by a silver stream moving through the trees at the edge of the clearing. He could hear it making its way over rocks and roots and wondered how he'd missed the sound before. Was he so dependent upon his eyes, he wondered, his other senses so stunted, that he could not recognize something until he'd seen it? But this alarming new tendency toward introspection made him uncomfortable, even irritable, so he shook himself all over, threw his head back, and yawned.

Forsaking the privy with a chuckle, he relieved himself in the bushes and then, on an impulse, dropped his blanket and his shorts at the edge of the stream, waded into its icy current, and began to splash himself clean.

"Holy shit," he screamed, prancing out of the icy water and, in the process, tripping on a tree root, badly wrenching his toe. For the second time since his arrival at Ian's campground he fell to the ground, this time bashing his knee, and then rolled about like a worm that's been halved by a spade, shivering with cold and pain, coating himself with mud and rotting leaves. When his pain had subsided, he stood up and looked down at his wet, muddy body.

"*Why* am I so damned stupid?" he whimpered. He washed himself off, picked up the blanket, and draped it around himself, but it did little to warm him and furthermore had snagged enough tiny twigs to make him feel as if he were wearing horsehair. Limping slightly, he made his way to the Schooner while his forgotten shorts slowly drifted downstream.

Small children oftentimes do not pay enough attention to how things work: which shoe goes on which foot, how a glass of milk on a table's edge is bound to be spilled, the hastened demise of bikes too often left in the rain. Older children, habitually rescued from their own inexperience by interfering adults, are equally prone to a debilitating brand of inattention. So it was that Joe had failed to notice how the side door to the Schooner—the one he'd used after leaving his bed—could be opened from the inside even while it was locked from the outside. And that once this door was firmly shut, it was automatically locked unless the small button set into its inner knob had first been released. And that to open this door, one needed the same key that was now languishing inside the pocket of the pants Joe had tossed on the foot of his bed the night before.

"Please, please, please," he intoned as he hobbled around, blue-lipped, to try the Schooner's front doors. They were locked. "Why, why, why," he whimpered as he hugged the blanket closer and circled the Schooner, confirming what he already knew: that every single window was closed up tight. The thought of fetching Ian was more than Joe could bear. So he sat down on a stump in the thin morning sun and thought it through. He didn't really want to smash a window, although this had been his immediate inclination. The Schooner was fairly old and might have parts quite difficult to replace. Maybe, he thought, the Schooner's former owners had hidden a key in one of these incredibly clever little magnetic boxes.

"Worth a look," he said aloud, once again breaking the vow of silence he'd sworn in the privy the night before.

He found the little black box on the Schooner's undercarriage after only a brief search. That it was rusted shut caused Joe no alarm. He was so pleased with his discovery that he barely noticed his fingernails ripping, dragging bloody bits of cuticle right along with them, as he forced open the rust-locked box. The key inside was in fine shape, for someone had had the brains to seal it inside a tiny plastic sack. Along with the key, Joe found a small sheet of paper folded many times. On it was written in green ink, *I told you so,* that was all, but the handwriting made Joe think that its author had been laughing at the time.

After he opened and unlocked the Schooner's door, Joe replaced the key where he'd found it and, for no reason he could put his finger on, taped the little note on the cupboard above his kitchen sink.

Then he took a proper shower in his slender stall, dressed in his last clean clothes, brushed his teeth and hair, and made himself a cup of terrible instant coffee. He carried it to the booth and sat down.

From his wallet, Joe took eight twenty-dollar bills, a ten, one fifty, a Mastercard, and a Visa card. He tossed the credit cards onto the kitchen counter. If the American Express was a dud, so were these. His father was a thorough man. But he was certain that $220 would be enough to see him through until he had a chance to cash a check.

"A check," he suddenly said, slapping an open hand to his chest.

"Oh, my God." He pictured his checkbook tucked into a drawer nearly six hundred miles away. "Good, sweet Christ," he whimpered, putting his head into his hands. The thought of going home broke, his tail between his legs, to live off the largess of a man he did not respect chilled him through. He didn't want to depend upon his father. But how could he live for long on $220? Would that even be enough to get him home? What if the old Schooner broke down? And if it didn't, what would he do when he got there? He had taken a great deal of money from his father and left without a word. Freed his sister. Dealt his father a nasty blow. Made him angry. Angry enough to cancel his credit cards. Angry enough to call the police? Angry enough to have them looking for the Jaguar? And if they found it, which they eventually would, angry enough to look for the Road Schooner? For the first time, the boy began to realize exactly what might lie ahead.

No. His father would not have called the police. To what end? He, more than anyone, would want to keep his secrets safe. But he would come looking. The serial numbers on the missing currency—something a man as thorough as his father would record and safeguard—would eventually take him to wherever Holly spent the cash, even if they didn't lead him directly to her. But Holly would be all right. She had proven her ability to look after herself and had enough money to do just that. But Joe had left his own trail and could imagine his father following it. Perhaps to reclaim his son. Perhaps to punish him. The point was moot, since the son did not intend to be found. Not yet.

For a while he'd be safe enough here in Belle Haven. It would take time for his father to conduct the kind of search needed to find one old motor home, tucked into a small, wooded refuge, endangered by random fire pits, in a town that warned strangers away, far from the last places where he'd used his credit cards and the innocuous lot where he'd traded away the Jaguar.

With a shudder, Joe realized then what would have happened if Frank at the gas station hadn't run a check on his credit card and discovered its cancellation. In a matter of hours his father could have learned his whereabouts and come, without warning, to find him. It became obvious to Joe that his father was not thinking any more clearly than he himself had been when he left without his checkbook, without taking more cash than his wallet would comfortably hold, without a backward glance. He imagined his father's rage upon coming home to find his children, his money, and his gold missing. He imagined, too, the rage that would greet him if he went home too soon, or if his father managed to find him before his fury had subsided. But Joe felt sure he could remain hidden for a little while, for as long as he chose to, for as long as he could get by with what he had on hand.

He could not apply for a loan, for that would involve using his real name. He could not wire his bank for money without revealing where he was. He was Joe, with no identification, no social security card, no credentials of any sort. Two hundred and twenty dollars in cash. "And," he said, reaching into his pocket, fingering the opal he had found in his father's cache. He had taken to carrying the gem with him as if it were some sort of talisman, but since this was not at all in character, he paid little attention to it. No more than to the change in his pocket or the storage of his keys. But he took a closer look at it now, wondered what it was worth, slipped it back into his pocket.

Two hundred and twenty dollars. Eight months before he could collect his trust fund. Only three before his senior year at Yale began . . . unless his father refused to pay for it. *Jesus,* he thought, dragging a hand across his mouth. *He wouldn't go that far.*

Clearly, he would have to go home. But not yet. In a few days his father would begin to calm down, to worry a bit. He would want his son back, despite what he was bound to consider a betrayal. A week should do it. By then this sojourn would be wearing thin. "Thinner," he amended. And then he would call home. Perhaps his father would be ready to face his problems. Perhaps he would even be glad that his children had forced the issue. But Joe knew better than to count on it.

He glanced around at his newly equipped Schooner. Why had he done all this? The Schooner itself . . . well, that was an impulse that he had always known could be corrected. Groceries were hardly optional. But why had he handed over much of the money in his wallet for a coffeepot, towels, a broom and dustpan? A skillet, for God's sake. (True, he *had* bought bacon, but was it actually necessary to *own* a skillet?) Thank God he'd put the toaster back. Things were already too far out of control. Why hadn't he thought so last night when Spalding had been here? It still surprised him that he'd invited the man in. It surprised him even more that Ian had asked no questions, voiced no suspicions about the reasons for his sudden arrival in Belle Haven.

So. Two hundred and twenty dollars. Enough . . . if he drove little, ate little, expected little. He could do it for a while. And in a week or so he'd call his father—perhaps from Randall, to be on the safe side.

He realized how difficult going home might be. There was every chance he'd have to act the chameleon, suffer his predatory father, until he was back at school and eventually twenty-one, wealthy in his own right. It would be a temporary sort of hypocrisy, the pragmatic choice, the only alternative to penury. But he could do it if he had to. And, once again, with deliberate enthusiasm, Joe imagined the possibility that his father might surprise him with a desire to make amends.

This settled, he felt so much better that he decided to take the Schooner into town for a really good breakfast.

"Angela's Kitchen," Ian had told him the night before, "is where you want to go for breakfast. Near Maple and Sierra. Better watch out for the trees on Sierra. Need trimming."

Joe had no intention, however, of taking his Schooner anywhere near Sierra and its overgrown trees. It was only 7:00 A.M., so there would be little traffic and plenty of places to park. As soon as he was within walking distance, he'd leave the Schooner and find his way to Angela's Kitchen on foot.

"Two hundred and twenty dollars," he figured as he drove carefully down the bumpy lane, through the trees, and onto the pale gray hardtop that led into town. "I probably shouldn't spend more than three bucks a meal." He had never had to price his food before. The effort made him hungry.

Chapter 10

"*I'll have two* eggs over easy, home fries, and toast. And cranberry juice—"

"We got any cranberry juice?" the waitress called over her shoulder.

"If it's not on the menu, it's not in the kitchen," the cook said mildly as she hauled a crate of grapefruits from the walk-in.

"No cranberry juice. Sorry," the waitress said. "But we do have orange, apple, tomato—"

"Make it orange, then," Joe decided, "and on second thought I'll have a cinnamon roll instead of the toast."

"Good choice. They're the best in town."

"I'll bet they are." Joe took a long look at the girl, at the way she was wrapped in her apron like a gift, and did not lower his eyes until she turned abruptly away and retreated toward the kitchen.

He opened his newspaper and skipped through the front pages, pausing at headlines. The world seemed to be going on without him. When he got to the bits and pieces of small news in the later pages he read more carefully but found nothing about a missing Christopher Barrows. Not that he had expected anything. But eventually, if he was reported missing, he might find a grainy likeness of himself on page 12 or thereabouts. God, he was hungry. Where the hell were his eggs?

Moments later, when the waitress carried Joe's plate over to the counter, he was immersed in his newspaper, which he had spread out in front of him, leaving no room for his food.

"Here you go," she said, holding his breakfast high in her hand. He raised his head, looked at her intently for a moment, and smiled. She was really something.

"Looks delicious," he murmured.

The waitress smiled back, her eyes narrowing. "You haven't seen it yet."

His smile stiffened. "I meant it *smells* delicious," he said.

She thought this over, her head cocked, one eye shut, mouth pursed. "No," she finally said. "I don't think so."

It startled Joe to see her slide his breakfast into the warming oven and pour out a large glass of milk.

"Here you go," she said, putting the milk down in front of him.

"What's this?"

"This," she said, raising her eyebrows, "is milk."

"Milk?"

"You were staring," she said. "At my"—she swirled her hands in front of her chest as if she meant to pull a rabbit out of a hat—"hooters. Knockers. Headlights. Coconuts. Lungs, as in, 'set of.' Ta-tas. Rack," she said and crossed her arms as if latching cupboard doors.

Joe wasn't sure what was going on. *Everybody* flirted. He'd watched his father treat a hundred girls the same way, and he'd picked up the habit much as he'd learned which fork was meant for his salad, which for his meat. But there was something in this girl's hipshot stance that made him think he'd chosen his target unwisely.

"I didn't mean anything by it," he assured her. He had not even been conscious of his actions, which made him wonder what else he commonly did to cause offense.

"Oh, sure you did, although I'm not sure what." She squinted at him as if he might just be one bug worth squashing, then turned to the oven for his plate. "I'll tell you what. You apologize and I'll give you your breakfast."

Annoyed with both the girl and himself, Joe said an unsmiling "Sorry" and held out his hand for his eggs.

"Oh, come on," the waitress scolded, shaking her head, holding the plate just beyond his reach. "Let's try that again."

Days earlier, Christopher Barrows would have done one of several things, depending on his mood: he would have walked out (without paying for his coffee); called for the manager; done his best to appease the girl. (The cook who stood several feet beyond the waitress, a spatula dripping in her hand, a look of uncertainty on her face, made the perfect audience: she watched, listened, did not interfere, posed no threat.) Christopher Barrows would never have been sorry, never have said so.

But Christopher Barrows would never have come to Belle Haven in the first place, much less to Angela's Kitchen.

"I'm sorry," said Joe. "Truly." With what was becoming habitual surprise, he felt a keen shard of admiration for this waitress. He had not met her like before or, if he had, had not recognized the breed.

"Much better," she said, and gave him his eggs.

Just then, a boy of about ten and a woman past sixty came down the stairs at the back of the pantry and tied themselves up in clean aprons. They said their good mornings to the cook and the waitress, smiled at Joe, and set to work. As if on cue, several farmers came into the shop to have breakfast, bringing with them the faint smell of Clorox, mud, gasoline, and sweat. Those who chose counter stools said good morning to the women, the boy, and nodded to Joe. For the first time since arriving in Belle Haven, he began to feel less the alien, a bit more the neighbor. He watched the waitress take a cantaloupe out of the cook's hands and slice it gracefully into perfect wedges before wiping her hands, removing her apron, and hanging it from a peg. She turned to the cook. "How much do I owe you?"

"For what? *You* made *my* breakfast, remember?"

"For the cinnamon rolls."

"Bah." The cook waved her hand impatiently. "Don't be silly, Rachel."

"Come over for brownies, then, and we'll be even," said the girl named Rachel.

The cook said, "It's a deal." And then, as if reminded that Joe had done nothing to earn *his* breakfast, she fished a pad out of her apron pocket, tore off a check, and tucked it under his coffee cup, face down. "Come again," she said, and turned back to her griddle.

Baffled by their conversation, Joe watched Rachel slip a flat wallet from the back pocket of her jeans and remove a twenty-dollar bill. She crumpled it in her fist and cautiously jammed it into a gleaming bucket that sat next to the coffeemaker. It made a crunching noise, like someone walking on gravel. When she caught him watching her, she slowly lifted one eyebrow, removed her hand from the bucket, and turned to the older woman who had come in with the boy to help and was now filling small silos with sugar.

"Rusty and I are going to the movies tonight," she said. "Want to come along?"

"Do we get popcorn?"

"Goes without saying."

"Count me in. Be nice to give Angela an evening to herself."

"Hang on a minute," the cook said, gently flipping an egg. "I don't want an evening to myself. It's Thursday, Rachel."

"Good grief," Rachel said, smacking her forehead. "So it is. I'll meet you back here when I drop off Dolly and Rusty after the movie."

"Fair enough," said Angela, the cook. "See you then."

"And I'll pick you two up at seven sharp," Rachel said, waving at Dolly, the silo-filler, and Rusty, the counter boy. "See ya later."

As Rachel walked out of the shop, Joe wolfed down the last of his breakfast, scrambled off his stool, still chewing, wrenched his wallet out of his pocket, and thrust a ten at the boy. Then he quickly pocketed the change and rushed out after her, leaving neither thanks nor tip behind.

Chapter 11

Out on the sidewalk, Joe looked up and down the street, as excited as he'd been as a boy spotting his first doe. He finally saw her, a block away. Hurrying to catch up, he noticed that she was standing absolutely still and staring across the broad street into a small parking lot tucked between a hardware store and Paula's Beauty Salon.

A man and a woman said something to her as they walked by, looked back at her as they continued on, but she seemed not to notice them. She was still standing there, her arms hanging loosely at her sides, when he slowed, wondering what to say. Finally, he called her name. It felt like a song on his tongue. "Rachel?"

She didn't answer but, after a moment, turned her head to look at him. What he saw on her face, the anger there, stopped him in his tracks.

"Did you want something?" she asked him, distracted and impatient.

He thought she might still be angry with him. He wondered if he ought to say no and go on his way. But he didn't want to do that, and he rarely did things that he didn't want to do. Instead, he said, "I'm sorry about that stunt I pulled back there."

For a moment she looked confused. Then, "You already said you were sorry."

"Well, I was hoping you'd maybe have lunch with me or something. Give me a chance to atone."

She turned again to look across the street. "We'll see," she said.

"Or if you're not busy right now I could buy you a cup of coffee."

"I've already had too much." Still without looking at him, she said, "You're a reporter, aren't you?" It had the sound of an accusation.

"Why would you think that?"

"They do stories about the fire sometimes." Now she turned back toward him and put her hands on her hips. "Most of them have lousy manners."

Joe, too, put his hands on his hips. They looked like kids at recess, squaring off. "Well, I'm not a reporter." The men at the gas station and, later, Ian had not seemed reluctant to talk about the fire out under the fields, but perhaps this girl Rachel was a more suspicious sort.

"You really want to do penance?" she asked, turning away from him once again, still absorbed with something else, something that had nothing to do with him, he now realized. He waited. After a bit she said, "Come on, then," and stepped off the curb.

With Joe following, Rachel walked quickly across the street and up to the door of the hardware store. "Damn," she said softly when she found it locked. She glanced at her watch. Joe glanced at his. Eight-fifteen. The store opened at half past. Rachel backed up to the curb and squinted at the windows of the apartment above the store. They were open, their shades up.

"Earl!" she called. "Earl, it's me, Rachel."

After a moment, a balding, fiftyish man appeared at one of the windows, a mug in his fist. "Why, Rachel," he said through the screen. "I must be dreaming. You finally ready to run away with me?"

Rachel smiled at him. "Do me a favor and open up early," she said. "It'll just take a sec. I need something in a hurry."

"For you and you alone," he sighed, a hand to his chest. "Be right down."

As they waited in silence for Earl to unlock the door, Joe tried to guess what kind of bee had landed in this girl's bonnet. She fidgeted impatiently, seemed angry all over again. But she had left the coffee shop smiling, her eyes glad. He stood and watched her expectantly. She looked ready to spring.

"Come on in," Earl said as he held the door open for them, looking curiously at Joe. "Morning."

While Earl switched on the lights, Rachel walked unerringly to a display of spray paints, all colors. After a moment, she handed Joe a can of red, one of yellow, tucked a green and an orange under her arm.

"You're a pal, Earl," she said as she paid for the paints, then collected her change and headed for the door. "Say hi to Mag for me."

Out the door, down the sidewalk, and into the adjacent parking lot they went. "How are you at butterflies?" she asked him.

"Butterflies?"

"You know. Butterflies. Can you make butterflies?"

"Well, I can't say—"

"Here, you can have red and yellow. Or would you rather have these?"

"No, I—"

"Just make sure you shake them up real well first."

And then, as he was about to write her off as a complete lunatic, Joe saw what Rachel had seen after she left Angela's Kitchen.

On one side of the parking lot, Paula's Beauty Salon presented a scarred, brick flank, innocent and bland but for a single emblem. It was an irregular circle of black paint about four feet across. Inside it were three *K*'s, the middle one bigger than the others, like a monogram of sorts.

Rachel shook one paint can in each hand, the little balls inside sounding like tap dancers. Tentatively, Joe followed her lead. Rachel uncapped both of her cans. Standing directly in front of the wall, she spent a minute or two contemplating the graffiti, giving the cans an occasional shake, then suddenly lifted her right hand and in one swift, unflinching movement turned the largest of the *K*'s into a bright orange *B*. To the spine of the *B* she added a mirror image. She swirled color, the green can hissing wildly, into each quadrant. Topped her butterfly with drooping antennae, fleshed out its body, obliterated the black of its skeleton. She was finished before Joe had even uncapped his cans.

"What are you waiting for?"

"Should you be doing this?" he asked, glancing over his shoulder. "I mean, aren't you worried someone will see you?"

"Worried someone will see me? You think I should be worried?"

"Well, these people can be pretty vindictive, can't they?"

"Oh, I suppose," she said, setting her paints at her feet and taking his from his hands. She gave them a vigorous shake and pried off their caps. Shouldering him aside, she began to work on the second *K*. "We outnumber them a hundred to one, but we act like a bunch of sheep. Too scared to rock the boat. Well, it's my boat, too, and I'll damned well rock it if I want to."

To Joe, her butterflies were inescapably ugly, for he had seen their larvae. But they had a frozen sort of dignity, like fossils or dead trees.

"You think I should be afraid of them?" She added a flourish of yellow to a fresh wing. "I'd rather be afraid of them than afraid of me."

Joe picked up a can of paint.

When they were finished, three ungainly butterflies struggled to breach their bizarre cocoon.

"Come on," Rachel said, rubbing colors between her palms. "Let's get cleaned up."

It wasn't until they had crossed Raccoon Creek and turned up her hill that Joe suddenly realized he'd never told Rachel his name.

"I'm Joe," he said.

"I know." She smiled. "Pleased to meet you."

"How'd you know my name?"

"Belle Haven's a small town," she said. "Not much happens around here without everyone hearing about it in pretty short order. For instance." She glanced at him without breaking stride. They were walking at a good clip up the steep road, and both of them were breathing hard, spending wind on both work and talk. "I know you arrived in town last night, driving a mobile home, got stuck on the bridge"—she tossed her head in the direction of the creek—"and ended up out at Ian's campground."

Joe whistled through his teeth. "This is a small town."

"Which means you won't get away with anything while you're here. At least half a dozen people saw us go off together in the direction of my house." She grinned at him. "Do you think I'd be walking up this hill with you otherwise?"

Joe shrugged. "I had wondered," he said. "I figured you were a trusting sort of person."

At which Rachel laughed. "You got that part wrong," she said. And then, after a pause, "But not entirely."

At the top of the hill and the end of the road, Rachel's house sat by itself, the nearest neighbor halfway down the hill. She led Joe across her front yard and onto her porch.

"Won't your family mind you bringing a grimy stranger home so early in the morning?" He pictured a mother in curlers, father unbathed, children, perhaps, intent on their morning cartoons.

"I live alone," she said. The door was unlocked, the windows wide open to the breeze.

Suspicious or not, Joe thought, *she feels safe enough up here.*

But Rachel suffered a moment's unease as she opened her door to this stranger—for despite knowing a thing or two about him, that's still what he was—yet the hair on her neck refused to rise, and any second sense she possessed seemed content to trust her first, more experienced instinct.

"Come on in," she said.

As he followed her into the house he was tempted to ask why she was living alone, at her age, in a house so clearly meant for a family. But he had only just met this girl and had no more intention of asking questions than of answering them. Instead, he said, "I got the impression from the signs on the road into town that this whole place was on the verge of going up in smoke, but all I've seen so far is a couple of hot spots way out in the middle of fields."

"The fire's not a problem in this part of town," she said, leaving him at the kitchen door as she pulled two jelly jars out of a cupboard, filled them with tap water, and drank one down. She held the other out in his direction. He had not realized he was thirsty until he began to drink. It was well water. Cold and somehow thicker than city water, with a taste like stone.

"It's not really a *problem* anywhere," Rachel was saying about the fire. "Once in a while a basement heats up, out at the far end of town where the tunnels are. Or a tree suddenly begins to die." She paused, took a sharp breath. "A church out that way has a hot graveyard, and there's talk about the coffins breaking up. Maybe sinking a little deeper than they ought to be." She glared at the back of her hand, used the pad of her thumb to massage a smudge of paint from the cleft of a knuckle. "Some people are thinking about moving the bodies somewhere else, but no one really wants to mess around with them unless they have to. So they keep on burying people out there and hope they'll stay put." Rachel gave herself a little shake and turned on the taps again, ran the water warm, fetched a bar of hard yellow soap from under the sink. "I'll bet you don't especially want to hear about all that."

It was true. Joe didn't really want to hear such things. Not on a full stomach. But he found himself fascinated by this strange fire, and he was curious about the kind of people who lived with it, cheek by jowl.

"No, I'm very interested," he said. "I'd never heard of any such thing as a mine fire before yesterday."

Rachel turned from the sink to look at him. "Where are you from?"

He had anticipated this question but had not settled on an answer. "The East Coast," he replied.

If Rachel found his answer vague, she did not say so. Turning back to the sink, she beckoned with an elbow. "Come get cleaned up," she said, making room.

Feeling a bit like a surgeon, Joe scrubbed the paint from his hands, now and then casting sidelong glances at the girl by his side. Her face, in profile, had a deliberate, pleasing topography of smooth lines, of features that suited one another like mountains suited their valleys, oceans their shores. Her hands, under their lather, were long and graceful with short, orderly nails. Both elegant and capable.

"Nobody's too worried about this fire," she said, as if she'd been chosen to speak for every man, woman, and child in Belle Haven. "Even before it started we sometimes had trouble with the ground giving way a bit from all the mining."

"Giving way?"

"Every mining town in America has some lousy soil. Loose, from the coal underground being removed."

"Anybody ever get buried?"

"Alive?" Rachel laughed. Shook the water from her hands. "Not even close. And no one's been burned either." She took a clean towel from a drawer by the sink, dried her hands, offered it to Joe. "As long as you aren't sitting right above a mine tunnel, you're as good as gold. And even then, you're safer than you would be living in the city." The more she talked about the fire, about her town, the more her slight accent strengthened. Her speech lost some of its edge. The tips of her words nudged one another, like beads in a necklace.

His hands tingling, Joe pulled out a chair at the kitchen table. He sat so that he could watch her as she hung the towel to dry and watered a primrose that was showing off on the windowsill.

"You must be used to it by now," he said.

"I am," Rachel said. "It's no big deal. Really," she added, as if he needed convincing. "Although . . ." She stretched the word out, tipping her head and appraising him with a long look. "I *could* tell you some stories . . ."

Joe appraised her right back. "Such as?"

She closed one eye, considered him soberly through the other. "I don't want to give you nightmares."

Joe grinned at her. "Don't worry about me. I'm a big boy."

Rachel smiled like a cat. "It's not a very nice story."

But Joe could not imagine that she knew any stories to compare to the ones that had sent him to Belle Haven in the first place.

"Shoot," he said.

Rachel pulled out a chair at the table. Sat down across from Joe. "When I was eleven years old," she said and was momentarily silenced by the look on Joe's face. "Is something the matter?"

She had sounded so much like Holly. *When I was eleven years old . . .*

"Go on," he said. "Nothing's the matter."

Which Rachel did not believe for a second. She watched him rearrange his face, fold his hands on the table in front of him. "Do you want some coffee?" she asked, more to give him a moment than anything else.

"Sure. If it's no trouble." He was startled by his own good manners.

Rachel got up and took an old percolator out of a cupboard beneath the sink. "The fire started when I was ten, so I guess I was ten when this happened. Maybe eleven." She cocked her head. "Thereabouts anyway." She filled the percolator with water. "I was playing at my friend Lynn's house. Lynn Cooper. She lived out near the tunnels, and north of town, where the fire started. We usually played here at my house because her brothers always pestered us, but her dog, Elvira—"

"Elvira?" he said. "They had a dog named *Elvira?*"

"I know. Don't ask me. Anyway, she had a litter of new pups in the coal shed, and I wanted to see them. We kept trying to sneak a look, but Elvira went nuts if we got too close. She was a good mother."

Rachel poured coffee directly out of a can into the basket of the percolator. She didn't bother to measure it. Joe watched her hands as she made the coffee. She handled everything with the same sure, steady touch.

"She was a good ratter, too, which was a good thing for the Coopers. Lots of rats lived in the tunnels, and when the mines shut down and there were no more lunch scraps for the rats to eat, they had to come up for all their food. But Elvira didn't have any trouble keeping them under control until the fire started. After that, the rats had to completely abandon the tunnels. People living near mine shafts, like the Coopers, suddenly had a real rat problem. Ever seen a mine rat?"

Joe shook his head. He thought about asking her to stop. "No, I never have."

"Lucky you." Rachel made a face. "Big as cats, some of them. Mean as spit. So up they came, looking for food and a new place to live. The Coopers had plenty of garden and a big barn, too. Rat heaven. Within a week of the fire starting, there were rat holes all over the place. Lynn's father was afraid they'd find a way into the basement, especially when Elvira was so busy with her pups. And Lynn kept having nightmares about one of those enormous rats eating the puppies. So her father got it into his head to wipe out the rats, once and for all." Rachel held the basket of coffee in one hand but had clearly forgotten it was there. She had gone pale with remembering. Joe watched the basket of coffee the way someone watches a long cigarette ash.

"First," Rachel said, "he filled in all the rat holes he could find, except two. Then he attached a hose to the tailpipe of his truck and stuck it down one of the two open rat holes. And then he started up the truck and left it running while he ran over and stood next to the other rat hole with a paddle in his hands."

She lowered her face to the coffee grounds, took a long breath, and, straightening up, refreshed by the smell of the grounds, dropped the basket onto its stalk inside the pot. Crammed on the lid. Plugged it in. Almost immediately, the percolator began to gurgle and spit.

"God, it was awful," she said. "We all sat on the back steps to watch—Lynn and I, Lynn's mother and her three brothers. Like it was 4-H or something." Rachel made a sound like there was something clinging to the lining of her throat. Joe wondered what 4-H stood for.

"I'll never forget . . . Lynn's father was wearing waders to keep the blood off his pants, and one of the boys kept yelling, 'Batter up!' "

It was at this point that Joe became aware of the eggs slowly liquefying in his stomach. Rachel, too, suddenly looked very grim. She swallowed so hard Joe could hear it above the grumble of the percolator.

"The first rat came scampering up out of that hole like the hounds of hell were after it," she said. "Lynn's father took a huge swing at it, but he hadn't expected the rats to panic. He thought the exhaust would slow them down, blind them. And he missed. And in the next second he realized what he'd done." Rachel took a quick step backward. "He started screaming for us to get in the house, but I was up off those steps and through that door before the words were out of his mouth. We all were. Then we watched from the windows." The coffee gurgled in its pot. Joe could hardly wait for the taste of it. "There were hundreds of them. *Thousands.* They came out so close together it was like watching a black river gushing up from the ground. We watched for over an hour before they stopped coming up out of that hole. And they ran out into the fields, into the barn. Elvira stood in the door of the coal shed and fought off the ones that came her way. Lynn's mother got on the phone and called the nearest neighbors to warn them what was coming. It took about a year and all kinds of exterminators, but we finally got the mine rats under control. I haven't seen one for years. Although now and then one will show up in somebody's garbage and everyone will act like there's a gargoyle on the loose." Rachel took a pot of sugar and put it on a tray. "But that's the worst thing that's ever happened.

"Go on out to the porch," she said, "and I'll bring the coffee."

And although Joe, too, saw that things could have been much worse for Belle Haven, he took a long look through Rachel's screen door before he opened it on this particular corner of the world.

The balance of their conversation that morning was full of the courtesy of strangers, of curiosity unappeased. They spoke some more about the town but little about themselves. Joe was reluctant to reveal his reasons for coming to this town. Rachel was so undecided about her future that she preferred to dwell on the here and now. So they talked about the fire, about the Schooner and the bridge, about Angela and Earl, about Ian Spalding and the demise of his campground.

"How does he make a living now?" Joe asked.

"He's a part-time schoolteacher, nearly ready to retire in any event." Which Joe could easily believe, for Ian had a teacher's way about him: he explained things well, seemed happy to share what he knew, had a voice made for the ear and an easy way about him. Joe thought he would be hard to ruffle. But he was also aware that he cared what Ian thought about him, which was unusual for Joe. Perhaps this was because Ian was so much older, so respectable-looking: his cuffs buttoned, sparse hair nicely cut, matching crow's feet around his kind eyes. Or perhaps because he had taught school for so long that he had learned the trick of treating others as he himself wanted to be treated: with patience and respect.

"The campground wasn't anything more than a way for Ian to keep busy during the summers and make a bit of extra money," Rachel said. "It was never very popular anyway. Just people passing through on their way somewhere else. But nobody passes through here on purpose anymore." She wondered if Joe was an exception, and if so, why. But she figured he'd tell her if he wanted to.

After their coffee was gone, they grew awkward with each other and Joe realized it was time to leave. "I guess I'd better go fetch my Schooner," he said. "I left it over at the A&P. Too bad Ian lives so far out. I'd rather not drive the Schooner into town again if I can help it, but I can't see walking all that way."

Rachel thought about that for a moment and then reluctantly said, "I guess you could borrow my father's bike. If you promise to take good care of it." She had mixed feelings about this man. One minute he was saying something to offend her, the next smiling his winsome smile, looking at her with those remarkably blue eyes, daring her to think ill of him.

He made her wary, suspicious, but she was tempted to trust him with small things. As if he were an ex-con or a friend known to lie. She had allowed him into her home. She would lend him her father's old bike.

"You'll need to walk it down to Frank's," she warned as they hauled the bike out of the cellar. "The tires need air, and I'll bet the chain wants a bit of oil."

"This is wonderful," he said, meaning it. "I'll take great care of it. Thanks."

Before he went away, she gave him her phone number (she'd thought about the wisdom of that while bringing out the bike and decided it could do no harm). "It's such a small town you shouldn't have trouble finding anything you need, but call me if you do."

"Thanks, Rachel. Ian's right there, but thanks. Maybe I'll see you at Angela's again."

She watched him walk off down the hill, wheeling the old bike that had been her father's for so many years. She liked Joe despite herself. "I'll have to watch that," she thought. The day stretched ahead of her with no reason to hurry, no plans or commitments. She sighed and turned back toward the porch.

"That damned step," she muttered when it sagged under her weight. "Today's the day I fix that damned step." Ed would be disappointed, she knew. It gave him something to complain about when he brought her mail. "One of these days it's gonna go," he often warned her. "Someone's gonna get hurt." And he was right, of course. The step was rotten with worms and wet. So she gathered up her tools and set to work.

With a crowbar, she pried and tugged and cursed until the top plank of the step gave way, splintering and shrieking, flakes of old paint flying. As she worked, she began to remember herself as a small girl. Struggling with her father's hammer. Handing him nails and clapping her hands over her ears as he pounded them in. Trailing her small paintbrush along the wood, leaving grasslike streaks that skipped against the grain. Strangling with pride when he admired her work. These had been their steps, the ones they had built together. This rotten plank had been measured by his hands, fashioned with his saw, borne his weight, her mother's, hers. This rotten plank. She set it to one side and looked straight into the sun. It was nothing to the brightness of her memory.

And suddenly it seemed to Rachel that she simply could not leave this place. The thought of going back to school again while this house stood here, locked up, mute with dust, made her sob aloud. She would stay, she decided. She would stay right here where she belonged.

As if afraid that her resolve might waver, she sprinted inside the house, up the stairs, and into the small study that overlooked the woods behind the house. Two blue jays were wrestling in the branches of a big maple. Rachel kept an eye on them as she rolled clean paper into her mother's old typewriter and began to compose her letter to Dean Franklin. It thanked him for three good years, informed him that she had decided to postpone the fourth. She wouldn't be wandering through Europe or getting the jump on her career, she wrote. She'd be catching her breath. Getting her bearings. She would be back, she assured him, when the time was right. If they would still have her.

She signed the letter, sealed it up in an envelope, stamped it, put it out on the porch for Ed. She felt better than she had since arriving back in Belle Haven, as deliciously guilty as a child who is kept home from school for a fever but does not yet feel any pain.

Before heading out to get a piece of lumber for the new step, Rachel wandered about the house looking for other things in need of repair. She had never done this sort of thing before, still had trouble thinking of this house as hers, not theirs. She had never before questioned the furnishings, the wallpaper, the way things were arranged. Now, suddenly, she began to become excited by the prospect of making this house her own. She would keep some of the furniture, things that reminded her of her mother and father. And the artwork, such as it was: faded prints of bucolic scenes, simple watercolors here and there, several black-and-white photographs of dead relatives posing arm in arm. The braided rugs would stay. Certainly the curtains, stitched by her mother. Most everything, in fact, now that she came right down to it, reminded her of them. But once she had given away some of the weary old furniture, there would be room to add some things of her own. More art. More books. More color.

First, the step. She had all the time in the world to feather her nest. "Just keep your distance," she said softly, looking out toward the horizon where a thread of smoke wavered like a cobra. Then she turned her back and went about her business.

Chapter 12

After leaving Frank's Gas 'n' Go, Joe pedaled over to the A&P. He hadn't ridden a bicycle for ages and felt such a sense of liberation as he flew down the streets of Belle Haven that he waved to an old woman sitting on a bench in the sun.

Since the Schooner's stern was equipped with a bike rack, it took Joe no more than a minute to stow his new transport and get under way. He had no good reason to linger in town: no money to spare, no errands to run, no appointments to keep. And, considering how small Belle Haven was, he was loath to do any more exploring than he'd already done. He would save the rest for the days that waited ahead, empty as drums.

Once back at the campsite, Joe parked the Schooner as before. With the bicycle Rachel had lent him, he probably wouldn't have to drive it for days—if his father came to fetch him, perhaps not ever again. He paused to consider this idea, to plumb its depths, then briskly disembarked and began to make a less impermanent camp.

First, he unfurled the Schooner's red-and-white striped awning and was relieved to find it clean and intact. Under the awning and next to a flat-topped tree stump, he set up the cheap lawn chair he'd bought in town. Then he mixed himself a glass of instant iced tea and carried it outside. The chocolate bar he'd bought at Frank's and carried home in his shirt pocket was soft and warm. He ate it slowly, sipping his cold tea, and stared at the sunlight on the stream. With the exception of a damaged cuticle, his entire body felt marvelous. He was aware of each breath lifting his chest, the smooth, uncomplicated function of his elbow, the way his brilliantly designed toes lay alongside one another and how the lenses of his eyes—the miracle of his eyes—brought to him so unerringly the majesty of the trees.

For the rest of the morning, Joe did nothing more than putter around his Schooner and make it more his own. He took an empty pop bottle and filled it with stream water and Queen Anne's lace for the sill of his kitchen window. He read the side panel of his carton of laundry soap, measured out what he needed, and washed his clothes in his new laundry tub. Then he rinsed them well and pegged them to the line he'd hung between two obedient pines in the middle of the sunny clearing.

For his lunch he had two bacon sandwiches with a cold bottle of beer, washed up his frying pan and dishes, dried them and put them away. He wiped the crumbs off his kitchen counter, squeezed out his sponge, dried his hands on a crisp tea towel, and hung it on a rack to dry. He dusted every surface, shook out the door mat, swept the Schooner's steps, and opened all the windows to let the breezes through. When he stumbled across the letter he had scribbled to his father the day before, Joe was taken aback. It still said what he wanted to say, but he was no longer so eager to make contact. In a week or so he would find a phone and courage enough to call home. Until then, he didn't much want to think about what he'd done or what he would say when his father answered the phone. He stuffed the letter into the glove compartment, slammed the door, and forgot about it.

At one-thirty on the afternoon of Joe's first full day in Belle Haven, he realized that he was both content and something akin to lonely. An early morning spent with Rachel had made the day seem unusually long and quiet. So, without thinking much about his intentions, he locked the Schooner and walked through the woods to Ian's house.

"Good afternoon," Ian said when Joe knocked on his back door. "How you making out?"

"Fine," Joe replied, smiling. "Feel like taking a walk?"

So the two of them strolled out across the fields that ringed the campground, wended their way through stands of pine and birch, and finally sidled up to a small hot spot that had opened in the bottom of a shallow ditch like a drain hole filled with flame.

"Yikes," said Joe, appalled. "I can understand why people stopped coming here to camp."

"That's nothing. You can't even get near the big ones, they're so hot. And they can come up so fast that even when you're well clear of the tunnels it's impossible to know where it's safe to camp. Except where you are," he amended quickly, seeing the look on Joe's face. "At least I think that spot's okay. It's hundreds of yards from the closest tunnel. And even though the fire branches out a bit, I've never seen any sign of trouble anywhere near there, maybe because of the stream, although I don't know how a shallow little creek could discourage a fire that runs so deep. But it seems to."

"I'm surprised no one's been killed by one of these things."

"Well, like I said, most all of them are within spitting distance of a shaft or a tunnel, and we all know where those are, give or take. Easy enough to steer clear of them if you know where they're bound to be. Remind me to give you a map later on."

"Uh-huh." Joe nodded, his skin clammy.

"Plus," Ian said, clearly accustomed to describing the fire and its habits, "the fire usually gives some warning on its way to the surface. Sort of like a whale coming up for air. The ground gets hot, of course, and softer, and sometimes buckles a bit right before the fire arrives. We get a few big hot spots around the tunnels because of the way the coal was mined. Traditional room-and-pillar style." He looked at Joe for any sign of comprehension. Found none. "That's when they leave pillars of coal to support the surface. The theory is that long, thin coal veins that didn't get mined are carrying the fire out from the tunnels and lighting these pillars. Or sometimes a skinny vein will travel underground for a while and then head for the surface, where it makes a smaller hot spot." He rotated his hands, one around the other. "Which in turn burns for as long as the coal vein lasts, peters out pretty quickly, the burned-out vein collapses in on itself, and the hot spot disappears as fast as it came. Leaves a bit of a crater, is all. But a lot of coal veins never hit a pillar or run near the surface so the fire doesn't often break through." Ian looked at the hot spot with grudging respect.

"You must get scads of geologists poking around out here. What do they think about all this?"

"I can't really say. They don't talk to us, you see. They don't seem to care what we think about the fire, what we've observed, what we want to do about it." He pulled a blade of quack grass from its sheath. It slid out smoothly, with only a single squeal of protest, as if designed for easy destruction. "There's a man named Mendelson you'll see around if you're here long enough. Don't know where he is right now. Probably off somewhere trying to sell his latest scheme for putting out the fire. He's an engineer, I guess. The government sent him in years ago, right after the fire got started, to dig a trench and cut the thing off before it spread. That didn't work. They filled the trench back in. So then they tried to drown it with water, stifle it with fly ash, which is little particles of ash that fly up when you burn something solid."

"Hence the name."

"Right. It won't burn, fly ash, so you blow in enough of it and it smothers a flame. Only it didn't work with this fire. Nothing has worked too well. Those boys go away for a while, and no one sees them around. Then, after a few months, back they come to try something new. Mendelson's always with them. Seems to take a personal interest in our little fire." He put the grass between his teeth. "Pretty soon they're going to have to make up their minds what to do next."

"About the fire."

"About the fire." Ian nodded. "About us. If the fire gets bad enough, heads into town, we'll all have to go somewhere else, I suppose. People who live out here where the fire already is, and along the edge of town, too, anywhere near enough to the tunnels . . . well, we look sharp. Take nothing for granted. Watch our step."

"Literally," Joe said, nodding.

"Any way we can," Ian replied as he backed away from the fire, Joe following, and turned toward home.

They said little on the way back. The sun was hot, the grass full of bugs that flung themselves out of the way as the men walked by.

"I met a girl named Rachel this morning," Joe said, following Ian across a plank that bridged the stream behind his house. "Know her?"

"Everybody knows everybody in Belle Haven, at least their faces. Rachel I know straight to the bone. I was her teacher in high school. Smart as a whip, that girl. Charmed me right down to my socks. Not a mean bone in her body. Probably the best student I ever had."

"How come she didn't go to college?" Joe asked as they crossed Ian's yard.

" 'Course she went to college. She'll be a senior in the fall. What made you think otherwise?"

But Joe had no idea why he'd got it wrong. "Maybe the way she seems so rooted here. She's got a house of her own, lives alone, didn't say a word about ever having lived anywhere else. I don't know, I guess . . . I don't know what I thought. I met her at Angela's Kitchen. I thought she was a waitress, but . . ." He looked at Ian from under the visor of his hand. "She's not a waitress, is she?"

"No, she's not a waitress," said Ian, smiling. He stopped by his back door. "Got any plans for tonight?"

"Actually, I don't. Why? Is there a ball game on or something?"

"I have no idea. I only ever do one thing on Thursday nights. You're welcome to join me. It would be a good way to get to know some people from around here."

"What would?"

"Thursday night at the Last Resort. It's a bar down by the tracks. Not much to look at, but the beer's cold."

"What's so special about Thursday nights?" Joe asked, grinning because Ian was.

"They have live music on Thursdays, is all," Ian said. "You coming?"

"Sure. We can take the Schooner, park near the bar, won't have to drive home if we have too much to drink."

"Now, that is one hell of an idea," Ian said. "Not that I ever have too much to drink, but just in case."

"Exactly," Joe said. "I'll see you back here at, what . . . nine o'clock?"

"On the dot," said Ian, and waved Joe on his way.

Chapter 13

Some people are born too late and miss the pocket of time that would have suited them best. Others, born far too early, never know what's to come and so perhaps don't feel the lack so keenly. Others miss the mark by just a decade or two and live to see what might have been. For them, there is sometimes much to regret.

Ian Spalding, born in 1919, first heard the word *astronaut* when it was far too late. From the time he was five years old he had looked at the heavens the way some people look at the sea. He thought of the stars the way others thought of the continents. And he considered the planets to be destinations only temporarily beyond his reach. Decades too early for *Apollo,* Ian decided that he would learn to fly airplanes, master the sky, and be ready for the first spaceships. He was only twelve when he made these decisions. He did not know about such things as odds or impossibilities. He only knew that if he did everything right—kept himself fit, studied hard, read every word ever written about flight, and somehow found his way into the sky—he would be a worthy pilot, perhaps a great one.

Each day, after his early chores, after school, after his late chores, after supper, Ian would sit on the edge of his bed and read books without number. He knew about Kitty Hawk as if he had been born there. The Wright brothers were his own brothers by everything but blood. Lindbergh was his hero, and the *Spirit of St. Louis* history's most heavenly vessel. There was nothing on earth, for Ian, to compare with the realm of the sky.

His father, a farmer with only one son and an ailing wife, knew that to farm, a man had to be tied to the land with a real bond, a sure commitment. Farming broke hearts and spirits. That's what it meant to be a farmer. And only those who loved the land could bear it, whether they called the bond love or something else. So he did not insist that Ian farm. He expected his son to help with the chores, but he did not look for anything more and he was not bitter. When his wife died and as he grew older, he allowed more and more of his land to go to grass and clover, or rented it out to neighbors, or planted it in trees. He loved his son and, though he never admitted it to himself, envied him, too. There was such great enthusiasm in the boy, such determination. To fly had never been the father's wish, but because it was the son's, it fired them both. While Ian worked and studied and dreamed, his father saved every spare nickel, and though there weren't many of these, there were enough to grant him one small wish of his own.

Living alone as they did, Ian and his father had learned to cook a dozen meals extremely well, exactly to their liking. They rarely fiddled with other possibilities. They saw no need. They had far too much to do to worry about what they ate, as long as it was good. On the third Friday in June 1935, they sat at the kitchen table eating oven-fried pork chops, mashed potatoes, baby limas, and store-bought bread. Ian's father was drinking his Friday-night beer.

"School's out next Friday," he said.

"Don't I know it," Ian said, buttering his beans.

"Sounds like you'll be glad to be out."

"Not just out this time. Done."

His father smiled. "Our first high school graduate." He pronounced it "graj-e-at."

"Soon to be a college man."

"Soon to be a college man." His father put a crust of browned pork fat in his mouth. "I don't know if I've told you how proud I'll be to have an educated son," he said after a moment. "But I will be. Already am."

"I know, Daddy," Ian said, unabashed, grinning with his mouth full of mashed potatoes.

A week later, when Ian graduated from high school, his father gave him a compass. "So you'll know it when you're facing Belle Haven," he said.

Two weeks before Ian was to leave for college, his father gave him a new suit of clothes and a small suitcase for his travels. "I've never in my life owned a suitcase," his father said. "Never went anywhere." But he said it without rancor.

Ian was touched by each of these gifts and was sincerely grateful, but it was what his father gave him on the eve of his departure that made Ian understand forever the mettle of his father's love.

Ian was packing his new suitcase when he turned to find his father standing at his bedroom door, looking all at once sad and delighted. A rare look for his father.

"Hey," the boy said.

"Almost packed?"

"Yessir. Not much *to* pack."

"Well, lights out soon as you're done, boy. Big day tomorrow."

Ian glanced at the clock by his bed. "It's only nine, Daddy. If I go to bed now, I'll be up at four."

His father nodded.

Ian had somehow thought that on the coming all-important morning he would for once be excused from his regular chores, but he corrected himself and returned the nod. "You're right," he said. "That'll give me plenty of time to catch the eight o'clock bus."

Ian's father shook his head, never taking his eyes from his son's face. "That'll give you just enough time to catch the five-thirty plane."

Ian straightened up. The shirt he'd been folding fell out of his hands.

"What plane?" he said. He did not appear to be breathing.

"Man named Stephens down in Bolton is making a cargo run to Pittsburgh. He takes a passenger whenever he can. Helps pay for the gas. Tomorrow he's taking you."

"Oh, God, Daddy," was all Ian said, unable to move, for every part of him—heart and head and soul—had already, impatiently, taken flight.

"And oh, my, what a flight it was," Ian said to Joe as the Schooner carried them toward the Last Resort that Thursday night, nearly five decades later. Ian tipped his head back and shivered briefly, all over. "Nothing I had ever read or ever heard or ever done prepared me for that flight. Nothing even came close. I thought I knew what it would feel like to ride up into the sky, skim the clouds, split the wind. But, oh, dear Lord . . . it nearly killed me."

"*Killed* you?"

Ian chuckled. "Nearly messed my pants before he even had that thing in the air. An old bucket of bolts, it was. I still think it's the ninth wonder of the world that I didn't throw up all over western PA."

"What, you were scared?"

Ian snorted. "You could say that."

"I guess you changed your mind about being a pilot, then."

Ian nodded. "Didn't give it too much thought while I was in the air. I think every circuit in my brain had blown. But after we landed and I'd spent half an hour breathing into a paper bag, I made a vow that I'd never get on one of those damned things ever again. Not ever. Amen."

"But you did, of course."

"Nope. Never. I hitched back and forth from home to school for the first three years. Then my daddy died and I drove his truck until it died, too. And then I came back to Belle Haven to teach school, and I've never gone so far afield that my own two feet or four Goodyears wouldn't get me there."

As Joe eased the Schooner into town, he wondered how different the wheel under his hands would feel if he ever decided to forego the world's mightier machines.

Joe had never seen a bar like the Last Resort, except maybe in the movies. He'd gone slumming before, but the Last Resort was in a class by itself. This place was, he realized, no different from thousands of other bars in thousands of other tiny towns across the U.S. of A. (as they called it around here), but it was something new to him. Without Ian by his side, he never would have entered such a place. Its walls were unpainted cinder block, its windows glass brick, its roof warped and rotting tiles, its parking lot mud, refuse, and slag. It seemed intentionally ugly, unforgivably squalid, unconditionally decrepit.

"Are we really going in?" Joe whispered as they approached the door.

"Well, of course we are," Ian said, clearly surprised. "That's what we came for."

"But what kind of music could they possibly have that's worth spending time in a place like this?"

"Probably the worst music you've ever heard in your life." Ian was laughing as he pushed Joe into the one bar in the world that he would come to love, heart and soul.

It was smoky inside the Last Resort. The floor was bare plywood, the walls unadorned. The horseshoe bar left little room for the unseated patrons who clotted the corners, drinking beer out of long-necked bottles. In a far corner of the room was a large doorway leading to a second room. Several people stood by this doorway, looking in and laughing at something that Joe could not see. He could hear the music coming from the other room: a guitar, a piano, some brass, an unlikely fiddle. And then someone began to sing the opening bars to the most appalling rendition of "Rambling Man" he'd ever heard.

"Jesus God," he gasped. "That's horrendous. Even I can sing better than that."

"Well, we'll just see about that," Ian said, and led the way into the crowd.

Most of the men were a good deal bigger than Joe, with heads that sat directly on their shoulders. They wore jeans, short-sleeved work shirts, belts with big buckles, dusty boots, and, a few of them, Stetsons. There was, as well, a leaner breed among them: smaller, with slim hips, arms that were brown and beautiful to look at, hairless faces, colorful eyes. The women had clean, shining hair, ironed jeans, crisp cotton blouses, too much makeup, and a few of them, too, Stetsons. No one seemed to mind the smoke, the mournful music, the bare-bones decor. As Ian had said, the beer was cold, the music terrible, the opportunity to become acquainted with a few Belle Haven natives too good to pass up.

"We'll just see about what?" Joe shouted into the din.

"It's amateur night, my boy," Ian fairly chortled as they finally reached the doorway into the back room. "One giant shower stall. Ain't it grand?"

Along two walls of the back room, twenty, maybe thirty people sat around narrow tables that were draped in long sheets of thin, white paper anchored with the biggest ashtrays Joe had ever seen. Everyone had either a beer in a bottle or something stronger in an uncomplicated tumbler. There was not a lime or a lemon or a swizzle stick in sight. There were baskets of pretzels on the tables, the air was awash with smoke, and a stupid breed of moths wandered through a propped-open fire door.

At the far end of the room a quartet of sweating musicians struggled valiantly to keep pace with a young man in a big hat who was singing so badly that many of those listening winced and writhed in their chairs. One older man covered his eyes with his hands. The musicians swayed in their folding chairs and thought about the beer and ashtrays tucked behind their heels. Spare instruments lay about, an empty guitar case doubled as a footrest, and in the shadow of an old upright piano, a little girl lay curled up on a blanket, impossibly asleep. There was a small patch of bare floor in front of the band, but no one was dancing.

After a final, prolonged yelp, the young man in the hat surrendered the microphone, bowed to a bit of belated applause, and took his seat. He was flushed, exultant, mortified. With one arm tucked across his belly, the other busy with his drink, he moved his head this way and that, careful not to look around at his neighbors but not at all sure what to do, where to look, how to settle himself. He took a long drink and calmed down a bit, leaning back in his chair, as a woman wearing jeans and rhinestones stepped up to announce the next performer.

"That's Amelia," Ian said. "Plays the organ at my church. She and her husband, Jim, own this place. Their son—the one with the fiddle—got together with three of his friends and started playing here Thursday nights. For beer money, you know. They're not too good, and they've all got day jobs, but we like them well enough. For a buck, they'll play backup. Pick a song from the list on the table there, and they'll give you lyrics and a microphone. The whole thing works out great."

"Ed?" Amelia called, peering through the smoke. "You out there?" When Ed sidled up to the microphone, staring at it in terror, Amelia turned to the band. " 'Tie a Yellow Ribbon,' " she said.

"Ah, shit," said the guitar player. "Not again."

"One of my all-time favorites," Joe said, grinning, his thumbs in his belt loops, chin in the air.

As he looked around at the patrons of the Last Resort, watched the man named Ed falter and fumble through his song, Joe wondered how many of them had ever been more than a hundred miles from Belle Haven, ever seen a ballet, ever read *To Kill a Mockingbird*, ever learned the exact configuration of the fifty states.

"These are the diehards," Ian said, waving an arm at those seated in the back room. "They're on deck. You in good voice tonight?"

"Not bloody likely." Joe snorted. "Come on. Let's get something to drink."

A few minutes later, not paying much attention to the onslaught of sound from the back room, Joe suddenly noticed that the bar had become quite still. People were turning toward the back room and around again. Then the stillness was gone and the din back, as before, but Joe, curious, got up to have a look at the man who was taking a turn with the band.

He was not a young man, not an old one. Neither plain nor fancy. He had a hard face, a hard body, clean clothes, lots of sun. He was bowed a bit with drink. Joe could see the weave of his shoulders and the lazy slide of his eyelids. But there was nothing sloppy or weak about this man. And the way he was singing "The Green, Green Grass of Home" made Joe think that maybe he had someplace he'd rather be.

"Who's that?" he asked Ian back at the bar.

"That," said Ian, "is Mendelson. The man I told you about this afternoon."

"The firefighter."

"The firefighter," Ian sighed. "After a fashion."

Mendelson had a good voice. He put the rest of the singers to shame. But he sang with his eyes closed, clearly unconcerned with the reaction of the audience, attentive only to the words he was singing and, perhaps, the way the microphone trembled in his hand, the way the sound came back to him from the walls, the way it feels to sing a song you love.

Later Joe watched Mendelson return to his stool at the bar, pick up his drink, light a cigarette, and stare into the middle distance. He was alone. He talked to no one and no one talked to him. After a while he got up, put some money on the bar, and walked out. Before the door had shut behind him, his drink had been cleared away, his stool occupied, and the sound of his voice purged by a fat man who had a twang like a banjo and could barely sing for hiccups.

Anthony Mark Mendelson had at one time been known as the Centurian, the finest wrestler in his corner of Kentucky and for a hundred miles beyond. Had he been an indifferent competitor, less able, less ambitious, he might have spent some of his youth exploring other arts. But he was a great wrestler, and that was enough.

Wrestling is an odd sport, not quite fighting, not quite not. A quiet sport, but for the grunting and the slap of flesh. An unflattering, unglamorous business, memorable for the sight of buttocks, of tendons rigid as machinery. But to wrestlers, it is a sport like no other. Its roots twine back through the ages, touch Olympia, blend the salt of dead champions and live boys, herald the unaided, unadorned, unqualified virtue of might. Throw in nicknames like Gibraltar, Pretzel, the Centurian, and wrestling becomes, to even its youngest and its most ungainly participants, a secret society, closed to outsiders, sacred and sublime.

When too many pulled hamstrings, too many displaced joints, too many hernias forced Anthony Mark Mendelson to give up the sport he loved, he continued to think of himself as the Centurian. Tony was not such a bad name. He had always liked it. But to settle for Tony seemed like a surrender. He had wanted to wrestle for the rest of his days, even bald and incontinent, and he was angry to have been denied this intention. He was a disappointed boy who gradually became dissatisfied with nearly everything about his life. Nothing sat quite right. So, at the age of eighteen, what he could change, he did. His hair, his habits, his name. When he left high school, he became Mendelson. Period. It sufficed.

After high school he joined the army, learned all there is to know about intimidation and a great deal about engineering, missed Korea by a handful of years, and—both too old and apathetic—skipped Vietnam. Working for a mining company suited him better, was far safer, more lucrative, more satisfying: in the rolling hills of Pennsylvania, he commanded all manner of men and machines.

He had a fondness for big dogs, small women, meat of any kind, and country music. Each Christmas he traveled home to see his senile mother, his sister and her brood, old high school friends. Some had once wrestled with him, and he was pleased to see them approaching their middle years flabby and slow, while he was still as muscled and fit as a young dog.

When he was thirty-five, Mendelson was called back to a site he had once worked for a short while before its closure. A fire had taken hold in the Belle Haven mines, and Mendelson had been nominated to contain it.

Mendelson had never fought a mine fire before. He'd observed a few, monitored the long, tedious struggle to extinguish them, and therefore welcomed the explicit instructions he was given by the committee of his colleagues, local officials, and fire specialists too busy with other mine fires to take on this one. "Dig a trench," they told him, and told him how. And so he did.

Things might have gone well for Mendelson, had he not still thought of himself as the Centurian. The aging miners who lived in Belle Haven knew its mines better than their own backyards, and they were waiting for him when he arrived. "Here's where you want to dig," they told him, uninvited. "Go deeper than that," they said, catching wind of his instructions. "Farther south," they said. "Dig fast, or it'll run right away from you."

To which he replied, lighting a cigar, squinting at the lot of them, very aware of his youth in the face of their decline, "I know my business. Get on with yours."

Although they had thought themselves more concerned with their town than their reputations, the miners were silenced by their pride, by their desire to see what this young stranger was made of. Each morning they would arrive to watch the digging of the trench. They would sit in their old trucks and drink coffee, smoke cigarettes, condemn. When the work crew broke for lunch each day, the miners found their fingers itching for picks and shovels. To a man, they longed to leap from their trucks and raise a ruckus, demand a greater effort from the uninspired crew. They were afraid of this fire and what it might someday do. But their pride was formidable. And so they sat quietly in their trucks and watched the goings-on like predators picking out the weakest, best candidate for a chase. But Mendelson would not run.

Day after day, their eyes upon him, Mendelson came to realize that he felt younger and stronger than he had since his wrestling days. Each morning he checked in with his advisors in Harrisburg, gave them a progress report, sought their allegiance, which they pledged. "You're doing fine," they said. "Right on schedule." It was easy for him to ignore his doubtful audience. Even easier to feel inspired by their lack of faith. He often paused in his work to picture their retreat, the fire cut off, the trench more daunting than a wall.

On the day that the trench was due for completion, Mendelson woke earlier than usual. He shaved carefully, dressed silently, walked to the diner next to the Randall Inn, where he was staying, and had eggs, sausage, home fries, toast, three cups of coffee, and, on his way out the door, a banana. Driving over from Randall, he sang his favorite songs and smiled a lot. He was happy. Everything had gone well. He'd done a good job. Soon he'd be headed somewhere else.

Old memories came up out of their black space as Mendelson crossed the boundary onto Belle Haven land. He had worked hard, as a boy, to earn his own pocket money, enough to pay for a yearly baseball, perhaps a comic book now and then, more likely food, which was sometimes scarce at home. He charged a dollar to tend a grave, turn the topsoil each spring, dress it with forest mulch, plant new grass and flowers as ordered. For another dollar, he would keep it tidy all season. For a buck and a half he would shovel a load of coal down a chute and into a coal cellar. He walked dogs when no one was home to tend them, split firewood, painted fences, ran errands. Sometimes he took home a licorice whip for his little sister, but mostly he spent the money on himself. He had, after all, done the work.

Even then, work had felt good, but not like the big work he did now. The way the earth trembled when his machines smacked it, the way he could point and the men would simply go, do what he told them to do: these things made him feel so strong that his work was his pleasure. He was good at what he did.

It was only seven o'clock when Mendelson arrived at the trench, but everything was white and hazy with August sun. The dew on the field grass looked like flint sparks. Sometimes, when Mendelson was the first to arrive, deer stood grazing at the edge of the far woods. But he had lingered over his substantial breakfast and was not so early this morning. Instead of deer he found his crew waiting for him in their trucks, which was odd. The old Belle Haven miners were all standing at the edge of the trench, looking in. This, too, was unusual.

Like a moose facing an onslaught of wolves, Mendelson was suddenly sorry that he had loaded his gut.

"What's wrong?" he said as his men joined him.

One man crooked a finger and, turning, led Mendelson toward the trench. The others stayed where they were.

It was not such a big trench. By all estimates, the fire should have been confined to one main tunnel at the extreme northern end of the Belle Haven mines. North of that there was too much granite for mining or, everyone supposed, a mine fire to spread. There were other, parallel tunnels to the east and west of the fire, but so far they were cold and empty and, everyone supposed, far enough away to be safe. It was to the south that the danger lay. On its way toward Belle Haven, the burning tunnel eventually intersected with the other tunnels. Once the fire reached this intersection, it would spread east, west, and carry on south toward the western edge of town. Mendelson had dug the trench well north of this intersection, to cut the fire off before it could contaminate the entire grid. So, although it was deep, and it sloped gradually up at either end to accommodate bulldozers and trucks, the floor of the trench was only about as large as a basketball court. The burning mine tunnel lay just beneath this floor. This was to have been the day when they would hit the tunnel, slice right through it, scoop out a gap where they'd made their cut, plug both portals with clay, and thereby prevent the fire from traveling any farther south. Once they had contained the fire, they would go back to its origin and begin pumping in water, or fly ash, or maybe just seal off that end, too, let the fire suffocate. These had been their intentions.

Mendelson looked down into the trench. At first he saw nothing. Rocks, clay, occasionally a squiggle of coal. Then, from the floor of the trench, he noticed an exhalation.

It was simply a small puff of smoke, and Mendelson suddenly imagined some mythic figure—Paul Bunyan or perhaps a breed of insect-man—sleeping on his back just beneath the dense soil, snoring smoke from his muddy lips in puffs like the one Mendelson had seen from above. In a moment there was another small exhalation. He waited. Another. The fire had come too quickly. And there was nothing for it now but to turn away from the sight.

The miners stood a few feet away. For all his years of training—as a wrestler, then a soldier, then an engineer—Mendelson was not able to still a momentary spasm that moved like ill wind across his face. The miners, seeing it, at once forgave him for his inadequate trench. Their pity rose clearly in their eyes.

"Fuck off," Mendelson said, and left them standing at the edge of the trench.

They were, for the second time, thoroughly offended by the anger that Mendelson had acquired in his youth and tended ever since. They were not, now, inclined to be so tolerant.

"No call to be rude," one of them said, more mildly than he felt. "We warned you this would happen. Nobody's fault but your own."

"When you're ready for a second go, let us help," another said.

"We know about this mine." But he did not try to hide the contempt or the fear that he—that all of the miners—were feeling.

Mendelson never even bothered to look back. He got into his truck and drove to Randall, called his superiors in Harrisburg, told them the bad news, and then spent the rest of the day in his motel room, thinking about how to go at the fire next.

It was what he would spend part of every one of the next dozen years doing: thinking about the fire, plotting, planning, swearing promises, wondering about the endless possibilities that waited underground.

And for those dozen years, it would be the habit of the people of Belle Haven to treat Mendelson with a mixture of pity and loathing. To shy away from him, set him apart, at best offer him the packaged friendliness generally bestowed on strangers. Those who tried harder got no thanks for their trouble.

This was why, whenever Mendelson made his infrequent trips to the Last Resort, for reasons he himself could not quite articulate, he drank alone, sang only to himself, and always went home thirsty.

Chapter 14

An hour after arriving at the Last Resort, Joe realized he was enjoying himself. He'd met some people, had some beer, come to like the look of girls in hats, and heard some of the best jokes he ever hoped to hear.

"I got another one," Ian said, twisting with glee. "Two guys are on safari when one gets bitten by a snake, right on the end of his manhood. Falls to the ground, writhing with pain. Yells to his buddy, 'Quick! Get help! Get a doctor! Run!' So the other guy runs like hell until he reaches a village, finds the doctor, tells him what happened. 'First,' the doctor tells him, 'you have to make two cuts, like a cross, where the snake bit him, and then suck out the venom.' Back the guy runs, just as fast as he can. When his friend sees him coming, he says, 'Thank God. Did you find a doctor?' 'Yep,' says the other guy. 'Well, what did he say?' says the first. His friend looks at him, shakes his head, says, 'Sorry, but you're going to die.' "

Joe was laughing, his heels on the rung of his stool, turned so that he could watch four young women belting out "Stand by Your Man," when he felt a current of clean, cool night air pour over him. He turned toward the door of the Last Resort and saw Rachel step inside, Angela with her, both of them smiling.

He had not given her a thought for hours now. He did not know her last name, her politics, or whether she liked to dance. But he remembered that she had a small, crooked scar on the back of one wrist—her right wrist—and that her ears were unpierced. The sight

of her made him feel as if he'd smelled lilac for the first time. She
looked as if she were made out of forest: her hair and eyes, even her
skin, fashioned from different strains of wood, different shades of
brown from almond to bay, but each of them rich and smooth and
polished. She made him wish he were an artist, or a father, or a gar-
dener capable of raising up out of rawness something so refined.

She frowned when she saw him. Then Ian called her name, she saw
that the two of them were together, and she laughed out loud. The
sound of her came tumbling through the motley chaos of the bar-
room. And in a moment she was by his side.

It seemed quite mysterious to Joe that in the hours he'd spent
away from Rachel she'd somehow latched on to his soul. He now suspected that it had been she who had led him to the Queen Anne's lace
that grew alongside the stream. She who had prodded him out into
the unmown fields where the cicadas screamed for summer and the
hawks killed with grace. She who had lured him into his simple companionship with Ian and, now, into an unkempt bar, which for all its
shortcomings promised to be the site of his undoing.

"Now I know what's so special about Thursday nights in Belle
Haven," he said blandly, his breath shallow. "I thought Angela
wanted you to set her hair or something."

"Oh, I get it," Rachel said, smiling wrathfully. "Bingo. Tractor
pulls. Church socials. Home perms. Boy, Joe, you sure got us pegged."

"Now, now, Rachel, cut the boy some slack," Angela said, waving
at the bartender.

"For the love of Pete," Joe spluttered. "You are without doubt the
most thin-skinned woman I have ever met."

"Thin patience," Rachel said coolly. "You have a habit of making
things a little harder for yourself, Joe. Go easy. Try to think before
you speak."

"Fair enough." He sighed. "Buy you a drink?"

"All right," Rachel said, willing, it seemed, to speed the water under the bridge.

It wasn't until Joe took out his wallet to pay for their drinks that
he remembered his budget. "To hell with it," he muttered to himself,
anchoring a twenty under his empty bottle.

It took a while for him to feel as cavalier about a turn in the spot-
light. "You want me to be a what?" He laughed, choking on his beer.

"A Pip," Rachel repeated. "You and Ian. You don't even have to sing.
Just do that rolling thing with your hands. Angela and I'll do the rest."

After several drinks and much persuasion, he finally agreed. "I'm going to regret this," he said through his teeth. And when, a few minutes later, Amelia called out, "Rachel, Angela, Ian, and Joe. Come on up here, now. The midnight train to Georgia's movin' on out," they had to drag Joe off his stool.

"Wait a minute," he bawled when Amelia handed him a microphone. "I thought I didn't have to sing." But Rachel, holding the other microphone, only smiled. The band began to play. Angela laid her palms on her lean hips, tapped her booted toes. Ian trotted first to one side, then the other, hands rolling. He was making trainlike noises. "Whoo. Whoo. Whoo."

"L.A." Rachel sang, rather badly,

proved too much for the man.
He couldn't make it, so he's leaving a life he's come to know.
He said he's going back to find what's left of his world.
The world he left behind, not so long ago . . .

Angela made a fair echo as Rachel sang. Ian stumbled around behind them, botching the lyrics and grinning. And Joe stood silent, rooted, watching the three of them in astonishment.

He could find in them no vestige of modesty or even self-awareness. They were immersed in the song, right from the get-go, all smiling, all having the time of their lives. As they warmed to the song, Joe noticed in the eyes of the onlookers an amused admiration for his companions, derision for himself.

I am smarter than any of these people, he reminded himself. Richer. Better. Pretty soon I'll be gone. I'll never see any of them again as long as I live.

And with that, he surrendered to the moment, gave himself up to fate, and began, slowly, to dance.

It would take him years to reach the conclusion that had he not been such a bred-in-the-bone snob, he would never have allowed a song, a woman, a run-down watering hole called the Last Resort to pierce the thick muscle of his heart and lay their claim. He would never have let his laughter reach up into his eyes. He would never have danced, sung, celebrated as he did that night.

Later, when Rachel and Angela left the men at the table to sing alone together, Joe wondered at the song they had chosen. But he felt inexplicably close to tears as they sang "Moon River," a song he had never really listened to before, a song that first silenced the people in that bar, then gently warmed their throats, brought them up off their stools singing, sent them slowly out into the night air dancing, closed Rachel's throat and made her stand there and cry while Angela wrapped her arms around her, singing as if her heart were breaking.

> *Two drifters, off to see the world.*
> *There's such a lot of world to see.*
> *We're after the same rainbow's end*
> *waitin' 'round the bend,*
> *my Huckleberry friend,*
> *Moon River*
> *and me.*

And when the song was over and Rachel had dried her eyes with her hands, Joe could not speak for minutes on end, could not look at them, at any of them, could not swallow or lift the mighty weight of his arms. For he had found himself, somewhere in the midst of that lovely old song, begging for a way to draw out this night. To keep his feet upon this undemanding floor. To stay inside the Last Resort until the rest of the world had found a way to match its matchless charm.

Chapter 15

Had Joe gone straight from the Last Resort to his bed that night, to sleep, to an awakening less magical, less potent than the undiluted night, his memories might have passed themselves off as dreams. He might have come to doubt what had taken place inside the Last Resort and inside his ringing skull. He might have deemed the whole thing a good time, nothing more.

But he did not go straight to his bed. He went with Rachel, and Angela, and Ian—singing still—down the street to rouse his patient Schooner, make for them a plate of sandwiches and a jug of sobering lemonade, explain to them the cryptic note taped to his kitchen cupboard, reveal with confused misgivings and uncomplicated trust the reasons for his arrival in their midst.

"I don't regret what I did," he said haltingly. "Just how I did it. I didn't think things through. I was too impulsive. And now . . . I feel like I'm at my father's mercy. I haven't got enough money to last me for very long. And I'm not sure what's going to happen next."

For a minute or two no one said a word. Joe guessed, quite accurately, that they felt for him a hybrid sort of pity. Their sympathy was tempered with scorn, as if Joe were an adolescent brother: arrogant, selfish, charming, much loved. He had been thoughtless to them in small ways, but for his sister's sake he had been brave, choosing her comfort over his own. When they pictured his merciless father, they planted their elbows on the Schooner's Formica tabletop and felt their hackles rise. And when he finally lifted his eyes to theirs, they closed ranks, he among them.

"If I were you," Ian said, "I'd go over to the Gas 'n' Go right now and call the man. Get it over with."

"I was planning to give him a few more days to cool off."

"Uh-uh. He's likely to be worrying his head off by now. And the more worried he gets, the angrier he'll be when he finds out you were sitting here the whole time, safe and sound."

"I don't know," Joe said. "I'm not sure he'd worry. He might, I suppose. I'm not sure I can rely on anything I thought I knew about the man."

"I don't envy you, Joe." Angela sighed. She'd been thinking about her long-gone husband and her son. "What a time you've had the last few days. It's hard to have so many things thrown at you at once." She slid out of the booth and looked at her reflection in the dark window. It made a kind mirror. She looked less tired, much younger than she felt. "I can understand you wanting to lie low for a while and let the dust settle. But I also think Ian's right. It might be better to go at this whole thing straight on, get it over with, thrash it out with him before things get worse."

After a moment, Joe turned to Rachel, who was sitting alongside him in the little booth. "Well?"

"Well what?" she said, startled. "What do I think? I don't know. I've just been trying to put myself in your shoes, but I can't quite manage it. You really did all these things without a second thought?"

"Afraid so." Joe leaned his head against the back of the booth and closed his eyes. "It seemed like the right thing to do at the time."

"And it's turned out all right so far, hasn't it?" she asked. "I mean, you're alive and well and in good company. Nothing wrong with that. If you'd done nothing, stayed where you were, Holly would still be counting down the days, you'd be as good as dead, and your father . . ." Rachel shook her head. "I know he's your flesh and blood, Joe, but he got what he deserved. And if there's any decency in him, he'll take it from here, get himself some help, and thank you in the end. If not, then it's good you left."

"Saved your life," Ian said, nodding.

Joe rubbed his eyes. It was three o'clock in the morning. His father would be sleeping. Dreaming, perhaps, of an absent son. Unaware of the rioting stars—distant, hot, noisy suns that from earth looked like chips of ice and diamond. Unaware of the treasure his son had some-how struck, on this journey, in his own neglected bones. Unaware of the choices his son was contemplating, like a farmer whose crop is nearly ripe.

"Who's got a dime?" Joe asked, and went out into the night while his friends sat and waited.

They waited for a long time.

"Think he got lost?" Ian finally yawned.

"Maybe he just chickened out." Rachel sighed. "He's probably wandering around like a goat, trying to figure out what to do next."

"Nice."

"Well, shoot me, Angela. I like the guy well enough—don't ask me why—but we've known him all of a day. He's already rubbed me the wrong way more than once."

"He's a stranger," Ian said. "There's no reason in the world we should be here waiting for him in the middle of the night, worried about him, looking for ways to help him. But I don't need a reason to like the boy or give him a hand if he asks for it." He paused and ran his finger around the rim of his empty glass. "Do you?"

"Well, no," Rachel said, somewhat petulantly. "I already said I like him, didn't I? I'm just a bit more skeptical than you, Ian."

"Maybe we should go look for him," Angela suggested.

At the sound of the doorknob turning, Rachel looked up, frowning. She was annoyed at herself for the softness of her heart. Her pleasure was scarred by indecision. Her instincts collided like the wakes of boats on separate courses, all foam and disturbance. She was prepared to meet his return with nonchalance, even disinterest. But she was not prepared for his sorrow.

He was weeping as he walked in the door. Rachel reached him first and did not think as she opened her arms and took him in. He was heavy and cold. His cheek against her neck was wet.

He was talking to himself, his voice so hoarse and exhausted, so clotted with tears that she could not understand what he was saying.

"It's all right now," Rachel murmured, helping him to his bed. When he lay down and turned his face to the wall, she covered him with a blanket and stood looking down at him.

She imagined that his father had lashed out at him, disowned him, torn at his heart, and she was right. But she also imagined that Joe had heard only what he'd feared, and in this she could not have been more wrong.

Book
Two

My crown is in my heart,

not on my head.

—WILLIAM SHAKESPEARE,
from King Henry VI, Part 3

Joe let his hair grow all through the long, hot months of his first summer in Belle Haven. While most of the other men in town had theirs clipped down to let the air touch their sweating scalps, he let his go its own unruly way. He let his beard grow too, for a while, but it made him feel like a stranger, and since he'd had enough of that, he cut it off sometime before July.

He borrowed a shovel from Ian, turned over a few bits of ground around the Schooner, and carefully transplanted clusters of wildflowers from the fields and woods.

He bagged groceries at the A&P, hauled ice in a worn-out truck, picked strawberries by the hundred-quart, and shelved books at the library. A few hours' work here and there. He fed himself, mended his berry-stained trousers, went to bed as soon as it was dark.

"My son, Rusty, hates to read," Angela said to Joe one day when he stopped in to buy a paper. "Which makes me sick at heart, Joe." She wiped one glistening cheek with the back of her hand. "I can't afford to pay you, but I'll feed you supper every day of the week. Anything on or off the menu, long as the fixin's are in the fridge. Ice cream if you're good." She smiled tiredly. "Read to him. At least once a day. You choose the books. Or let him. Whatever you want. Read to him. Talk to him. Tell him stories. I don't care what you do, just get him in love with books. Would you do that for me, Joe?"

He would have done it for nothing. He did it for her. For her cooking. He didn't really know the boy yet. Had he known him, he would have done it for the boy, and for no other reason.

He started with books gathered by the town's eager librarians, books that made Rusty wince when he saw them coming and made Angela shake her head in doubt. Big, heavy books with somber leather bindings and pages that creaked like long-locked doors. *The Last of the Mohicans, The Yearling, Treasure Island, Kidnapped.*

"I like comic books," Rusty said, looking a bit like he'd stepped out of one. He was small for his age, crowned with a cowlick, his jeans cuffed up, his face freckled. He sat across from Joe in the Kitchen's only booth, the books scattered across the table between them.

"So do I," Joe said. "I also like these."

Rusty picked up *The Yearling* with both hands. Pasted on the front cover was a large illustration of a boy and a deer. He turned it over suspiciously.

"What's this one about?"

"What do you think?"

Rusty looked at the picture again. "A boy and a deer."

"And?"

"And what?" Rusty gave Joe a sour look. He glanced over toward his mother, who was polishing the chrome on an enormous blender, but she ignored them both. When Joe did not answer, Rusty sighed and said, "How am I supposed to know? You're the one that read the book. You tell me."

Joe picked up the book, weighed it in his hands. "I could tell you this story, in a hundred words or less, and you'd forget it by bed-time." He leaned toward Rusty and lowered his voice, as if he had se-crets to share. "Or you could read a couple hundred thousand words instead and never forget the story as long as you live."

Rusty snorted, crossed his arms over his chest. "Hundred thou-sand? You gotta be kidding me."

"Hey, look, kid. I couldn't care less if you read comic books and ce-real boxes the rest of your life. But I do care what I read, and I'll be goddamned if I'm going to spend my summer reading trash." He stopped. Rusty looked at him across the table as if it were a conti-nent. "All right, let's start again," Joe said, running a hand through his willful hair. He thought for a minute or two while Rusty waited. He seemed to be good at waiting.

"All right," Joe said again, taking the book up against his chest and closing his eyes. He held it there for a moment while Rusty won-dered whether he was supposed to do something to get them both past this bad beginning.

Then Joe opened his eyes and smiled.

"What would you do," he said, "if you were out in the woods, deer hunting with your father—"

"I don't have a father," Rusty said. He said it simply but as if he wanted to get that one thing straight right up front. "And I don't like it when people try to act like they're my father either."

Joe had never had a conversation like this before. He couldn't remember the last time he had spoken even a single word to a child, let alone discussed great literature and the unfortunate lack of fathers.

"I don't blame you," Joe said. "And if it matters, I don't really have a father either. Not anymore."

Rusty looked as if he wanted to ask a question, but he had enough sense to keep it to himself. "So I'm deer hunting with my father, and?"

"And you've wandered pretty far from home. There's no one else out in these woods. No phone. No car. Just the two of you and your guns. And all of a sudden, your father gets bitten on the leg by a rattlesnake. He's going to die if he doesn't get help quick, but he knows that the faster he moves, the more the poison will spread. And then, even though he's dying of this snakebite, your father picks up his rifle and shoots a doe. Kills it. And starts limping toward its body." Joe stopped short and waited. He, too, was learning how to give people room.

Rusty was not too proud to meet him in the middle. "Why would he shoot a deer when he's dying of snakebite?"

Joe held the book out toward Rusty, who looked at it with a little less loathing than before. "How many thousands of words do I have to read before I find out?" the boy asked.

"They'll fly by," Joe said.

Within the month, Rusty had taken to waiting for Joe on the steps of the Kitchen, light pouring out of his eyes. He now carried his own library card with him everywhere he went and had begun, unbidden, to read. Books from the school library that smelled like french fries, with sticky, ragged pages. *James and the Giant Peach, Island of the Blue Dolphins, The Call of the Wild.*

As long as they stayed within the boundaries of stories, in the company of characters like King Arthur and Daniel Boone, Joe and Rusty got along like bread and jam. But on occasion, when Joe forgot the rules and was heavy-handed, acted too much like a father, or when Rusty asked Joe about his boyhood, forgetting for a moment that Joe would not answer . . . when either of them trespassed on such forbidden ground, a wall went up between them, leaving them stranded.

"Hey, Rusty, this book is a week overdue." It was a blazing August day, and neither of them was in the mood for anything but Raccoon Creek and a rope swing. But as much as they could, they stuck to their habit of meeting at the Kitchen for an hour every other day, usually to read together in easy partnership, sometimes to talk about what they'd witnessed between the covers of their books.

"Big deal. A nickel a day. My mom'll pay for it."

Joe thought about Angela, hard at work long before dawn every day of the week.

"You ever take a good look at your mom's hands?" he said. "I don't think she should have to do even thirty-five cents' worth of work just because you're too goddamned lazy to return a book on time. You were my kid, I'd make you pay the fine yourself out of money *you* earned."

Rusty picked up the library book. Got out of his chair. "My mother and me are none of your business," he said. And walked out the door.

Joe sat in the Kitchen for another ten minutes, thinking about his own mother. And about his father. Then he got up and went looking for Rusty.

He found him coming out of the library. When Rusty walked past him, Joe took his place by the boy's side and they walked up Maple Street without a word. When they got to the bridge over Raccoon Creek, Rusty shimmied down the steep bank and straight to the water's edge. He took off his shirt and shoes, wedged them in the fork of a tree, and stepped into the cool creek water.

Joe stood on the bridge and watched Rusty from above. He was afraid to make matters worse between them, worried that what had started over a library book might end in a place they wouldn't easily get beyond. Not unless he chose his words carefully.

"I'm sorry, Rusty," he said, leaning on the rail of the bridge just over the boy's head. "I like your mother a lot, but I'll never love her one millionth as much as you do." Rusty had found a stick and was stirring up the water along the bank of the creek, hoping to spook crayfish. He didn't look up, give any sign he was listening. An old man, walking along Maple Street, glanced twice at Joe as he passed, wary of someone who made speeches from a bridge.

"I never earned a nickel in my life, until I came to Belle Haven," Joe said. "Which makes me something of an idiot to be preaching at you." He had seen Rusty working in the Kitchen and had never heard him complain about it, not once. When he thought about it, Joe realized that it was not only understandable but entirely reasonable, even desirable, for Rusty to misbehave now and then, especially with someone who could be counted upon to let him.

"I will mind my own business," he said. "From now on. I promise."

Rusty finally looked up.

"It's okay," he said after a moment. "I don't much mind."

"Good," Joe said. "And while we're at it, it's 'My mother and *I* are none of your business,' not 'My mother and *me.*'"

At which Rusty picked up a clod of creek mud and lobbed it at Joe, who ran down the bank hollering and into the creek, shoes and all.

In September Angela asked Joe to tutor Rusty in other subjects. "He's a smart kid, and he does pretty well in school. But it's not enough to be smart and I don't give a good goddamn about grades. He loves to read now. I want him to love to learn."

So Joe and Rusty continued to meet at the Kitchen, on the ball diamond, on the banks of Raccoon Creek. Joe made the town's meadows into classrooms, teaching Rusty about the migration of hummingbirds, the stunning unlikelihood of metamorphosis, the indispensable gift of bees. He made baseball a matter of math and physics as well as of pure, immeasurable joy. Together they catalogued the clouds and the leaves of the trees, sought the burrows of earth dwellers, studied the kingfisher taking its plunge.

"I used to know a lot about frogs," Joe said as they waded along the bank of the creek one day in late September. Rusty had caught a fat frog and held it cupped between his hands. Its legs dangled between his fingers, and its head popped through the collar Rusty had made with his thumbs. He held the frog's face up close to his own and studied the speckles on its cheeks, the twin globes of its frightened eyes. "We dissected them in biology class when I was in eighth grade," Joe said, the remembered tang of formaldehyde stinging his nose.

"Cool." Rusty looked at Joe with envy. "I'll bet the girls screamed a lot."

"I went to an all-boys school," Joe said.

"All boys?" Rusty looked as if he were weighing the pros and cons of such a place. "No girls at all?"

"The lunchroom ladies."

Rusty snorted. "They don't count."

"I do remember one French teacher . . ." Joe made an hourglass in the air.

Rusty grinned. "But no real girls?"

"Nary a one."

Rusty turned the frog this way and that, upside down, and then set it free. It sat on the bank, getting its bearings for a moment, before leaping into the rushes that grew along the water's edge. "I don't think I'd like that too much," Rusty said. "Sounds boring."

"It was," Joe said.

They both realized, suddenly, that except for the one brief reference to his father, this was the first time Joe had spoken to Rusty of his past.

"I don't remember a single thing I learned from picking a frog to pieces," Joe said.

And for the rest of the afternoon, they scoured the banks for amphibians, scrutinized them gently, and then went home empty-handed.

Joe had not asked Angela about her absent husband. He had quickly learned that the people who lived in Belle Haven did not like to be questioned even though they were, as a rule, a talkative bunch. And despite the fact that he had been schooled among rude young men—perhaps because of this—Joe knew without thinking about it that to speak casually of Angela's husband would be like speaking casually of the newly dead. Angela herself was the one who brought it up.

"Has Rusty told you anything about his father?" she asked Joe at the end of summer while they sat together in Angela's living room, waiting for Rusty to come home with a Sunday trout. It was the only supper that the Kitchen did not serve—Sunday supper—and Angela's only chance to sit down to a proper meal with Dolly, Rusty, and, quite often now, Joe.

"No, not really."

She lit a cigarette, killed the match. "Has anyone?"

"No, Angela." Joe liked to say her name. He had decided that the

women in Belle Haven had the nicest names he'd ever heard—
Rachel, Angela, May, Coral, Ophelia, Anne, Helen, June. "And you
don't need to tell me anything either," he said.

"Well, maybe I do," she said. She smoked her cigarette for a moment, never moving it far from her lips. "You may eventually hear
something or other, and you need to know what's really true and what
you may hear from Rusty."

"The two aren't the same?"

"Not like I wish they were." She sighed, went into the kitchen to
fetch some more iced tea.

"It was the strangest thing," she said, coming back. "Buddy was a
really good boy. Buddy . . . that was his name. Still is, I guess. He
had beautiful manners. Never got into any trouble. Got along with
his folks. But so . . . so *exciting,* too. I'd never met anyone quite like
him. I saw him for the first time at a corn festival in Randall, where
he lived. We were both sixteen. We were watching a tractor pull, and
I got splashed with mud. He ran and found a wet cloth somewhere
and helped me get the worst of it off. And then we began to see each
other the way young kids do, at movies, ball games. He played the
harmonica. Looked a lot like Jimmy Dean. I was in love with him
and him with me before we turned seventeen, and it was the real
thing. Didn't matter how old we were. Not then." Angela took a
long swallow of tea and put her bare feet up on the coffee table. Joe
sat with his back bowed, his head hanging, his elbows on his thighs.
It was how he listened, now that he had learned how.

"We got married, right after high school, even though everyone
wanted us to wait a while, especially Buddy's folks. Buddy was good
with cars, so he took a job at a garage in Randall. I sold stuff door-to-
door. Makeup, mostly. Had to get all painted up and walk around in
high heels." She made a face. "I'd drive Buddy to work and then take
the truck around Randall, Fainsville, Jupiter. But the outfit I worked
for didn't like the idea of an old pickup, so I had to park it somewhere and do each block on foot." Angela held a foot in the air,
turned it one way and then the other. "By the time I got home at
night my feet looked just awful. God, they hurt." She took another
drink of tea.

"Then I got pregnant with Rusty when I was still only eighteen
and after about a month I got fired, which saved me the trouble of
quitting. I kept having to stop to throw up in somebody's petunias.

And my feet got much worse. It wasn't working out at all. After that we couldn't afford to pay rent on our own place, and Buddy's parents didn't have any room, so we moved in with my mother. She was still living down by the school at the time, in the house where I grew up." She glanced over at Joe, smashed her cigarette in a tray as big as a football.

"Before you have kids, you just can't know what it's going to be like to have a baby come along and change everything. Everyone told us what was coming, but hearing about it didn't do a thing to prepare us—not for the joy *or* the hurt. And Buddy was so excited about having a kid, always walking around with a big smile on his face. He didn't seem to mind living with his mother-in-law. He watched me get big as a house and lose all my color and have my hair falling out all the time, and he treated me like I was a goddess of fertility or something. He had stars in his eyes. I was very happy that whole time, thinking about what kind of father he would make." Angela lit another cigarette.

"In the first few days after Rusty was born, Buddy could barely speak. He was absolutely overcome. He had this perfect little son and I was okay and everything was fine." She hung her left hand on the back of her neck. "And then Rusty got the colic and cried for four months straight.

"After the first month, Buddy started sleeping at the garage or out in the truck or sometimes on his parents' couch. He'd come home and try to help me, but he just couldn't stay. He tried, though. I'll give him that. But there was something very wrong, all of a sudden. He came home one night when Rusty was about twelve weeks old, and the poor little kid was bawling his head off. Buddy had a beer and he watched some of a ball game on TV. And then he came over to where I was rocking the baby and he picked him up—I thought he was just going to walk him a bit—and he started to shake Rusty so hard his . . . his little head was snapping back and forth. I thought it was going to break right off." Angela tried to smoke her cigarette, but it fell out of her lips and she had to scramble for it. "I finally got Rusty away from him and I ran into the bedroom and Buddy stood out in the living room and screamed until he was hoarse. He kicked in the television and he threw a lamp through the front window, and then he sat down on the floor and cried." Angela rubbed some flakes of ash into her blue jeans. "When he came around he got really scared and ran out of the house, bunked with a friend for a couple of days. Then he finally came back home and we all sat in the living room and stared at each other. Me, Buddy, Rusty, and my mother. She sat in the corner and didn't say a word, but she wouldn't leave us alone either."

Angela smoked her cigarette some more. "You don't know her very well yet, Joe, but my mother is one hell of a woman. Quiet. Keeps to herself. But she's as solid as a rock. Sold her house so I could buy this place. I never even had to ask." She stared, remembering. "Anyway, she sat there with us so Buddy would behave himself, I guess. I had Rusty in my lap. He'd been crying all day, and he still was. Buddy got down on his knees and begged me to forgive him, and I did. I was feeling pretty desperate myself, and I thought I could understand how he had lost control for a minute like that. But after an hour in the house with Rusty crying the whole time, Buddy all of a sudden started to look wild again. My mother went in the nursery with Rusty and shut the door, and I stood outside it while Buddy paced around the house, pulling on his hair and cursing and looking like he was going to break something. And then he left the house and got in the truck and drove off." Angela's cigarette was all ash now.

"I know it doesn't seem very likely that a man would run off over a crying baby. But that's what Buddy did. I didn't believe it at first, had the police looking for him for weeks. But about six months later I got a letter from him. Even when I sat down and read it, I had an awful hard time believing that the man I had known so long could suddenly change so much. He hated Rusty. He hated him. And of course he hated himself—I mean really *hated* himself—for feeling that way about our little baby. But there was something . . . *wild* about Buddy by then. He was like a grizzly or maybe a hyena. Some kind of animal that kills its young." She closed her mouth, and Joe could see that she was chewing the lining of her cheeks.

"If it's one thing having a child has taught me," she said, "it's not to judge other parents. I used to see people in the grocery store or on the street with their children, and I'd think, 'I'll never act that way when I have kids.' But now I lay off. Nobody else can know how a child can change you. Turn your life inside out. Thank God, I'm one of the lucky ones. From the time that boy was a knob in my belly I've loved him as much as I can love. And when he is an old man, if I am still alive to see that, I will still love my boy with every bit of my flesh and every particle of my spirit. And I know Buddy loved him too. He *had* to. But to him Rusty was like a magnet, or a lightning rod. Every regret that Buddy had ever had, every doubt, every complaint, every kind of anger was unleashed on our baby. It was a horrible thing to watch. And I know that is why Buddy left. He would have learned some control, Rusty would have outgrown his pain and that incredible selfishness that infants have, but Buddy would never have been able to look at his son without knowing what he was capable of doing. Without remembering those bad early days. Without longing for a different sort of life." She picked up her glass of tea and drained it.

"Rusty thinks that it was me his father left. And that, too, is the truth."

When Joe put his arms around Angela, he had to fight not to pull immediately away. It shocked him deeply to feel how thin she was, how hard her muscles, and how strong the shudder that ran the length of her. But then he felt her relax, her head grew heavy on his shoulder, and he found that he was gently rocking her, and she him, and that he, too, was comforted.

By the time Rusty came home with the trout, Joe and Angela were laughing, and neither of them ever mentioned the absent Buddy again.

"You have a good knife?" Rusty asked Joe as they picked their way through Ian's pumpkin patch the day before Joe's first Halloween in Belle Haven.

"I guess," Joe said, turning over a nice pumpkin, looking for rot. "Want to carve it at the Schooner?"

"Sure," said the boy. "It'll be easier to cart home that way. We can carve one up for you, too."

But it turned out that Joe did not have a proper knife. Nothing quite sharp enough or small enough for pumpkin teeth or fragile pumpkin brows.

"Here," said Rusty, pulling a whittling knife from his pocket. It was very sharp. "My grandma taught me how to carve walking sticks out of sumach when I was a kid. Sumach looks like deer antler, has real velvety sort of bark, comes off smooth as you like. The stick's no good for anything but a day's walk. After that it dries up. Warps. But it's a pleasure to carve."

Joe sat and looked at the boy, found it hard to believe he was just ten. It must have been the talk of knives and carving. Men talked of such things. Yet these things were foreign to Joe. The knife was heavy in his large palm. He snapped it open on its capable hinge. There were no notches in its blade. It was a good knife.

They spent an hour on the pumpkins, scooping out their pulpy meat, saving their seeds for the oven, and making elaborate faces in their rinds until the light began to fail.

"That's a good knife," Joe said, wiping the blade on his pant leg and snapping it home. He held it out to Rusty.

The boy looked at the knife. He looked at Joe's face. Perhaps he was remembering how little Joe had brought along with him from wherever he'd been.

"You keep it," Rusty said, wedging his pumpkin into the basket of his bike.

"Don't be silly," Joe said, holding out the knife. "I can get another one."

"I'm not being silly. I know you can get another one. Have this one," Rusty said, turning his bike so it faced the lane and home.

Joe remembered the small apartment above the Kitchen, Rusty's tiny room, how neat it was. ("I thought kids' rooms were supposed to be messy," he had said the first time he'd gone upstairs. It was only later that he realized Rusty did not own enough things to make a mess, or to neglect them.)

"Thanks," Joe said, slipping the knife into his pocket. It was the first thing Rusty gave to Joe and perhaps the most important gift he would ever receive.

"Whittle something and you'll see for yourself how nice it is," Rusty said as he left. "It makes you nice and sleepy if you do it on a doorstep. Especially if the lightning bugs are out." And Joe breathed in relief to hear Rusty speak like the boy he was and ought to be for some time to come.

There were no lightning bugs out that night, for they were all mated by now and content. But there were still crickets out flexing their harplike legs, spiking the night with raspy love songs, and no one believed that snow was mere weeks away. Joe sat on the steps of the Schooner with a narrow trunk of sumach and Rusty's smooth-handled knife. The sun had set but not departed. The sky was nearly green. Birds in flight were black against it. The blazing trees stood still, barely breathing. One star appeared. Another. The knife's silver blade stroked the wood. The flesh underneath the bark was soft, cool, and very white. Ribbons of bark fell at his feet like garlands. And the moon came calmly up into the sky. Rusty was right. Joe had never felt more solitary. Or more content.

When the cold finally came to Belle Haven, Joe spent his spare hours wandering through the woods and fields, collecting stones as big as grapefruits. He lugged them home in a satchel, a few at a time, and piled them in the middle of the clearing. When he had enough, he made some mortar and built a fireplace of sorts, big and deep enough to shield a fire from the wind and the snow. He topped it with a chimney, capped that with a vent to keep out the wet, let out the smoke, encourage an upward draft.

On many cold winter nights, Joe built a beautiful blaze in his fireplace and sat bundled before it, whittling and wondering what went on in other places he had been. When it snowed, he stayed indoors, listened to his small transistor, read book after book after book. He did not own a calendar and tried hard not to think about his approaching birthday. Or about Christmas. Or about the twin he would now never know any better than he knew Angela. Not even that well. Not nearly as well as he knew Rachel.

Something had happened to them on the night back in May when he'd called his father. She had sat beside him on his bunk for a long time, stroking his hair, holding his hand for the last hour of darkness and long into the dawn until he finally fell asleep. He had opened his eyes to find her sleeping in a chair beside him, their hands locked, Ian and Angela gone. He had barely moved for an hour or more, afraid of waking her. Had watched her face, studied the way her thick, cinnamon hair coursed down her neck, marveled at the way she curled, cat-like, in the unyielding chair. After a while, she had opened her eyes, taken a moment to decide where she was, and looked down at their clinging hands. When she had gained her bearings, she smiled at him uncertainly and yawned.

"Get dressed and follow me," she'd said after a bit, and he had.

She had taken him back to her house on the hill where there was plenty of hot water, a good shower, and breakfast in her garden. They had not spoken of his father or anything else from his past. And, in part because of his reluctance to talk about such things, she had not revealed much about herself either. They would discover what was important, in their own good time.

By Labor Day, Rachel and Joe were the kind of friends who unabashedly tell each other when they have something stuck between their teeth. They played late-night Scrabble and outdoor cribbage, did the crossword puzzle every Sunday morning, read each other's palms, cut each other's hair.

Joe felt, with Rachel, as if he had been taken apart, bone by bone, and put back together again in a far less imperfect way. She felt, with him, as if she would live forever. They had each had good friends before, but neither of them had ever had this. They didn't even know what to call it, so they didn't call it anything at all.

It was Rachel who tried to convince Joe, as they sat on her front porch paring apples for a pie, to call his faculty advisor at Yale, for the fall semester was scheduled to begin in just a few days. He was no longer concerned about revealing his whereabouts: his phone call to his father had already left traces and had, furthermore, convinced him that no one was likely to seek him out. But the thought of calling Yale made him hurt. It made him feel unwell.

"All of that's over and done with," he told her. "Besides, I'd hardly qualify for a scholarship."

"You're just looking for an excuse," she insisted. "If you want to go back to school, just take out a loan until your birthday. By then you'll have money of your own. Loads of it. Good God, man, it would take you ten minutes to get tide-over money. Probably less. I don't know why you haven't already gone ahead and done it. You're not worried about your father tracking you down anymore, so why not call up your banker and get some money?"

He looked at her carefully. "You're a terrible actor," he said, taking her hand and putting it to his lips. "You would go mad without me, and you know it."

"Go take a flying leap," she said and burst out laughing. "Pig." She threw an apple peel at him. "You still haven't answered my question."

"I'm doing just fine on my own," he assured her. "The money will still be there when I want it. And so will Yale."

"Well, to tell you the truth, I do understand how you might feel that way."

And that was when Rachel finally told Joe about her parents: their lives, deaths, legacies.

Joe had already heard these things from Ian and Angela but had waited for Rachel to be ready to tell him herself. Like Angela's story about her husband, and like Rusty's gift of the carving knife, knowing about Rachel's loss had so softened Joe's heart that he now felt newly saddened. As she spoke about her parents, tears in her eyes, his own lips trembled. His own chest ached.

"Oh, Christ," he said. "How did you bear it?"

"I didn't have any choice," she said.

He didn't ask her about the money she'd inherited or what she'd done with it. It wasn't something he wanted to know about. It wasn't something he envied. It was almost something he feared.

In the end he decided not to call Yale, not to answer the questions that were bound to be asked. He'd let his father worry about that. So he sent a postcard instead, requesting a last-minute leave of absence, not really caring much whether it was granted.

With his mind made up—not only to stay in Belle Haven but to make it his home—Joe felt himself lighten as if he had shed a heavy winter skin. He began to breathe all the way down to the cradles of his lungs again, for the first time in years. He woke each day with an appetite and a curiosity that was easy to calm with small things— like walking straight out into the morning to sample the weather, following whatever temptation crossed his path, and embracing every chance to pair the days of his past with better ones in this, his new life. There were many such days that fall, and the promise of more to come.

Rachel and Joe spent Christmas together, invited Angela, Rusty, Dolly, and Ian for dinner at Rachel's house. That night, after the feast, they all went out to the Schooner and built a big fire in Joe's fireplace. Joe had decorated the pines at the edge of his clearing with tinfoil stars. They flared in the firelight, turning in the cold wind, and the clouds scudded across the dazzling sky. Wrapped in blankets, they sang Christmas songs and drank hot wine. They threw pinecones into the fire and waited for them to pop. They were silent and listened to the wind. Then they staggered to their various beds, sated with joy, and were asleep before the cold, hard, invigorating sheets had warmed.

Chapter 17

In January, one week before Joe's birthday, an old woman named Sophia Browning, who lived a fair distance from the nearest mine tunnel, was mixing up cookie dough when she found herself short an egg. So she went out into the snow to buy a dozen and a quart of milk to go with the cookies. She planned to eat them hot. She left her little house, its lights throwing golden patches on the snow, and her cat, Moushka, asleep on top of the refrigerator.

Sophia's late husband, Otto, had been a friendly man who nonetheless valued privacy above most things he could hold in his hands. He made sure that the walkway he built from the road to the front door of their house was wide and welcoming and that the porch light was turned on at dusk, but he also planted a border of spruce trees around the house and tended them with care until they eventually made the loveliest sort of wall. They cast fragrant shade, gave the birds shelter, tempered the cold winter wind. Sophia liked to look at the spruce trees. They reminded her of Otto.

As she walked back from the store with her groceries tucked into the crook of her arm, Sophia admired the spruces from a distance, was captivated by their silhouettes against the pale night sky. They seemed, tonight, in the hard January freeze, to be edged with gold. As if the sun were rising behind them. Quite beautiful. Actually, she decided, quite odd. When she reached the brick walkway that Otto had built between the spruces, Sophia peered uncertainly through the trees and saw that her house was in flames.

Her neighbors, who had by then run from their houses, had to hold the old woman back. She kept calling out to her cat and to her small house while the fire grew with extraordinary speed into a shimmering, shrieking rage.

By the time the fire truck arrived, Sophia's house was far beyond salvation and the spruces that had for so long graced it were blackened, mostly spoiled, their branches cooked to spars.

In the morning the fire inspector, surprised that the house had burned so quickly, traced its source to Sophia's basement. Near the furnace.

"There was absolutely nothing wrong with my furnace," Sophia insisted, her cold hands tucked under her chin. "Nothing whatsoever."

She looked upon the black and broken hull of her house, the ring of ruined trees, every standing remnant wrapped in dazzling, tumultuous ice, and was unable to see the accidental beauty wrought so suddenly during the night.

A few blocks away, Joe walked into Angela's Kitchen to find the breakfast crowd talking about the fire.

"Think it came up from underground?" he asked no one in particular. People shrugged, frowned, ate their eggs.

"Don't think so," said Ed, the mailman, who drove past a dozen boreholes every time he delivered the mail. "That fire's been burning for a coon's age, Joe. It's not going anywhere. Not doing too much harm. Never come anywhere close to Sophia's place before. She's a good bit east of the tunnels."

"What about the coal that was never mined? How do you know how much coal is buried right down under our feet? How do you know the fire's not going to come and get it?"

"Well, we don't," said Earl, who made sure his hardware store was always well stocked with smoke alarms. "Things are okay so far, Joe."

"I'm not sure Sophia would see it that way, Earl."

"Fires do happen for all kinds of reasons, you know," Angela said with Rusty by her side.

Cal, who ran the A&P, chuckled into his coffee cup. "Sophia's living with her son and his family now. Probably rigged the whole thing."

"I can't believe you people," Joe said, swiveling around on his stool. "There's a great, big fire down there, and all any of you ever do is make jokes about it."

"What're you doing about it, Joe?" asked Earl.

"Come on, Earl. All I've got to worry about is an old motor home."

Earl ate his eggs.

"What do you want us to do, Joe?" Angela sounded angry, looked angry, kept her hand on Rusty's shoulder. "You think we should leave everything on the chance that the fire might decide to come this way?"

"Seems to me you're taking an awful risk," he said.

"Seems to me you are, too," she said with a certain satisfaction.

And for a while everything in town was relatively quiet.

Chapter 18

On the last Sunday in April, Joe decided to clean out the Schooner, stem to stern, and usher in the warming breeze. His landlocked ship was full of winter dust and smelled like dirty laundry. So he opened all the windows, dusted off the screens, polished the panes, shook out his blankets and pegged them in the sun. He scoured the bathroom, swept the floors, scrubbed the countertops. He cleaned out his small fridge, washed his clothes and his curtains, and made everything tidy.

He rarely stepped foot in the Schooner's "wheelhouse," as he liked to call it, for he seldom drove anywhere, even in winter; he biked or hitched instead and was usually content to leave the dusty dashboard to the spiders and the windshield to the frost. But spring cleaning was spring cleaning. So he filled a pail with soapy water, grabbed his sponge, and headed for the bow.

He sponged down the dashboard and the vinyl seats, swept the leaves out from under the gas pedal, washed the windshield inside and out. He polished the mirror and dusted the visors. Threw out the junk that accumulated in the glove compartment, including the letter he'd written to his father nearly a year ago. He did not read it first.

"Done," he said, his mind on a hot shower and a cold beer. But there was one more thing he knew he really ought to do.

To the right of the driver's seat, bolted into the floor, was a wooden trunk about the size of a sewing machine. It was handmade of hard wood and brass hardware, one of the things that Ian had noticed right off the bat, Joe's first night in Belle Haven. Someone had taken great pains to build and install this trunk, presumably for valuables. But there was nothing in it now. Nothing but a few maps that Joe had transferred from the Jaguar. He was fairly certain about this. He tried to think back to that day when he'd pulled into Big Al's, to remember whether the trunk had been empty when he'd dumped his stuff inside and slammed the lid. Later, just as he was about to drive the Schooner away, Al had called out to him. "That lockbox up front there? The previous owner had that installed—for cameras and stuff, I guess. It's got a good smart lock on it. Combination's on a slip of paper taped inside. Don't worry, I didn't peek," he'd spluttered, his tongue showing.

But since Joe had not consulted any maps on his headlong flight from home, he had had no reason to open the box as he made his way toward Belle Haven. And by the time he had acquired enough possessions to need the trunk for storage, he'd somehow managed to spin the wheels of the sturdy little lock—nudged them as he edged his way into the driver's seat, perhaps. The trunk had become locked with the combination inside. And so it had remained for the better part of a year.

But it was a beautiful trunk, and Joe regretted its inactivity. And there was something more besides. Something that he felt he ought to remember. Something that nagged at him every time he glanced at the trunk. He had no idea what it could be, but he was now determined to find out.

He figured that the numbered wheels could not have been knocked too far off course. So, to prevent himself from making matters worse, he wrote down the numbers that were up and then began, very methodically, to try out different combinations. From 5–8–9–4, he went to 4–8–9–4, then to 6–8–9–4, then to 5–7–9–4, then 5–9–9–4, and so on until he had tried out a dozen combinations and yet failed to unlock the safe.

At this point he put away his cleaning stuff, took a shower, and ate a bowl of tomato soup with cheddar cheese melted in it, a stack of crackers, and a fistful of carrots. Then he went back to the box. Ten minutes later, when he was about ready to borrow Ian's crowbar, he turned the dials to 3–7–0–3 and found that he'd finally got it right.

Inside the trunk were several maps of New England states, a nearly new flashlight, which pleased him greatly, and beneath these things, the cardboard box that he had been surprised to find under the driver's seat of the Jaguar. As soon as he saw it, the nagging feeling that had inspired this whole investigation was relieved. Some part of him had remembered this box and wondered about it for months now.

When he lifted it out of the trunk, he was again surprised by its heaviness. He carried the box to the kitchen table with both hands, slid into the booth, untied the strings that held the lid on tight, and finally opened it. Inside, a folded piece of notepaper sat atop a tissue-paper nest. He opened the note and began to read.

Dear Kit, it said, and he had to stop for a moment to say the name out loud.

> *You are an unpredictable boy. To surprise me like this, just when I thought I had you pegged. It's quite the nicest thing you've ever done for me. The loot is wonderful, too, of course. It will take me clean away from here and let me get on with my life. I'm only sorry that our reacquaintance will have to wait. Not for long, I hope. Go off and wander around for a bit—it will do you good— but then come find me. I'll be in San Francisco, I think, or possibly Mendocino. Somewhere along that coast. I shouldn't be too hard to find. If I haven't heard from you by our birthday, I'll write to you at Yale. Or I'll call. One way or the other, I'll let you know where I am. In the meantime, watch out for the riptide. Don't get dragged back down. Use this to have a summer beyond his reach, if such a thing is possible. It's not much—I've kept most of the treasure, since in truth, I need it more—but it should be enough to keep you going if he "cuts you off without a penny." Which he may do for a month or two. If you find yourself in trouble, call Emily's parents in Newport. George and Ardith Corrigan. If you've lost the number I gave you tonight (which you probably have), they're in the book. They'll know how to find me.*
> *Be good.*
> *Holly*

For a long time, Joe sat in his kitchen with the letter in his hands and thought about his sister. Pictured her placing the box on the Jaguar's back floor. Pictured her smiling with satisfaction. Pictured the box sliding under the driver's seat as he hurried out of town that night.

He could almost feel Holly's eyes upon him as he turned back the petals of tissue and saw the trio of sleek gold wafers, the crisp coins that nestled inside. He had taken them for her. Now they were his. And there would never be a way to give them back to her.

He put the letter back into the box and the box back into the trunk, shut the lid, walked out of the Schooner, left the door swinging on its hinges.

When he reached the sloping fields beyond the stream, he began to run. At the edge of the forest on the far side of the fields, he grabbed the purple bramble whips that gave most intruders pause and tugged them aside with his bare hands. As he stumbled into the shadowy cathedral of the trees, he was not looking for solace. He wanted immediate distance, a degree of oblivion, exhaustion. He was hoping that the impartial trees would simply shield him for a while from the scrutiny of the world. But he did not reckon on the uncanny knack of forests to hone the truth, or the power of solitude to magnify remorse.

Chapter 19

When peace, like a river, attendeth my way
When sorrows like sea billows roll —
Whatever my lot,
Thou hast taught me to say
It is well, it is well with my soul.

It is well
It is well with my soul, with my soul,
It is well, it is well with my soul.

"*Baptist?*" *Joe queried* as he and Rachel strolled up
the walkway and through the open doors of the church. It was
Mother's Day, and the nave was full of pastel, canary-faced women,
wet-headed men, children in their Sunday best.

"If I bother at all, I usually go to the Presbyterian church where I
always went with my parents," she said, "but I'm afraid I'd get pitied
to death if I went there today. Besides, since they died I've become a
more generic sort of Christian. And today I'm in the mood for Baptist. They have the nicest music." She took Joe's hand and led him
through a narrow passageway, up a winding stair, and into the small
balcony at the back of the church. "The view's better from here," she
whispered as they sat down in a shadowy corner. They'd both dressed
up for the occasion. Rachel wore an iris blue skirt, an azure blouse,

and a straw Easter hat, Joe a nut brown oxford and a pair of fawn corduroys, both of which were now too big for him. They looked as if they had traded colors for the day.

When Joe had balked at the idea of church, Rachel had dismissed him with a wave of her hand. "Suit yourself," she'd said. "Spend the morning slobbering in your bed, like you do every other Sunday, gobbling down sausages, dragging your ass around 'til noon. *I'm* going to church."

"Why? You hardly ever go to church."

"Because it's Mother's Day," she'd said, and he had suddenly remembered the look on his sister's face as she worked her knuckles through their mother's vow-heavy rings.

From the balcony they listened to the drone of the sermon and grew as drowsy as babies in the sun. They sang, sharing a hymnal, and Joe had to admit that the choir sounded fine and the songs themselves were sweet.

> *I come to the garden alone,*
> *While the dew is still on the roses;*
> *And the voice I hear, falling on my ear,*
> *The Son of God discloses.*
>
> *And He walks with me, and He talks with me,*
> *And He tells me I am His own,*
> *And the joy we share as we tarry there,*
> *None other has ever known.*

He recognized a couple of selections—the Doxology and "Holy, Holy, Holy"—from the Christmases and Easters of his childhood. He sang "Amazing Grace," unconcerned with the vagaries of his voice, until the grief in Rachel's eyes closed his throat. And then, when he thought that the service was at an end, the preacher smiled down upon his flock and said, "I have a special surprise for you. A busy man, preaching and teaching in Philadelphia. An important man with little time to spare. But he's back here in his hometown for a visit, and I know you'll be glad to see his face again and share his wisdom. The Reverend Gerald Cryers." He opened his arms to a pudgy man who was making his way up to the pulpit. "Welcome home, Gerry."

"Thank you," said the Reverend Gerald Cryers. He grabbed the front edge of the pulpit with both of his sweating hands and leaned scowling toward the congregation.

"It's true," he finally said. "I've been away for quite a while. And many things are different around here. Little things, like a house that's changed color or a tree that's died. New faces, older faces, new children." He paused to bat his eyes at a little girl in the front pew who was drawing a camel on the back of an offertory envelope. "But some things never change. Like the sanctity of motherhood," he announced, quite predictably, since it was Mother's Day and the sermon had already reminded everyone of that fact. "You women who have brought children into this world have received God's blessings in a most tangible way. He has given each of you a part of him, blessed you with his love, made you a tool . . . a conduit . . . a vessel to carry his most precious gift.

"Mothers!" the preacher suddenly thundered, the sweat quivering on his lip. "There is another gift He has given you. When you look upon your children, remember the giver of the seed. Remember the protector, the provider, the man who took the world upon his shoulders that you might bear your young in peace."

As the preacher paused and focused his glare, Joe was startled to hear Rachel suddenly make a small retching sound. She didn't look sick, but there was a certain twist to her mouth that Joe had seen before. "Oh, Lord," he whispered to himself.

"Close your eyes!" the preacher commanded. "Bow your heads and close your eyes. Close them as tight as oysters, and consider where you would be without fathers for your children, without bread upon your table, without a strong shoulder to lean on and a sturdy paddle in the storm."

Joe looked down upon the congregation and was amazed to see that nearly every member sat with bowed head, men as well as women. Only the smallest children, watchful as owls, disobeyed.

"Consider, on this Mother's Day, the blessings granted you by the Father of us all, and by the fathers who walk this earth with one perfect rib long since surrendered. Who look into the hard, scowling face of the world with dry eyes. Who look upon their women and children and see before them the grace of God embodied."

At this point, Rachel made as if to rise up out of her seat. But then, inexplicably, she checked herself, tamped herself down, and put her hands into her lap.

"Raise your hands," exhorted the preacher. "Mothers! Mothers! Raise your hands. Let your open palms wave like flags of gratitude, emblems of praise for your stalwart husbands, the fathers of your priceless children. Raise your hands if you know, in your deepest heart of hearts, that without them lies poverty and sorrow and fear."

As if from a vast clutch of closely packed eggs, three hands hatched out of the nestled congregation and reached tentatively upward. No more than three. But to Joe's astonishment, the preacher began softly to applaud.

"Before me rises a sea of waving hands, acknowledging, celebrating the bond between us, the certainty that it is the marriage, the collaboration of parenthood, and not the woman unto herself that we are honoring today. A sea of hands. A sea of hands. This sea of hands rejoicing. And another. And another. And another."

Rachel had known liars before. She had been lied to, fooled, shamed—not often, but often enough. Never, though, had she spoken up, drained her fury. Contained, it had achieved a greater potency, a stronger proof, than it merited. It had tainted the vessel that held it, embittered her, occasionally made her bold.

And yet, in this place, Rachel was mute. She wanted so badly to face this man. But she simply could not. And she was not even sure why.

"Come on, Joe," she said, stamping her feet solidly as she rose, so that the thump of them echoed through the church. "Church is over."

Rachel let her heels knock on each step as she led Joe down from the balcony. At the door, she turned. She looked straight down the aisle toward the pulpit. The Reverend Gerald Cryers was counting on his fingers the merits of the assembled men, calling out their praises to the congregation who still sat, heads bowed, obedient as calves. He watched Rachel and smiled uncertainly. She leaned her back against the church door so that it began to open, creaking. One man at the end of a pew swung his head into the aisle, leaning around to see who was sneaking out early, like a horse looking out of a barn door, eye mostly white, mane twitching. He too watched Rachel for a moment and then swung back around, surveyed his neighbors. She saw him counting the hands raised for fathers on Mother's Day. Seven.

In a moment, when the minister arrived at his reluctant "Amen," every head came up. There was a great shuffling of feet. It was time to go home.

Rachel walked out of the church into the drenching sunlight and was immediately warmed. There were bees in the air and the smell of new grass.

"You know, my father was a splendid man," Rachel said, as she and Joe turned onto Maple Street and toward the creek. "But this is Mother's Day," she said, throwing up her hands. "*Mother*'s Day. Not Father's Day. Not Columbus Day or Veteran's Day or some president's birthday. Not Saint Patrick's Day. *Mother*'s Day. A measly twenty-four hours in which the mothers around here get flowers and cards and chocolates and get to cook themselves their favorite meal or maybe even eat out. What in the world would move him to meddle with that?" She was walking fast, looking straight ahead.

"I mean, imagine all those women sitting there, happy that this is their special day. And then that bozo starts telling them that without men, they're nothing. Dross. Sheep. Imagine." There was awe in her voice. "And then they've got this absurd choice: raise their hands . . . and they might as well just bleat at this point . . . or sit still. Which is like saying, 'No, I don't honor my husband.' When maybe they really do."

She was silent the rest of the way back to her house, and Joe left her alone. He knew that she was lecturing the Reverend Gerald Cryers, walking off her fury like a cramp, and he did nothing to distract her, although he suddenly felt as if there were things he ought to tell her. About his own mother, and especially about himself.

When they got to Rachel's house, Joe led her around back and straight to her hammock. "Have a rest," he said, gently taking off her hat, slipping her shoes off her feet. "I'll fix us some lunch."

"Peanut butter and jelly," she said with her eyes closed. "Milk if it's really cold."

They ate in the hammock, swinging slightly, and then went into the woods together.

When they reached a patch of moss under a giant pine, Joe put out a hand to stop her. He tilted his head back and saw the blue of the sky through the branches of the tree, heard the gentle conversation of mourning doves, felt the chill of shadows on his face, and could not stand it for a moment more.

He turned to Rachel and, although he knew that he should give her some warning, gentled one hand along the back of her neck, put the other on her hip, and kissed her with such longing, with his lips moving so softly against hers that she stood very still and did not stop him. Their chests touched and parted, touched again. Rachel felt the space between them closing. As he was kissing her, she took a small step forward so that she suddenly felt him all along the front of her body, from her thighs to her throat, felt the pressure of his hands behind her, one still along her neck, the other flat against the top of her thigh, holding her gently, pressing her gently against him, as astonishing as brands.

She had had no inkling of this and wondered if he had known it would happen. She hoped that he had not. She hoped that he had walked into these woods unknowing. She held herself in check for a moment more as she pondered these things with a sliver of her mind. And then she opened her lips as slowly as a space between clouds, moved her hands around him as unerringly as vines, and closed the last of the distance between them.

Joe felt Rachel make her decision and was as moved by the knowledge as by anything he could remember. He lifted her up against him and carefully laid her down on the moss. It took him a long moment to open his clothes, lift her skirt like a veil, slip her blouse over her head. And then, as he laid himself down on her, she stretched her arms high above her head and parted her legs until the eventual, mild protest of her hips, as if she were making an angel.

Muscled in the way that men who pick corn and shovel snow and tote ice are muscled, Joe mourned the lack of a blanket between Rachel's back and the million stems of moss. He wanted nothing to distract her now, not a single, small discomfort to refract her attention. So, even as he made himself as close to her as it was possible for him to be, he rolled with her deeper into the bed of moss so that she soon lay atop him, gasping, and immediately began to love him in the fashion of females.

It was, perhaps, nothing more than this simple reversal that accounted for the intensity of Rachel's arousal. While the blue jays screamed and the trees shuddered in the wind, Rachel regretted the fact that there was no way to press herself any closer against Joe than she already was. But it was more than their coupling that aroused her. It was that this was Joe. This was her Joe. These were his hands holding her down hard against him, his belly straining against hers. When she sat up suddenly and put her freed hands down against the place where they were joined, felt it wet with her own thick juice, smelled their raw smell, she could not prevent herself from panting lightly, like a cat. When Joe heard her, he grabbed her hips and she could see the muscles in his belly harden like the ribs of a seashell. She clenched him, and he dug his fingers more insistently into her, closed his eyes, and began to rise up from the moss, lifting her with him.

Joe had done something, moved against her in some way she could not isolate, and she quickly lowered herself back down along the length of him. She laid her hands on the smooth caps of his shoulders, tucked in her folded arms, and as she gently kissed him, made love to him in an entirely selfish, inexperienced way that seemed to be exactly what he needed. As her rhythm became more emphatic and her mouth grew suddenly slack, he took her head in his hands and lifted her face away from his so that when she opened her eyes she saw, in his, the unbordered scope of his desire.

Chapter 20

"None," she said as they walked back through the woods toward her house.

"Jesus Christ, Rachel. What do you mean, 'none'?"

"I mean none. That's what I mean."

"You're not on the Pill?"

"No." She snorted. "I'm not. I wasn't expecting to have any sex this month, and even if I had, I wouldn't be on the Pill. Why should I pop hormones every day of the year on the off chance that I'll be ravaged under a pine tree on Mother's Day?"

"I can't believe this," he said, stomping into her kitchen and letting the screen door smack shut behind him.

"I don't understand." She took two bottles of beer out of the fridge and handed one to Joe. "You mean you haven't ever bothered to think things through?"

"*Things.* I hate it when you do that. What are *things?*"

"How can you go around making love to people and not be prepared for fatherhood? Seems to me you should have given some thought to procreation before you took off your pants."

"Look who's calling the kettle black."

"No, I'm not," she said, taking a long drink of beer.

"Of course you are." He set his bottle down on the counter so hard that the beer foamed up and out of the neck. "Maybe I was wrong to assume you'd . . . taken care of things—"

"No maybe about it."

"But what you did was worse. You *knew* what kind of chance we were taking, but you took it anyway."

She nodded. "I'd be quite happy to have a baby anytime soon," she said calmly. "Wed, unwed, whatever. I've got plenty of money, a house, friends, and I've wanted a baby ever since I was twelve. So if I get pregnant, that's fine."

"But you're only twenty-one, Rachel. Barely that."

"I'm an old lady, Joe. My body just hasn't caught up with me yet. I'm temperamental. Set in my ways. Not very wise, but I will be." She sat down at the kitchen table and rubbed the cold bottle of beer up along the inside of her arm. "I saw a woman named Mrs. James in the park last week," she said, smiling. "She was walking very slowly, as if her hips were locked. But when she got to the swing set, she settled down onto one of the seats and began to work herself up into the sky. She grabbed hold of those two chains with her old-bird hands, leaned back so far I was afraid she'd fall, and stretched her legs out to get herself going. She was wearing horrible, thick stockings and big, heavy black shoes. She swung as high as anyone I'd ever seen, with her sweater flapping out around her and her hair coming loose. And then, after a bit, she slowed down, had to wait until she had stopped completely, and then she got off the swing and hobbled away down the path." Rachel looked up at Joe and shook her head. "It was like looking into a mirror, Joe. It was just like looking into a mirror."

"Then that's even worse," he said, taking her cold hands in his.

"What do you mean?"

"It's not safe for old women to have babies," he said.

That night Rachel did some thinking. She sat on her moonlit porch and thought about lying with Joe on the moss in the woods, resting, letting their bodies cool. She thought about the differences between the first time she'd been with someone—with Harry—and this second time, with Joe. She remembered how terrified she'd been, for two long months after Harry (through the death of her parents and the long gray days that had followed) when she'd had no period to end things properly, completely. She remembered her explosive relief when she'd felt the first hot blood seeping, finally, and had moved a great step further from that dreadful time.

How different those ghastly final months of college had been from her first extraordinary days away from Belle Haven. Despite her reluctance to leave home, she had almost immediately felt a great freedom, a great release, an enormous excitement. Every choice she made filled her with pride and satisfaction. Every new friend, every good day, every letter home that spoke of what she'd learned and what she'd gained compounded her certainty that this new chapter of her life was one she'd be sorry to end.

And now it all seemed so long ago and far away, almost as if it had never happened. As this Mother's Day waned—as the feel of Joe holding her faded—Rachel wondered how her awful humiliation and disappointment at Harry's hands might also have diminished if she'd only had the chance to ride them out, go on to better things, return to the sound habits and safe choices that had brought her such satisfaction.

But her parents dying—when and how they had died—had made it impossible for Rachel simply to pick up where she'd left off. She had changed. She could not ever retouch the way things had been. They were there in her mind, sharp, stuck images: Harry laughing with the next girl; the slick, hot feel of Skip tonguing her ear; Paul turning her out of his car; ashes rushing downstream.

And now, Joe. Now she had Joe. This afternoon she had done something she'd sworn never to do in haste again. But Joe was not Harry. Not at all like Harry. She'd known him for a whole year already, and she felt that she knew him through and through.

So why, even as they had nestled on their bed of moss, even as he had lazily combed her hair with his fingers, had she felt her lingering curiosity begin to harden into clots of doubt?

It's no good, she thought, watching the moon. I can't just hope for the best.

The next day, when Joe came to her, his eyes alight with memory, she sat with him in the hammock in her backyard, let him lace her fingers with his, and asked him for the hundredth time, "Why are you here?"

" 'Cause I finished turning over Mrs. Grant's garden early and Ian doesn't need me to do his until two." He rolled out of the hammock and pulled her shrieking into the grass.

"Stop it, you fiend." She laughed.

"Not until you admit that you didn't sleep at all last night."

Which sobered her, for indeed she had slept very little. Yet he was smiling when he said, "Every time I shut my eyes I was back in those woods with you."

"What I meant was, why are you here in Belle Haven?" she said, rolling way from him, gaining her feet.

When he lunged for her again, she stepped out of reach. It was difficult to look at him, at his smile, without returning it.

"Come with me for a minute," he said, taking her hand and pulling her toward the trees. "I want to show you something."

"I'll bet you do," she said, resisting, half laughing.

"No, nothing like that. God, what a mind you have."

Reluctantly, she let him lead her into the woods. But before they'd gone far, she asked, again, "What are you doing here? Really."

"Oh, for Pete's sake, Rachel. Not this again."

"Well, if you'd ever give me a straight answer, I wouldn't keep asking."

"How straight do I have to get? I'm here because I want to be here. That's it. That's all there is to it."

"But I still don't understand why you didn't go back to school."

"Why *I* didn't go back to school? Why didn't *you*?" He paused to bend an unruly branch out of her way.

"If you're suggesting that our answers are the same," she said, stepping past him, "you're wrong."

"I am not wrong. We're both content to be where we are. We both have better reasons to stay than we do to leave."

"But I *live* here," she said. "I've always lived here. This is my home."

"Mine too."

"But that's what I'm talking about. Why have you made *this* town your home?"

"Look, Rachel. I don't understand what you're getting at." He grabbed her by the arm to slow her, took up his place beside her on the narrow trail. "Why can't you accept my decision to stay?"

"Oh, come on, Joe. You're a rich boy who belongs here about as much as I belong in Manhattan."

"That's not fair," he said, and she could tell that she had hurt him. "Who are you to say who belongs here and who doesn't? Besides, you're not exactly poor yourself."

"Which has absolutely nothing to do with this. There's no question that *I* belong here."

"So you've said, over and over and over again. Which makes me think you need to hear it more than I do."

"What's that supposed to mean?"

"Nothing." He sighed. He stepped quickly in front of her, took her by the arms. "Why can't you take things for what they are?"

"What are they?"

"They are . . ." he said, shrugging, twisting with frustration, "what they are. And if you would simply admit that I do belong here too—"

"But you don't. You never have. Not really. You came here unintentionally, to some extent against your will, and I think maybe you would have gone home by now if your father had asked you to."

"Not true," he said, leading her slowly along the rabbit trail again, up through the sloping woods. "I've stayed here because I've wanted to."

"But that's what I'm asking you. Why? Why have you wanted to stay in this particular place? When you could go anywhere, do anything you want to do?"

"Why don't you ask yourself the same question?" he said, but before she had a chance to reply he stopped suddenly and turned again to face her. "Hang on a minute," he said. "I have a favor to ask."

"What?"

Ahead of them stood a huge old black walnut tree with a trunk as big around as a barrel. It spread its great, heavy branches out in all directions as if it wanted a partner.

"I'd like your permission to build Rusty a house in this tree," he said.

Impatient with this diversion, she barely looked at the tree. "Way up here? Why not closer to the Kitchen?"

"There aren't any trees like this down there. None that I could build in, anyway. This is a nice patch of woods. And besides," he said, "this place is far enough from home to give the kid a thrill but close enough to you to be safe. What do you say?"

"I say 'Of course,' of course." She looked at the walnut tree carefully for the first time, looked at Joe looking at the walnut tree, saw him planning the house he would build for Rusty, and thought she had her answer. She was thrilled by it. To be thinking of tree houses, of building something that would last, he had to mean what he'd said. Belle Haven had become his home in the best sense of the word.

But she was wounded by this answer, too. Undone. For if she had anything to do with his decision, so did Rusty, and Angela, and Ian, and, for all she knew, the taste of Belle Haven's corn, the music of its birds. Much as she valued her self-reliance, Rachel wanted to be at the center of someone's world. At the center of Joe's world. But she was not yet ready to make Joe the center of hers.

She did not know that he, too, was torn. That he prized his hard-won independence as much as he yearned for a bond that would not erode it. That he was wary of trusting too much. In these things, they were alike. But while Rachel was still somewhat cautious about Joe, he was reluctant to put all his faith in a town that could one day be swallowed by flames. He had made it his home, and he was prepared to invest in it his labor and his love, but he would not expect too much of the future.

He would simply stay as long as he could, for all the reasons he had given Rachel, and others, too. One of which lay concealed in a pocket of trees on the far side of Ian's fields, where the fire had made its in-delible mark and Joe, just as clearly, was carving his.

Chapter 21

By the time he discovered his sister's gold, Joe had spent nearly a year in Belle Haven, riding the bicycle Rachel had lent him or hitchhiking to a dozen farms out of the fire's range, harvesting whatever the ground yielded: strawberries, corn, cauliflower, beans, apples, pumpkins, fresh, fragrant Christmas trees. When snow flew, he shoveled it. When the breeze warmed, he pruned a thousand apple trees and cleared the brush from unkempt orchards, acre by acre. With time, his speech became more like that of his employers: soft, mumbled, loosely strung with a subtle, northern twang. And with the money he didn't spend on his food and keep, he bought from Earl a sheaf of sandpaper in various grades and a small collection of carving tools, including a hatchet and a tiny plane.

The Schooner had taught Joe how to take care of the things he owned. The tools taught Joe how to cherish those few possessions that bridge the gap between the thinking mind, the prismatic idea, and creation: tools like the pen, brush, harp, camera, forge, or blade. His most valuable tool was the knife Rusty had given him for whittling. Joe had spent the winter and the spring carving litter from the woods—small branches, broken sticks, even logs—until he began to realize, like Michelangelo, that a sculptor or a carver discovers as much as he creates.

On the day that Joe had fled from Holly's gold through the fields and into the forest, he had come across a graveyard the likes of which he had never seen. Here the fire had arched upward, scratched the surface with a blackened fin, and left behind not a crater but a small plot of dead trees like tombstones among the ferns. There were perhaps a dozen of them, quite perfect without their leaves, dead from the roots up, bloodless, not yet brittle. A single dead tree might have gone unnoticed, but a dozen, surrounded by their verdant neighbors, caught Joe's attention. When he stumbled upon them on the day that he opened the box of gold, he saw, in those trees, what he might never have seen before Rusty's knife had made him into a carver.

From the moment Joe had read Holly's letter, his memory of her face had become as clean and clear as a reflection. And when he saw the murdered trees splintering the sunlight with their black shadows, he once again saw her face reflected. As he approached the trees, he took Rusty's knife from his pocket and opened its blade as if he were breaking bread. He walked past the first of the trees, and past the second, stopped at the third, and with scarcely a pause, lifted his blade.

It was not nearly as easy as he needed it to be. He needed it to be quick and faultless, and when it wasn't he had to struggle not to hack at the wood and ruin both the tree and the knife. He forced himself to go slowly and not to mind the delay. He convinced himself to stop often and catch his breath, blow on his blistering palm, and walk the blood into his legs. When it became dark, he wiped his knife on his pants, closed it, put it back in his pocket, and left the woods.

Early the next morning he got out of bed wearing the clothes he'd gone to sleep in, gathered up his carving tools, and walked through the soaking fields to the woods. The light was different now, and for a moment he could not see Holly in the monument of dead wood. But then yes, there she was, waiting. And he took up exactly where he'd left off the day before.

By the third day, Joe had lost his job as a bag boy at the A&P. Rachel, when she came looking for him, found Ian instead, sitting under the Schooner's awning, smoking his pipe.

"There's something the matter with him, Rachel," he said. "He keeps going off into the woods, and he won't talk to me."

"Maybe he's having second thoughts about all this," she said, her belly lined with dread.

"I don't think that's it," Ian said. "I think maybe he's staking some sort of claim."

She thought about this for a bit and then said, "Tell him that I was by, Ian. He'll talk about it if he wants to."

At the end of the third day, Joe came out of the woods and found his way home, slept the night through, and then went back out into the world to work.

He spent the first days of May in dirt of one sort or another, his boots heavy with mud, his fingernails so packed with earth that they ached. He helped a farmer plant potatoes in the rain and hang a new barn door. He turned over a vegetable garden for Mrs. Sapinsley, who lived next to the elementary school and had sciatica so bad she could no longer wield a shovel. He dug a new grave in the Baptist church-yard and then filled it back in the next day. And every evening, after he had fed himself and washed the dirt from his eyelashes, he gath-ered up his tools and hurried across the fields, scattering birds and big-eyed mice as he ran.

Rachel had not asked him about the silence or the absence he'd maintained for that handful of days. But after Mother's Day Joe de-cided that it would cost him nothing to make a pact with her.

"I think I can make you understand why I've stayed in Belle Haven, Rachel," he said to her one day in June. "But it will mean telling you things I'd rather not talk about, so don't ask me any more questions after this."

That afternoon Joe led Rachel to the woods on the far side of Ian's sloping fields. He walked carefully, on the sides of his feet, as if he were stalking deer, compelling her to do the same. She was taut with anticipation and found that she had to make a conscious effort to breathe deeply. *What is all this?* she asked herself, unable to believe that Joe could have any secrets from her when he'd already told her so many.

Through the green galaxy of maple leaves, she thought she glimpsed a face up ahead, watching them, but in a moment it was gone. The light was growing brighter, she realized, and the under-growth less dense. Someone—Joe, she presumed—had beaten a path through the ferns, which made their travel easy and certain. I'll be able to find my way back here, she realized.

Then Joe came to a stop, moved to one side, and Rachel saw before her an austere collection of small, dead trees, all the more unlikely for the attendance of their robust neighbors. It was an eerie, quiet spot. The dead trees were very still. Very stark. She wondered why Joe had brought her here.

She looked to him for some clue, but he was standing as quietly as the trees, looking into their branches. So she turned to them once more, and that was when she saw what he had accomplished.

Given the chance, weather and time would camouflage Joe's creation so well that a person could walk right by it without ever knowing it was there. But although the wood was dead, it had not yet completely grayed and the places that Joe had carved were a different color from the bark he'd left untouched. It was this different color that drew Rachel's attention. Once it had, she was so startled that for a moment her heart stopped beating.

She was immediately reminded, when she saw what he had done, of a photograph she'd once seen, of a cliff of red clay tumbling down into the sea. Nothing but mud, chunks of it, boulders of it. And then, when she'd stopped looking at the photograph so hard, she had seen among the rubble a fantastic sculpture of a mermaid sitting on a rock. The tide had taken most of her tail, but her magnificence had been unimpaired. Rachel had not forgotten that photograph, just as she would not forget this.

She had never seen Holly or any likeness of her, but she knew that this was Joe's sister among the trees. It wasn't just the imperfection of her face, although that made Rachel certain. It was the way Joe had carved her, so that she was less beautiful than striking, and with a look of such yearning on her face that Rachel crossed her arms over her chest.

Joe had carved the trunk of the small tree so that it merely suggested a woman's body, but he had given her a face of such acute detail that for a moment Rachel found herself questioning Joe's part in its creation.

"You did this?" she asked him.

"I can hardly believe it myself," he said. "I've been carving things for months now, but I had no idea I could do anything like this. Nothing at all like this. I feel like a man who goes to bed one night a cripple and wakes up with wings."

"I don't know what to say, Joe." She walked up close to the statue and, glancing at him for permission, ran her finger along its jaw.

"It's not just carving this that has me so excited, Rachel," he said. "It's the idea that if I can do something like this when I never, ever suspected that I could, there might be other things waiting ahead. It's incredible." He ran his hands down a dead maple. "What if I had never come to Belle Haven? What if Rusty had never given me that knife? What if I had never found these trees? What if I'd lived and died without ever knowing how unbelievably satisfying it is to make something like this?"

He sat down and stretched his long legs out in front of him, tipped his head back so that the sun struck his face. "There have been lots of times in my life when I've done something beautiful in my head, but I've never come close to achieving the same perfection outside of my skull. When I was a kid, I thought up the most wonderful birdhouse, but when I tried to build the thing, I simply made a mess. French. That was another thing. After four years of classes, I could speak it so well in my head, but when I opened my mouth, it came out lousy. Although I suppose those things had more to do with inexperience than anything. But there's more to most things than experience. If there weren't, there would be thousands of Mozarts."

He looked at Rachel to see if she understood what he was saying, but she was still gazing silently at Holly's face. He trailed his fingers absently through the grass. "I've painted paintings in my head," he said, "composed music, designed machines. All things that should not be so difficult to lift from my mind and make. That's the only part I couldn't do: make the thing, whatever it was.

"But there's a synapse. I don't know what to call it. A hiatus. Even in the making of a birdhouse, even if you know how to use a hammer and where to place a nail, there's something else you have to have in order to do it right. With a birdhouse, maybe it's nothing more than a knack. In the case of a symphony, a really good symphony, you have to have knowledge, and experience, and whatever bridges the hiatus. I don't know what to call it." He shook his head. "It sounds too pretentious to call it a gift. But I think that I may have been given a little piece of it. Just enough. And there's only one thing that ruins it."

Rachel turned away from the carving.

Joe pulled his knees up to his chest. He shook his head. He looked everywhere but at Rachel—the sky, the trees—and finally closed his eyes. His hands lay still in the ferns. Rachel could see his throat working.

"What ruins it?" she said, moving next to him, kneeling by his side. When he made a small sound in his throat and dropped his head into his hands, Rachel put her arms around him. He tucked his head into her neck, and Rachel was reminded of the night a year earlier when he had called his father.

He had never told anyone, not even Rachel, what he'd learned that night. But now he did.

"When I called my father last May," he said, his voice terrible, "he told me that Holly had died."

At which Rachel pulled back sharply to look into his face and then took him again into her arms, shutting her eyes. "Oh, my Joe," she said. But he did not seem to hear her.

"He told me that she had been in a terrible car accident in San Francisco. Right after she arrived there. Right after she left home. She wasn't driving. She didn't have a car and I'm not even sure she knew how to drive. But there was a lot of fog. It was late at night." He took a long breath. "No one was sure what happened. And I don't really remember what else my father said about it. He told me a lot of things that night. He told me that she had already been cremated. Everything over and done with." (And here again Rachel felt as if she had slipped backward through the months to arrive at the feel of cold water around her bare ankles and the sight of ashes moving like a bird's shadow downstream.) "He told me that if anyone was to blame for my not knowing, it was me. I was the one who had left without a word. I was the one to blame for a lot of things." Joe lifted his head. "And that's what ruins this." He looked into the gallery of trees.

"But I still don't understand why."

Joe gestured impatiently toward the dead branches. "Everything I've done here is tied to what I did back there." He scoured his face with his hands. "If I hadn't given Holly the money, she wouldn't have left, she wouldn't have gone to San Francisco, she wouldn't have died. And if she hadn't died, I might . . . I'm sure I *would* have left Belle Haven a year ago, or at least never stayed anywhere near this long. If she hadn't died, I might never have discovered that I could do something like this." He nodded toward the carving among the trees. "If she hadn't died, if I hadn't stayed in Belle Haven, maybe there wouldn't have been anything to discover."

"Is that what your father told you that night?" she asked, looking again into his face. "That it was your fault Holly died?"

"I don't want to talk about him anymore," Joe said.

"What a bastard," she muttered, shaking her head. "You can't avoid being involved in other peoples' lives. Especially when they're your family. But that doesn't mean you're to blame for Holly's death, or that your"—she swept a hand toward the tree—"your ability is tainted by it."

"It feels that way. Holly simply wouldn't have died when and how she did if I hadn't meddled with her life."

"No," Rachel admitted. "She wouldn't have died then and there. But that doesn't mean you killed her. It just means that you were involved in your sister's life and therefore in her death."

They sat together in the hot grass, considering the trees clustered around them. "It would be different," she said after a bit, "if you had expected to gain something by giving Holly your father's money. But you yourself told me that what you did was one of the few unselfish acts of your life. The first in a very long time. It was a risky thing to do. You didn't do it for profit."

"Of course not. What difference does that make?"

Rachel plucked a brittle frond from a dead fern and began to crumble it between her hands. She thought of Joe lying with her in the woods behind her house, leading her to the huge walnut tree where he had already begun to build Rusty's house. "I'm sure it made a lot of difference to Holly. She probably valued your motives far more than she valued the money itself."

"That may be true," he said impatiently, "but my sister is still dead. And I am responsible."

"You had no way of knowing what would happen." She cast the broken frond away from her. "Just as I had no way of knowing that my love for apple cider would get my parents killed."

They sat together for a while longer, matching Holly's gaze.

"Where is she buried, Joe?"

This startled him. It was a question he had asked himself more than once, but he had always imagined Holly lying next to their mother, safe again. Whatever else their father had done, however righteous he might have felt when his children had fled, surely he would have brought Holly's body home.

"I don't know," Joe said. "But we had a family plot. It's where all of us were meant to be buried. Holly must be there." He watched a hunting spider lurch along his bootlace and disappear into the grass. "Why do you ask?"

Rachel chose her words. She wanted nothing less than to feed his guilty assumptions. "Did you ever look for anything about the accident in the paper? Was there a death announcement?"

Joe looked into Rachel's face. He became completely still. "No, I didn't look. Why would I look?"

Rachel shrugged. She laced her fingers. Waggled her head. "She was your sister, Joe. Didn't you feel horribly . . . removed from what was happening?"

"Removed? That's not how I felt. I didn't feel removed. I felt as if I had exploded into a million parts. Even so, I would have done more than I did, if I could have. But she had already been buried by the time I found out. Everything was over and done with and there was nothing I could do about any of it. And a death announcement would not have put me back together again."

"But didn't you want to know for sure what happened?"

"Know for sure?"

She looked back at him. Saw how pale he had become. She realized that some small part of him had already faced the possibility that his father was not to be trusted. But she knew as well that it was unnatural to assume the worst of a parent . . . or a child.

"Jesus Christ, Rachel, he's not a monster. You think he killed my sister?"

And then she knew for sure that she should let this go. It would be cruel to speculate about things he had laid to rest. Joe had shouldered all the hurt he could. He couldn't take on any more. Not right now. And she also knew that as much as Joe might seem to be defending his father, he was in equal parts protecting himself.

"Of course not," she said. "The thought never entered my mind."

She watched Joe's body relax. She watched his chest expand.

"There's one thing I don't understand, though," Rachel said. "I thought you were bringing me out here to explain why you've stayed in Belle Haven."

"That's right."

"But you decided to stay over a year ago, Joe, long before you started carving like this. And a minute ago you said that it was that phone call you made to your father—learning about Holly's death— that made you stay. So why bring me out here? Out of the blue? As if this"—she gestured again toward the blackened grove—"as if this is your explanation?"

"Because it *is*. The best one I can give you. Of course Holly's death changed things. Of course I found it impossible to go home after . . . after the things my father said to me that night. But there's more to it than that." He took a deep breath. "Almost from my first day in Belle Haven, I've felt like a changeling. Things have been cooking inside me all along. It's hard to be sure about the reasons I've felt this way, but I have. And I have the feeling that there's more to come."

Joe took one of Rachel's hands in his. He felt that her arrival had extracted from this place a portion of its magic. But her presence and her admiration had also affirmed what he had done. If it was less magical, it was also more real. Something he could count on. Something he had not imagined.

"I want to do this for the rest of my life," he said, kissing her palm.

She was not certain, as she brought her other hand up to cradle his face, what it was that he meant.

Chapter 22

When Angela saw the package Joe had brought Rusty on his eleventh birthday, she nudged it with a knuckle and leaned close for a better look.

"Ask a man to fix a carburetor, barbecue a steak, mow a lawn," she said, "and he breaks out all over in Y chromosomes, his biceps swell, pecker perks up, grunts like a caveman. But ask him to preheat an oven, buy a box of tampons, wrap a birthday present . . . his eyes glaze over, his palms sweat, 'I don't know how,' he says. Which he'd never dream of saying if you asked him to build a rocket ship. The stronger sex. The world's rulers. I give you"—here she bowed to Joe, who sat scowling at her kitchen table—"the answer to every woman's prayers."

"Oh, shut up, Angela. I did my best."

"That's what's so amazing, Joe," she said, kissing the top of his head. "I'm sure you did. But Jesus, honey, you must've been wearing boxing gloves."

"Anyhow, who cares how it's wrapped? Look at him. He's ripping it off faster than a raccoon husking corn."

"Oh, my," Rachel said laughing and clapping her hands softly, "I do believe he's made the leap, Angie."

"You think? I don't know, Rachel. Say *wash*, Joe."

"Warsh," he obliged.

"Well, tie me to an anthill and stuff my ears with jam. I'd never have believed it a year ago." Angela picked up her camera and aimed it at Joe. "Say *wash* again, Joe. This one's for my scrapbook. Think of a caption, Rachel."

"Something simple," she said. "How about, 'Just Joe'?"

"That's to replace the one you gave me," Joe said to Rusty, ignoring the women.

"It's great, Joe. Mom, look at the knife Joe gave me."

"Oh, Lord, Joe. I should've known you'd give him something I've got to worry about."

"I have something else for you, Rusty, but it was too big to wrap."

"A horse?"

"No, not a horse. Good grief, boy, what do you think your mother would do to me if I gave you a horse?"

"She'd make you take care of it," Rusty said.

"Exactly. Now finish your cake and we'll all take a walk up to Rachel's place."

Angela lifted her eyebrows at Rachel, who shrugged and smiled and filled her mouth with cake.

After the cake was gone and the dishes washed and put away, the four of them walked down the street, over Raccoon Creek, and up the hill to Rachel's house. It was just approaching twilight, for Angela had closed the Kitchen up early in honor of her son's birthday and the August evening was long and light.

When they reached the house, Rusty started up the front steps, but Joe called him back and led them all around the house and up the path into the woods. It was clear that the boy was mystified and excited in a way peculiar to children and a very few adults. He walked directly behind Joe, bumping into him now and again, not at all distracted by the lightning bugs that flashed along the edges of the shadowed trail like channel markers.

When they passed the big pine and the bed of moss, Joe turned around and gave Rachel a slow smile.

"Much nicer than flowers, Rachel," Angela whispered; she knew why this particular tree, this exact plot of moss, made Joe smile, Rachel slow her step.

Rachel slid her hands into her pockets. "Much," she said.

When they reached the huge walnut tree, Joe turned quickly and clapped his hand over Rusty's eyes.

"Only two things you have to promise," Joe said. "No fires, and no girls for a while yet."

"Done," Rusty promised, and pried Joe's fingers from his eyes.

He was speechless, at first, when he saw the house that Joe had built in the tree. He blinked, gaped, took a slow step forward. Then he let out a whoop of delight and ran for the tree, launched himself up the ladder, onto the sturdy, railed-in deck and through the door.

In a minute he appeared on the deck again.

"You *got* to see this, Mom," he called down, dancing from foot to foot. "It's fantastic."

So Rachel and Angela and Joe climbed up the capable ladder and onto the small deck. Angela cast a mother's eye over the rungs, the rails, the beams that fixed the house to the ancient tree, and nodded her approval. Rachel, who had seen the house in various stages of construction, was nonetheless surprised to see it done, for Joe had finished it with the sort of details seldom spent on animals or children.

The door had wooden handles inside and out, a hardwood dolphin for a knocker, and the single word—RUSTY—carved on a small plaque above the door frame. He had made the door full size, furnished it with a lock, and carefully fit door to frame so the boy inside would not be bothered by mosquitoes or weather. For the same reason, Joe had bought three small glass panes that were set into metal, hinged frames. They fit snugly into the square holes cut in the walls, swung outward on their hinges, and came with braces so they could be propped safely open on windy days.

The house was an eight-foot square with a peaked, shingled roof and a smooth wooden floor. Joe had paneled it from the outside with wood he'd begged from farmers with fallen barns, loaded into Ian's pickup, and carried into the woods, plank by plank. He had chinked the cracks between the weathered boards but had not paneled the inside of the house. In between the vertical supports of the frame he had built small shelves and cupboards and stocked them with books, licorice, a lantern and extra batteries, a tablet of writing paper, and a jug filled with sharp, fragrant pencils. There was a small table and a matching chair, a cot folded up and stashed against one wall, and in another corner the wooden trunk that Joe had carefully removed from the Schooner and carried up into the tree.

It was plain to see that Joe had learned a lot in the months he'd spent working with his hands. Helping farmers and neighbors with the heavy work of building barns, of fixing things broken by weather or age, had taught Joe how to earn a living. But as he had come to know about wood and tools and sweat, he had also come to know things about himself. He liked what he had learned, and he knew that he would always love this tree house as much as any other dwelling on earth.

"Earl gave me all kinds of stuff I needed," Joe offered. "Nails, lots of hardware, lumber for the frame, lent me his drill, a couple of saws. He also helped me with the hard parts. So it's really his birthday present, too," he said to Rusty. "Don't forget to thank him."

"I won't, Joe." He looked around the house one more time, turning on his feet like a boy in a music box, and then put his arms around Joe and laid his head against his chest. "Thank you," he whispered. "I'll never forget you as long as I live."

"You won't need to," Joe said, his hands in Rusty's sleek hair. "I'm not going anywhere." Then he put the boy away from him. "Listen, Rusty," he said slowly. "I know that you might have preferred something a little less . . . refined. You know: a rope ladder, apple crates. Don't think you have to keep it this way just to please me. It's your house. Do whatever you want with it. I just couldn't help making it this way. For some reason I just can't help thinking of you as much older than eleven."

Rusty looked as if he would explode. "It's perfect," he said.

"One more thing you haven't seen," said Joe, leading him out onto the deck and lifting his chin up toward the pinnacle of the tree.

"A crow's nest!" Rusty cried, scrambling farther up the walnut's massive trunk, rung by rung, to where it was encircled by a sturdy, narrow walk. From his perch Rusty could look through the walnut's upper branches, over the tops of its smaller neighbor trees, and down the gradual slope of the hill. In one direction he could see the top of Rachel's house and, beyond that, a distant field, moving with wheat and a mare's tail of smoke drifting in the breeze. When he looked quickly away toward the town he could see more, for the hill sloped sharply down to Raccoon Creek. As the walnut's upper branches soughed gently the boy caught glimpses of his own rooftop.

"You can send me messages, Mom," he called down. "We can learn Morse code and use flashlights."

"Uh-huh," she said, looking up, her feet making continuous small adjustments like an outfielder gauging descent. She held the back of her head in both hands, her fingers buried in her sandy hair. "Just watch yourself on the way back down, Rusty."

By now it was well and truly sundown, and somewhere below them a choir of frogs began its fervent evensong.

They all climbed down from the old black walnut. Rusty kissed his smiling mother, Rachel took Joe's callused hand, and the four of them walked along the well-worn path and out of the woods. At the edge of the trees they were silenced by a sunset as gaudy as a parrot's wing and felt themselves slipping from long practice into uneasy admiration of the fine, polluted light that swept slowly toward Belle Haven.

Chapter 23

That night, in a field not far from town, not even as far as Ian Spalding's campground, alongside an old stone wall that had mostly tumbled down, a doe stopped grazing and lifted her head. Her companions, loitering in the near distance, paused to watch her. The ones closest to her began to tremble. The doe gathered herself to flee. For one silent, enormous moment, she knew nothing but terror and the exhilarating notion that she could save herself. But even as her hooves braced themselves against the ground, it melted away like sand touched by tide. Where the deer had stood was nothing but a dissipating spout of smoke.

A few more stones had fallen from the mossy old wall. The site of the deer's abduction was oddly bare. But there were, otherwise, no signs to caution passersby that this was a place best avoided. Just as flags were lacking in a dozen other scattered places waiting for unlucky strays.

Chapter 24

It was the middle of August, and Joe had not been up
to the second floor of Rachel's house since Easter.

"I'm redecorating," she'd said in the spring. "No going upstairs
until I'm done." And Joe had been aware, all summer long, of panel
trucks parked by Rachel's house, trails of sawdust on her front porch,
the sound of hammers coming down the hill as he biked into town.

With her house in such disarray, Rachel sometimes drove out to
the Schooner to spend a short summer night, cook with Joe, play
crazy eights, maybe dance in the clearing. And on nights when the
moon was big or the days so hot that the streets melted, Joe often
showed up at Rachel's door and led her to the moss in the woods or, if
Rusty was in his tree, lay with her on her cool kitchen floor.

He had long deferred to Rachel's wish that they—neither of them—
spoil their lovemaking with concerns about the future. It wasn't that
he no longer cared whether or not Rachel became pregnant, but the
thought of a child no longer alarmed him as it once had. If Rachel
didn't worry about it, neither would he. They were already a family of
sorts, married or not. More, in some ways, than the one he'd lost.

These notions of family had made Joe miss the house on the hill,
where everything was both a source and an extension of Rachel, and
he was glad when she invited him to see what she had done with it.

Rachel was unlike anyone else he'd ever known, but Joe somehow
expected to climb the stairs into the upper regions of her house and
there encounter something predictably feminine. Pretty. Charming.
Full of mirrors and scent. He felt strangely gratified to be joining the

fraternity of mated men who are presented with such emasculating bowers and are expected, unconditionally, to applaud.

As they climbed the winding stairs together, Joe felt a great tenderness for Rachel. She had seen his work unveiled. He readied his smile and his kindest words as he climbed toward hers.

"Well," she said, watching his face. "What do you think?"

At one time there had been, at the top of the stairs, a hallway joining two bedrooms, a study, and a sewing room. All of that was gone. There was, instead, one large open space. The main supporting beams remained, as did a portion of the ceiling that had before entirely hidden the attic and roof above. The bare wood floor, too, had been exposed but had then been sanded and finished to a gleam. The windows, drapeless, sparkled. They were filled with the blue of the sky and the myriad greens of the trees, as if they were changeable paintings.

One end of the room held a polished brass bed, its immaculate white spread stitched with a wreath of roses. Next to the bed, a simple wooden table held a lamp made from a bottle of red glass and a painted shade. There was a small wicker wardrobe, a braided rug, a jug of clover on the windowsill.

On the other side of the room, in one large corner, was a hodge-podge of bookcases, all filled with books. Each case was topped with motley stuff: colored bottles shot with sunlight; a spiny blowfish; a coffee mug full of birds' feathers; a large conch shell; a fan of coral; a childish purple crock. On the floor was a plain blue rug. On the rug was an old rocking chair. On the chair was an open book.

The rest of the room was filled with odds and ends, piles of colorful pillows, good prints, a huge desk heaped with books and papers, and, against one wall, a deep fireplace of red brick with a simple wooden mantelpiece. Over the fireplace hung a portrait of a young man and woman with their arms around each other.

"That was my one extravagance," she said. "I had it painted from a picture I found in my mother's scrapbook. The rest of this stuff I bought at flea markets or rummage sales."

"It's really something," Joe said, wandering around the room. Above them, in the part of the room that had no ceiling, the peaked roof of the house seemed high. "You won't be too cold in the winter?"

"I had them insulate between the rafters before they paneled the inside. I think it'll be okay."

"What's the loft for?" In one half of the room the wooden ceiling and attic remained but had been finished off with a triangular wall. "And how in the world do you get up there?"

Rachel pointed toward a slender, rod-shaped handle that hung down from the ceiling. When Joe pulled on it, it brought a portion of the ceiling about as big as a door slowly downward on a set of hinges. As this hatch tilted open, a set of stairs, built on rollers and fixed to runners on the upper face of the hatch, slid gently down until the bottom step came to rest on the floor below. "Ingenious," said Joe.

"It's just for storage," Rachel said. "I keep the other seasons up there."

"Other seasons?"

"This is summer," she said, looking around the great room.

In October Rachel traded the wicker, the white spread, the blow-fish and the seashells, the colored glass and pillows for a big wooden blanket box, cream-colored drapes, a patchwork bedspread, an over-stuffed chair, and the dozen wooden creatures that Joe had carved for her during the summer, among them a sandpiper and a miniature cat.

Rachel was curled up in the fat chair, reading a book and half sleeping one Saturday morning in October when she heard a knock at her door, the sound of it opening, and a voice, down below, yelling, "Hey, Rachel. It's me, Angela. Come on out and play."

"Go away," she yelled back.

"No kidding, Rachel. Get your ass down here."

Which is when it occurred to Rachel that Angela should have been at the Kitchen, busy with the last of the breakfast crowd.

"What's wrong?" she said, hopping down the stairs with her shoes half on.

"Everything or nothing, depending."

"Depending on what?"

"Depending on how you feel about Belle Haven's dearly departed." She opened the door and stepped out onto the porch.

Rachel threw on her coat. "What?"

"Just follow me, pal," Angela said, her apron hanging out from underneath her coat, nurse's shoes on her feet. "And bring your keys."

They took Rachel's truck down the hill, over the bridge, past the Kitchen, toward the western edge of town, to park outside the church where Rachel's parents had always taken her. There were already a number of cars along the street, and the church lot was full.

"Come on, Angela. What's going on?"

"I honestly don't know for sure, Rachel. Rusty came busting into the Kitchen a little while ago with some wild story about skeletons surfacing out here, and everybody decided to come and have a look, I guess. Ophelia didn't even finish her waffles, which is a first as far as I know. Rusty was back on his bike before anybody could get another word out of him. So I finished making pancakes, left my mother in charge, and decided to see what's up. Not skeletons, I hope."

Rachel didn't say a word. She knew how Angela must be feeling, despite the wisecracks. Angela's father was buried here. So were her grandparents. Rachel's, too. There was nothing to be laughing about, if what Rusty had said was true.

It was, but the state of things in the graveyard at the edge of town might have remained hidden forever if not for the fact that Sophia Browning missed her husband.

After her house had burned ten months before, Sophia had moved to Randall to live with her son and his family. She had missed everything about Belle Haven, but most of all she had missed her daily walk to the graveyard to visit her darling Otto, talk to him, cry for him, remember him. It was so difficult, now, to come every day from Randall. She could not drive; her son and his wife were too busy to take her more than once a week. And so, even though she had never imagined leaving Belle Haven herself or disturbing her husband's remains, she had finally talked to the authorities about the laws that governed the handling of the long dead.

What she discovered alarmed her: that the fire far underground—never any worse than a bit of smoke and a bad smell—may already have displaced the remains interred in Belle Haven's Presbyterian graveyard. "We've warned people, the last five years or so, about such a possibility," she was told. "But people just ignore us, generally."

"Nobody ever warned me," Sophia protested.

"When did your husband die?" they asked her.

"January, 1965," she said.

"Well, there you go," they said. "The fire hadn't even started yet back then."

"But what is there to worry about, anyway? I don't care if the coffin's a bit singed, as long as it's in one piece. As long as it can be moved." As she talked, she tried to pretend this was not her Otto they were discussing. She tried not to think about him at all.

"Ma'am, we think that maybe some of the remains may have been *displaced*. That's what we're talking about here."

"Displaced! What do you mean, displaced?"

"Gone," they said.

And so she had made up her mind, right then and there, to move Otto. It might have been difficult anywhere else, but Belle Haven wasn't like anywhere else. All it took was permission, quickly granted, and hired people who knew how to manage such things. It surprised Sophia that there were such people, and that they were listed in her yellow pages.

"I want to be there when you move him," she insisted, and so she was. Much to her endless regret.

Otto had not been displaced. Not really. But his coffin was simply gone, reduced to ash and splinters. By the time their shovels reached him, Otto had been for years exposed to the heat of the fire and the brutal invasion of underground things. Not expecting this, one of the diggers had scooped Otto's skull onto the blade of his shovel. There had been no coffin to slow his stroke, and he had tossed the skull out onto the grass before he'd even realized what he'd unearthed.

Sophia, closer than she should have been, saw the skull roll across the grass, flakes of dirt falling from it as it bumped along. She screamed at the sight and then ran away, around the church and straight into it, screaming all the while.

It took no time for the news to spread, for a crowd to assemble at the hot little graveyard. Angela and Rachel arrived as Sophia emerged from the church, her son and his wife at her side.

"Put him back," she told the diggers, who had covered the skull with a bucket. "Put him back carefully, just the way he was, and fill the grave back in." At the look on their faces, she bared her teeth and shook her head. "I'll pay you for your time," she said, and went on back to Randall.

"What are you going to do?" Rachel asked Angela on their way back to the Kitchen.

"Fix lunch, I guess."

"About your *dad,* Angie."

"About my dad? What's there to do? I'd rather be boiled in oil than dig him up. If he's like Otto is . . . well, I guess it doesn't make much difference to him. And if he's not there at all, I really don't want to know about it. I happen to believe that there's nothing really important down there anyway."

"Me, too," Rachel said, thinking of her grandparents, the cast-iron ring that hung next to her kitchen sink, and the sight of her parents' ashes as they'd melted in the icy water of Raccoon Creek.

Chapter 25

Always an especially spooky event in Belle Haven, Halloween that year was truly unnerving, for Otto's exhumation was still on everyone's mind and those who had seen his skull come pitching out of the grave could not forget it. Some of the smaller children, too nervous to go trick-or-treating, had Halloween parties at home. Even the older children stayed clear of the land above the tunnels, for it was a moonless night, full of wind and raccoons on the prowl.

Rachel, in the willow tree in the park, was busier than she'd ever been. She had made herself an octopus costume, with tentacles that she draped over the branches, a huge, bulbous body, red eyes, and a sharp beak. To make up for the tardy moon, she put fresh batteries in her biggest flashlights, stretched red cellophane over their lamps, and taped them to the tree trunk above her so that she was bathed in a red glow.

The children were impressed.

"Golly, Rachel, is that you?" asked Rusty.

"Who's Rachel?" she croaked, weaving and nodding in the tree above. "Come a little closer now, and I'll give you a sucker."

When the children sidled up, she let out a shriek and swung a tentacle at them, which they loved. Then she tossed down some lollipops and sent them away.

This was a strange night for Rachel. Halloween always had been. As a young child, she had toddled around the town with the other children, collecting candy, saying Boo! at people. But when she was nine, several things had happened.

First, she had wanted to be Captain Hook, but her mother, insisting that no little girl could be a pirate, had dressed her as a milkmaid instead. Swinging a metal pail, she had gone out after sunset with her friend Caroline, who was dressed as Red Riding Hood. Before they'd gotten very far, Caroline had stumbled on her cloak and fallen, bloodied her nose, skinned her hands, and banged up her knee so she could barely walk. Rachel had helped her home and left her there, intending to join the next batch of children that came down the street. But, standing in Caroline's front yard, she had become captivated by the stars and by the feeling of being completely alone, invisible in the night, on her own.

It had taken her only a few minutes to scamper down the street to the park and up into the branches of the big willow where her father had taught her to climb trees. From there, she had watched the other children making their way down Maple Street. She had heard Frank up at the Gas 'n' Go, howling his werewolf howl. She had giggled softly at the sound of shrieks and monstrous growls. It was fantastic. No one knew where she was. No one could see her up here. She had collected a little bit of candy before Caroline's fall, which she now ate. It was the best candy she had ever eaten. Nothing, in fact, had ever tasted so good.

She had stayed in the tree for a long time. Even when her muscles began to cramp and her tailbone to tingle, even when Frank had stopped howling and porch lights had begun to go out, Rachel stayed in the tree. The wind sounded different in the darkness than it ever had before. This could almost be a different town. She could almost be a different girl. But not a milkmaid.

When she got home that night, later than they'd expected her to be, Rachel's parents had scolded her mildly. "We were starting to get worried," they said. "Is that all the candy you got? You ought to have a bushel by now."

"My shoelace came untied on the bridge," she told them, "so I set my bucket down on the rail and I tied my shoe and then I knocked the bucket over by accident and the candy fell into the creek. Most of it anyway." She pulled a few crumpled wrappers from her apron pocket. "I ate the rest," she said. It was the only lie she could ever remember telling her parents.

The next year, and for every year after that, she made sure to collect plenty of candy before parting company with her friends and heading for the willow tree alone.

Now, grown up, her parents dead, Rachel did not consider it odd to be sitting in the old willow, an elaborate octopus, a cherry lollipop in her mouth, waiting for children to seek her out. No odder, at least, than Frank in his werewolf costume or Joe as a troll laying claim to the bridge. Belle Haven, she thought to herself, tentacles swinging lightly in the black breeze, is a town that praises its oddities. "I am what I am," she said out loud, somewhat fiercely. But it came out as Popeye always said it—"I yam what I yam"—and, spoken by a young woman dressed as an octopus, clutching a lollipop, it lacked what she had intended: conviction at least, if not certainty.

Inside, somewhere near the place where memories of Otto Browning still lingered, Rachel felt a hollowness that her solitude could not in any way explain. But then a new passel of children came across the park toward her, and there was suddenly no reason to be anywhere else.

Chapter 26

As winter approached, Rachel climbed up into the loft at the top of her house and brought down her cold-weather things. At the windows, she hung sapphire blue drapes. In front of the fireplace, she placed a huge oriental carpet (her second extravagance), two comfortable chairs, an old butter box full of books, and a good floor lamp. To her bed she added a comforter half a foot thick, for the room was not quite as warm as she'd hoped.

The basement was not so cold, for the old furnace ducts passed through it on their way upstairs. Gloomy as it was, and sometimes damp, the basement was where Rachel spent a good deal of her time that winter, for she had bought herself a potter's wheel and a kiln, put them in her basement, and picked up right where she had left off in the eighth grade, making pots and plates and vases for no other reason than that she liked to. She liked the feel of the cool, wet clay. She liked the way it evolved so quickly from one shape to the next with the slightest movement of a finger or a wrist. She liked not knowing quite how something was going to turn out until she opened the lid of the kiln.

Sometimes, after the Kitchen was closed and while Dolly tended Rusty in the apartment above, Angela would climb the hill to Rachel's house with a bottle of questionable wine and a bucket of chicken.

"Yessir, this is just what I thought I'd be doing in my twenty-ninth year. Sitting in a moldy basement, eating cold chicken out of a pail, watching you make whatever the hell that is you're making. What the hell is that, anyhow?"

"It's a honey pot."

"A honey pot." Angela poked through the chicken in search of a leg. "A honey pot? You're sitting here in your basement making honey pots? While the infamous, luscious Joe walks the world above? You're off your nut, girl."

Rachel let her wheel spin, picked up her wineglass with wet, gray fingers, and took a long drink. "Yech," she said. "Next time bring beer."

"Pardon the hell out of me." Angela finished the chicken leg and washed her hands in the laundry tub. Her knuckles were red and scaly from too much washing. "So where is Joe tonight?"

"How should I know? I see him when I see him. He never calls, never tells me where he's going to be or when he's coming by. He just shows up here."

"Hmmm. You don't sound too pleased about it."

"That's because I'm not."

Angela poured herself another glass of wine. She wandered around the basement, liking the feel of the hard dirt floor under her feet and the smell of cold stone. "Let me ask you something, Rachel," she said, cocking her head at the ceiling. "Which would you rather have: a man who loves you truly but doesn't always act like it, or a man who's not really in love with you—and you know he's not—but he does everything right. Flowers now and then, slow sex, conversation, the works."

"God, what a question."

"Well, here you are complaining that Joe doesn't pay enough attention to you, but we both know how he feels."

"We do?"

"Well, *I* do."

"He's never said he loves me."

"That's my whole point. Would you rather have someone who truly loves you or someone who makes all the right moves? And don't say both. Such things have been known to happen but hardly ever."

Rachel stared at Angela, the pot spinning between her palms. "It sounds to me like you've given this an awful lot of thought, Angie."

"Yes, I have."

Rachel lifted her hands and straightened her back. "Okay," she said. "I guess if I had to choose, I'd keep what I've got."

"Of course you would."

"Which doesn't mean it's perfect."

"I never said it was."

Rachel thought a lot about such things that winter. A week before Christmas, when Joe showed up at her house to bake cookies, she was at first tempted to send him home. She hadn't heard from him in days, but she knew he'd been to town: Angela had fed him supper more than once, and Earl had sold him a new chisel. But there he stood on her front porch, his cheeks blazing, his shoulders hunched against the cold. Ian's truck sat in her driveway, knocking softly. Looking past him, down the hill toward her neighbors, Rachel could see chimney smoke. The cold night air was tinted with the color of Christmas lights. Joe opened the paper sack in his arms: he had brought with him sugar, flour, butter, chocolate chips and coconut, raisins, even vanilla, dear as it was, and the first set of cookie cutters he'd ever owned.

"Come on in," she said after a moment and led him to the kitchen.

They baked Toll House cookies, cinnamon stars, butter thins, pinwheels, and maple curls. It took them hours. By the time they were finished, the kitchen was hot and gritty with spilled sugar, but there were cookies everywhere, cooling, and Rachel was glad he had come.

"I missed you this week," she said to him, around midnight, as they sat at the kitchen table, eating cookies and drinking cold milk.

"But you slept, didn't you?"

"Of course. Didn't you?"

"I suppose," he said. "It wasn't easy."

"I'll bet that Schooner is damned cold," she said, grinning.

Joe put down his milk and picked up her hand. "I have a lot of good reasons for living out there, cold as it is, but it's hard to remember them when I'm here with you."

He stood up and leaned across the table, pulling her toward him so he could kiss her. She licked a trace of sugar from his cheek. "You taste good," she murmured.

"Come on," he said, leading her toward the stairs.

Her bedroom was very cold. As he took off Rachel's clothes, Joe could feel her warming the air around them. He felt incapable of letting her go, even for a moment.

When she wrapped her arms around him so that her breasts swept across the cloth of his shirt, Rachel felt herself loosen inside. She stepped back then, quickly, to help him off with his clothes and pull the blankets from her bed. When they lay down on the freezing sheets, they gasped and shuddered. It was so cold, their bodies so insistent, that neither of them wanted to wait another moment.

Joe lay down upon Rachel and she was instantly warmed. She brought her legs up around him, stroked him with her thighs, with both hands pulled his head down and kissed him slowly, her lips slack, every inch of her drenched in longing.

As much as they could, they made love gradually, each stroke bringing sounds from their throats. But when Joe paused to give himself time, to slow his body, Rachel slapped her hands down against the small of his back and hurried them so that it was quickly over, leaving them sated, smiling, wrapped together until their skins began to chill, and then, beneath the blankets, they were asleep.

After a while, Rachel woke and remembered the cookies in the kitchen below. She crept downstairs and put them all away, then returned to Joe where he lay, deeply sleeping, as perfect as she needed him to be.

She lay next to him for a long time, thinking about the question that Angela had asked her, and about Joe's reasons for staying in Belle Haven, and about her own.

The next morning, after Joe had left, Rachel got into her truck and headed for Randall. There were two things she wanted to buy.

First she went to see Mr. Murdock, the lawyer who had helped put her parents' affairs in order and who was now helping her to manage her own, considerable estate.

Rachel had always impressed Mr. Murdock as being a very sensible young woman: she had invested her money wisely and then left nearly all of it alone, comported herself well, did not seem given to costly whims or gestures. Which is why he was so surprised by the request she made that morning.

"I'm not sure I understand," he said. When he raised his eyebrows, his forehead wrinkled up into his thinning hair. "You want to buy up Belle Haven?"

"Not right now," she said, aware that he would think her odd no matter how she explained herself. "And not all of it. Obviously I can't afford more than a few pieces. But what I'd like you to do is start investigating whether or not the government has any plans to relocate or otherwise meddle with us. I've seen a lot of unfamiliar cars around town and too many strangers in city clothes. They've been asking a lot of questions, writing down the answers. They aren't reporters." She was not concerned with Mr. Murdock's opinion of her, but she could not help seeing herself through his watchful eyes and she knew she would have to forgive him for the look he now gave her. "And the man who has always been in charge of fire intervention, as they call it—although he hasn't done any intervening to speak of—has been around a lot, too, even though he doesn't seem to have any new project in the works."

"All of which you take to mean that the government has thrown in the towel, given up trying to fight the fire, and is now trying to identify residents who may soon be at risk." Rachel was pleased to hear how it sounded coming from him.

"Actually," she said, "the government seems to think that some of the families living over by the tunnels already *are* at risk and ought to be moved. At least that's my impression."

"What gives you that impression?"

"I just told you."

"Well, Rachel, a few strangers in town doesn't necessarily mean that the government's planning to relocate anyone."

Rachel looked at him. "You heard about the problems in the graveyard?"

Mr. Murdock began to straighten a paper clip. "Yes, of course."

"Things have been different since then. The families out around there *have* heard from the government."

Mr. Murdock sighed. "All right, Rachel." He thought through his questions and ordered them quickly. He was a good lawyer. "You've talked to these families?"

"A couple."

"And do they want to be moved?"

"No."

"They don't consider themselves to be at risk?"

"No more than for the past eight or nine years. They want to stay right where they are."

"How many families are living directly above the tunnels?"

"Directly?"

"Yes."

"Four or five, spread out, on big lots. And the church, of course. A few more families close by. Maybe half a dozen."

"And the government has approached all of them?"

"Some sort of surveyors have. From the Department of Community Affairs, whatever that is. They're asking how people would feel about selling their property if conditions worsen, is how they put it."

"Like if people start getting sick or their houses start burning down."

"I guess that's the kind of stuff they're suggesting might happen."

"I see." Mr. Murdock leaned back in his chair and tossed the paper clip onto his blotter.

"So if I confirm that the government does indeed have a plan to buy out these families, you want me to . . ." He made a beckoning motion with one hand.

". . . get there first."

"Buy their land?"

"Buy it in my name, pay whatever the government is offering. More, if those people really are at risk. Whatever I can afford. We can talk about the price when the time comes."

"Mind if I ask why?"

"Why do I want to buy their property?"

"For starters."

"Because once the government gets a foothold in Belle Haven, once it's had to dish out money for some 'worthless' land, it will find a way to turn things to its advantage. What good are a few acres of land over a burning mine? But several hundred acres—*all* of our property—would be worth having. And once people are running scared, they'll probably sell out for a lot less than their land is worth."

Mr. Murdock rocked forward again and planted his elbows on his desk. The young woman across from him looked so earnest that he was tempted to see the situation her way, take her word for things, say something to make her smile. But he was a lawyer.

"Forgive me, Rachel. I know Belle Haven is your town, and it's a beautiful place, but the government won't be able to force any of you to sell your land unless there's an authentic threat. A serious one. And if that's the case, why would the government want the land? Why would *you* want to own it either, or to stay on it, for that matter?"

Rachel was glad to find that for each of Mr. Murdock's questions she had a ready answer. "I think it's reasonable to assume that the government would be interested in cheap land that's probably still got plenty of coal in it. As for the threat, the degree of it . . . ever since the government realized the fire was going to be difficult and costly to contain, we've been hearing various official assessments of our situation. Ten years ago they told us the fire would spread along the coal seams that radiate out from the tunnels and we'd all be forced to leave, probably within a year or two. Five at most. Well, it's true that the fire runs off course and burns along coal seams and comes up in odd places, but it has never wandered far from the tunnels. Even the people who live right above them have never seen more than smoke out there, and the only reason there's even smoke is because the government drilled holes to vent some of it. So why should I be alarmed by what they tell us?

"There may be a threat to Belle Haven," she said, leaning forward in her chair, "and the government is certainly broadcasting that fact, but it's a distant one at best that has not yet harmed a single living soul. In other places, there are all kinds of threats—crime, pollution, poverty—but because these dangers *are* so pervasive, so *visible,* and because no one can be sure who will be the next target, the government doesn't bother to broadcast the danger or buy out potential victims.

"Given the choice between staying in Belle Haven where I've been pegged as the eventual target of an invisible threat or moving to some place where statistics *claim* I'll survive a million *visible* dangers, I'll stay right where I am."

Mr. Murdock raised an eyebrow and sighed again. "There's no law that says you have to move to a city," he said in a reasonable tone. "There are lots of nice, safe, friendly little towns around here."

"Of course there are," she said. "But can you guarantee me that if I move, someone won't eventually come to my door with the news that I'm living too close to some toxic dump or power lines, or that they're going to build a highway through my backyard? I've thought about this a lot, Mr. Murdock, and I'd rather stick with the devil I know."

Sensing that there was nothing he could say to her that would weigh more heavily than her own conclusions, Mr. Murdock simply picked up his pencil and opened a fresh file.

"If it's taken ten years for the government to get this far, it may take them another ten to take the next step," he said.

"That's what I'm hoping," she said. "For once I'm glad the wheels of government turn as slowly as they do. But I'm sure they'll be watching things closely and that if the opportunity arises to take control of Belle Haven, they'll move far more quickly than they have so far. Which is why I want you to be ready when the time comes."

Mr. Murdock stopped himself from shaking his head. He tried not to sigh. "You know you're right when you say you could never afford much of the town."

"No. But if I can buy enough key properties here and there to prevent them from obtaining a solid block of land, they might not try to buy any more than the few pieces where the threat from the fire might actually materialize."

Determined to be sure that he understood her, and she him, Mr. Murdock said slowly, "But if the government says that the threat *is* real and offers to buy people out, and if you can't afford to buy up all of their land, you do acknowledge that some people *should* sell to them."

"You're worried that I might become a rabble-rouser, organize some kind of protest?" She shook her head. "I won't interfere with a legitimate plan to assist people at risk. But I don't believe the majority of people in Belle Haven will ever be threatened by the fire. And if they aren't convinced of a serious and immediate danger, most of them will never choose to leave. Never."

Mr. Murdock looked at her carefully, his smile in check. "You seem to expect the government to exaggerate the danger in order to obtain land, Rachel."

"I think such a thing is conceivable."

"You don't have a lot of faith in government."

"If they had spent enough time, money, and effort on Belle Haven in the beginning when the fire was just getting started, we wouldn't be having this discussion. As it is, they've spent far more than that in the past decade, playing catch-up. And they haven't caught up yet."

He'd asked good questions. She'd given him complete answers. Still, he was convinced that there was more to this than met the eye. Here was a young woman, a beautiful young woman, who had chosen to leave school a year shy of her degree and live on her own in a town too small and too remote to provide the culture or the excitement—or the opportunities, for that matter—that she might be expected to seek.

He didn't know that she had isolated herself in other, even more unusual ways. He didn't know that most of her friends—like Angela and Ian and Earl—were older than Rachel by years. He didn't know that she had drifted clear of her childhood companions in favor of these mentor-friends, or that, with the exception of Joe, she'd felt close only to those who had known her parents well and understood the depth of her love for them. She had always felt different from her classmates, but she was now unwilling to overlook these differences. If old friends like Estelle were puzzled by her, so be it. She didn't care.

Had Mr. Murdock known these things, he too might have found Rachel even more puzzling than he did. But she would not have cared about this either.

"You're determined to stay in Belle Haven, then?" he asked. "Despite everything?" He was talking about her parents but could not bring himself to say so.

"It's where I belong," she said.

As Rachel was leaving his office, Mr. Murdock called her back. "You haven't told me what you plan to do with all this land . . . if people are forced to sell it . . . if you buy it. Or haven't you thought that far ahead?"

"That's the easy part," she said, smiling. "I'll just keep it until they're ready to buy it back."

Of all the things Rachel had said to him that morning, this last was the part that troubled him most.

"Have a nice day," he said, but she was already out the door.

After leaving Mr. Murdock's office, Rachel went straight to the Randall animal shelter to get Joe a Christmas present. It was not easy for her to choose one: every puppy, seen through the bars of a cage, looked desperately in need of a home. A few of them were recognizable breeds in their trademark coats and bones, but most were unapologetically mutts, cheap, their lineage uncertain, unique.

Rachel held each of them before finally settling on a young mutt, a female, who looked into her eyes with great confidence and laid her tiny muzzle against Rachel's neck.

Rachel was afraid to keep the pup at her house for fear it would quickly come to think of it as home and Joe as some sort of substitute for her. So she drove out to Ian's place on her way back from Randall and found Joe at the Schooner, fixing his lunch.

"Good, I'm starved," she said, stepping inside. "What are we having?"

"Soup."

"Perfect." She lifted the lid off the pot and let the steam bathe her face. "What did you do this morning?"

"Helped fix a barn roof over in Jupiter."

"Jupiter? How'd you get way over there?"

"Bike."

"Holy cow! Ten miles each way? In this cold? Are you out of your mind?"

"The Schooner gets touchy in this weather. And Ian went off early in the truck. But it wasn't so bad," he said, smiling, his teeth still chattering as he boiled water for their tea. "Better than walking."

It was at times like this that Rachel felt uncomfortable about her money, his lack, and the impossibility of offering to help him. She suddenly realized how difficult it might be for him to feed a dog, especially if the pup that waited out in her truck grew up to be a big one.

"Before we eat," she said, "I want to give you your Christmas present."

"No way," he said, putting out bread and butter. The table was already set with a jug of milk, cheese, and apples. "Nothing before Christmas morning. That's the rule."

"Not this time," she said. "Stay right there. And no peeking." Joe watched the door swing behind her and thought about his great good fortune.

A moment later she stuck her head into the Schooner. "Ready?" she asked.

"Ready."

"Close your eyes."

"Didn't you even wrap it?"

"No, I didn't wrap it. Shut your eyes."

Joe closed his eyes. Rachel stepped into the Schooner and shut the door behind her, the puppy inside her coat. When she stepped close to him, Joe swung his arms out toward her, eyes still closed. "Let me guess," he said. "You. In Saran Wrap."

"Wrong, you oaf. You can open your eyes now."

Joe opened his eyes. "Well?"

"Merry Christmas," Rachel said, stepping closer, and opened her coat just enough to let the puppy poke its nose against Joe's chest.

He gently lifted the puppy up against his neck and held it there for a moment, speechless. Even though he could not yet know what this dog would come to mean to him, he felt an immediate and escalating happiness that moved him nearly to tears.

"Thank you, my wonderful girl," he said, kissing her, while the soup bubbled over and the teakettle screamed. "He?" he asked.

"She," she said, smiling, tending to their lunch.

"What'll we name her?"

"How about Noël. For Christmas."

"Nah, that's a real girl's name. She's got to have a dog's name."

"What, like Bowser?"

"Better than Noël," he said, setting her down gently on the floor, where she immediately peed.

"Marking her territory," Rachel said, stepping out of range.

Joe said, "That's all right." He cleaned up the mess, poured a bit of milk into a pan, and began to warm it. "Fortune," he said. "How's that sound?"

"She's your dog," Rachel said, pouring soup.

Joe watched the pup waddle around the Schooner. "I wonder what she'll look like when she's full grown."

"Like a bigger mutt," Rachel said.

"Perfect," he said. "Friendliest dogs on earth."

"You can't leave her alone in the Schooner all day, you know. You're going to have to take her with you places or find someone to look after her when you're working."

"No shit, Einstein. I'll rig up a carrier on the back of the bike for when she's tiny. When she's big she can run. And I'll drop her at your place on really nasty days."

"I have an idea. Why don't you drop her at my house on really nasty days?"

"Wish I'd thought of that. Thanks, Rachel. You're a pal."

"Now *there's* a better name."

"Pal?"

"Better than Fortune."

"I suppose." And he did call her Pal, for all her born days.

Chapter 27

When spring arrived, Rachel took down the blue curtains, shook them clean, and stashed them up in her loft. She made long and narrow ceramic bowls, filled them with water, white pebbles, and flower bulbs, and put them to wait on the windowsills. She rolled the oriental rug and lugged it up into the loft, swept the fireplace clean. At a garage sale in Fainsville she found a lemon yellow throw for the bed, hung rounds of stained glass in the windows to enrich the thin April sun. She topped her bookshelves with more of Joe's creations: a mermaid, a perfect acorn, a horse's hoof, a polished bowl that she put odd pebbles in. Of these, the mermaid was and always would be her favorite.

When she planted seeds that spring, she put some into urns and jugs she'd made on her wheel and set them out in the sun. She didn't give much thought to her reasons for doing this. She liked her pots and thought they looked lovely in her garden.

"Nobody just suddenly decides to plant a moveable garden," Joe said as he lay in her hammock with Pal and watched her transplant a clump of pincushions into a big purple pot. "Not without a reason."

"Why do I need a reason?"

"Forget it," he said, closing his eyes. He was tired of talking. There were too many things that Rachel would not discuss, too many things he could not disregard. Like Otto Browning's detached skull. Like the mine rats that were suddenly much more numerous—much more alarming with their slick pink tails and their white-thorn teeth—than they had been since their first exodus from the mines over a decade earlier. And, most recently, like what had happened at the Hutter place, and then soon after to Rebecca Sader.

On the day of the first good thaw that spring, when the last stubborn inches of snow had melted off the grass, a man named Bill Hutter, who lived four long blocks from the mine tunnels, had gone outside to find a sheet of ice across his lawn. It was a good inch thick and too hard to break with his boot. Nobody else had ice. Everybody else had good, wet grass, already greening under the snow. His, through the ice, looked gray.

Nobody could think of an explanation for the ice except that something had melted the snow that lay closest to the ground and that the slush had frozen solid soon after. Rachel was not interested in explanations. When Joe brought it up, she changed the subject. And before long it became old news, for the ice melted in the strengthening sun and the lawn beneath it survived.

The greater mystery, the one that Joe had brought to Rachel this very morning, having heard about it from Angela over breakfast, was stranger, more frightening.

Rebecca Sader was not an overly dramatic woman. She was not flighty. She was, in fact, sensible, practical, and calm. But according to her husband, Doug, she had gotten mixed up somehow, the night before.

"She nearly cooked herself in the shower." He pronounced it *shar,* waited while Angela warmed his cup. "You know how you do something a million times without even thinking about it, but as soon as you give it any thought a'tall, you're not quite sure you're doing it right?"

Angela nodded, her ponytail bobbing. "Happens to me all the time."

"Well, Becca was in the shower last night, and after a while it started to get too hot. So she turned back the hot a bit, but that didn't help. So she turned up the cold. It just got hotter, she says. So instead of just turning it off she got all in a tizzy, and I guess she got the handles mixed up and shut off the cold, left the hot on by mistake. I don't know. She ended up doing the standing long jump outta the tub. Anyway, I was already in bed, sound asleep. First thing she says this morning when we wake up is, 'Doug, there's no cold water.' 'Whatdya mean, no water. The well can't be dry.' 'No *cold* water,' she says. 'Whatdya mean, no cold water?' I says. 'How could you run outta *cold* water?' She gets outta bed, drags me into the bathroom, turns on the cold tap, and whatdya think comes out?"

"Cold water?"

"Cold water," Doug said. "Cold as you please. But don't tell her I told you. She made me promise to keep my mouth shut."

But it was Rebecca herself who spread the news. She knew how it sounded. She knew people might think she'd made a silly, stupid mistake by nearly scalding herself, by talking about it afterward. But she knew—she *knew*—that she had made no mistake. The water that had come boiling down on her back had come straight up from the well, and it should have been cold. Somehow, the water in the well had become hot and then, by morning, cold again.

But as soon as she began to talk about the fire coming up under the well, people stopped listening. Sophia Browning's house had stood three country blocks from the tunnels. Bill Hutter's ice-locked lawn was just a block farther away than that. But Rebecca and Doug Sader lived a *half mile* from the nearest tunnel. Lots of people lived closer, and none of them had ever had hot wells. Unless you counted the people right over the tunnels, who had to be careful whenever they ran a bath. But that was different.

"Why is that different?" Joe had asked Rachel when he'd brought her the news about the Saders' well.

"All kinds of things go on out over the tunnels. Their gardens aren't much good anymore. Their basements are hot sometimes. That's to be expected. They're used to that sort of thing. But you can't go around assuming that every odd thing that happens in Belle Haven has something to do with the fire. Especially not as far from the tunnels as the Saders live."

Which is when Joe suddenly rose up from the hammock and asked Rachel why she was digging up her garden and putting it, piecemeal, into pots.

Chapter 28

By July Rachel had decked her room out in its summer things again and Belle Haven was ready to celebrate Independence Day in its own, inimitable way. The country was turning 206 years old, the fire 12, and the people of Belle Haven made the most of both events.

There was, of course, the parade down Maple Street. There were picnics and baseball games, fireworks and painted faces. But there were other things, too: things that did not take place in other American towns. There was, every Fourth of July in Belle Haven, a gathering over an obliging hot spot. When night came on, enough wood was pitched into the glowing hole to make a magnificent bonfire. Everyone sang "The Star Spangled Banner," "America the Beautiful," "My Country 'Tis of Thee," marched around to "You're a Grand Old Flag," while the volunteer fire department tossed small fireworks into the hot spot and let the fire set them off. No rockets, though. Nothing meant to fly. Just color, and light, and enough bang and sizzle to make the babies cry.

It was at these outlandish fireworks that Joe finally met Mendelson, the firefighter.

They had, of course, heard of each other. Belle Haven was too small for anonymity. They had seen each other, too, from time to time. But they had never before met.

Joe had gone out to the hot spot—which had come up in the middle of a big tomato field—to please Rusty, but after a while he said good night.

"You're not leaving yet?" Ian was sitting in an old lawn chair with his pipe and a supply of sparklers. Rusty stood behind him, chewing on a stem of grass, his face bathed with firelight. Angela and Rachel were over with the firemen, begging them to throw something more dramatic into the flames: what, they did not know. All around the hot spot, the tomatoes had baked black. At a safe distance, the spectators, all of whom understood the value of farm goods, had carefully taken up posts in between the rows of plants, like an eccentric battalion.

"I guess I am," Joe replied. "If I could just look at the fire from the ground up, like you all do . . . but I can't. It's too spooky, to me."

"You think that's how we look at it? From the ground up?"

Joe stuck his hands in his pockets, looked back toward the fire. Rachel and Angela made precise, black figures against its glow. "Look at them, Ian," he said. "You think they're afraid?"

"Things aren't always how they appear," Ian said. Rusty watched the fire, waited patiently for the firemen to throw something into the flames.

"Well," Joe said, "Pal's a little nervous, too, so I think I'll take her home."

"Where is she?" Rusty asked.

Joe whistled, and Pal came trotting into the light. But when an emerald plume came whistling up out of the hot spot, she stopped short, wheeled on her hind legs, and plunged away. "Come here, you big chicken," Joe called, but Pal stayed where she was. "So long," he said, stepping carefully between the crowded tomato plants. "You going after trout tomorrow, Rusty?"

"You bet."

"Can I come along?"

"You bet."

"Good night," Ian called after him, lighting his pipe. "See you back at the ranch? For a nightcap?"

"In the words of Belle Haven's finest trout fisherman," Joe called, without turning around, "you bet."

He found Pal cowering among the infant pines at the edge of the woods. A single touch of his hand behind her ear calmed her. The scent of him made her smile. "Come on, girl," he said, walking along the border of the tomato field, toward the road. It wasn't far from here to Ian's, and it was plenty warm, beautiful, a good night for walking. When he reached the road, he had nothing on his mind except the way the trees looked in the reddish glow. He did not notice Pal stop suddenly. The first he knew of Mendelson was the sound of his laughter, close by.

"Hello, Joe. Had enough?"

Joe stopped, Pal caught up with him, and the two of them stood looking at the man in the road. "Who's that?" Joe asked.

"We haven't met," the man said, stepping forward. "The name's Mendelson."

"Ah," Joe said, taking his hand. It felt as if it were skinned with hoof, hard and dry and cold. "I've heard a lot about you."

"I'll bet you have. And I've heard a lot about you."

"Have you?"

"Well, sure. Strange young man shows up out of nowhere, no last name, no visible means of support. Curiouser and curiouser."

"Not really," Joe said mildly. He couldn't see much of the man's face, but now and then, as Mendelson turned his head, the firelight caught his eyes. "I just got tired of living where I was, so I left."

"And now you're here," Mendelson said.

"And now I'm here."

Mendelson spread his feet and crossed his arms, something that smacked of the military. "I'll bet you didn't know that some of the locals called you in to the FBI."

Joe raised his eyebrows and smiled. "Did they?"

"Yes, indeed. Thought you might be one of the ten most wanted or something, looking for a place to hole up."

"And what did the FBI tell them?"

"Said they didn't want you, but thanks anyway."

"How could they know that, without taking a look?"

"Fingerprints."

"Fingerprints?" Joe began to wonder if Mendelson might not be crazy.

"From a butter knife."

Outside of the Schooner, the only Belle Haven butter knives he'd ever touched belonged to friends.

"Do you always do this when you meet new people? Invent some far-fetched tale, see how they'll react?"

Mendelson chuckled. "I've been accused of a lot of things, Joe, and many of them are true, but I've never been known to lie."

"Uh-huh. Well, it was a pleasure to finally meet you, Mendelson. See you around."

"That you will," he said as Joe walked away. "That you will."

As he made his way home Joe wondered if someone might really have sent his fingerprints to the FBI. The thought made him laugh aloud, but this was an odd place, full of people with odd habits. Anything, he thought, was possible. Mendelson—now there was an eerie man. Standing in the shadows, watching. A flat, awkward laugh, unlikely to spread. A man who had dealt with the same fire for a decade, never making any headway, had to be unhappy in some ways. The way the dark air still looked red, this far from the hot spot, made Joe feel sorry for Mendelson. People seemed not to take this fire too seriously, but surely Mendelson did. Joe himself did, more and more the longer he stayed in Belle Haven.

By now he knew the names of every street in town and of a great many people who lived there. He knew where all the boreholes were, where Mendelson and his men were drilling, measuring, mapping. He knew all about the hot spots as they came and went. And he knew, as few others seemed to know or admit, that the fire was not abating. If anything, it was growing stronger. Or so it seemed to Joe.

The road twisted around a small hollow and rose, gradually, up the slope of a gentle hill. When it flattened out again, Joe could see Ian's fields up ahead and the shape of the woods beyond them. He stopped and looked back toward the town, which cast its own faint light upward, like a dome. In the distance, Rachel's hill rose smoothly up. Narrow valleys here and there plunged down and away. Small fields lay flat and fertile under the sky or sloped up to meet it. And all of this was cast in a subtle shade of orange, as if a foreign moon were preparing to roll up over the horizon.

Always before, as he had crossed Ian's fields with his carving tools, on his way to the dead trees in the woods, the occasional pit of flame in the distance had been easy to avoid, if not ignore. Like a horse with blinders, he had walked the land, the smoke or the fire passing away at the edge of his vision, less commonplace than lightning. But lately, when he glanced back toward town, the tools in his hands felt oddly like weapons. And when he looked at the land that stretched between him and the distant houses, he now felt as if he were on the far side of a border that absent statesmen had only recently laid down.

It was with a sense of relief that Joe reached the Schooner and settled down with Pal to wait for Ian to arrive. This was a place where he had always felt safe, where he knew what to expect and what was expected of him. But for the first time he wondered how much of his comfort depended on the wheels that could someday take the Schooner on its way.

Chapter 29

Out in the woods beyond Ian's fields, in the stand of dead trees, Joe's statue of his sister had weathered to a softer mien, tranquil, as gray as clouds gathering rain. Beside her, Joe had carved a charming, elfish Rusty, unmistakably bright. Next to him Rachel stood wrapped in the bark of a young, dead oak tree, crowned with fragile branches, her eyes all challenge and entreaty. A fourth tree, awaiting its own face, bore the first of Joe's incisions.

It had been more than a year since he had discovered Holly's gold and the site of her resurrection, but in all that time he had brought only Rachel into the woods. He had satisfied Ian's curiosity by telling him he'd found some good wood to carve and would take him out for a look someday.

For Christmas he'd carved for Ian, the stargazer, a plain wooden star from a flawless block of mahogany. The star was as smooth as Rusty's young skin, its undulating grain as alluring as Rachel's hair. "It will always be my Christmas star," Ian had said, turning the polished wood in his gnarled hands. He was silent for a moment or two, and then he said, "I want to see what you're working on out in the woods. When it's all right with you."

On the first Sunday after Independence Day, Joe washed his breakfast dishes, made his bunk, and set out for Ian's house with Pal at his heels. It felt like a good day to take Ian to the woods.

Ian's pickup was in the driveway, and there was a shovel thrust into his garden, but when Joe knocked first on the front door and then the back, Ian did not come.

"Ian," Joe hollered through the screen door. He cupped his hands against the screen and peered into the house. The bathroom door on the far side of the kitchen stood ajar, the shower dry. The cellar door was shut, the bolt shot. "Ian," he called, backing away from the door.

He looked out across the fields, thinking that Ian might have gone walking. "Ian," Joe called, walking toward the plank that bridged the stream at the edge of the fields. Pal, ahead of him, stopped suddenly and looked back over her shoulder.

Ian, who had offered Joe sanctuary, who had seen how alone he was and offered him allegiance, was lying on his back in the clear, restless water of the stream. At first Joe thought he had simply become hot while gardening, fancied a moment in the cool waters of the stream, and become caught up with such dreams and diversions as water often inspires. He thought that Ian simply had not heard him calling, did not hear him at the stream's edge, for he was lying in the shallow water with his ears submerged, his short hair waving like an un-pinned halo, his face dry and pale in the sunlight.

But in the water next to Ian lolled an upended pail. On his hands were gardening gloves. On his feet, good boots. His red shirt and old jeans were swollen with cold water.

"Ian," Joe whispered and went down on his knees. A jay landed on a rock near Ian's boot, jabbed its beak at a stem of berries arcing over the water's edge, and then hopped onto the toe of the boot to ruffle its plumage in the breeze.

Joe waited until the bird had flown, waited until his heart had stopped trembling, and then stepped down into the water of the stream. He gathered Ian up against his chest and staggered onto the grass. He knew he would never be able to carry him to the house alone. He was a heavy man, in wet clothes, his body weighted with the gravity of the dead, impatient for the earth.

Joe knew that if he dragged him, even in a barrow, the sight of his friend bouncing lightly, his hands dragging in the grass, losing their gloves, his heels rutting the lawn would haunt him for the rest of his days. This was Ian, drinker of brandy, singer of songs, teacher, confessor, companion, the sort of man Joe had made up his mind to be.

He sat down with Ian stretched out beside him on the grass, attended by wildflowers, and closed his eyes. He had not prayed much in his life, but he prayed now. He prayed that Ian was somewhere good. He sent a bray of anguish and longing skyward. And he began, quietly, to cry.

He thought of Ian lying alone in the beautiful water, dying, perhaps by conscious degrees, his eyes full of sky, his ears memorizing the sound of pebbles as they shifted in the current, his heart flooding with blood. He thought of Ian realizing that these were his last moments. Giving up his claim to flesh and land and voice. Sorry for the lack of warning, for the fact that he was leaving things undone, yet at the same time grateful to be leaving quickly.

"Good-bye, Ian," Joe said inside his chest. "Good-bye and good-bye and good-bye." And as he gained his feet and started toward the empty house, where he would find a coffee cup on the kitchen table and on the desk a letter just begun, he knew with exhilarating certainty that someday, in the far, immeasurable distance, he would see his friend again.

Chapter 30

"*Ian was my* teacher," Rachel said, looking at the faces of those assembled around his grave. "He taught me about Henry the Eighth and the fall of Rome, showed me how to make pickles, taught me the proper way to splice a rope.

"I never had any uncles, but Ian was a lot like one to me. He and my father were friends, so I got to know Ian pretty well over the years. After my parents died, he told me I could depend on him if I ever needed anything. And I knew I could. He was that kind of man. I never expected him to die so soon." She plucked at the damp sleeve of her dress. It was too hot for long sleeves, but Rachel didn't notice. She had cried for Ian as she had not cried for her own parents—shock and anger over losing them leaving her too clenched for tears—and her eyes were swollen and red.

"I didn't expect him to die at all," she said. "When he did, I sat down and tried to write a poem to read at his funeral. To read here. I sat up all night thinking about Ian, remembering. That's as far as I got. What's in my head wants to stay there.

"But a few days ago I read something that reminded me of Ian. I think he would have liked it, too. It has no title." She opened a small book to a dog-eared page.

Joe, who had been looking at the clouds, lowered his gaze slowly toward Rachel, who stood a bit apart from him, closer to the edge of the grave. From where he was standing he could see part of the page she was reading from and the poet's name at the top of the page.

H. Caldwell. The name stirred something in his brain. But then Rachel began to read, and once again Joe was overcome with thoughts of Ian, and the fact that this was his funeral.

In the thick of the screaming, impolitic gulls
sat a boy
sand on his feet, hair sticky with wind
arms sleeved in salt
clutching in his hands
a bag of old bread.

He tore off a crust, peered at the birds.
Threw it and the wind swept it back.
The birds converged. The boy hastily drew in his feet.
Drew out another bit. Thought about the wind.

His second throw took the bread well out to the birds,
who fought over it as if the sea held nothing to compare.
They paid no attention to the boy.
Their eyes, like fish eyes, left sticky impressions on the bag.

The boy wanted to feel the tops of their heads,
run his hands along the feathers on the tops of their heads.
He wanted them to come closer, orderly like,
and stand still.
He took another crust from the bag and tossed it on the sand.

Then a girl who had been watching from nearby rocks
walked through the mob of birds and spoke quietly to the boy.
Looked out toward the sea. Gestured at the sky. Glared at the birds.
And walked away.
The boy watched her go.
Looked at the birds for a very long time.

Then he threw the feast high through the sun-sated air
and walked away slowly, the bag balled in his pocket,
his arms straight out at his sides,
his hands sweeping through
the most uncelebrated region of the sky.

Rachel closed the book and slipped it into her coat pocket. A woman near her turned and looked into her husband's eyes. He gave a small shrug. Rachel, noticing, smiled. She turned, walked away from the edge of the grave, and stood with Joe while the minister invited the mourners to throw flowers or earth down onto Ian's casket. Without a word, Rachel and Joe declined.

One week later, Joe woke up in the middle of the night and opened his eyes. He lay quietly, waiting for whatever had awakened him to resume. There was thunder in the far distance, but he did not think he had been awakened by thunder. Acorns and twigs sometimes fell loudly onto the Schooner's roof, but there was no wind. On occasion, an arrogant raccoon would scratch its irritable hide against the Schooner's bumper and set everything rocking. The first time this had happened Joe had nearly fainted from fright, but he couldn't remember the last time a raccoon had brought him up out of sleep into this kind of wakefulness.

Gradually, he grew sleepy again. His body grew heavy. His breathing slowed. And then, as his eyelids slid to a close, he remembered.

He climbed out of his bunk and turned on a lamp, pulled an apple crate out of the back of his closet, and removed from it several dusty books and a bouquet of winter gloves. In the bottom of the crate sat the box of gold. Still inside was Holly's letter.

He carried it back to his bunk, sat down, and read it through, once, twice, once again. Then he put the letter back into the box of gold, replaced the books and gloves, slid the crate into the closet, and began to dress.

Rachel awoke to the sound of someone banging on her door. The air pulsed with the sound of the hammering. When she heard a man calling her name, she was certain that his voice was a stranger's, it was so hoarse and terrible.

"Who is it?" she called with both of her palms flat against the door.

The banging stopped. "It's Joe," he said.

When she opened the door, he grabbed her by the hand and pulled her up the stairs, past her cooling bed, and into the corner where she kept her books.

"What's wrong?" she gasped as they stumbled through the darkness. "For God's sake, Joe," she cried as he knocked over a lamp and scrabbled for it in the dark. "Tell me."

"That poem you read at Ian's funeral," he said, breathing more slowly, finding the lamp and switching it on. He got up from his knees, put the lamp gently on the table, and turned to the nearest bookcase. "Would you please show me the book it came from?"

He had terrified her. For a book. And it was in Rachel to throw him out, kick him down her front-porch stairs, sweep sand into his eyes. "You had better have a goddamned good reason for this," she muttered, reaching for a slender book with blue binding.

He seized it from her, turned it over in his hands, opened it. He flipped impatiently past the first page, the second, paused at the third, closed the book, and sat heavily on the floor.

"What did you do with the jacket?" he asked her, using his mouth carefully.

"It was in my way," she said. "It's"—she strode across the room to her desk—"right here." He made no move to regain his feet. She brought the jacket to him, put it in his hands, felt her anger abating as she watched him slowly look at every part of the jacket, read every word on it, and carefully set it aside.

"These poems were written by Harriet Caldwell," he said. "My sister's name was Harriet. Her middle name was Caldwell, my mother's maiden name. My sister was a poet. And I think I was that boy on the beach. The one who didn't understand about birds." He held on to the book like it was a lifeline. "I have to use your phone," he said, and started for the stairs.

Chapter 31

"Mrs. Corrigan?"

"Yes?" the woman said, her voice rough with sleep.

"Ardith Corrigan?" he asked, paused, switched the phone to his other ear. "Look," he said, when she did not immediately reply. "I know it's the middle of the night, but it's important that I speak with Ardith Corrigan. Emily's mother. Are you—"

"Has something happened to Emily?" she said in a rush and then, almost immediately, asked, "Who is this?"

"I'm sorry, Mrs. Corrigan. My name is . . ." And here he had to stop, had to open the lexicon of his former life. "My name is Christopher Barrows." He was astonished that, with Rachel nearby, he had lowered his voice.

"Christopher Barrows?" She was silent for a long moment. Then, "What do you want?"

Taken aback by her tone, he too paused before saying, "If you *are* Emily's mother, I hope you'll be able to tell me where I can reach her."

"Why?"

"Well . . . it's a long story." He was beginning to think he had made a terrible mistake. "I'm trying to find Emily so I can talk to her about my sister, Holly Barrows. They were roommates at Bryn Mawr. Emily—"

"Look, young man," the woman interrupted. "I don't know who you are or what you want, but you had better leave Holly alone."

His hand trembled. He grabbed his jaw. "She's alive?" he asked.

"Who?"

"Holly."

"I'm going to hang up now," said Mrs. Corrigan. It was clear that she was nervous, angry, afraid.

"Don't," he said. "Please listen to me for a moment." He carried the phone over to Rachel's kitchen table and sat down awkwardly, as if his brain were too consumed with what he was saying and what he was hearing to manage anything more. "My name is Christopher Barrows," he said once again. "Most people call me Kit. Or they *did*," he amended. "I have a different name now. I last saw my sister, Holly—Harriet—over two years ago, and a few days after that I learned that she had died."

He heard the gasp, had expected to hear it.

"But she didn't die, did she?" he asked, and even though he had come to suspect this, it wasn't until he heard her say, "Of course not," that he allowed himself to believe it, truly to believe it, and then his relief was so enormous that at first he did not understand what she said next.

"But you did," she said quietly.

"Excuse me?"

"You did," she repeated. "*You* died. Holly's father tracked her down, told her that you had died in a car wreck the day after she left home."

"He told her . . ."

"That you had died. He told her you had died."

"And he told me that she had," he said.

"Oh, my God," Mrs. Corrigan whispered fearfully.

"My own father. My own goddamned father," he said, standing up in the middle of the small kitchen.

"Oh, you poor, poor children," Mrs. Corrigan said, and he heard her begin to cry.

"It's all right, Mrs. Corrigan," he assured her. "Everything's going to be all right now."

And in a safe corner of her own, warm kitchen, Rachel felt the marrow of her bones grow cold.

Almost immediately after calling Mrs. Corrigan, Joe fell asleep on Rachel's couch with Pal at his feet.

As she had on another night, long ago, when Joe had called his father and learned of Holly's death, Rachel sat nearby and watched Joe sleeping. He had changed since that earlier time. Grown thinner. Stronger. His hair was longer, brindled with sun. His hands showed signs of work. And the arrogance that had once hardened his face had been replaced with sensibility, so that even in sleep he appeared to be aware of the world.

Before she returned to her bed, Rachel stopped in front of the mirror at the foot of the stairs and looked at herself. She did not seem to have changed nearly so much.

In the morning Rachel gave Joe breakfast and listened when he told her again, in fits and starts, what his father had done. Through all of it he was preoccupied, dazed. She watched him carefully the way a mother watches an ailing child. She waited for him to touch her, and when he did not, she closed her hands into fists and crossed her aching arms.

After breakfast she waited outside while he called his sister. She waited for a long time. Then she drove him out to the Schooner so he could pack a small bag, took him back to town afterward, to her bank for the money he'd need to get to San Francisco.

"What am I supposed to call you now?" she asked him as they waited for the Greyhound in front of Frank's Gas 'n' Go.

When he turned to her, she saw the sudden warming of his eyes. "Call me what you've always called me," he said, putting his arms around her. "Joe. Just Joe. I love that name." But even as he kissed her she felt him again retreating. And at the sound of the approaching bus, the light again receded from his eyes.

When they could no longer see the bus, Rachel and Pal walked slowly down the street to Angela's Kitchen. She was not hungry, wanted no food, but was not quite ready yet to be alone.

"Joe's gone to see his sister for a week or so," Rachel said. She had decided to spend the afternoon helping Angela make peach cobbler and corn bread while Dolly took care of the tables. It was a hot July afternoon, and the few customers who straggled in off the shimmering street ate cold sandwiches, drank their lemonade from weeping glasses, and wandered off in search of shade.

"His what?" Angela asked, her mouth full of peach.

So Rachel told her what Joe's father had done.

"That son of a bitch," Angela said. "He ought to be shot."

"Well, maybe." Rachel nodded. "He won't see his children again. Or grandchildren, if he ever has any." Rachel chose a peach from the basket at Angela's elbow. "He's a director of several large corporations. He's a trustee at some posh university. One of the Ivies. And he's a consultant for the government. Joe's going to collect his trust fund and put it somewhere safe, and then he's going to write a few letters. Let those places know what kind of a man his father really is."

"Might work," Angela said, her hands glazed with peach juice. "Might not. You know how the world works."

"Maybe it'll make Joe feel better," Rachel said, shrugging.

"You all right?"

"Sure. Why wouldn't I be?"

Angela just shook her head, wiped her hands on her apron.

By the time the supper crowd began to arrive, Angela's face was white, glistening, with red patches mottling her cheeks. She poured a tumbler full of cool water and drank down another tablet of salt.

"Why the hell are we baking corn bread on a day like this?" Rachel muttered. Her thick hair was tied high off her neck, but enough had escaped to cling wherever it touched her hot skin. "Get away from that damned oven, Angie, before you fall in."

"Quit yelling at me," Angela growled. But she closed the oven door, dropped her mitts, and ducked under the counter. "Move over." Rachel made room for her under the ceiling fan. "My kingdom for an air conditioner," Angela groaned.

The next day, a Sears delivery truck pulled up in front of Angela's Kitchen. The driver opened the back doors, pulled down a ramp, hopped inside the truck, and soon reappeared with a big box on a dolly. On top of the box he set a toolbox and a coil of thick yellow extension cord.

"She's a right good girl," Angela said under her breath as she headed for the door.

But Rachel always did the best of her deeds when she felt the devil in her rising.

She knew she should be glad for Joe and Holly both, but instead she felt cranky and spiteful. She wanted to sit in her kitchen and eat everything in her cupboards, jar by jar. She wanted to sleep all day and lie awake in the hammock all night, watching the bats that were a shade blacker than the sky, wondering what the night birds thought of them. Wondering what papayas tasted like. Wondering anything but what Joe was doing without her.

She wanted to feed Pal with tenderloins and fresh eggs until she stopped sitting by the door, her ears cocked toward the road, waiting for the sound of Joe's return. She wanted to go about her business, get on with her life, but she felt too listless to bother with much of anything.

In the evenings she sat on her front porch with Pal, listening to her parents' old records, one after the other, until the stars eased through the fabric of a sky made threadbare by approaching night. The songs left her so sad that she felt almost afraid for herself. She listened to Ed Ames singing "Try to Remember," Andy Williams singing "Moon River," Judy Collins singing about sons.

At night she lay in her bed and imagined Joe eating crabs on Fisherman's Wharf, dancing at a diner in Sausalito, laughing with strangers. She imagined him standing on a beachhead, looking out over the extraordinary Pacific, letting the cold, salty air rush over him, his back firmly toward the east. But most of all she imagined him with Holly.

She couldn't stop thinking of the two of them, a continent away, linked by blood and adversity, two of the strongest bonds there are. Rachel could not imagine that Joe would spend any of this time away thinking about Belle Haven or about her, unless it was to rehearse how to say he wouldn't be coming back. The more she thought about this, the more convinced she became that Joe would be seduced by the West, commit himself to the sister he had long thought dead, and put Belle Haven behind him. She was not hurt that he had gone without her, for it had never occurred to her that she too might go. But it hurt that he had gone at all, even though she understood why he had.

For three days she listened for the phone to ring, and when after that Joe had not called, she unplugged her phone, gagged it with its cord, and threw it under a chair.

On the third night since Joe had left Belle Haven, Rachel dreamed that he was lying in her hammock with his hat over his face, his hands behind his head, his long legs crossed. When she sat down beside him, the hammock tipped him over so that he had to grab her around the waist to keep from falling. And when the hat fell to the ground, she looked down, laughing, and saw that it was not Joe lying there in her hammock but the young man who had fed her ice cream from an unclean bowl, whose sheets she had bloodied, whose face she had all but forgotten. Harry's face. Harry Gallagher. Whose name tasted like bad meat in her mouth.

On the fourth day since Joe's departure, Rachel awoke to the sound of birds outside her window. Listening to the sound of them, she remembered the feel of Joe in her arms.

She knew why she had mixed him up with Harry in her dream, but as she lay in her bed she wondered why Harry's common brand of barbarism had stayed alive in her blood for so long. Perhaps, she thought, what he had done seemed more heinous in the context of her placid adolescence. People had always been kind to her. Belle Haven had been a wonderful place to grow up in. Perhaps, she thought, she had been too lucky. She had certainly been naïve. This town, which had kept her safe, had also kept her from knowing the world. Perhaps, in consequence, Belle Haven had made her a perfect mark.

The birds were still singing. A shaft of sunlight slowly approached her bed. There was a cool breeze coming through the nearest window. "Enough." She sighed, pushing the sheet down and away, swinging her legs off the bed and rising.

She missed Joe. She was angry with him. She wanted him back. But on that spectacular morning she tied back her hair, cuffed her sleeves, grabbed a wicker basket from the pantry, and slammed the door shut behind her. "Never waste a summer day," she said out loud and bounded down the steps into the sunshine, stomped down the hill, and headed for Caspar's Hollow.

Rachel had accomplished a great deal in the two years since she'd left school. She had raised funds for special door-to-door bus service for the elderly and the handicapped, fattening the pot with money of her own. She had spent scores of hours in Belle Haven's single library, scribbling down the titles of essential books she could not find, and had then donated them all, boxes and boxes of them, and new shelves to hold them. She had bought dozens of flowering trees and arranged for them to be planted wherever there was room: along the creek, in the park, outside the post office, throughout the town. She had taken a course in CPR. She had spent a hundred afternoons with the kindergarten class—singing, painting, storytelling. And every Thursday

morning for two years, she had walked down along the old, meandering, leaf-slick cow path that led into Caspar's Hollow to sit with Mr.
Caspar and hold his knotty hand, water his plants, make sure he had
enough to eat.

Ross Caspar was too old to do any more farming; his wife had died
a long time ago, and his children had moved away. So he lived alone
on his hill-bound farm with a passel of dirty black kittens and an
attic full of bats. When the batteries in his hearing aid went dead, he
simply turned up the sound on the television and made Rachel look
straight at him when she talked. When the television went dead,
Rachel brought him a book and began to teach him how to read. And
when he finished reading his first good story, he laughed and cried
and beat his fists on the arms of his old chair until the air became
foggy with dust.

"You're on your own now," Rachel had said.

"Don't I know it," the old man had replied, wiping the tears off his
baggy face. "Bring me some more books, Rachel, next time you're
out this way."

And she had. Every Thursday morning. For two years. Rain or
shine.

It had been weeks now since anything unusual had happened in
Belle Haven. The grass had grown back over Otto Browning's grave.
The water in the Hutters' well was fresh and cold. Even at the edge of
town, boreholes that had once fairly whistled were often quiet now,
and the fumes they vented were mild, the smoke infirm. In the face of
all this, Rachel had allowed herself to be seduced by summer: by the
scepters of corn that raced upward, creaking and snapping, through
the quiet summer nights; by the children stalking crayfish along the
shady banks of Raccoon Creek; by the black storms that blew in from
the west, lifting the branches of the trees, flashing the white, warning
backs of the leaves.

As Rachel headed for the hollow, she thought only good thoughts,
put Joe and Harry Gallagher out of her mind and with them, unknowing, the lesson Harry had taught her: that seduction can come
with fangs.

On the way through the town, Rachel bought a dozen hot rolls
from Angela, a slab of honey ham from the grocery store, and a bottle
of homemade grape juice and a quart basket of tomatoes from a farm
truck parked at the side of the road. She packed the food into her bas-

ket and lugged it across a wide field and down into Caspar's Hollow, taking turns with her arms, watching for the copperheads that liked to nap on bits of hot slate.

As she came through the trees at the bottom of the hill, Rachel looked up smiling. She took another step, still smiling. Her eyes saw that something was wrong, but her feet kept moving. Her lips kept smiling. Her heart kept beating. There, on the left, across a small field of clover, was the old barn where the black kittens were always born. There, to the right, was the flower garden that grew to a luscious tangle, seeded itself unaided, offered itself to the honeybees and the birds. The house where Ross had always lived should have been there too. It should have been near the garden. But it was not.

Rachel dropped the basket and ran. She tripped in the clover and raced on again, screaming for Ross. Where his house had been she could now see, amazingly strange, the peak of the roof with its old, mossy tiles poking up through the soil, the top edge of an attic window, unbroken, the brick of a chimney rising up out of the ground as if it offered passage to the center of the hot, revolving world.

Rachel was brought up, panting, by the sight. The bit of roof, the chimney, that was all. The soil was gray all around where the house had been. Rachel took a step onto the strange ground, and her foot disappeared, she began to sink, quickly, her other foot bracing against the lip of firmer ground, her arms flapping in the air, hands wild, mouth working. She threw herself backward, scrabbled at the sparse grass, rolled away from the big grave where Ross Caspar was now buried, turned toward the hills, and ran.

She ran past the basket where she'd dropped it, ran up the path through the woods; ran until her lungs were seared. Then she ran some more, her mouth full of paste and heat, her bare legs scratched, sweating, stuck all over with seeds.

At the top of the hill, in the field of tall grass, Rachel lay down, choking on hot phlegm and the memory of Ross's rooftop. There was, here, no stink or commotion. The birds around her were content among the seeded stalks of grass. But Rachel was badly afraid. She spread her body out in all directions like someone caught on thin ice. She gripped the ground with her fingernails and dug in her toes. And then, remembering the sight of that chimney rising up out of the corrupted earth, she scrambled to her feet and fled.

Book
Three

Ah, when to the heart of man

Was it ever less than a treason

To go with the drift of things,

To yield with a grace to reason,

And bow and accept the end

Of a love or a season?

— ROBERT FROST, *from* Reluctance

Chapter 32

Joe stood at the door to his sister's apartment and wondered how he had gotten there. The long trip west, which had felt endless, now collapsed into a single, ponderous moment. Despite having traveled the world, he was bewildered to be in a place thousands of miles from where he had been that morning. His senses told him that it ought to be dark by now, but with the change in time zones and the length of summer days, it was still light in Northern California. Night would already have fallen in Belle Haven. He would call Rachel as soon as he could. He didn't want to wait too long and risk waking her. Then Holly opened the door.

"My God," was all she said at first. She said it as she looked at him standing there. She said it again as they grabbed each other and he lifted her off her feet. She said it as she led him inside and closed the door.

"I don't think I believed you were really alive until now," she said, taking his face in her hands and looking at his eyes as if to be sure they matched her own.

"Quit saying everything I'm thinking," he said, taking her hands in his. "Even if that's what twins are supposed to do." He'd never called her his twin before, and she knew it. It was the first clue to the changes in him.

They stood looking at each other for a long moment. After two years of mourning each other, they were easily silenced by the shock of meeting face-to-face.

"Are you hungry?" she finally said.

Which seemed to awaken Joe. He blinked. Took a deep breath. "As a horse." He looked around him suddenly. "But I think I'd better get my bag before someone walks off with it."

"Oh. Sorry." Holly waited while he went back out for his bag. "I'm a bundle of nerves, Kit. This is all so strange. He said you were *dead.*"

"He said you were, too," Joe said, putting his bag by the door. The "he" hung in the air between them. "You called me Kit, didn't you?" He massaged his temples. "No one's called me Kit for two years. Except Mrs. Corrigan, last night. Was that only last night? Jesus, Holly. I feel like my head's about to explode."

"Mine too." She rolled her eyes. "This is getting ridiculous. Last time I saw you we had nothing good in common. Now I feel like I'm looking in a mirror." She touched the ruined side of her face when she said this.

"Me too."

Which made Holly grin. "So what do you want to eat? There's a great little Thai place on the corner. Or I can make us a pizza. Or . . . what? You name it."

Joe suddenly found himself thinking about Belle Haven. A town that lived on corn-fed beef and homegrown crops, plenty of bread and butter, whole milk, and fruit pies. The lure of Thai food, so spicy it cracked lips, was incredibly strong. He felt disloyal. He felt hungrier than he had in years.

"Thai," he said. "That would be perfect."

And it was only after they were out the door and down the street that he remembered he hadn't called Rachel after all.

Somehow being in the restaurant together made it easier for them to discuss what their father had done. The place was crowded and noisy, the air so full of pepper it stung their eyes. Holly had been there enough times to know what to order, to set things in motion as soon as they were seated, which meant that for every awful thing they discussed that night, there was a chance to say, "Good God, that's hot," or "Water just makes it worse."

Still, it was hard to say out loud that their father had hurt them as badly as he knew how. It was hard to say that, having done such a thing, he had never made any attempt to right the wrong. Had never sought forgiveness. Had never even tried to find out what had become of his children.

And it was hard, as well, to acknowledge that they had accepted their father's lies without question, had never tried to find out for sure what had become of each other.

Joe, who had accepted nearly everything his father had ever told him, was nonetheless horrified that he had not questioned the news of Holly's death. And Holly, who had for years known that her father was a cruel and dishonest man, was astonished that she had taken him at his word. True, by the time he had called with the news of her brother's death, she had spent weeks building a new life and trying her best to forget the one she'd left behind. True, too, that the sound of her father's voice alone had so shocked her that the words he had fired down the telephone line had shattered, one by one, against her skull until she felt as if she had been caught in an explosion. In defense, she had retreated, shut down, sealed off her past and refused to look back at it for a long time. She now confessed to her brother that she had been too afraid, in those days, to dwell on his death or on anything else their father had last said to her. Even now, she could not easily speak of such things.

Yet as she unburdened her heart, Holly felt herself lighten. Her sorrow over her brother's death had lasted all this time, even if it had lessened somewhat, but as she sat across from him she felt the last of it dissipate. She had not accepted the blame that her father had tried to inflict on her, the shame of participating in her brother's death, but she had still been scarred. Now, as her scars peeled away, she felt well and strong where they had been. The fury she had felt since learning—that very morning—of her father's lies was coupled with an equal measure of joy over having her brother back.

But he, who had known the same sorrow and shame, the same fury and joy, reacted differently as he sat with Holly and tried to articulate what they had suffered at their father's hands.

As he told Holly about the night he had called their father and learned of her death, he remembered what kind of person he had been back then. He remembered what had made him leave home in the first place, the long and terrible story Holly had told him in the gazebo that morning, how their father had tried to rape her, the threat he had been to her for years. Joe remembered how he had doubted Holly, had even accused her of lying. He remembered defending his father, but he could not remember why.

As he told Holly about Ian, Angela, and Rusty, described the fire that was growing beneath Belle Haven and what the town had come to mean to him, he found himself wondering whether he had outgrown his deep-seated proclivity for looking the other way. And as he spoke about Rachel, he realized that he had always forgiven her habit of denying what she feared because he had for so long done the same.

"I wonder if I do that because it makes me feel better about my own faults," he said absently, the food on his plate forgotten. He put his hands in his lap. Looked at his sister. "I thought I'd come a long way since I left home," he said, "but now I feel like I'm right where I started."

"Don't be so hard on yourself," Holly said, reaching across the table to touch her brother's cheek. "I am a thousand times happier than I was back then, and that's mostly because you helped me leave. Ultimately, you did believe what I told you. Even though I heaped on you in one morning what I'd spent years getting used to. None of what we've been through was easy, Kit. But what doesn't kill us makes us stronger."

"You keep calling me Kit. I feel like I'm splitting down the middle."

The look in his eyes frightened Holly. He was so obviously confused that she wanted to get him home quickly, send him off to bed. They had said too much, too soon.

"Let's go home," she said. "Everything will seem better in the morning."

But it didn't.

For the next three weeks Joe said very little. He appeared not to listen to what was said around him or even to him. Holly's friends, after meeting him for the first time, avoided her eyes, for they sensed that her brother was not quite whole.

Holly suspected that her brother was simply trying to make sense of their father's senseless lie. To do that, he would have to understand his father. And to do that, he would have to take a long and honest look at the kind of person he had been before leaving home, for it was in those days that he had been most like his father, had seemed content with following in his footsteps regardless of where they led. He had taken such a look immediately after leaving home, but since then he had put as much distance as possible between himself and the person he had been, which meant that he had tried not to look back, or at least not too closely.

Now, as he peered beneath his own scars, Joe saw his father and himself very clearly. Perhaps time had provided this clarity. Time and therefore some objectivity. Or perhaps living in Belle Haven had given him a different perspective so that, like a tourist abroad, he saw things the natives missed. What he saw did not surprise him, for he'd caught enough glimpses before. But it did frighten him, for he now admitted to himself that no matter how much he had changed, no matter how hard he had tried to better himself, he was still capable of repeating his worst mistakes.

He had once accepted things as they were, had done nothing to improve them, and had not been the only one to suffer the consequences. And he was doing it again in Belle Haven. The difference was that, under his father's roof, he had been able to claim some ignorance, to hide somewhat behind his youth, to beg the excuse that it was natural—perhaps even commendable—for a boy to be loyal to his father. What excuse did he have now for looking the other way while the fire made its way closer? For taking part in a conspiracy—if only because he did so little to dispute it—that seemed sure to hurt those he loved? He still felt that he was a better man now than he had once been. But this only made his collaboration seem worse.

Holly watched her brother as he spent endless hours on her small balcony, looking out over San Francisco. She imagined that he was still straining, quietly, desperately, against his father's stubborn grip. Even after all this time. Even after everything that had happened. And she was right.

But she remembered the night he had arrived on her doorstep, how much he seemed to have changed since they had last seen each other. And she was convinced that her brother's silence was a good thing, a sign that he no longer took things lightly. She knew, because she had spent years doing so, that it was better to face difficulties than to look away. After what he had been through, he was giving himself a chance to heal before going forward. Time to sort himself out. And again, she was right.

Three weeks after he'd arrived on her doorstep, he startled Holly by singing "Moon River" in his morning shower, by shaving carefully, by sitting the wrong way in a kitchen chair, so that his chin rested on its back, and declaring that he was famished. Over a feast of eggs and pumpkin bread, he told her that he wanted to go home.

"What are you talking about?" she cried, angry and alarmed. "You promised me you wouldn't go anywhere near him again."

"Oh, no," he said, reaching one arm over the back of the chair. "No. Not there," he said. "I want to go back to Belle Haven, Holly. As soon as I can."

She sat down, shook her head. "Sorry," she said. "I wasn't thinking." She looked straight at him and frowned. "Don't you want to hang around a bit longer?"

"I'm okay now," he said to the uncertainty in her eyes. "Honest, Holly. Even better than okay." He smiled at her in a way she'd never seen before. He looked happy. "And besides," he said, "I have something important to do."

It took Joe two weeks to reach Belle Haven, for he stopped along the way to spend a great deal of his inheritance. It made him feel good to shed his wealth, for it was not really his. He had not earned it. Or if he had, it was by doing things he wished he could undo, following his father without question. Like the Jaguar he'd traded away, the money was tainted by its source, but he hoped that what he had bought with it would lead him entirely beyond the borders of his father's shadow.

It was only when he saw through Rachel's eyes what he'd done that he wondered whether he'd someday rue its price.

Joe arrived back in Belle Haven at the end of August. He had been gone for more than a month and was thinner than when he'd left. Paler. He moved a bit more slowly, as if his thoughts were sucking the blood up from his legs.

As the Greyhound bus pulled away from Frank's Gas 'n' Go, loud and stinking, Joe waited impatiently for the air to clear and the sounds of the night to return.

It was only about ten o'clock, but there was no one around. He had decided, on the bus, to walk up to Rachel's house and surprise her, collect Pal, maybe stop and say hello to Angela and Dolly and Rusty on the way, see who might be sitting out on their porches, enjoying the cool night air and the white of the stars. But as he picked up his bag and turned to go, he saw, leaning up against the back of the bus-stop bench, the bicycle that Rachel had lent him so long ago. He had left it at the Schooner.

He looked at the bike, looked down Maple Street toward the creek and Rachel's hill beyond it. He did not want to ride all the way to his hot Schooner, his bag making the trip a chore. Out there, so close to Ian's empty house, he knew he would not be able to sleep. But something told him to go anyway. Something told him the bike had been left here so that he would.

He met no one on his way out. No cars. No hand-in-hand strollers. No dogs after mice in the grass. There was no moon. Only the lingering warmth muffled the brilliance of the stars. There was no wind, no sound loud enough to challenge the rattle of the old bike on the road. Even when he stopped to switch his bag to his other hand, Joe heard nothing. Saw nothing but an orange sheen in the air, reminding him that there was fire out here. He felt as if he were the last person alive on earth.

When he reached Ian's lane and turned in, Joe was surprised to see light shining through the front windows of Ian's house and the shape of a car parked by the door. As far as he knew, Ian had died with neither heirs nor will. He and Rachel had taken on the dreadful task of going through Ian's house after his death, emptying his fridge, looking through his papers, watering his plants. Perhaps, Joe thought, some distant relatives had been found.

He turned down the bumpy lane that led through the woods to the Schooner, struggling to steer with one hand. Then up ahead there was the Schooner, waiting for him, and he was glad to be home.

There was a note wedged into the crack around his door. He carried it inside, put down his suitcase, switched on a light, and sat down to read it.

> *The land you're parked on has been sold,*
> *Joe. If you need more than twenty-four hours*
> *to leave, we can talk about it. Come see*
> *me when you get back. I'm living in the*
> *Spalding house.*
>
> *—Mendelson*
>
> *P.S. I'll let you know what's owing on the electric.*

Joe threw the note away and opened his windows wide. Someone—Rachel, he presumed—had come around to close them to an inch or so and had also taken from his cupboards things that might have rotted, emptied out his small fridge, opened its door, unplugged it. He undressed and lay down on his stale bed. Through the nearest window he could see a piece of blackened sky.

For some reason he was afraid. Having to move the Schooner upset him, for he liked this spot by the stream and the way the fields looked in a storm. Pal, too, would miss it, her only home. But it was time to move, and move he would.

Something else was wrong. Something that awakened the remnants of his ancestors within him: those newly down from the trees, who stole the fur from bears and ate beetles, whose instincts made them bare their teeth and run, peeing down their legs, when the earth shuddered under their feet. Something that made Joe sweat heavily and lift his head suddenly off his pillow, again and again, throughout the long and empty night.

Chapter 33

"*Ah,*" *said the man* who answered Ian's door, his face half-lathered, a razor in his hand. "Joe."

"Morning, Mendelson," Joe said.

"I heard you rattle by last night. About ten-thirty, wasn't it?" The man spoke through the screen, did not open the door.

Joe nodded. "That's right," he said.

"You'll be out by tonight, then?" It wasn't a question. "That'll be twenty-four hours. Actually, that'll be about two weeks since I moved in. I was tempted to have that old heap of yours towed off long since, you know."

Joe looked closely at the man in the doorway. The screen made him look all gray. "An odd thing to be tempted by."

He turned and walked away, back through the woods to the Schooner, and began to break camp. He lashed his outdoor furniture to the top of the Schooner, coiled up his clothesline and stashed it inside, shook his awning free of leaves and acorns and furled it up tight. He unplugged his electric feed and retrieved the jacks that kept the Schooner level and bore some of its weight. Then he started the engine to make sure it would run. He always warmed the engine at least twice a week, listened for a lazy battery, checked what needed checking—but he'd been away for a month and was relieved when it started up. It had been much longer since he'd actually driven the Schooner anywhere, and the tires were mushy, but as he cast off it rolled smoothly over the bumpy ground, rocking a bit, unperturbed.

As he drove slowly along the narrow lane that led through the woods to Ian's and on out to the road, Joe watched the tall grasses bend down before him. In his mirror, he caught a last glimpse of the place where he'd lived for more than two years now, of the fireplace he'd built, of the outhouse where Ian had found him in such an unusual state. He laughed aloud at the thought, his eyes full, and did not spare a glance at the man who stood out in front of Ian's house, stiff-legged, like a dog.

Chapter 34

To Rachel, it would always seem odd, somehow pre-arranged, that she was once again lying in her hammock, her mouth full of sweets, when she heard the sound of the Schooner coming into town. She heard it come down Maple Street. She heard it approaching the bridge. But this time, when it reached the foot of her hill, it turned up toward her and came on slowly, laboring, edging up over the crest of the hill like a benign beast, and finally stopped alongside her house. Joe looked small and fragile through its vast windshield, as if he were starting his boyhood all over again.

At the first rumbles of the approaching Schooner, Pal had suddenly come bounding out of the woods, nearly singing with excitement, and Rachel had felt herself surrender to Joe's proximity. Now that he was back in Belle Haven, now that he was within her reach, all the tempests knocking up against her ribs, twisting her gut, had calmed. Away, he had seemed so prone to villainy. Returning, he was ripe for pardon. The sight of him resolved things for her, took them clean out of her hands.

When he walked across the yard to her, she knew immediately that he was changed. But when he knelt down beside the hammock in the thick grass and laid his head on her belly, she put her hands on him and did not care.

Joe and Rachel spent the rest of that day together. They were never far apart and often found themselves wedged in the same chair, or

standing flush up against each other, or even more frequently locked
in deliberate embrace. They ate from the same bowl, did not answer
the phone when it rang, did not go beyond the borders of her land.
They lay in bed in their hot, summer skins and talked and made love
over and over again.

Joe had not yet told Rachel about his weeks away, but she already
knew quite a lot about them. She knew he had done something about
his father. What it was she didn't know, but she sensed in him a se-
renity he hadn't had before, certainly not in the hours before he'd
gone away. She realized that he had put all of that part of his past
where it could not hurt him as it had before. He seemed happy in a
mild, peaceful, lasting way. He seemed sure of himself. He seemed
wise.

Reluctant to tell Joe about Ross and everything that had happened
since that day down in Caspar's Hollow, Rachel had decided to wait
until they'd had their fill of reunion. But Joe, too, could tell that
something was different. He remembered the fear with which he'd
slept the night before and saw, in Rachel's eyes, its twin. She, who
had always been so certain, so self-assured, seemed newly timid. Distracted. As if she were listening for something, even in the midst of
laughter.

After supper, when they took their tea out onto the front porch,
Joe went to the Schooner, returned with a box, and put it into
Rachel's lap.

"Open it," he said, and told Rachel about the gold she found
inside.

"Holly doesn't want it, and neither do I," he said. "Do you think
Angela would use it for Rusty's education?"

"What's to think about? Of course she would."

"Then how about you sneak it into her tips bucket for me. You're
always messing around back there behind the counter."

"Why don't you just give it to her yourself?"

"Nah," he said, seemed about to elaborate, in the end did not.

"All right," she said after a moment or two. "I guess you don't
really need this, now that you've claimed your inheritance." She laid
the heavy box on the floor.

"Oh, that," he said, blowing on his tea. "I've already spent most of
it."

"Spent it?" She had always imagined that there was a great deal of
money involved, and in this she was right. "For God's sake, on what?"

"I invested it."

"Invested it." She nodded. "So you'll live off the dividends?"

"No dividends."

"What the hell did you buy, then?"

"A piece of land," he said, grinning. "Prettiest land you ever saw." But he did not tell her where, or why, he had bought it.

She pictured the bald, golden hills of California rolling into the tumultuous sea and could not really fault his impetuosity. But she put the image immediately out of her head. He would tell her about it when he was ready. She would listen when she had to.

"So now you'll have to work for a living." She snorted.

"Which I've been doing for two years now, going on three," he said, reaching down to stroke Pal's ears. "What's wrong with that?"

"There's not a thing wrong with that. Matter of fact, I think that's great. Better than sitting around, living off the interest like me. Jesus, Joe, you make me feel like a wastrel."

"Not at all," he said mildly, sipping his tea. "I'm sure you have all sorts of plans for that money of yours. None of my business, anyway."

"Damn straight," she said, bracing her feet against the porch rail, tipping her chair up on its hind legs.

They sat for a while, watching the day go down into dusk. The sky became tarnished, everything colorful bled, and into the still air came the sound of cicadas, like mutant violins.

"I guess it's time I let you know what's been happening around here," Rachel said with a sigh. And told Joe about Caspar's Hollow.

She told him about the roof jutting up through the gritty soil like the bow of a sunken ship. "It was the strangest thing I'd ever seen," she said. And she told him how she had unwisely stepped onto the insubstantial ground and nearly been buried alive. "Like Ross."

Joe didn't move once as he listened to Rachel tell the story. He pictured her sinking into the earth, the dirt creeping along her body, up her neck, over her lips. Her eyes. He felt sick. He wanted to weep. He could hardly believe it when Rachel then began to talk about the aftermath, as if there was anything left to say except, It's time to leave.

"A whole bunch of new people arrived a couple of days afterward," she said, bringing her chair down on all fours. "Government people, scientists, geologists. Same as Mendelson and the rest who've been out here before, only now there are more of them and this time they mean business. They didn't pay too much attention when cows went missing, but a dead man is different." She bit her lip. "They dug for

Ross's body, but it's long, long gone. Almost lost someone looking for him, so they quit. They left his house just the way it was when I found it. Nothing much they could do. But up here in town they've been going around from house to house, interviewing everybody who will talk to them. They've taken a health survey, put together a medical profile—"

"A medical profile?" Joe asked, his skin crawling.

"Seems there's more cancer in Belle Haven than there should be, according to these new people. But mostly out near the tunnels."

"And this is news to you?"

Rachel shifted in her chair. "There's a lot of black lung around here. In the old men. That I already knew. But I didn't know that there's more cancer—especially breast cancer—than there ought to be, and I'm not surprised. I mean I'm not surprised that I didn't know about it. It's not the sort of thing people talk about. And besides, there still isn't all that much. It's the percentage that's high."

She paused. He said nothing.

"They've also put a monitor in everybody's cellar," she went on, not looking at him. "They're saying that carbon monoxide could kill us in our sleep if we don't turn them on. They've got everybody scared stiff." She rubbed both eyes with the heels of her hands. "The government has no business here."

From the hilltop, Joe could see that the sky above the distant fields was tinted with orange.

"There are more hot spots now, Joe," she said, following his gaze. "All of a sudden."

"Oh, come on, Rachel. There have been more and more hot spots for months now. But Ross dies and suddenly . . . there they are! Even Rachel Hearn sees them. That must mean they're really there. Are you ready to talk about the fire now as if it really does exist? Not just 'out there' somewhere, but maybe everywhere by now. Do we get to do something, finally, instead of sitting around, knocking our knees, waiting for a sign from God? Which, as far as I'm concerned, you've had. Take your pick—rats, fires, sinking houses." He shook his head at her. "Jesus, Rachel, you're not stupid. You must have known this would happen sooner or later. You can't save a town built on top of an inferno."

She stared at him. "I don't know what you're talking about. This *town*'s not built on top of the fire. A few houses are. Which is why I— and a lot of other people—aren't about to panic. Caspar's Hollow is a good half mile away from here. Maybe the fire's getting bad out there, but that's out *there*. Not here." She peered into her empty cup. "Even so," she said, "we've decided to buy another fire truck for the town. And if there ever is a problem with gas coming up, those monitors will give warning in plenty of time."

"And if another house goes down like Ross's?"

"I can't see that happening."

"Oh, I see. You're the expert now. Then tell me why Ross's house went down. How close was he to a tunnel?"

Rachel looked away from him. "Well, there's the strange part," she muttered. "His house wasn't actually close to a tunnel at all. They're all west of his hollow. He must have been sitting above a long coal vein, a big one that went right up to the surface, which is very unlucky, of course. I'm sure the chances of the fire coming up directly underneath a house are pretty slim. It's never come near us before."

"Who's us?" Joe snapped. "Obviously not Ross. Sophia? What about Sophia? Or Bill Hutter? Or the Saders?"

"You don't know why Sophia's house burned down, Joe, or why there was ice on Bill's lawn, or why Becca Sader's goddamned shower was too hot."

"That's right. I don't. You don't. Nobody does."

"Look, I'm sorry for Sophia, and I'm sick about Ross, but the fact remains that the fire is nowhere close to most of this town. You look at the maps of the tunnels, and you'll agree. They're not a threat to most people."

"Most people?" Joe pulled his chair up closer to Rachel's so he could see her face more clearly, and she his. Pal, awakened, took up a fresh post at his side. "What about the ones who *are* at risk? A minority you're prepared to sacrifice, I take it." As she opened her mouth to speak he rose to his feet. "And what about all that coal down there?" he demanded. "You're sitting up here on your hill, safe and sound, telling people to wait until their shoes start smoking before they run. Looking down your nose at anybody who's got the good sense to be worried. While Angela and Rusty and all the rest of your pals down there walk around on top of a time bomb." He glared at her. "Goddamn it, Rachel, grow up."

She watched, speechless, as he stalked off the porch and into the Schooner, held the door for Pal and then shut it sharply behind them. He did not reappear for as long as she sat there alone in the darkness, stunned, furious, and for the first time sorry that he had come back to her changed.

Chapter 35

Rachel slept little that night. Her belly gurgled with acid, and her eyelids seemed to repel each other like mismatched magnets. Around midnight she heard Joe start up the Schooner and drive away. He drove out of town the way he had come in. She imagined that San Francisco had recalibrated Joe's vision, had cast Belle Haven and all of its citizens—including Rachel herself—in a new, unfavorable light. She imagined that he was, at this moment, bound away, across the farmland, toward the nearest city.

The Schooner was the first thing Angela saw the next morning when she came down from her apartment above the coffee shop. She unlocked the front door and walked straight across the sidewalk to Joe's door. She knocked, waited, knocked again.

"How do you want your eggs?" she asked when he opened the door.

"Good morning, Angela," Joe said, knuckling his eyes. "Some law against sleeping past the crack of dawn?"

"Yep," she said. "Never park your disreputable caravan outside my front door after a month's absence unless you mean business. I've been itchin' to talk to you, boy, and I hate to be kept waiting."

"Don't you want to know why my lovely caravan is parked outside your disreputable hash house?"

"All in good time," she said, smiling. "Eggs?"

"Scrambled," he said. "With cheese on top."

"Ten minutes." She turned on her heel and disappeared inside the coffee shop.

By the time Angela had fixed his breakfast—eggs with cheese, fried tomatoes, toast, coffee, and cranberry juice—Joe had showered, dressed, fed Pal, bought a paper.

"I know all about Holly," she said, bringing him pepper. "And I know all about Mendelson moving into Ian's place," she said, back at the grill, busy with bacon. "But I don't know why you're here eating my eggs instead of up with Rachel where you belong."

"We had a fight," he said, drinking the cold juice. It was like liquid rubies. "I take it I'm the first to tell her how stupid she's being about this fire business."

"I don't know as how I'd call her stupid." Angela began to brew a second pot of coffee as a couple of farmers came in, corn silk on their sleeves. She took the first pot to their table, said hi, filled their mugs, put menus in their hands.

"You got to understand something about Rachel," she told Joe. "And it's not something I've ever said to her, because I think in time she'll work everything out for herself and rushing her won't help. But it's my opinion that the way Rachel is acting about this fire has a lot to do with the way her parents died. Actually, more to do with *when* they died. She was beginning to outgrow this long habit she had of always doing the right thing, being so reliable it about made you sick." She glanced over at the farmers, who were waving their menus at her. "Keep your shirts on, I'll just be a sec," she called. "But she was on her way, starting to outgrow all that, when *bang.* Her parents got killed in a pretty horrible way. Right on the heels of a miserable time at school. And right before my eyes she did this incredible flip-flop. Instantly. All of a sudden she's stubborn as a mule. Pigheaded. Absolutely set on doing things her own way." Angela waggled her head. "All in all, a pretty reasonable reaction, wouldn't you say?"

Joe shrugged.

"Besides," she said, poking a stray wisp of hair back into place. "She's not the only one dragging her feet. We all are. Some people can't see that there's any problem at all. Some are bent on looking the other way. Some see it all right, but it's like they're looking through binoculars from the wrong end. Some see a problem like this and they get their backs up. Rachel's one sort or another, I'm not sure which."

"And what sort are you, Angela?"

"Hang on a minute." She went back to the farmers, took their order. "I," she said, cracking their eggs onto the grill, "am the sort who's gotten very good at knowing when to throw in the towel. And I'm not there yet, that's for damned sure."

"Don't you think you ought to get Rusty and your mother out of here?"

Angela put bread into the toaster.

"I like you, Joe. You know that, right?"

"I guess."

"You guess. Shit, boy, you *know* I do. But keep your goddamned nose out of my business." She flipped the eggs with one smooth turn of her wrist. " 'Course I'm worried. But we like it here. And besides, what choice do we have? No one in their right mind's going to buy a square foot of Belle Haven land until this fire's dead and gone. Certainly not my disreputable hash house. So you want to tell me how we're supposed to start over somewhere else?"

He put down his fork and wiped his mouth. "What about the Schooner?"

Angela turned from the grill to look at him. "What about it?"

"It's not much, but if you have to go somewhere else, it will get you there."

Angela frowned at him. The eggs sputtered for attention. "You offering me your Schooner?"

"If you need to get out in a hurry," he said.

She looked at him some more, thinking it through. "You planning to buy a place with your trust money?"

"Don't worry about me," he said, impatient.

Angela watched the bacon fry. "Thanks."

"Don't mention it. What do I owe you?"

"Not a thing," she answered. "It's on the house."

They talked for a while until Angela got too busy and Dolly came downstairs with Rusty to help out.

Before he left he asked, "All right if I park the Schooner here for a bit while I look for someplace more permanent?"

"I have a better idea," Angela said, carrying a plate of flapjacks to a man in a bright orange feed cap. "See if Earl will let you park at the back of his lot. It's never been full, not once in all these years. Tell him you'll stock shelves for him one night a week, something of that sort. He's likely got an outlet you can plug into, long as you pay for the juice. And when it's too cold to put a hose on his outside tap, you can use my shower upstairs if we're not in it, no charge." She came closer and lowered her voice. "You can even, ah, wash up in the back whenever you need to."

"Thanks. I've got that part under control, Angie."

"Enough said."

"All right, then," he agreed, smiling, pulling on his earlobe. "I'll go talk to Earl."

"Fine with me," Earl said, dusting a pyramid of paint cans. "Long as you don't mind paying for the electric and the water. Never mind using the lot. That's what it's there for."

"How about I shovel your walkways come winter and keep the lot clear?"

"Now, there's a thought," Earl said, his eyes gleaming. "There is a thought."

"It's a deal, then," Joe said. "Let me know if you hear of anyone hiring, Earl. I need a bit of a job."

"I'll do that," Earl said.

As it turned out, Joe simply began to do what he'd done before: some of this, some of that, plenty to keep himself in soup and bread, soap and razors, new laces for his boots, the occasional carving tool, gasoline and oil for the Schooner. He mowed lawns, drove old ladies to the A&P and home again, picked late peaches and early apples. School started after Joe had been back only a few days, and Angela again offered to feed Joe for time spent with Rusty and his books.

"That's ridiculous," Joe said. "I'm the one getting an education. Rusty's smart as a whip. He doesn't need my help."

"Don't argue with me."

"Fine. Okay." He held up his hands. "If you really want to make a trade, Rusty can watch Pal for me once a week. I've got some stuff to do out of town, and she hates driving."

"Pal drives?"

"Very funny." He was surprised when she didn't ask what he'd be doing out of town, but he was also relieved. There would be a time and a place to tell her, but this wasn't it. "And I will use your shower, if you don't mind. But that's more than enough. Way more."

And so things went.

A few weeks earlier Joe would have mourned the loss of his lovely camp: the sound of the stream and the blowing trees, the sight of deer at the edge of the woods, the fireplace he'd built, the place he'd made for himself, bit by bit. But he had come back to Belle Haven treasuring more than anything else the people he encountered, even those who failed to win his affections, for they all impressed him with their inimitable bones, the oddity of their notions, with their very human fragility. And of all the people in his life, he marveled at himself most of all. At the smoothness of his fingernails, the random lunacy of his dreams, the way the smell of oranges made him think of his mother.

He still knew how to appreciate the beauty and the genius of trees, blackbirds, other live things. He still loved music and color and art of all kinds—his own included. But the impressions these things left on him were as important to Joe as the things themselves. The memory of them as precious. And the idea of things to come as rewarding as their arrival. He asked little of the world, cared little if he left it different in his wake.

Rusty, Rachel, Holly, Angela, Ian, and his father, in their various ways, had taught him to waste no time, for there was none to waste. They had taught him to do whatever made his sleep easy and his appetite strong. They had taught him to yearn but not to crave. To feed and feel as if he'd feasted. To lay open the fragile membrane of each and every cell in his body and draw in all light, all sound, all substance— but not to overlook the dark, quiet emptiness between the stars.

The days since he had fought with Rachel had been like a fast, but even as he hungered for her, Joe was content with what he had. He stood by his choices: to leave home, to live simply, to spend his inheritance on something worthwhile, even if it might mean losing Rachel for good . . . and now to dispute the choices *she* was making. If he wanted to be able to live with himself, he had to risk living without her.

Then, one night, he found himself remembering the Jaguar he'd left back in a lot somewhere east of Belle Haven. He remembered the feel of it, the sound of it, the joy it had brought him. A car. A way to get from one place to another. Rubber and steel and leather. Glass and paint. Plastic. *Plastic.* But he had loved it and missed it for a long time.

He knew then—and realized that a part of him had always known—what Rachel saw when she looked down from her hill and out over the fields. She saw something coming for her. For the house where her parents had lived, where she had made a place for herself. For the trees and the cats and the houses. For the people she knew and loved so well.

She did not see their destruction, or she would surely be nearer flight. She saw, instead, a kind of foreclosure, a species of theft, and she clung on, she dug in her heels and wrapped her fingers tighter, and bared her teeth like even the gentlest of dogs are known to do when threatened.

She had much more to lose than a car.

As Joe walked across Rachel's front yard that night, pushing her father's old bike, Pal trotting alongside, he saw her watching him from the porch.

"I'm sorry," he said, leaning the bike against the porch rail.

She thought about that for a bit. "That's good. Because the only way I can take you is whole and entire. I can't just rope off little sections of you and say, well, that part's no good, so I won't touch it. That part's broken, so I'll leave it alone."

Rachel watched Joe mull this over. Had she been able to read his thoughts—to know that he was forgiving each word as it left her mouth and promising her time to grow out of her tyranny—she might well have struck him. Instead, she leaned over the railing and offered him her bottle of beer, which he took. "I don't mind fighting with you, but if you are truly as disgusted with me as you seemed to be the other night, I want nothing to do with you anymore." She smoothed her hair behind her ears. "Have you gotten over all that?"

Joe sighed and handed back her bottle, sat down on the porch steps. He watched Pal move silently off into the night. "Oh, I don't know, Rachel. You made me mad with all that talk about letting the fire run around like a rabid dog. I happen to think it's going to kill some more people. I hate to think about that, or about you being swallowed up like Ross was. Take me down to his house and look at it with me and tell me you're not scared stiff. Tell me that, truthfully, and I'll keep my mouth shut."

They shared the beer. She sat down next to him on the steps.

"I'm sorry," he said again after a bit. "I should have remembered that you were patient with me once."

"I don't need your patience, Joe," she said wearily.

"Well, maybe not. You're a grown woman. You do what you have to do."

He went inside and came back out with a second beer.

After a while, she said, "How do you like living in a parking lot?"

"It's better than a stick in the eye."

She laughed and laid her head against his arm.

"The best part about it is the view," he said, which made her laugh harder. But when he said, "I can see your butterflies from the window by my bed," she first looked up, confused, and then became still, remembering.

"What about your statues, out in Ian's woods?" she said after a bit. "Does Mendelson know about them yet?"

"I don't think so," Joe said, drinking his beer, running the bottom of the bottle down his thigh. "I barely spoke to the guy. I wonder why he'd want to buy Ian's place, what with the fire and everything."

"He didn't," Rachel said. "The government did, from a cousin Ian has, had, out in Wyoming. He didn't want the place, and the government got to him before any of the rest of us even knew the land was for sale. Now Mendelson's living out there with a few of his crew. He's supposed to figure out what happened to Ross's house and plan what to do about the fire, once and for all. He's the one who's going to recommend what happens to this town." She held her bottle with both hands. "Which scares me more than just about anything else." Neither of them spoke for a while. Then Rachel said, "It shouldn't be too hard to sneak out to the woods."

"Sorry. You lost me."

"To work on the statues."

"Oh." He nodded. "I don't want to sneak out there," he said. "And I'm not going anywhere near those hot spots again if I don't have to."

Rachel frowned. "Think about it, Joe. It's probably safer out there in those dead trees than anywhere else around here. The fire's already eaten up any coal in that spot."

"I suppose."

She gave a little grunt of exasperation. "Are you saying you don't want to go back out there? I thought you loved carving those trees. They're beautiful!"

"Yes, I think so too. But I can carve things right here."

"You can't mean you're going to leave that last statue unfinished."

"It's a statue, Rachel. It's dead wood. The worms are out there right now, and so are the woodpeckers. In a year or two those trees will be down and rotted."

"How can you think about it like that?" she cried. "You were so excited, that day you took me out there to show me that first carving of Holly. Don't you remember talking about how good it felt to make something so beautiful?" She was close to tears, suddenly, and for that he was sorry. "What's happened to you?" she said.

"I'm the same as I always was," he said gently, "only better."

Rachel looked into his face, unsmiling, and slowly turned away. "I don't understand you anymore."

"And I feel the same way about you," he said. "I hope it's like a temporary sickness and that we'll both get better. But right now, you seem to be paralyzed by the prospect of leaving here." He reached for her hand. "Don't you think I ought to shake you out of it? Isn't that what you would do for me? Isn't that what you *did* do for me?"

She took her hand away. "I'm not paralyzed, Joe. But I'm not leaving either. I'm going to do what needs to be done."

"About what?"

"About the fire, for Christ's sakes. Isn't that what we're talking about?"

"But what can you do?" He was bewildered.

"I don't know," she said, although the look in her eye made him think she had something in mind. "But if I do eventually leave, it won't be like some goddamned lemming."

"What the hell have lemmings got to do with this?" He made no attempt to hide his exasperation. "Can't you admit that there are plenty of good, rational reasons for leaving Belle Haven? Even if there were no fire, there would be plenty of reasons to go somewhere else. Good grief, Rachel, this isn't the only decent spot on earth. If anything, I'd say you're acting like a lemming by *staying* here."

"You don't understand." She stood up, looked down at him. "This town isn't just the place where I live. It's part of me." She shook her head impatiently. "The willow in the park where I go on Halloween . . . that was where my father taught me how to climb trees. I had my first haircut at Paula's. I remember thinking my hair was going to bleed. I grew up on cider from those apples"—she pointed toward the trees—"and huckleberries from every backyard in town." Her voice thickened. "I grew up knowing that there was a fire out under the fields, and waiting for it to get here has been terrible. But if it finally does, I think I'll be relieved. I feel like a sailor who can't swim, who's terrified of the goddamned ocean and gets sick of shore after two days home."

To Joe, the simple porch suddenly felt like a stage. He knew that she had allowed herself to be swept up in her dilemma, as if in a net made of her own hair. Listening to her now, he could only imagine what she sounded like to herself. And yet, at the same time, he be-lieved a part of everything she was saying.

"So don't you treat me like I've lost my senses," she said angrily. "You think I should leave Belle Haven? This place has made me what I am. Where am I going to find another Angela? Or another Rusty? What other place has roads my father walked on, trees my mother planted? Where on this entire earth will I ever find a place to com-pare with this one?" She looked at him sadly. "I would have bet any-thing you'd understand what I'm talking about. I thought you loved this place, too, for the same kinds of reasons."

He could see in her eyes that she had begun to agonize, but he did not see any way around that. "Jesus, Rachel. I *do*. But you were one of the people who taught me that if you can live with yourself, you can live anywhere." He reached up and pulled her down beside him on the step, pushed her hair away from her face. "This is only a *place,* Rachel. A few acres of ground." He took her by the shoulders so that she had to look at him. "You can't let your roots tie you down."

She shook her shoulders free. "What do you know about roots?"

He looked at her steadily. He knew a lot about roots. "I know that the best ones grow inward," he said, "and stay with you wherever you happen to be. It's not the place that's important. It's what it means to you." He put his hands on his chest. "And even when you leave, you won't leave that behind." He had not come to plead a case, but he feared that this might be the last time she would hear him out.

She stood up, stepped toward the door, looked down at him. "All you've talked about since you came back is how we ought to leave this place, which you claim to love. I don't know what to think, Joe." Again she said, "I don't understand you."

But he only shrugged. "I can't help that."

When she went inside the dark house, he stayed for only a moment more and then stood abruptly, set down his beer bottle, and, whistling for Pal, walked away, leaving her father's bicycle behind.

Two hours later, when Rachel returned to the porch, exhausted, sick of her bed, she looked out toward the land that had belonged to Ian and saw a new landmark. Hot and orange, this one reached up-ward, violent, as if it came not from under the ground but from the world above it, fed with boundless air, strengthened by wind, and fortified by the rigid flesh of trees.

Chapter 36

When Mendelson walked into Angela's Kitchen the next morning, stinking with sulfur and cologne, Joe put down his fork, wiped his mouth carefully on a clean napkin, and took a long swallow of water.

"Give me a bag of hot cinnamon buns and fill 'er up, Angela." Mendelson left his thermos by the register, moved down the counter to a stool next to Joe's. "I thought I might find you in here," he said.

"Morning, Mendelson."

Mendelson spun slowly on his stool until he sat with his back to the counter, elbows cocked and braced on the Formica, legs crossed at the knees. "You know, the oddest thing happened last night, out in the woods at the edge of my spread."

"Ian's place."

"Used to be, yes," he said, nodding. "Someone started a pretty big fire in the middle of the night. Enough fire around here as it is, but some dumb bunny can't get his fill, I guess. Know anything about it?" He peered at Joe, one eye shut, his curiosity real.

"Why ask me?"

"You used to live out there, is all. Thought you might've seen something of this sort out that way before."

Joe finished his breakfast, drained his mug. "Probably just a hot spot, Mendelson."

"Not this one." He shook his head, sent his stool into another lazy spin. "Somebody made a fire out of old wood, tended it, banked it.

Left a bunch of stumps and a nice, tidy pit of ashes, sort o' like a druid hangout or something. Not the way kids would have done it, but I guess it might have been kids."

Angela put a fat brown paper bag and a full thermos in front of Mendelson. "Post this in your window, Angela," he said. He handed her a printed notice, paid for the food. "Guess I'll be sleeping with one eye open from now on," he said and left.

"There's going to be a meeting in the school auditorium. Tomorrow night," Angela said, reading. "I guess they've finally got something to tell us."

Joe picked up a salt shaker, put it down, watched Angela looking at the notice in her hands. "You going to go?" he asked her.

"Not until I have to," she sighed, and missed the sight of Joe bowing his head.

"This'll go a whole lot faster if you'll all shut the hell up." Which did shut everyone up. They looked up at the stage and gaped at Mendelson, who stood and glared down at them all, breathing heavily through his mouth. "That's better," he said.

He looked at the papers in his hand. "Just shut up and listen, then I'll go on home to bed and you folks can bitch at each other as long as you like. Jesus Christ," he muttered to the man from the Department of Community Affairs, who stood nervously at his side. "Have you ever in your life heard such a load of crap?"

Had Mendelson paid closer attention, he might have noticed in the eyes of the townspeople a sudden shift, a change in temper, a clear, unmistakable signal that their silence meant anything but surrender.

"As usual, you all seem bent on confusing the issue, so let's start over. At the beginning. And get things straight." Teacherlike but not kindly, he said, "Ever since I walked into this school I've been hearing the same tired complaint. That the government has ignored Belle Haven. Which is simply *not* true. Hell, we've been fighting this fire for a dozen years! We tried sealing the shafts with clay. Not our fault the soil around the mine's so porous it let air in anyway. Nothing we could do about the breathing room left when the coal's burned away. No way to stop the fire from nipping up to the surface and leaving a vent behind. Plus, where it's hot enough, the ground cracks like a bad brick, which lets air in too. Throw in a few thousand drilling holes left behind when the mining outfits quit, and you've got dandy conditions for a mine fire to spread." He slapped a hand against his chest. "None of which is *my* fault."

He drew breath as if to continue but suddenly turned instead to the man from Community Affairs who had begun to shift his ample weight from foot to foot. He said, as if there were not hundreds of others looking on: "Did you know there's an Australian mole that actually *swims* through sand, breathing tiny pockets of air caught between the grains." He made stroking motions through the air. "Amazing."

The fat man beside him nodded uncertainly. The audience, torn between fascination and an accelerating impatience, leaned forward in their chairs as if they did not trust their hearing.

"Anyway," Mendelson muttered, "where was I? Oh, yeah. We couldn't choke off the fire. Right. So." He smacked his hands together once. "Next thing we did was we sunk a barrier to keep it away from the town. Fire went under it. So we tried drowning it with water. Fire came right back, like that." He snapped his fingers, and a moth that was beating its dizzy way across the stage veered into the shadows. "Tried suffocating it with fly ash. Waste of time. We even thought about building a power plant right on top of the fire, giving it a boost or two, using its power and letting it burn out. But we were afraid that doing that might make things a whole lot worse." He did not mention the trench that he had dug before taking any of these other measures. The room was silent.

"So all this talk about the government wasting time and money is nonsense. We've been trying everything possible to put the goddamned fire out. And while we've been trying all these things, Belle Haven's been pretty lucky. Up until now, the fire's been taking its time, meandering around out there, generally keeping out of town. Coal veins carry it up where it doesn't belong, stink things up, spread it around out in the fields a bit . . . big deal. No harm done, am I right? Hell, the boreholes at the far end of town didn't even go in until three, four years ago, and they're not so bad.

"You want to know how lucky you are? Take a look at India." He held his arms out as wide as they would go. "They got whole villages sinking into coal fires that make ours look like a weenie roast. They've got such bad fires in Jharia that if they were flooded and every air vent was packed with sand, they'd still stay hot for eighty-five, ninety years. Hot enough to reignite if they were exposed to air. And the coal beds are so hot they ignite other beds without even touching them." Mendelson's eyes were gleaming. He shook his head but it was not clear whether in admiration or more impartial wonder. "By comparison, you haven't been bothered much at all.

"That's because when *this* fire finally made its way down to the tunnels under the edge of town, the cupboard was almost bare. Most of the coal out there had already been mined. So what if the tunnels were on fire? Without a lot of coal, there wasn't that much heat. The fire moved slowly. And if it was spreading out from the tunnels, it was headed toward the fields and around the hills where there's still some coal left and close enough to get at.

"But things are different now," said Mendelson. "And if you don't believe me, ask Ross Caspar—if you can find him." An old woman in the back of the auditorium got up, sat down again, began to rummage through her purse.

"He probably thought he was in the catbird seat. Plenty far from the nearest tunnel . . . farther than a lot of you, if you care to check the maps. Snug as a bug down in that hollow of his. So what happened? That's the question. What happened." He plucked a fat marker off the lectern and tapped it against his chin.

"Here's what happened," he said, turning to a flip chart. At the top of the chart he made a squiggly line. "Here's where the fire started, where it's been burning all along, about two miles from here, give or take." Toward the bottom of the chart he drew a long, sloppy rectangle. "And here's the town proper." Above the rectangle, more toward the left than the right, he drew something like a kidney. "Here's Caspar's Hollow." In the open space on the chart, mostly at the top and down along the far left edge, he drew thick stripes. "And here are where most of the tunnels are, quite a ways from Ross's place." He turned back and looked at the audience. "But when we went into the hollow to look at the situation, we found the kinds of things we're used to seeing way out in the fields: hot ground, soft ground, a bit of smoke coming up here and there. No flames, mind you. No fire visible from above. But an awful lot of heat. An awful lot of heat." He paused, rolling the marker between his palms.

"What we did then," he said, "was send up a plane, take some infrared pictures, and make a thermal map. Like we've done before over the tunnels. And what we found was just exactly what we expected to find: that the fire has branched out in a southeasterly direction—in *this* direction"—he stamped his foot—"even though there aren't any tunnels leading into town and even though we thought there wasn't enough coal left around the southernmost tunnels to let the thing spread this way. But it must have worked its way out to a helluva coal seam that sent it branching out into Caspar's Hollow.

"Which means that Belle Haven proper is a sitting duck. Because there are no tunnels underfoot, we can't tell you where the fire will eventually hit. We'll take some pictures, by and by, but we'll be seeing where the fire *is,* not where it's going. It will no longer be a predictable, traceable fire. It will no longer be the fire that's way over there on the edge of town, out in the fields, anywhere but *right here.* It will be like a jack-in-the-box, poppin' up. Boo!" He threw his arms up in the air. "There's quite a lot of coal down under *this* end of town, you know. Quite a good bit. And all it's going to take, you see, is one little ribbon of coal bringing the fire across that last bit of distance between Caspar's Hollow and here." He breathed deeply.

"And then there's another angle to this thing," he continued. "If the fire's headed this way, what's to stop it from hitting Fainsville to the south? Just two miles south. Hop, skip, jump . . . *kaboom!* That fire decides to pick up speed, and Fainsville's a goner, too. And don't forget, folks, that between here and Fainsville there is a vast, virgin coal deposit. It's been sitting down there, safe and cold, and no one's ever worried much about it because it's a good piece from the Belle Haven mines and there's more clay than coal in between. But it's an awfully big lot of coal. Enough to keep that fire going forever and ever, Amen.

"It's too bad that coal wasn't mined. And the coal straight down underfoot, too. Would'a been, I guess, if the company had gotten to it before they went belly up. Maybe not. Who cares." He flapped a hand. "The point is, it's too close for comfort. Now that the fire's taken this new turn away from the tunnels, it's like a rogue elephant. And you shoot rogue elephants." He grinned. "Which is where I come in."

Mendelson took another deep breath, and when he spoke again, it was more loudly than before. "Before very much more time passes—maybe a month, maybe a year—some of you are going to die. Your cellar walls will collapse. Your yards will cave in. Hydrogen gas, highly combustible stuff, and carbon monoxide, which will poison you to death, will come pouring up through the dirt like something right out of the Bible. Only you won't see it," he added mildly. "In the wintertime, when you close your windows, it'll be like nailing a lid on a coffin. Tap, tap, tap. Good night, Irene."

A man in the front row crossed his legs, uncrossed them, folded his arms over his large belly. "How come that's never happened out over the tunnels?" he asked. His neighbors nodded.

Someone said, "That's right."

"Because out there"—Mendelson knocked a knuckle on the left side of the drawing—"the coal doesn't amount to much." He spoke as if to children. "Over here"—he ran his hand over the place where they were sitting—"there's just loads.

"Now," he said. "Is that clear?" He smiled at their silence.

"The monitors we sent around'll give you some warning, but I'll bet dollars to doughnuts half of you never even turn 'em on." He sighed heavily, turned to look at the man by his side, who had, from time to time, taken a step forward, opened his mouth as if to speak, and then settled back again as Mendelson carried on.

"I suppose what you do with those monitors is up to you. Whether you stay in Belle Haven or leave is also up to you, at the moment. But if the fire reaches the coal straight down below here—and I, for one, am sure it will—you'll have to go. You *will*. On foot or in boxes, one way or the other."

"We understand." From where she was sitting in the front row, Angela could see that some of Mendelson's fingernails were very long. "We understand that there could be trouble," she said. "But the fire isn't here yet. The monitors sound like a good idea. We'll need to know if the fire ever makes it this far. But maybe it won't. Or maybe it won't get here for another dozen years. And yet here you are saying we're going to die soon." She lifted her shoulders. Opened her hands. "People get killed in cars every day, but we all drive them. People drown, we still swim. It's the way of the world. So I'm still waiting to hear why you think *we* should leave when *you* ought to be out there putting the goddamned"—she caught her breath—"putting the fire out."

"Well, I'm trying to tell you. I really am," he replied, smiling at her. "It's not easy, trying to explain some things to people who won't listen to reason. And you'll appreciate that I've been trying to ease my way into the nuts and bolts, 'cause if you all can't even agree that there's a problem, you're sure not going to agree with the solution. But maybe I should just get on with it, let you all go home to bed."

He looked around the auditorium as if he might want to remember the sight.

"As I said, Fainsville may soon be at risk—and there's no way we can let the fire hit the big coal between here and there. A lot of other small towns may soon be at risk. Belle Haven," he said, lifting his eyebrows high on his head, blowing out some air. "Belle Haven is beyond salvation. It simply isn't going to survive this. And if we let the fire get past here, it will gather such strength that we'll never be able to stop it."

He let this sink in, heard the crescendo of whispers, and began to speak again. "But, I'll say it again, that's where I come in. My men and I. What we plan to do is dig a trench." There was a sound from somewhere in the room, which he ignored. "A very long, very deep trench—four hundred fifty feet deep, five hundred feet across, a mile long. Now, *that's* a trench." He chuckled. "Maybe we'll dig several trenches. Wherever they're needed. Cut the fire off and let it burn itself out. That's it. That's what we're going to do."

"So go ahead!" Earl yelled from the back of the room. "Get on with it. Don't you think we want to stop the fire before it gets here? Hell, that's what you've been trying to do all along, and we've never once objected!"

"Jesus H. Christ!" Mendelson said, running his hands through his hair. "For the last time, listen. Listen!" He pointed at his ears, became red in the face, slapped the flat of his hand against the flip chart. "Belle Haven is *done.* Finished. Kaput. How many times do I have to say it?" He lowered his voice some. "It'll take quite a while to dig this trench, it's going to be *that* deep. So, one"—he held up a finger—"we've got to dig it a good distance from the fire so we'll have time to get it finished before the fire travels that far. And two"—he held up another finger—"we've got to dig it where it will keep the fire from reaching the big coalfield south of town, now or ever. There's only one way we can kill both birds with one stone." He stopped to let this sink in.

"Do you mean that you're going to dig the trench *south* of town and just let the fire come and get us?" asked a boy along the aisle who could not have been more than twelve or thirteen.

"I'm afraid I do." Mendelson nodded. "And once that trench is dug, it'll act just like a wall. The fire will hit that wall and maybe pile up, maybe burn out, maybe make a run straight back this way. I'm afraid I can't tell you for sure."

Rachel rose to her feet and took a step up the aisle toward the stage. "What have *you* got to be afraid of?" she said. "You're a contractor, aren't you? How much money have you made over the last twelve years? You say you've tried every way you can to put the fire out. Now, *that's* nonsense, if anything is. You were the one who dug that first trench. You could have had the fire out before it spread too far, but you failed. There were dozens of miners who had worked in those tunnels who knew, who *told* you, that you had to keep digging and you had to dig faster, shifts around the clock, no time off, no holidays, no goddamned lunch breaks. You had enough men. You could have had it out before it got anywhere near us, Mendelson. But you did too little, too late. And now look at us.

"Stopping the fire would have meant stopping the gravy train," she said. "Stopping the fire would have put you out of a job. Digging this new trench, on the other hand, will keep you and your people busy for a long time to come. And once you've dug that trench, you'll no doubt mine all that lovely coal. That's the real issue here, isn't it, Mendelson? There's a fortune down there waiting to be made, and you're the one who's planning to make it. You and Uncle Sam."

Mendelson folded his papers and slipped them into his breast pocket. "Night, everybody," he said, waving. "It's been fun."

"Everybody knows something's got to be done for us," Rachel said as he walked past her, down the aisle toward the doors. "Everybody knows the government's going to have to spend some money on us. So they figure, why not make back thirty, forty, sixty million while we're at it? Dig the trench north of here, save the town, and what does the government get? A few hundred votes, maybe. Dig it south of here and make a killing. There's no profit in trying to save this town. Right?"

Mendelson stopped, turned to look down the length of the room. "Right," he said.

From where he sat in a shadowy corner, Joe watched Mendelson's departure. The man wore his clothes well, was lean and shaven, held his head up, did not slink. He looked capable and calm. He was clean. He had not lifted a hand against anyone. But as Mendelson walked toward the back of the auditorium, Joe found himself breathing lightly, through his mouth, as if newly aware of a stench. He, too, had noticed Mendelson's long fingernails. He had seen, through Ian's screen door, Mendelson's eyes. Joe knew all about contradictions, knew how it felt to harbor them, knew that they were as much a part of human chemistry as blood, marrow, and elation. But Mendelson's incongruities were less savory than most, less acceptable, like a froth of grime on a bar of white soap, and Joe looked upon him with great unease.

He heard the door close as Mendelson left and watched Rachel standing in the aisle, her arms hanging at her sides, one foot pointing in. Then, as the people around her rose suddenly to their feet and began loudly to debate the proportions of their predicament, Rachel seemed to melt down to nothing, as if drawn in all directions, diluted, and absorbed by their immediate, collective need.

Chapter 37

"Why didn't you want to go, Gran?" Rusty and Dolly sat side by side on the couch, waiting for *M*A*S*H*. She was drinking a Dr Pepper out of a bottle. A slice of pizza drooped in her hand.

She had been married for nearly twenty years before having Angela, against all odds, and was therefore a much older grandmother than she might otherwise have been. But she had a knack for putting herself in other people's places. She was a quiet woman who listened well and thought before she spoke. And she had won Rusty's confidence as well as his heart. He never lied to her.

"You first," she said.

"I was going to go." Rusty went into the kitchen, came back with a sack of ginger snaps and some milk. "Want one?" He tipped the sack her way.

"Maybe later," she said. She was thin, like her daughter, but darker, her hair the color of cinders and ash.

Rusty settled down with the sack in his lap. "I would have gone," he said. "But Mom didn't really want me to. She said there wouldn't be any kids there." He put a cookie into his mouth, whole. "I know some kids who were going with their parents, but I let her decide. I guess she's got a reason for wanting me to stay home." He dunked a second cookie in the milk. "Well, actually"—he turned his head and grinned at her—"I didn't want to go. Mendelson's a creep. And I'd rather stay here with you."

Dolly dusted the crumbs from her hands.

"Took the words right out of my mouth." She drank the last of the Dr Pepper. "We probably should have gone, though. Your mother talks tough, but the fire's got her scared."

Rusty huffed with impatience. "I don't see why," he said. "It took years and years for the fire to come a mile. It ought to take years for it to come the rest of the way into town."

"Ought to." Dolly held out her hand for a cookie. "Two words that don't amount to a hill of beans."

"You two eating all the cookies again?" Angela stood in the doorway, unaware of the catastrophe of her face.

"Never, my girl," Dolly said, rising. "Come sit down here. I'll make some coffee."

Angela sat down, eased off her shoes. "What's on?" she asked, looking at the TV.

"*M*A*S*H*, in a minute."

"Good." She reached for a cookie.

"So what happened?"

"If it's okay with you, Rusty, I'd just as soon not talk about it right now."

He hadn't wanted to hear about it anyway, knew that he would soon enough, but he said, "Why not?"

Through his father's long absence, through the perpetual struggle to make ends meet, through housemaid's knee, the parching of her skin, the way her body was slowly bowing to gravity, Rusty had only very rarely seen his mother as she was now. When he turned to her, all innocence, for his answer, he was unprepared for the sight of her, immobile, her hands in her lap, her head nodding heavily, her face slack with worry and fatigue.

"Never mind," he said quickly. But she either had not heard him or intended, by her silence, to pardon his mistake. It was, more than anything, this silence, this distance, that finally convinced Rusty he had something to fear.

In the morning, toting eggs and home fries to early risers, Rusty heard about the trench. A sentence here, there, and, later, straight talk from Joe told Rusty what his mother had not. The talk startled him, silenced him, sent him out in search of Mendelson and his crew.

Like many children, Rusty believed that Saturday mornings were the most tangible, most reliable embodiment of freedom. To spend one in pursuit of a man he despised so he could talk about a situation he deplored seemed a lot to ask. But to wander through the day without voicing his objections seemed worse still. So he packed a pear, a meat-loaf sandwich, and a thermos of milk into his bike basket and set out toward Fainsville. He saw plenty on the way to make him glad he'd come: a penny-colored horse; a black snake that crossed the road ahead of him, as long and liquid as a whip; a fat hawk after mice in the grain.

It didn't take Rusty long to reach the region where Mendelson meant to dig his trench. The boy assumed that the land they had chosen would be pasture or cropland, since digging up trees would make for much harder work. He wondered about the farmers whose land was to be sacrificed, whether they had sold their land willingly.

Rusty left his bike at the edge of the road and walked into the fields. He didn't really know where he was going. He didn't really know if he should expect to find anyone out here. He wasn't even sure, suddenly, why he'd come. Perhaps he had come out here too soon. Perhaps they would not start to dig for weeks yet. He looked for flags, stakes, markers of any sort, but saw none. He saw no machines. There was no one around, not even a farmer, not even a dog out trotting.

He lay down on his back in the tall grain. The patch of sky above him was shaped vaguely like his shadow, edged with the neat heads of the grain. On every side he saw the stalks of the grain, heard the movement of grasshoppers and birds. He sat up, ate his sandwich and his pear, drank some of the milk and capped the rest. He had waited long enough. It was clear that Mendelson was not out in these fields.

He did not feel as if he were sitting on top of so much coal. He had expected to feel it from afar, as if it were alive, as if it were moving. Set afire, it would send up signals. He was sure that it would. He did not believe that a massive fire, even one deep underground, could pass unnoticed. He was sure that he would know when the fire worked its way into town. Lying back again in the golden grain, warm and drowsy, he was simply not so sure that it ever would.

When his mother asked him, later that day, where he'd been, he told her that he'd gone out looking for arrowheads.

Rusty let a few days go by and then returned to find the fields of grain shorn down to stubble yet much as they had been. He smiled, turned to go, and that was when he saw, farther south, a bit of smoke rising, heard the grunt of machines, felt a trace of something disturbing the ground beneath his feet. So he rode farther along the road to where it sloped slowly down and turned before flattening out through a nice stretch of bottomland where black cows were known to graze. It was here that Rusty found Mendelson, the earth all in a shambles, the machines already digging, and not a cow in sight.

He had intended to talk to the man when he found him, to register his protest, probe for a soft spot. But when he saw the long, black incision they had made in the flat belly of ground, he knew that nothing he could say would make any difference at all. Not to Mendelson. And if he had anything important to say, if he wanted to speak his mind, bare his soul, expose his heart, he would, he decided, do better with someone who loved him.

He went back to Belle Haven, straight to his mother, and told her about the trench.

"What are we going to do?" he asked. "We're not leaving, are we?"

Angela was mixing up a vast bowl of tuna salad. Dolly sat at the far end of the counter, rolling quarters. She looked up, listening.

Angela gazed at her son for a moment, turned back to the bowl. "You don't want to leave?"

He pulled up the bill of his cap, scratched his forehead with the back of his thumbnail, pulled the cap back down. "No," he said. " 'Course I don't want to leave. Do you?" He looked at his mother, at Dolly, at his mother again.

Angela dug at the salad with a massive spoon. Her forearm was as muscled as a farmer's. "I don't think this is something you have to worry about just yet," she told him. Dolly set aside a roll of quarters and began the next. "There's time for us to decide what to do. The fire's not here yet. It may never come this far," she said.

Rusty grinned. "That's just what I was thinking," he said, then he kissed his grandmother and headed for the door.

Chapter 38

It couldn't have been Ian, or Rachel, or Angela. They were the only three people who had fed Joe, in those early days after he'd arrived in Belle Haven, but they were also the only three who knew why he had come. Even if they had not believed his story about a bad father and a disfigured sister, none of them was the sort to sneak away from the supper table with a dirty butter knife, wrap it carefully, and send it off to the FBI. He simply could not believe such a thing. Dolly? This, too, seemed fantastic. But Rusty could have done it. He was a boy with an imagination and a mind of his own. It could have been no one else.

Rusty looked up from the comics and caught Joe watching him.

"What?" he said.

"What what?"

"Do I have a booger in my nose or something?"

"No, you don't have a booger in your nose or something. Can't I look at you?"

"Suit yourself." Rusty went back to his comics. He was sitting, cross-legged, on Joe's bunk, Pal with her velvet jowl on his thigh, while Joe sat in the kitchen booth with a cup of coffee and a letter from Holly. He watched the boy and wondered when his young voice would begin to crack. He was growing leggy and lean, like his mother.

Without looking up this time, Rusty said, "What?"

"You always get this shook up when people look at you?"

"Who's shook up? I'm trying to read, is all."

Joe folded Holly's letter and put it in his shirt pocket. "Your mother tells me you went out looking for Mendelson the other day."

Rusty sighed, put the comics away from him.

"Yeah, I did."

"You worried about all this?"

"All what?"

Joe put his coffee down on the tabletop and looked at Rusty for a moment. "All *this*," he said. "All this business about the fire coming in."

Rusty flopped onto his back, crossed his arms behind his head. "What's there to worry about? So far, it's all just talk. If the fire comes all the way in, we'll do something about it, I guess. Until then, why worry?"

"Just talk?" Joe slid out of the booth and walked over to his bunk. He grabbed Rusty by the wrist and hauled him to his feet. Pal leaped up.

"If you're going to come over here and read my paper and eat my cookies and listen to my goddamned radio and ask me about girls and practice swearing in my Schooner, you're going to have to play by Schooner rules." He let Rusty go. "Rule one," he said, pushing Pal's nose out of his hand. "None of this goddamned 'just talk' bullshit. The fire is nearly here, and that is all there is to it." He took a deep breath. "I don't go up to Rachel's house anymore. I haven't spoken to her for a week. You know why?" Rusty shook his head. "Because we can't talk about the fire without fighting, and I'll be damned if I'm going to keep my mouth shut. I don't dare talk to your mother about the fire, you know why? Because she's already scared to death and I love her too much to make things worse." Rusty seemed to grow smaller before Joe's eyes. "I'm sorry," he said quietly. "I'm sorry if this kind of talk scares you. But inside these four walls I speak my mind. This is my home. You will always be welcome here. And I will always do whatever you want me to do, to help keep you safe, to help keep you happy. But I won't lie to you."

Rusty had not once taken his eyes from Joe's face.

"Do you know why I came to Belle Haven?" Joe asked. Rusty shook his head.

"I had to leave home for a while because I found out that my father had been lying to me about some things. And then, after I got here, he told me another lie that kept me from going home. And when I finally figured out the truth, I made up my mind to face things, squarely, whenever I could. It is so much, so *much* worse, Rusty, to look the other way and hope for the best. And I only wish that I had had someone to teach me that when I was a boy." Pal put her nose into Joe's hand again, and this time he rubbed his fingers gently along her jaw. "Didn't your mother ever wonder why the FBI was writing to you?"

Rusty's eyebrows shot up, his jaw fell. "How'd you find out?"

Joe laughed. "Mendelson told me someone had sent in my fingerprints on a butter knife."

Rusty ran a fingernail down the grain of his jeans. "How'd you know it was me?"

"Wild guess," Joe said.

"You mad?"

"Mad? Me? At you?" He put one hand on the back of Rusty's neck. "Never."

It was Rusty, then, who began to talk about hot wells and poison gas, the house that was still sinking by inches deeper into the bottomless soil in Caspar's Hollow.

They talked for a long time, until Angela finally ran over in her apron to call Rusty home for supper, homework, and bed.

Asked to join them for chicken pot pie and cider, Joe had quietly declined. Here, in his Schooner, it had felt right to talk with Rusty about the things that Angela refused to confront. As he had taught Rusty about Mars and the Parthenon, so had he tried to teach him about the danger of blinders, and of embracing the shadows they cast. But to sit in Angela's Kitchen and eat her food—payment for the instruction he gave her son—when he knew full well that she had resolved to shield Rusty from certain knowledge . . . this seemed like a betrayal. And so, alone in his Schooner, he ate stew from a can. And wondered why it was that he had spoken so long and with such certainty to Rusty when such talk with Rachel always, always led him to retreat.

Chapter 39

While Mendelson began work on the giant trench, other, milder men came into town to hold town meetings and offer the people a loathsome trade. The government, they said, would pay people to leave Belle Haven. By the head. Twenty-five thousand per adult (forty for anyone living alone). Ten thousand for each of no more than two children.

Those with the most land and the nicest houses went inside them, shut their doors, and roared with disgust. Those with the mean lots, poor houses, especially those living over the tunnels, counted themselves lucky.

"It's only fair," the strangers from Harrisburg had said. "Starting fresh somewhere else shouldn't mean starting from scratch, no matter what kind of house you're leaving behind."

Or, if they preferred, people could trade their houses outright for brand-new prefabs that the government planned to erect at the edge of a new development twenty miles east, right outside of Spence.

"We'd like to maintain a sense of community," the government men said. "To relocate not only the people of Belle Haven but its heart and soul as well. To preserve its integrity and maintain its heritage." They were even willing, they claimed, to move one or two important structures: one of the churches, perhaps, or the old train depot, charming and defunct.

It didn't take long for people to take sides. There were some surprises: a few parents with young children who wanted very badly to stay in Belle Haven; a few old people who had lived in Belle Haven all of their lives but had reluctantly decided that their final days might be spent more wisely in a safer place. Mostly, though, the town divided much as everyone had thought it would. Old miners, many dying slowly from black lung, intended to stay. They were not afraid of coal or coal fire. Young, able-bodied families began to talk about departure. Some widows and widowers finally picked up their phones and called their far-flung children. If it comes to that, would you take me in? they asked, afraid of whichever answer they might hear.

For many, the decision of whether to stay or leave was easy compared to the choice between striking out alone or relocating to the Spence development. Alone, elsewhere, they had the chance of finding a good home in an authentic, rooted, albeit foreign community. In the Spence development they saw dreariness and woe. They would become, they feared, a collection of refugees with only two things in common: having lived in Belle Haven and having left it.

And so the debate began. It was kept alive between the cashiers and the customers at the A&P, the farmers baling their hay, the breakfast crowd at Angela's, the children in their classrooms. We should leave, some said. We should stay, some said. They all felt it best that they stay together, but they could not agree on the best way to stay alive.

"Houses are full of gases. It's natural," claimed a large woman named Ruby who had come into the Superette for some Pop-Tarts. "Furniture, rugs, insulation . . . everything gives off gas of some sort or other."

"Dogs, beans . . ." said Lenny, behind the counter, grinning.

Ruby laughed. "Whenever I give Tom beans for supper, he goes off to watch TV with the dogs, I hide the matches." She trembled with mirth. The Pop-Tarts rattled in their box.

At the Baptist church the next Sunday the preacher, thinking he might unite his flock with hope and gumption, tore it right in two.

"I have spoken to Mr. Mendelson," he said when he had put his sermon to bed. "And I have learned that Belle Haven will not be declared a disaster area. Not even if the fire gets as bad as he claims it will. He wouldn't tell me why, but I think I know. When the government declares someplace a disaster area, the people who live there, or who must leave there, are given replacement value for the homes they've lost or left. Which is quite a bit more than some of us have been offered.

"The upside is that we don't *have* to leave unless our houses are condemned, which I am confident will not happen. We can stay put, if we like. Those who sell out and leave—well, their houses will be torn down right away. Mendelson says the idea is to tear them down so they can't catch fire and cause bigger problems. So what will we have, those who stay? We'll have our homes. And around our homes we'll have empty lots. So here's what I propose." He paused, smiling.

"I propose that we set out to beautify our town. In every empty lot— and, God willing, there won't be many—we'll plant new grass and flowers, trees, make parks. None of us wants to see our neighbors leave, but if they do, we'll heal up the wounds with our own hands, keep Belle Haven from scarring. That," he said, smiling, "is what I propose."

The next Sunday, half of the pews in the church were empty. Missing were those who thought that no one, much less a preacher, had the right to shame or tempt anyone into staying in a place that they had begun, reluctantly, to fear. Husbands were there without their wives, wives without their husbands. So far, there was no proof that there was any more fire under Belle Haven than there had ever been, but it felt like maybe there was.

Some people, already weary of debate, declared themselves in more subtle ways. Fran Harkley was seen putting a hundred new tulip bulbs in her front garden and a ring of daffodil bulbs round the birch by her porch. The Danielses put a new roof on their house. And Sarah Clemm ran an ad in *The Randall Recorder. Fire Sale! Swing set, kiddie pool, TV antennae, porch swing, you name it. Everything must go. The house, if you want it. Sat. 9–5.* But she didn't sell much. Someone said it felt too much like a foreclosure.

Halloween—Joe's third in Belle Haven—brought a respite. No one had yet left town. No one was even packing. The monitors were all quiet. Wherever the fire was, it had not yet surfaced the way Mendelson said it someday would. So the town turned its attention to the annual business of horror and delight.

Rachel, dressed as a tiger and with a huge sack of candies in her paw, climbed the giant willow in the park and settled herself in a roomy fork. Joe hung himself with tattered furs, sooted his face, gave himself sharp nails and teeth, green hair and a club, and toted his bushel basket to the tree stump by the bridge over Raccoon Creek. Ghosts and corpses dangled in the trees along Maple. Jack-o'-lanterns glowed on every front porch. Earl leaned out of his window above the hardware store and dropped rubber spiders onto the heads of passersby, then reeled them back in again, laughing like a child. Angela had painted the big front windows of the Kitchen so it looked vaguely like the gingerbread house in "Hansel and Gretel." But the sky, in the distance, glowed with the light of hot spots, many now closer than anyone liked to see.

The odd light made the children walk quickly and laugh nervously, without reason. It made them quite literally jump when Frank rushed out of the Gas 'n' Go in his werewolf costume. "Grrr," he said, chasing them around the gas pumps. Their screams could be heard all the way down to the creek.

The mothers in town, accustomed to sorting out the cries of their children, stood on their porches and listened to the screaming and were not sure what to think. They had never before minded Frank's high jinks or those of the other grown men who jumped out of their shrubbery when children walked past, or dressed like scarecrows and draped themselves in lawn chairs, springing to life when the children came their way. But this year such antics seemed stupid.

So did thirteen-year-old Jake McKinnen. He'd read all about the boy who cried wolf and should have known better than to start a fire in a trash can behind the library. "Help! Help! Fire!" he cried, throwing sheaves of newspaper into the flames until they soared.

Nearby children, hearing his screams, ran in all directions, shrieking, while grown-ups froze in their doorways, candy spilling from their hands, and then raced toward the light and smoke, white-faced.

"What the hell's the matter with you!" Jake's father snarled, dragging him home past a dozen shaken neighbors who had taken up posts along the sidewalk.

"It's Halloween, Dad," the boy whimpered, his arm hurting, at which his father snorted, "Not anymore. Halloween's over for you."

It ended early for everyone that year. When their children hurried home, tripping over their costumes, long before they were due, most parents shut their doors, turned off their porch lights, and called it a night. They felt a little silly, letting themselves be spooked by Halloween. At their age. But they looked forward to morning, nonetheless.

Joe, too, was glad when the last of the trick-or-treaters had made their way home. For weeks now he had spent too much time alone, working on farms here and there, passing his evenings in the Schooner with Pal and a book for company, and going to bed early. He sometimes visited Angela at the Kitchen or shared his newspaper with Rusty at the Schooner. And once a week he left Pal with Rusty and drove the Schooner out of town for the day. ("I've got an appointment," he would say, leaving visions of doctors and dentists in his wake.) But more often than not he was alone.

He had not spoken to Rachel, had not heard her voice, since the night in the auditorium when he'd watched Mendelson tell her that her town was going to burn. When he saw her walking on the street, she was always on the other side. Whenever he went to Angela's, it seemed she'd just left. Inside him, there was a longing as keen as winter wind, but in his head all was peaceful. He knew he'd been right to speak his mind.

Still, here he was, sitting alone on a tree stump, Pal shivering at his knee, and he had to admit he'd had better Halloweens. "Time to pack it in, girl," he said. She had long since pawed away the paper horns he'd tied to her head. The apples he'd collected held no attraction for her. When he climbed to his feet, she started off toward Rachel's hill, wagging her tail.

"No, Pal. This way," he said, hoisting the basket of apples to his shoulder and heading across the bridge. But he, too, had been tempted to go the other way.

Joe stashed his apples in the Schooner, cleaned himself up, and put on some proper clothes. "Now what?" he said, looking at Pal, who didn't answer. The Kitchen was closed. It was too early for bed. But there was always the Last Resort. "Don't wait up for me," he said to Pal as he headed out the door.

He did not pass a single soul as he walked through the town, and when he came within sight of the bar's lighted windows, he lengthened his stride. The place was even more battered and grimy than it had been the first time he'd seen it, two and a half years since, but he smiled as he put his hand out and pulled open the blistered door.

It wasn't until he had hung up his coat and turned to the bar that he saw Rachel in her tiger suit, whiskers painted on her cheeks and triangle ears pinned in her mahogany hair. Her face and lips were rosy, as if she'd just come in from the cold, and her eyes glittered with laughter over something Angela had said. She was sitting on a bar stool with Angela beside her, a bowl of popcorn between them, smoke swirling slowly above their heads like strange weather.

"Would you like to dance?" he said, his lips close to her ear, before she'd had a chance to see that he'd come in.

She turned so abruptly that she had to put a hand on his chest to keep from falling off the stool. "Joe," she said.

"Rachel," he replied.

She looked at him solemnly. "You want to *dance?*"

"I asked you first," he said, smiling.

When they reached the dance floor in the back room and he took her in his arms, she found that her fist was full of popcorn. She ate it slowly over his shoulder.

"Does this mean we're friends again?" she finally asked him. They were dancing to a slow Elvis Presley song. She was trying hard not to listen.

"This means we're not fighting anymore," he replied. They danced for a while, quietly.

Then, "I don't think we were fighting," she said. "I think things have changed so much between us that maybe we can't go on the way we were before." His shirt, against her neck, smelled like soap.

"You mean we can't be in love anymore?" He lifted his head away, looked down into her whiskered face.

"Is that what we were?" She had not been this close to him for weeks, and she allowed herself a moment to linger over his strong, sweet face, the wonderful blue of his eyes.

"That's what I was. That's what I am. You know that."

"Yes," she said, sighing. "I know that. But lately I don't know how *I* feel about anything. My head hurts from thinking so hard all the time. I get up in the morning and I don't know where to begin. I feel as if I've been told I have a rare disease that's been known to kill people, but it might not kill me. And even if it does, I won't know *when* until I'm already dead."

He thought of a thousand things to say. "So that means you can't love me anymore?"

"I don't know."

They danced to another song—afterward neither of them could remember what it had been—and then they returned to Angela. She was talking to a sort of cowboy named Sam who wore a Stetson on his head and a bronze lasso for a belt buckle. She seemed interested in what he was saying, and after a moment Joe and Rachel said good night.

It had grown colder, so Joe put his arm around Rachel, much as any friend might do, and hurried her to the Schooner, which was nearer than her house. Inside, he gave her a big sweater and made her some hot chocolate while she washed the whiskers off her face and took the tiger ears out of her hair. They talked for a while, about books they'd been reading and how much they missed Ian. Joe made them thick sandwiches and dished out some of the fat, crisp pickles she herself had made for him. At midnight they listened to *The War of the Worlds* on Joe's small radio.

"I'll walk you home," Joe said when it was over.

"No need," she replied.

"I insist," he said, one arm in his coat. "I want to."

"You misunderstand," Rachel said, walking close to put her hand on his cheek. "I'm staying."

Once again the world tilted on its axis and things shifted to where they'd been before. But like a forest altered by the seasons, the place they returned to was different now. Less certain. As if it would not take much the next time to cast them adrift.

Chapter 40

"It won't do you any good, Rachel."

Mr. Murdock was angry. At Rachel, mostly at himself. Once he had found out for himself how shortsighted and stingy the government had been in the matter of the fire, he had caught some of Rachel's feverish determination to keep Belle Haven intact and had been plotting, planning, and keeping secrets with her for almost a year now. Armed with her money and a lot of hard-won knowledge, he had been prepared to throw a monkey wrench into whatever plan the government was concocting to obtain Belle Haven. He had come to feel like a cross between Robin Hood and Karl Marx, and for a while he had liked the feeling. But when Ross Caspar's house went down, when Mendelson laid out the evidence of the fire's new and dangerous behavior, Murdock had balked. He had come, suddenly, to his lawyerly senses. He had returned to the pragmatism that had served him so well in the past. And now he was trying to bring Rachel along toward a more realistic attitude.

"It won't do you one little bit of good," he said to her, the day after the government had begun making bids on Belle Haven land. "You can buy half a dozen houses and maybe, after a few years as some sort of landlady, after the fire's out or gone, sell the land back to someone who wants to live there, restore Belle Haven to its former glory. Something like that." He slapped the air impatiently. "But it's a whole lot more likely that you'll go broke buying people out and then, when the fire comes to town, have all your property condemned and demolished. You'll still own the land, but no one will ever come back to claim it. It will be yours—not exactly worthless, maybe worth a whole lot if the government decides to try and salvage the coal down below—but for your purposes, it will be worthless." He gave her a hard look. "Buying land won't save Belle Haven as you know it. It will simply eat up your money and maybe even cause some ill will between your neighbors. You start paying top dollar for some houses and let the government buy the others for less, how do you think people are going to feel?"

It was unlike Rachel to sit still and listen to such things. But she sat in Mr. Murdock's office and said nothing. It was clear to him that she was angry, perhaps a bit afraid. He had expected her to fire him out of hand and was surprised that he had been permitted to speak his mind, encouraged by her silence.

He didn't know that from the moment in the auditorium when Mendelson had pronounced his sentence, Rachel had begun to change and that she often now, despite continuing resistance, imagined hot air swirling around her ankles, certain as a tide, bringing with it nameless things: black-eyed serpents, long-tailed devils, and flame. She hadn't admitted this to Joe. She saw no reason now to admit it to her lawyer.

"I wouldn't be doing my job if I didn't try to protect your interests," Mr. Murdock was saying. "My advice is that you wait and see what happens. There will be a lot of people who, like you, won't sell an inch of their land until they're convinced of immediate danger. The government's offer will probably even keep them on their land longer: knowing that they can sell out in a hurry and get something for their land, even if it's on fire, will encourage them to stay until the last minute. Personally, I think that's a very dangerous, foolhardy attitude, but . . ."

Even at this, Rachel did not speak. Mr. Murdock began to wonder if she was listening to him at all. "If you wait and see what happens," he said, "you'll still have plenty of time to buy up some land, break up the government's holdings, after the exodus has begun."

"If it begins," Rachel said, quietly. Mr. Murdock was both disappointed and relieved to hear her say it. She was not yet ready to give in and let go, but some of the spirit had gone out of her. She seemed close to surrender, and this pleased him. He was concerned about her money, about her contest with the government, but most of all he was concerned for her safety and her health. He wanted her out of Belle Haven, and he suspected that, given time, she would go of her own free will. She was still very young. She needed time to test her perceptions and discover for herself their faults.

"Give yourself some time," he said gently. "There's no hurry. And there's every reason in the world not to do something now that you're going to regret."

Rachel bit her lip and folded her hands. "All right," she said. "I'll wait for a while longer. But I'm not saying that I've changed my mind."

"I understand," he said. He walked her to the door. "But there's no shame in doing what you have to do to make the best of a bad situation. No one's going to blame you for looking after your own interests."

She turned back at the door. "That's what I've been doing all along," she said. "And I'm beginning to think that maybe there is some shame in it after all."

Chapter 41

The number of those who thought that relocation was wiser than resistance slowly grew as autumn aged into winter, but still no one left. Some focused all their attention on Christmas, vowing to get on with things once the holidays were past. But Christmas came and went without incident and without the departure of a single family. No one wanted to believe that the fire would get to be as bad as Mendelson claimed. No one wanted to give up and go. Above all, no one wanted to be the first to leave.

Before winter hardened the ground, seventy new boreholes were drilled in town and fifty more around the fields, among the hills and hollows to the north. Many backyards, most street corners had them. Government workers roamed the town like coyotes. They lowered instruments into the holes to see if the temperature down below was changing. Out closer to Ross's sunken house, they found that the fire was indeed moving slowly toward the town. Sometimes they found their gauges ruined when they hauled them back out of the boreholes. In such cases, "That's one hot fire" was as close as they came to a reading.

The people of Belle Haven became accustomed to sleeping with their windows cracked open. They grew sick of the ticking of the monitors, day and night, and of the frequent visits from the "meter maids" who assessed the safety of the indoor air. The sight of the borehole spouts was sickening, but most people found themselves unable to walk by one without taking a good look. Somehow, the absence of smoke did not placate them.

In February, faced with the news that a monitor in one of the houses not far from the tunnels had gone off, most people were stymied. A few months earlier they would have shaken their heads and, perhaps, sent a prayer skyward. A few months earlier they had thought of the fire way out in the tunnels as nothing more than a dreadful old companion that required a bit of watching and a slightly cautious tread. No one would have been terribly worried about an alarm out there going off. Odd things seemed commonplace when they happened near the mine. But now, seven months since the incident in Caspar's Hollow, since the rest of the town had begun to walk more softly, news of this first alarm was shocking.

"But why's everyone so upset?" Rusty asked his mother one morning before school. "The fire's been out there forever. It's nothing new. If the McCoys had had a monitor all these years, it probably would have gone off hundreds of times. Heck, they're glad it went off. They were all set to move out anyway. Now they'll get their check faster. It's not like a monitor in this part of town went off or something burned down or anything."

"Hush now, Rusty," Angela said, sliding a bowl of cornflakes in front of him. "You'll be late for school."

Joe, feeling Rusty's eyes upon him, ate his waffles and shrugged.

Joe had spent a lot of time at Angela's Kitchen since the cold had come into Belle Haven. There wasn't much work for him to do during the winter, for the crops were all in and graves that needed digging after the ground froze were given to backhoes. But he had cut Christmas trees if the farmers came to fetch him, helped Earl with his inventory, shoveled snow. And he continued to spend one day each week out of town. "Taking care of some business," he said if anyone asked. And Rusty continued to look after Pal while Joe was away, for she went nearly everywhere on foot, hated riding in cars, trucks, the Schooner especially.

These times away from Belle Haven, tending things that he had kept carefully secret, helped Joe stay out of the trouble the fire had caused among his friends and neighbors. Between sojourns, while those around him either prepared to leave or stubbornly set their anchors, Joe was quiet, mostly idle, carving small things, which he offered in trade now and then.

By March he had used up most of what he'd earned in the fall and was prepared to draw on what was left of his inheritance. But somehow Angela knew he was a bit short. Perhaps she had noticed the condition of his jeans or the splitting seams of his gloves.

"You going to call, or what?" she said to him one evening when Rachel had come down from her hill to join them at the Kitchen for poker and pie.

"Nah," he said, throwing in his hand. "Too rich for me."

Both women looked up in surprise, for Joe, normally thrifty, loved to gamble, win or lose.

"What's a buck or two?" Angela asked him. After a moment she put down her cards and ducked under the counter. "Be right back," she said.

When she returned from her apartment, she laid in front of Joe a roll of quarters and a single Krugerrand. "The quarters are for the game," she said. "The coin will keep you going for a while, just until you can get some farmwork."

"Where'd you get this?" he asked quietly.

"A friend gave it to me," she replied, cutting him another wedge of pecan pie.

"Well, you hang on to it, then," he said. "I still have some money left I can send for."

"Just take it." Angela picked up her cards and arranged them fan-like. "I don't like those Kruger-whatever-you-call-'em anyway. If I were that antelope on there, I'd take a flying leap somewhere else, go play with some deer."

"Springbok," Joe said, smiling at her.

"Whatever. Besides," Angela continued impatiently, "it doesn't matter to me how much money you have left. This is mine to give, and I want to give it to you. It's not often I can do such a thing, but I come from people who take care of their own."

Rachel, watching them, felt like she was invisible. "That's for Rusty's education, Angela," she protested. "If Joe needs anything, I can help him out better than you can."

They both turned to look at her. Joe picked up the gold and held it out toward her. "Then maybe you could drive into Randall for me and cash this in," he said.

Reluctantly, Rachel took the gold. "All right."

Although Joe never really thought about it, the gold that Angela gave him kept him suspended in penury. It paid his keep through the spring, allowed him the luxury of spending the little money he earned on good wood and a few more carving tools. It kept him from altering his life. It kept him content with things the way they were. But then, in the middle of May, came the change.

It must have started during the night. When people left their houses in the morning they noticed right away that one of the boreholes right smack in the middle of Belle Haven proper was suddenly spouting smoke. Not a lot: only a wisp now and then. But within two days there was a steady thread of smoke and, worse, a stink coming up out of the ground.

Ed Zingham, who had delivered mail in Belle Haven for fifteen years, lived in the house closest to the borehole, but he'd been walking past these things out by the tunnels for years and the sight of this one did not alarm him overmuch. When the smoke thickened and the smell began to bother him, he simply shut the windows nearest the hole and tried not to think about it. The people in the two other houses nearly as close as Ed's nervously followed his lead. They watched the borehole, listened to their monitors ticking, told themselves again and again that Ed would know something before they did.

Ed was dozing in front of an old spaghetti western one cool, wet Monday when he heard a brief squawk from down in his cellar, something like the sound of a foghorn. A moment later, the meter maid who was checking his monitor came quickly up the cellar stairs, her clipboard clutched under one arm. Ed watched as she rushed to the front door and flung it open.

"Hey!" he called, "what's your hurry?"

"When's the last time you were down to your cellar, Mr. Zingham?" she said, standing on the threshold.

"Um. Friday," he said. "I spent most of the weekend over in Randall with my sister. Why? Something the matter down there?"

"How long you been home?"

"I got home early this morning, went straight back out again to do my rounds, just got in about"—he glanced at his watch—"about forty minutes ago."

"Then I'd say you owe your sister one." She took Ed's coat off a hook by the door and tossed it into his lap. "Your cellar is hotter than hell," she said. "If you'd turned on your monitor, you'd know that your carbon-monoxide level is up to fifty parts per million."

"I turned it off for the weekend," he said, shrugging. "It uses up a lot of electricity, you know."

"But you didn't turn it back on when you got home, or the alarm would have gone off. Too much trouble. Instead, you sat down in front of the television, got nice and drowsy."

"Got a headache, is what I got." Ed put on his coat. "So how long do I have to leave before it's safe in here again? How 'bout I just go back to my sister's for another day or so? Leave the windows open while I'm gone?"

She handed him his hat. "You don't understand." She sighed. "You can't ever come back here again."

When Ed tracked down Mendelson, the man was unmoved. "I'm sorry as hell, Ed, but my hands are tied. You gotta know that. You're the one who delivered the policy statements all over town, Ed, and you've all had months to get used to the idea. Any house that registers more than forty-five parts per million and tops ninety degrees Fahrenheit and is adjacent to a borehole with a sustained output gets condemned." He took a rigid index finger and ran it like a knife across his Adam's apple. *"Fffft,"* he said.

Ed stared.

"I told you way back in September that this day would come, Ed. But don't worry." Mendelson slid his arm around Ed's shoulders. "You won't be the only one."

Indeed, before the week was out, six other houses on Ed's block wore red crosses on their front doors, as if they might be harboring medics or a renegade religious sect. Signs were posted in their yards warning people to keep out. An army of movers came and emptied out the houses in record time, carted everything off and into storage. The government put Ed and the others up at the Randall Motor Inn while they decided what to do next, and everyone in Belle Haven talked about them in whispers, as if they had died.

But neither Ed's house nor any of the other six was the next of Belle Haven's homes to sink, as Ross's had, through the earth's hot skin. That day was coming, though no one believed it yet. They knew the fire had arrived. And many of them prepared to leave before their own houses were condemned. But the exodus, when it began, was a slow and measured procession that stretched through the summer without mishap.

The government had purchased fifty of Belle Haven's houses by the end of August but had not kept them. Soon after each family left, a red cross was sprayed on the front door of the vacant house and a weary bulldozer smacked the house down to nothing, leaving an open cellar full of debris. Frank had long since emptied out the big tanks

at the Gas 'n' Go—he'd had no choice—so the vans and the bulldozers and every other piece of machinery in Belle Haven had to drive
over to Randall for gas. In the tiny clinic right in town, there were
more and more cases of nausea and dizziness, bronchitis, allergy. People who had never lived through a war began to speak as if they were
now part of one. But as the number of those still in Belle Haven
dwindled, their dander rose. "We'll leave when we're good and
ready," some said, narrow-eyed and nervous. "We're going to stay
right here," said others, "and we'll be here long, long after everyone's
done selling out. And we'll be the tightest, best little community
you could ever want to see."

"You study your geography," said Archibald Kreider, who had
been a miner for most of his life and told anyone who would listen
that it would take more than a mine fire to chase him off his land.
"All the best places on earth are a bit ticklish. People live on river-
banks. They get floods. People live on beaches. They get hurricanes.
People live on volcanoes. They get . . . eruptions." It was hard to tell
if Archie was laughing or coughing. "Some things are worth the
risk," he said, loading his jowl with tobacco.

He watched as his neighbors stripped their houses down to skeletons, hauling away lengths of hand-carved molding and mantelpieces
torn carefully from the walls. No one wanted to leave anything precious to the bulldozers. They took stained-glass windows, thresholds,
kitchen cupboards, weathervanes, even floorboards sometimes: whatever would remind them of the place where they had once lived.

And along with these forlorn treasures, each family leaving town
took a tiny garden grown in Belle Haven soil and cradled in Rachel's
unlikely pots. They took young huckleberry plants and tea roses,
Johnny-jump-ups and hollyhocks, pincushion flowers and dragon's
head, and herbs like coriander and mint.

Rachel left her hill less and less often as Belle Haven fell to pieces.
She could not bear the sound of the bulldozers or the sight of moving
vans. When she went to see Joe or Angela, she raced down the street
and no longer stopped to listen to the water flowing under the
bridge.

Every day she woke with the thought of calling Mr. Murdock,
telling him to buy something, anything at all, to slow this outra-
geous destruction of her town. But then she would recall his predic-
tion and reluctantly admit that to see Belle Haven's houses being

leveled was bad enough, but to make them her own and then watch them fall would be even worse. No one would be coming back to reclaim these ruined plots of ground. She knew this now. But even as she slowly, bit by bit, gave up the notion of keeping her town together, she grew more and more determined. She would salvage what she could.

Since their reconciliation, Joe had not spoken to Rachel about leaving. He had become a quiet man now that the fire had arrived, choosing his words carefully and listening with great intensity. He hated the bulldozers—heartless as big, hard, yellow hyenas—and the sound of nails torn shrieking from old wood. So, on many days that summer, Joe climbed Rachel's hill and walked farther, past her house, into the woods, to the tree house he had built for Rusty.

He had rarely visited the tree house since the day he'd given it to Rusty many months before. When he returned to it after this long absence, hauling Pal up under one arm, he found its shelves stocked with canned goods—beans and corn, stews and chowders, soups with noodles shaped like little sharks. He found a stack of musty blankets. A tin of kerosene and an old railway lantern. Several boxes of candles and a supply of wooden kitchen matches. Three gallons of water in plastic jugs. A bar of soap and a small towel. Hung on a peg in the corner, a set of foul-weather gear.

Joe looked everything over. He did not know what to think. He did not eat any of the food or disturb the careful arrangement of the blankets. Not yet. There might come a time when Rusty's preparations would serve a good purpose, but they were not meant for casual consumption or for play.

If Joe arrived at the tree house and found Rusty there, the two of them were content to pass the time together. They did not speak of the supplies Rusty had gathered. They behaved as if he had instead stocked the tree house with the more traditional trappings of boyhood: comic books and Cracker Jacks, muddy bottles, arrowheads.

Sometimes Joe stayed there alone with Pal, carving, reading, writing to his sister, sleeping when night came on before he'd noticed.

Eventually, when the gold was spent, when his clothes once again became somewhat threadbare and his hair untamed, neither Angela nor Rachel seemed to notice. Each of them was stricken with Belle

Haven's dismantling. Each waited in single-minded suspense for the time when they would all leave town. But as long as they were still there, often separate but always close at hand, none spoke to the others of leaving. Not yet.

It was strange how nothing had burned. The gases came up steadily, and the smoke pouring out of the boreholes was thick and grainy. But not a single house had actually burned. Perhaps that was the one thing that kept many of those still in Belle Haven from going.

Perhaps they had forgotten about the house in Caspar's Hollow.

Chapter 42

It was early October. More than a year had passed since the incident in Caspar's Hollow, since Mendelson had begun his new trench. Rachel had been to Angela's for an early supper and was hurrying home through the twilight. She thought of stopping in at the hardware store to see Earl and buy some lightbulbs, maybe spend some time at the Schooner, but Joe had not come to Angela's for supper and was, perhaps, enjoying his solitude. The street was nearly empty. Rachel, who so rarely came down from her hill these days, was the only one there when it happened.

As she approached the lot where Joe lived, Rachel heard Pal barking and, turning, saw her through one of the Schooner's windows, saw her head snapping as she barked. Rachel figured that Joe would be lacing up his boots, buttoning his coat, coming out in a moment with Pal at his heels for their evening walk, so she waited where she was. She'd walk with them as far as her hill.

Then, as she watched Pal becoming frantic, Rachel heard a new noise. It was something like the sound of a huge wind coming, or perhaps a train, but strangely distant, as if heard through a thick wall. She stood still and listened to it, tried to place it, found herself leaning toward the Schooner, when the asphalt beneath it buckled, a geyser of smoke shot upward, and the Schooner disappeared straight down into the earth as if it had never been.

For a moment Rachel stood unmoving, staring at the place where the Schooner had been and hoping that she was simply dreaming. In the next second a powerful wave of thick, hot air hit her in the face, choking her, minutely wounding her cheeks. As she ran across the street, bright flames snarled up through the crevice, something down below exploded, and the sides of the pit caved in. When Rachel sank to the sidewalk she could feel, through her knees, a distant rumble.

And then nothing.

When people began to run out onto the street, they smelled the terrible stench of the fire. And when Angela ran down the block in her apron to where Rachel knelt on the sidewalk, the smell was so bad that she gagged.

"Come on!" she yelled, dragging Rachel to her feet. "Come away from there. Rachel! Come on!" But Rachel could not stand up. So Angela and Earl picked her up between them and helped her back to the Kitchen.

Angela sobbed, "Goddamn, goddamn, goddamn," as she fed Rachel brandy and rocked her fiercely in her arms.

Rachel was shivering. "This can't be happening," she said, bent at the waist as if she'd been halved, hinged, swung shut. "He said we should all go before somebody else got killed." She clenched her fists. "I want him back." And she began to cry as if nothing on earth could stop her.

There were other people all around them, huddling together as if expecting bombs from below. The two women, unaware of Rusty sitting across the table from them with his head buried in his arms, unaware of the sound of a siren in the distance, unaware of the earth tumbling toward its own eventual demise, suddenly felt themselves wrapped in a cold embrace and heard the sound of Joe's voice: "I'm all right. Hush now," murmuring into their hair. "I'm all right. I'm all right . . ."

As Joe held them, they cried even harder and clung to him so tightly they left bruises on his arms.

He already knew about Pal. "I . . . I had some things I had to do this afternoon. And the Schooner didn't want to start. So I borrowed Frank's pickup. You know Pal," he said, the tears pouring down his cheeks. "I begged her to come, but she wouldn't go near the truck. And it was damp and cold. And Rusty was still at school. And I thought I'd only be away for a couple of hours. So I left her in the Schooner. I left her in the Schooner." He tipped his head way back, squeezed his eyes shut, and the tears rolled into his hair.

When Angela brought him a mug of hot, sweet tea, he opened his eyes, shook his head, could not help panting.

"I wasn't going to go away today," he said. "I didn't feel like it, and I should have been digging potatoes instead. But if I'd stayed home I might have been in the Schooner, having supper. I should have been in the Schooner." He began to tremble.

As she put her arms around him, Rachel vowed never again to risk doing him the least harm. But within days she had broken her vow and left on him his freshest scar.

Chapter 43

Joe slept at Rachel's house that night, although in fact he slept little. For hours he lay in Rachel's bed with her hair blanketing his shoulder and thought about the days that lay ahead. He had known for a long time that changes were coming, but it seemed that they were suddenly upon him and now he did not feel quite ready for them. It still did not seem possible that the Schooner was gone, Pal gone with it. He himself had predicted such things. Now he found them difficult to believe.

As he lay in Rachel's bed, he thought about how he had lived his life. He thought about the things he'd done since finding Belle Haven and about how some of them had angered Rachel beyond understanding. He looked frankly and fully at what she meant to him and he to her, weighed this in several lights, imagined what would happen when she found out what he had done on his way home from California and had been doing behind her back ever since.

In the morning, after Joe had washed and dried his only clothes, he went with Rachel down into town and found a red cross painted on the door of Earl's hardware store and another on the door to Paula's Beauty Salon, which stood on the other side of the ruined parking lot. A chain had been fixed across the entrance to the lot, and on it was a sign saying, DANGER! KEEP OUT! Earl stood on the sidewalk a few paces back, his hands thrust into his coat pockets, watching Mendelson prod gingerly at the ground around the cave-in. Earl seemed not to hear Rachel when she spoke his name.

"Leave him be for now," Joe said. "He needs to get used to the idea."

Joe himself had not looked right into the lot where the Schooner had gone down. He could not bear to think that the floor of it might have grown hot, that Pal might have felt the fire coming. And, too, although he had to a great extent forsworn the lure of possessions, for him the Schooner had been a treasure. And, as such, the memory of it would always fire his heart. And so he could not look at the place where it had been.

"They say the Lord looks after fools and little children," Mendelson said, stepping over the chain to join Joe and Rachel, walking away with them toward Angela's. "And considering how close you came to an early grave, I guess they're right, Joe."

"Did you want something, Mendelson?"

"Just to remind you that you're not eligible for any government assistance, Joe. I'm sorry as hell about that, truly I am, but technically you're not a resident of Belle Haven. And without you telling me your last name and your social security number, I can't do anything no way, nohow."

"Uh-huh." Joe opened the door to the Kitchen, let Rachel enter. "Not a problem, Mendelson."

"Well, I didn't really think it would be, seeing as how your girl's all set, money-wise."

Joe walked into the Kitchen and shut the door against the sound of Mendelson clucking his tongue as if he had run out of things to say but was still too full of noise to keep silent.

Fewer people in Belle Haven might have meant fewer people at Angela's, if not for the smell of cinnamon and coffee, the taste of good, hot food, the soothing wash of conversation: these were things that stood up to the fire and the fear of it. So there were quite a few people in the Kitchen that morning, a block away from the lot where the Schooner had been, and Angela was hot and busy. But at the sight of Joe, she said, "Hang on" to a man ordering flapjacks and sausage and came around the counter to kiss Joe and take his hands. "You're looking bright-eyed and bushy-tailed this morning, my darlin'."

Joe smiled at her.

"What can I get you two?"

"An apron," said Rachel, and Angela did not protest. "You, Joe?" she asked.

"Tea, when you have a second." Before she turned away, he said, "And what would you say, Angela, if I asked you to close up for a few hours tomorrow?"

"What for?"

"Something important."

"Ask me again later," she said, distracted by the man wanting flapjacks.

While Rachel helped Angela and Dolly, Joe sat at a small corner table, drinking his tea. Then, "I'll do the dishes when I get back," he told Angela, kissed Rachel's cheek, and left. But it was nearly lunchtime before they saw him again. It took him a good deal longer than he had thought it would to talk with the other people who had come to be his best and only friends, asking them to spare him some time, some trust, and to take, in trade, some of the luck with which he had been blessed.

"What's all this about, Joe?"

"I told you, Rachel. I want you to come somewhere with me tomorrow. It's a surprise." They were sitting in Rachel's kitchen, sharing a chicken pie they had made together and trying not to listen for the sound of Pal at the door.

"Angela's coming too?"

"And Rusty. And Dolly. And a couple of other people."

"Who?"

"Mrs. Sapinsley," whose garden Joe had worked so often that he thought of it as his, too. "Earl and Mag," whose condemned hardware store had provided him with the tools to do what he loved. "And Frank," who had been one of the first to welcome Joe to Belle Haven.

"You taking us to the circus?"

"The circus?"

"That's what my dad did when things weren't going particularly well, for whatever reason." Rachel pushed her food around on her plate. "He'd hustle me and my mother into the car, wouldn't tell us where we were going, and we'd end up at the circus or having a picnic up on top of a mountain or on a fishing boat out in the middle of some lake. He thought the adventure would snap us out of whatever sort of funk we were in." She put down her fork and smoothed her hair behind her ears. There were purple smudges under her eyes.

"Didn't work too well, though. Or I suppose it did, in a way. I'd feel so bad about how hard he was trying that I'd put on a good face and laugh a lot. Which is the sort of thing I used to do all the time. Worry about whether everyone else was happy. Just like he did, I suppose. Try to guess what would make things go along most smoothly." She put both hands down flat on the table in front of her, as if to be ready for anything. "But I've changed, Joe. You take me to the circus, and I'm liable to smack you right in the face."

Joe reached across the table and picked up one of her hands. "I already know that, Rachel," he said. "I don't think there's much you could do to surprise me. Not anymore." He held her hand tightly, looked into her face. "Will you come?"

She thought it over for a minute or two. "All right," she finally said, nodding. "Let's see if you have any surprises left for me."

It was seven-thirty in the morning. In the window of Angela's Kitchen was a sign that read, GONE FISHIN'. BACK BY SUPPERTIME. Since it was Saturday, the elementary school, where more and more desks sat stiff and empty, would not miss Rusty. Frank no longer had his gas station—just a pile of rubble—so he'd said, "Hell, why not?" when Joe asked him to spend the morning out of town.

Earl and Mag, who had emptied out the hardware store, put their furniture in storage, and were staying at the Randall Motor Inn, waiting for their check, drove into Belle Haven, unsmiling, to find out what Joe wanted with them. Betsy Sapinsley already had her check and was simply waiting out one final week until her son could find the time to drive over from Cleveland and take her home to his tiny apartment. She, who had not left Belle Haven for years, wondered what Joe could possibly have to show her, but he had been tending her garden for two years now, toting her groceries, shoveling her walks, and listening to her when she remembered being a girl. She would go with him for a few hours, gladly. All of them had gathered at dawn in the parking lot behind the school.

The grass on the baseball diamond was brilliant with dew, the cool, October sky nearly purple, the clouds immaculate, the breeze strong. It was nearly impossible to believe on such a morning that everything had gone so wrong, that the land beneath this particular piece of sky was dying.

"I'm sorry I got you all up so early," Joe said when everyone had arrived, "but I didn't really want anyone else to know about this. I couldn't invite everyone to come along, and I didn't want to make a big deal out of it. There's enough bickering going on in this town already." He gave a short, sharp dog whistle, and Rusty, hanging from the jungle gym, turned toward him, ears cocked. "Time to go," he yelled, and Rusty came running.

At Joe's request and with Joe's money, Earl had rented a van in Randall big enough to carry all nine of them. They climbed in and settled themselves, saying little, twitchy with curiosity. Even so, no one had tried very hard to find out where they were going, and Joe was amazed by this. He wondered what they were thinking, whether they had guessed his intentions, if not their destination. He thought that Rachel might have some idea, for she had chosen to sit at the back of the van with Angela and refused to meet his eye.

He saw that Mrs. Sapinsley was quietly smiling. Perhaps she was simply glad to be going somewhere, knowing that she could still return. She had told him often how much she loved to live alone, far from the nearest city, and how much she feared what her life would be like once she was stranded in Cleveland, a burden to her son and a stranger to everyone else.

As Joe drove out of town, Rusty, in the seat beside him, pressed his face against the window, staring out at the passing houses or at the foundations of those that were gone, as if he were looking at unfamiliar country. He guessed the names of the small rivers they crossed on their way north, away from Belle Haven, and exclaimed over the faces of deer among the trees. And then he grew silent, and Joe wondered if he had already begun to miss Belle Haven, so recently put behind them.

After a while, Rusty turned suddenly and asked, "Where we going, Joe?"

"Almost there. You'll see soon enough."

Rusty touched Joe on the arm so that he turned to look at him. "I want to go home," he said.

Joe saw in Rusty's face an unbearable blend of relentless hope and unfocused fear. Looking back to the road ahead, he remembered how it had looked through the Schooner's big, dusty windshield.

"When I was a boy," Joe said, "but much younger than you are now, my mother died. One day she was there with me—I can still remember how it felt to sit with my head against her chest—and the next day she was gone. There wasn't a single part of a single room in our house that didn't remind me of her. She had cut some flowers and put them in a vase in my sister's room the day before she died, and when the flowers wilted someone threw them away and I thought I would go out of my mind. I didn't ever want to leave that house. But then I changed and my life changed, and it wasn't until I got to Belle Haven that my mother's face came back to me, and the smell of her, and the sound of her voice, and the feel of her chest against the back of my head." Joe turned to look at Rusty, whose eyes were closed. "There are some things that stay with you forever," he said. "Even after they're gone."

They went on without speaking. Rusty leaned his head against the window, his eyes closed. He might have been asleep but for the flexing of his fingers.

Twenty miles from Belle Haven, Joe glanced in the mirror at his silent passengers. "We're here," he said.

Rusty opened his eyes and sat forward and was the first to see the gates, which were old and stood wide open. Joe eased the van through them, drove slowly along the dipping, uneven lane, and proceeded alongside a field of clover to the edge of some woods. "I don't think I'd better go any farther," he said. "It's pretty muddy along here right now, and I don't want to get stuck."

He shut off the engine and turned in his seat to face the others. Quite suddenly, he was afraid.

"I don't know if maybe I've done the wrong thing here," he said haltingly, astounding Rachel by blushing. "I thought, when I was visiting my sister in San Francisco last summer, that the time would come when you would all have to leave Belle Haven. Or at least ought to. So, since I had plenty of money, I decided to do something to help. I figured that it . . . that what I've built wouldn't go to waste, even if you stayed in Belle Haven. I thought that I could always find a use for this place, one way or the other. Or sell it. So don't anybody feel that you have to, you know, humor me or anything. If you like what you see, wonderful. If not, no harm done." He cleared his throat and ran a hand over his face. "We're about three miles south of Cookstown. There's a good school there. There's a hospital about five miles east of here, in Fairlawn. Fire stations, police, plenty of stores both places. This," he said, holding an open hand out toward the land beyond the windows, "used to be part of a small horse farm.

I bought the place on my way back to Belle Haven last August. There are several pastures with woods around them. And—"

But Earl, who hadn't said much of anything since finding the cross painted on the door of his beloved hardware store, suddenly shook his head, rose partway out of his seat, and held both hands over his head as if Joe had a gun on him. "Whoa, boy," he said, silencing Joe and forestalling Rachel, who had been gearing up to make a protest of her own. "Jesus H. Christ on a crutch. This is not Hollywood, Joe." He sat back down in his seat and put his hands on his knees. "This is not *Wheel of Fortune.* You are not Pat Sajak. And I am not some lady from Topeka with big hair and a pair of stretch pants."

Mag looked wide-eyed at her husband. "Earl!" she said, glad to hear him talking again but not much liking what she heard. "You want to lie down or something?"

"No, I do not want to lie down or something." He shrugged her hand off his arm. "Nor do I want charity, which is what I think I'm being measured for, am I right, Joe?"

Joe made a face. "That's not what this is, Earl."

"Then what? You pack us all in here and haul us outta town to look at something. What? Put a name to it, Joe. I don't like mysteries."

Joe knew Earl was not angry at him. Not specifically. But Earl was angry, and rightly so, and could not very well take it out on the fire itself. Joe didn't mind being a surrogate. Not where Earl was concerned.

"I don't have a name for it," Joe said. "And if it's all right, I'd just as soon show you as tell you what all this is about." He turned back around in his seat and stepped out of the van, came around to the other side and slid back the big side door. "Come and see for yourself. Then you can all go home." He sounded defeated, which made Earl mad at himself, too, and brought him out of the van without any further protest, Mag still watching him out of the corner of her eye.

The rest of them climbed out without a word, except when Mrs. Sapinsley thanked Joe for the hand he offered her, and Dolly said, "Watch your head, Angela," which was more than she usually said. The sound of Dolly's voice startled Joe, as it always did. But he never forgot that she was there, for he carried with him the image of her standing guard at the nursery door while her baby grandson lay on the other side and his father raged nearby.

Rachel didn't say a word. Angela looked like she was simultaneously experiencing every emotion known to man, from anticipation to regret, and was not enjoying herself much. Rusty, who loved being in the woods, seemed content to take things one step at a time: he was ready to look at what Joe had to show him but in the meantime was happy with the sight of the trees.

Joe led them all down the lane into the woods. Rusty walked alongside him. The others followed, picking their way carefully among the tire ruts and tree roots, keeping the pace slow so that Mrs. Sapinsley would not feel rushed.

The lane had been sculpted by the passage of large trucks, and the undergrowth that bordered it was dusty. It was clear that something had been going on in these woods, but it was not until they were nearly upon it that they saw, at the end of a narrow dirt laneway that led off into the trees, the first of the houses.

It was unmistakably new; there were still stickers on its window-panes, there was a swath of unplanted ground around it, and the rooms inside looked bare. But, solitary, tucked in among the trees, it did not have the raw look of houses assembled on the muddy, forsaken fields of retreating farmers. It had a wraparound porch with a beautifully carved railing, lots of windows, a big brick chimney, a roof shingled with precious cedar. There were shutters and window boxes at the windows, gables, a big oak door.

When everyone had stopped to have a look, Joe turned to Earl and Mag. He reached into his pocket and took out a ring of keys, sorted through them, and slipped one free. "Here," he said, holding it out to them. They stared at the key, Joe, the house.

"What's this?" Earl said.

"It's the key to that house," Joe said, trying to smile. "Why don't you go have a look."

"But whose house is it?" Mag asked, although the look on her face betrayed her. Feeling none of Joe's uncertainty, she did nothing to hide her own smile.

"Yours, if you want it," Joe said.

"What do you mean, theirs?" Angela, looking on, still doubted what was happening. She had been so badly disappointed in her life that she no longer assumed anything much would come her way.

Joe turned to her and shrugged. "Theirs," he repeated.

"Here we go again." Earl sighed. "If this isn't charity, then I don't know what the hell is."

But this time Joe was ready. The short walk into the woods had given him all the time he needed to find another name for what he'd done. "Let me ask you something, Earl," he said, fingering the raw notches on the key in his hand. "What did you charge me for parking the Schooner in your lot?"

"Nothing. It didn't cost me anything to let you park there. You comparing that to this? Apples and oranges if I ever saw 'em."

"And what did you charge me for the supplies and the work you put into Rusty's tree house?"

"This," Earl said with a snort, pointing at the house in the woods, "ain't no tree house."

"How much?" Joe repeated.

"Nothing." Earl threw up his hands. "But that was different. It was a good idea, building a tree house for Rusty." Neither of them said anything about the conversations they'd had, high up in the walnut tree, as they'd wrestled the beams of the tree house into place. Conversations about Rusty's father, who had not been seen in Belle Haven for over a decade. "It was my pleasure."

"And this," Joe said, nodding toward the house among the trees, "is mine."

Still, Earl did not take the key. He mashed his lips together and blew air out of his nose, like a horse.

"Thank you, Joe," Mag said, taking the key herself. "Shut up, Earl," she said, before he'd said another word. "I don't know what we'll do about this," she said to Joe, "but I must say there's not a thing wrong with your heart. It's in the right place." She turned to Earl. "And if you think I'm going to get back in that van without taking a look at that house, you're outta your mind. I've been living above a hardware store for twenty years, Earl, and they were twenty good years," which took the twist out of his mouth, "but I'm having a look at this house, and that's all there is to it."

And with that, she took Earl's hand and led him into the trees, although he went willingly enough. He'd made it clear he wasn't looking for a handout. No one could fault him for yielding to a wife who'd asked for very little in her life and would have been happy with less.

"Come on," Joe said to the rest of them, continuing down the lane, and they followed him in a ragtag sort of way, trying not to look too far ahead, but each for reasons that were entirely their own. Threading like a knotty ribbon through the woods was a string of ancient, overgrown apple trees. "Those trees still blossom in the spring," Joe said to no one in particular, but Rusty raised his head, listening.

The next house, on the other side of the lane from the first, was quite small. The garden, which appeared to surround the house, was if anything the bigger of the two. Around both was a low fence, sufficiently high to make rabbits think twice, with a gate and a trellis arching above it, asking for vines. A single step led to a front porch big enough for a rocker. Joe turned to look at Mrs. Sapinsley.

She looked at the house. She knew it was hers, but she did not believe it. "This is not for me," she said. It did not sound like a question, but it was.

"There aren't any stairs except that one at the porch," Joe said, searching for the right key. "And the grocery store will make deliveries. I checked. The garden's already been turned over, so it's ready for spring. I had a truck bring in a load of topsoil, but you'll have to decide what you want in it. Maybe you'd like to bring some of your perennials along with you?"

Mrs. Sapinsley looked at the big, empty garden. She thought of her generous son and wondered how much of him would be hurt, how much relieved, to hear that she would not be joining him in Cleveland.

"But you hardly know me," she said, feeling that she could not possibly accept such a gift.

Joe remembered the night he had called his father and been told that his sister was dead. He remembered stumbling back to the Schooner where Ian and Rachel and Angela waited inside. He remembered that the three of them, who had barely known him then, had done everything they could to help him find his way.

"I know you well enough," Joe said. When he took Mrs. Sapinsley by the arm and led her toward the house, she went with him willingly, beginning to be convinced that there was a way to leave Belle Haven without leaving her heart behind.

"I'll be along in a while to collect you," Joe said to her as they reached the porch. When he turned back toward the lane, Frank, Angela, Dolly, Rusty, and Rachel all stared at him in complete silence. But he could tell from the looks on their faces that for each of them the silence meant something different.

"Frank," he said, as he walked up to them. "If you could design your own house, what kind of house would it be?"

Frank, whose hands were still mapped with black from his long association with oil and old metal, grimaced as if he had a bad tooth. "That's like asking me what I plan to wear to the ball," he said. "Not something I figured I'd ever be called upon to do."

"Consider yourself called upon," Joe said. He wasn't smiling either.

After a long pause Frank said, "No, I don't think I can. I've lived in the same house all my life. And I do mean all my life, birth on up. I don't know anything else, and I don't really want to."

Which took Joe somewhat aback. Despite everything he'd seen and heard in Belle Haven, he had become convinced that everyone would eventually go their ways. In their shoes, which he in fact was, he would have spent time imagining his departure, planning the next part of his life, trying it on, making adjustments, aiming for the best possible fit.

"You don't mean you're going to stay in Belle Haven?"

"Yes," Frank said. "That's what I mean."

Rachel looked as if she wanted to move closer to Frank, take his arm.

"And do what?" Joe tried to sound simply curious, but this came out sounding like the challenge it was.

Frank gave him a sharp look and reset his cap. "You've done a nice thing here, Joe," he said, gesturing all around him as if Joe had been the one to plant these trees, sculpt this earth, brew this air. "But it's not what I'm after. To tell you the truth, I'm surprised you'd think of me. Do I really strike you as a man who needs minding?"

When Joe had imagined his plans going wrong, he had imagined something much like this, words of this sort, but spoken by someone else altogether.

"No, no, I never meant to imply you needed looking after, Frank. You or anyone else."

"Then how come I'm here?"

Joe had thought he knew the answer to this one but called upon to give it found himself at a loss.

"I don't have a lot of friends in this world," he eventually said. "But you're one of them."

Frank nodded, pleased with this answer, willing to accept it but not to be bound by it. "That's fine," he said. "And I thank you for the offer. But I'll be staying in Belle Haven for now. Maybe for good. I won't know till I'm dead or on my way, I expect."

And with that he headed back down the lane toward the waiting van, leaving Joe with a good deal of the wind knocked out of him, Rachel looking smug, Angela and Dolly and Rusty somewhat removed, as if they were waiting for their turn to make a decision but not entirely certain what it would be.

Now, with only four following him but they the four people he counted as family, Joe walked on down the lane. When they reached the next house, he lifted an elbow toward it but kept on going. "That would have been Frank's house," he said. Glimpsed through the trees, it seemed quite modest, as Frank was. Simple and straightforward.

Rachel, watching it as she passed, had to admit that Joe had a knack for summing people up. He seemed able to see to the core of a person, and he usually had no trouble accepting people for what they were. And yet for months now she had felt as if he was sitting in judgment of her, whether he had any right to or not. Frank, it seemed, could flat out say he'd be staying in Belle Haven and Joe did nothing, said not a syllable, did not protest at all. To Rachel, who had also been born and raised in one house, one town, one world, Joe had made a thousand arguments, all meant to speed her on her way. She did not consider this a sign of love for her. If he truly loved her, he would respect her as well. Accept her for what she was. Accept her reasons for doing what she did.

By the time they reached the next house, Rachel was preparing to do as Frank had done: say thanks, and mean it, but go her own way, which was back home. She had not imagined how it would feel to see Angela, and Dolly, and Rusty, who were her family, too, choose a different direction.

Joe stopped. The others stopped with him. He turned to Angela, who was clutching Rachel's hand like a child. "Hang on," Joe said, grabbing Rusty's sleeve as the boy lunged forward toward the house he could see among the trees. "Wait for your mother. And your grandmother," he added, beckoning Dolly forward. "Angela," he said, turning back to her and for the first time truly smiling, "I know you may not want this place. I know that already, so you won't kill me by saying no. But I loved building it for you. I really did." He took another key off the big ring in his hand and gave it to Rusty. "Now you can go," he said, and Rusty sprinted down the laneway toward the most beautiful cottage Rachel had ever seen.

It was all shingled in cedar that would weather to gray and had the look of houses built by the sea. Its windows were tall and thin, its porch wide and deep, and upstairs there was a small balcony with French doors, which would make it easy to hurry out into the morning or watch the flight of the moon. When Rusty appeared suddenly on the balcony, waving the key in his hand, Joe was reminded of the day he'd given him the tree house. And for the first time since leaving Belle Haven that morning, Joe thought that maybe he'd done the right thing.

Angela looked at her son on that balcony, looked around her at the safe and beautiful woods, and breathed a long, shuddering sigh. Then she dropped Rachel's hand, took her mother's, and the two of them walked slowly toward the cottage.

Joe watched them until they disappeared inside the house. He knew he had no choice now but to turn and look at Rachel, to see what waited on her face. He could hear her breathing. The branches of the trees overhead moved gently. The sunlight moved on the ground as if on water. There was no smell to the air except of damp earth. One of the best smells there is.

"Where are you going to live?" Rachel finally said.

Joe turned and looked at her face, but she avoided his eye. She was not smiling. She looked as if she never had.

"I'll show you," he said, heading farther down the lane into the woods. At a narrow path, Joe turned off the lane and led the way through the trees to a cabin. It was old but appeared sound, a little bit mossy, a little bit crooked, somewhat overgrown. It, too, had a porch in front, a garden wild with carrots and rampant beans, an enormous chimney. "It's where one of the trainers lived when this was a working farm. Wait until you see the fireplace," he said, heading for the door.

"Joe," she said, stopping him. He turned slowly. "I don't care about your fireplace. I don't care about any of this."

Joe opened his mouth and closed it again. Shrugged. "I was pretty sure you'd feel that way," he said.

"But you did it anyway."

He looked up, straightened his shoulders. "Why not? You know how I feel about staying in Belle Haven. It's a dangerous place to be. I don't want to lose the people I love. What's wrong with that?"

"Then where's my house? Didn't you build one for me?" She peered into the woods. "Or did you think I'd move in here, with you?" She looked at him. "Or don't I count as one of the people you love anymore?"

"Don't do that," he said. There was more anger on his face than she'd seen there in a long time. "Don't you *dare* do that. You've kept me at arm's length for weeks now. You've tried to make me feel how you feel, and I can't and I won't. Not anymore. And if I lose you in the process, then I lose you." He stopped to breathe. "But don't you dare suggest that I'm the one who's become hardhearted. That's you." He nearly drove her back a step with his fury. "Not me."

They stared at each other, Rachel trying to remember what she'd meant to say, Joe calming himself by degrees.

"If you knew how I would feel about all this, why did you bring me along?" she said.

Joe rubbed the back of his neck, shook his head. "I didn't know for sure," he said, unable to look at her. "I hoped after you saw this farm, you'd want to live here too. Near me. But on your own." He met her eye. "I didn't build you a house because you can afford to build your own house and I knew you'd want to be the one to do it."

"Don't tell me this has anything to do with money. If it was about money, you wouldn't have brought Earl and Mag up here. They'd be okay on their own. You'd have brought people like the Millers who live down by the tracks. I don't see them here, but they're the ones who need the most help."

"You're right," Joe said, a little of his anger returning. "It's not only about money. I'm not doing this just to help people. I'm doing it for them and me both. I chose people who get along well with one another, who are already friends and will look after one another. People I care about. Some of them need more help than others. I could afford to help them all, so I did. And if I've annoyed you in the process, I'm sorry."

"Annoyed? You think I'm *annoyed*?" she said. "I am annoyed by people who let their dogs shit where I walk. By slow drivers in the fast lane. I am annoyed by people who give little girls toy ironing boards for Christmas. I am not annoyed by what you have done. I am disgusted." She waved her arm at the trees. "By the way you have taken my friends and the only family I've got and my entire life and tried to make them all yours." She began to back down the path through the trees. "You don't like your life anymore, so you help yourself to mine. Buy people some houses, and they're friends for life. You spend a whole year building this place, and you keep it a secret. From me." She hit her chest with her hand. "From *me*! How could you do that? You know I'd do anything to keep Belle Haven from falling apart, but things have gotten to be too much for me. And now you're pushing them faster. You're making it so much harder.

"I trusted you," she said. And she turned away, walked off down the path and onto the lane, heading for the van.

Joe stood alone outside his cabin and watched her moving through the woods until he could no longer see her. Then he sat down in the leaves and put his face into his hands and did not move until he heard Rusty calling his name.

Chapter 44

There was no one in the lane, but as Rachel paced the length of it she saw her friends through the trees and was amazed by the ease and immediacy of their surrender. Earl and Mag were still circling their house, their faces serious but pleased, first one pointing up at the chimney, then the other at how the sunlight struck a window, as if they were saluting the house and all its singular merits. But it was Angela who stopped Rachel in her tracks, for she was lying full length in a bed of pine needles, their barbs weathered blunt, her eyes closed, her hands resting easily on her belly. She seemed to be smiling.

Rachel turned away and walked out of the woods. She walked past the van, through a field of long grass, and up over a rise.

Here, hidden from the woods where Joe had built his houses, was another house. It was big, sound, freshly painted, well kept. A vegetable garden to one side still had tomatoes, cabbages, a pumpkin or two, some Indian corn. On the other side of the house a few horses grazed in a fenced pasture. They were racers, lean and shapely.

She walked up to the fence and called to the horses. They ignored her so completely that she blushed.

Her head hurt. She felt as if she might throw up. Her toes were clenched so tightly that they strained the seams of her shoes. Everything had gone so wrong. What was she supposed to do now? There were things in those woods that Rachel had not reckoned on. No matter what she did, what she said, she would do some wrong, commit some injustice.

She had been unkind to Joe and it had come easy. She had not felt the slightest hesitation, no inclination at all to choose her words or soften them.

She cursed softly and smacked the top rail of the fence with the flat of her hand, but the horses did not spare her a glance. One of them straightened its legs and shook itself all over. Its mane was like a woman's hair.

Rachel suddenly became aware that there was an old man walking toward her along the fence. "Never mind them," he said, stopping next to her. "They play hard to get 'less you feed 'em."

"I'm sorry," Rachel said, stepping back from the fence. "I didn't mean to intrude."

"No intrusion." The man put out his hand. It was like wood. "Denver Simms."

"Rachel Hearn."

"Nice name, Rachel."

"Denver, too."

He looked at her closely. "You going to be one of our new neighbors?"

She looked away, toward the horses. "No."

"No?"

"No. I just came along for the ride."

He tipped his head toward the animals. "You like horses?"

"To look at."

"Ah, well, these are fine for that. Even better for riding. Fast." He hissed through his teeth, skimmed the air with his hand. "Smart, too."

"You breed them?"

"Did. Raced them, too. Trained them. Mine, other folks'. World's finest way to make a living."

"But you've sold your land."

"Oh, well. Ada, my wife, and I are getting on, and my son, Steven"—he rubbed the bridge of his nose—"well, he didn't really take to it. So, he's an architect and that's what he's good at so that's what he ought to do. And I'm proud of him, which is not to say I don't wish it were otherwise."

Rachel glanced back toward the van, but it was hidden on the other side of the rise.

"You nervous they're going to leave you behind?"

"No," she said. "They'll wait for me."

"They like the houses Christopher built for them?" Denver leaned toward her slightly, smiling, eyebrows lifting, pleased.

The *Christopher* had thrown her for a moment. Finally, "I guess," she said. Shrugged. Bit her lip.

"I'll tell you, Ada and I are very happy with the whole arrangement. We had plenty of offers from developers wanting to clear out all the trees and build a hundred look-alikes on our land. But I don't hold no truck with developers. Christopher, he's a different sort. He told us what he wanted to do, said we could keep these few acres, promised us there'd be only a few houses and the trees would nearly all stay. We said yes, just like that. And when he said he wanted to live in that old cabin in the woods, we approved. We understand about these things, Ada and I."

"So do I," Rachel said.

"But the thing that really sold us was the way the horses took to him. He walked up to the fence, about where we are now, and he made a little kiss sound, and they came ambling over, blowing, and stood still for him. They don't often take to strangers that way, not these horses. So if we needed a clincher, that was it."

Rachel tried to picture Joe—Christopher—to picture him with the horses, but she kept shying away from the thought.

"Well, I guess I'd better get on back to the van before they come looking for me."

"All right," he said, putting out his hand once more. "It was nice to meet you, Rachel. I hope we'll be seeing you again."

She liked the way he kept saying "we," as if his wife were never truly absent.

"It was nice to meet you, too," she replied. "Take care of your horses."

"You can count on that," he said, and she turned away.

On her way back toward the van, Rachel felt her fury resurfacing, but it was a pervasive, chaotic anger that seemed to have too many sources, too many targets, to contemplate. It exhausted her, made her feel truly desperate. And so she forced it down and thought, instead, of horses and of Denver's wayward son.

She was tempted to give up, give in, and not to mind that the people she had lived her life with had chosen to go their ways, too. But in the face of this temptation came a new resolve to resist any plot that was not her own. "I am not resigned," she said as she came over the rise and saw the van waiting below.

Chapter 45

October 18, '83

Dear Rachel,

I may not see you for a while. There's really no reason for me to go down into town anymore. I can't stand the sight of the bulldozers, I can't stand to be bothered by the reporters. I'll go down to see Angela and Rusty, help them move out, help everybody move out if they need help, but most of the time I'll be in Rusty's tree house, with your permission. It's on your land, I know, but I hope you won't mind that I'm out here. I won't bother you. I'll climb up over the hill, won't come through your yard.

But that's not why I'm writing.

I'm writing to say that there's land for you up on that farm if you want it. Always has been. I picked out a beautiful place alongside a stream. There's an old stand of holly trees nearby. Quite rare, really. When I was walking the farm, trying to picture where everything would go, I thought you might like that place, so I set it aside, had a well dug, brought the power lines out that far. Everything's ready whenever you want it. But maybe you won't.

I think I understand how you feel, at least a little bit. Like I betrayed you, took your friends away. Nonsense, really, but I can still understand you feeling that way for now. Get over it quickly.

Remind yourself that I love you. You know I do. There's nothing to be afraid of.

I hope this letter makes you truly furious. I hope you get so mad that you come storming out here and fight it out with me. Maybe then I'll be able to explain things to you. Though I shouldn't have to.

I don't believe in utopias and I certainly haven't tried to create one. But I had more money than anyone has any right to have, and so I spent it. It's as simple as that.

It occurs to me that maybe you had a similar plan in mind, a way to put your own money to good use. Did I steal your thunder? Well, I'm fond of thunder, too. Fire, no. You can keep your fire.

I'll be leaving Belle Haven whenever you're ready. You may not want me with you and I'll stay far enough away. But I won't leave you here alone. I'll be in the tree house if you need me.

If you change your mind, want to join us on the farm, you can stay in the house I built for Frank. I'd let you keep it, but it's meant for someone who doesn't have the kind of money you do. Someone like Ed Zingham, but he's already taken an apartment in Randall. Maybe you could call him for me and ask him if he wants it. Tell him where to find me.

Well, you're probably not interested in all this talk about the farm. I wish I didn't love you so much. Sometimes I wish I'd never come to Belle Haven. But most of the time I thank God I did.

Yours,
Joe

Chapter 46

"What do you mean, you're not leaving?"

"I'm not leaving *yet*, I said. My mother's going up to get the house ready. Earl and Mag will give her some help if she needs it. But Rusty and I are going to stay another week or so. I want to spend some time with Rachel, Joe. See if I can get her to change her mind. And Rusty wants a few more days with his friends. He's known them all his life, and he's never going to see some of them again. How can I say no?"

"Where is he now?"

"He's over at Mary Beth Sanderson's house. You know, over on Rachel's side of the creek. There's been no trouble over there. The nearest borehole is real quiet. The kids are just playing in the yard. Relax, Joe. Everything's okay."

He took Angela's hands. She noticed that his fingernails were torn. He was growing a beard. "Don't stay too much longer, Angie," he said. He never called her Angie. "I've got a bad feeling about all this."

Judy and Daniel Sanderson and their three children were among the hundred or so people still living in Belle Haven when the first cold nights came to town and the leaves began to turn. Judy, immense with her fourth child, had spent a whole week wandering through her house, looking at each room, checking to make sure the canaries were still on their tiny trapezes, trying to find the energy to pack everything up into the boxes she'd been collecting for months. It wasn't that she wanted to hang around any longer than she had to. With the A&P closed and the Superette always low on everything, even putting supper on the table had become a challenge. But the check from the government would be arriving any day now, and then they would go. Daniel would still have his job in Krebs Corners. They had found a house real close to his office, a good fifteen miles from the fire, and had all but paid for it. They had to wait for the check to arrive. Then they'd go. But she couldn't get organized. She couldn't stop thinking about that motor home going down the other day. Three blocks away, other side of the creek. Maybe the creek would keep the fire away.

She walked back down to the kitchen and stood at the window watching Mary Beth and Rusty in the backyard, sitting at the picnic table, eating grapes and reading comic books. Everything looked okay. But no matter how hard she tried, she could not stop thinking that maybe in the next minute, in the minute when she was not watching, the fire would come right up out of the ground. She looked down at the linoleum on the kitchen floor. It was blue and white and very pretty. She sat down in a chair at the kitchen table and took off her shoes. Took off her socks. Put her bare feet flat on the kitchen floor so she could feel the cool linoleum. And finally began to pack.

Angela, too, had begun to pack. She was still serving odd, scanty meals to use up everything she had in stock. She wasn't making any money, barely breaking even, but with her check on the way and the house Joe had given her outright, she was not worried. She and Dolly packed up everything in their apartment over the Kitchen in just a couple of days. They didn't have much to pack, really. Then Angela borrowed a big pickup, Joe and Frank helped her with the fridge, the beds, the heavy things, and they both drove up north with her to unload everything at the farm.

When Angela got back to Belle Haven, exhausted and pleased, she loaded up the pickup with smaller, lighter cargo, and drove north once more, this time with Dolly.

"Now, don't worry about a thing," she told her mother after they'd carted the last boxes inside. "And don't rush around trying to make everything perfect inside of a week. Rusty and I will be along soon. A few days more. We'll be fine staying at Rachel's house, and maybe, when we come up, we'll be bringing her with us."

Dolly took Angela in her arms. "Don't stay too much longer, girl," she said. "It's not a good idea to tempt fate."

"I know, Mother. I won't."

The next morning, Angela put a sign in the Kitchen's front window. It said, CLOSING DAY. EVERYTHING'S ON THE HOUSE. She served lots of eggs and ham, canned peas, raisin bread, cranberry juice she'd brought in for Joe. Odd stuff. Some of the people eating it were crying.

When she'd had enough, Angela and Rusty gave everyone something to take home: a sack of flour, sugar, salt, pickles, whatever was left. Then she sent Rusty on ahead to Rachel's house, watched him as he walked away.

"So that's it," she said, closing the door as night came on. She washed the dishes, dusted off the shelves in the pantry, scraped down the big grill, swept the floor, scrubbed the counter, set everything to rights before the bulldozers came in a day, a week, whenever they were through wrecking someone else's home.

Then she went upstairs one last time and sat on a milk crate by a window, her cheek resting on the sill, and looked down into the street where she'd been walking the day her water broke, looked over toward Raccoon Creek where she'd taught Rusty how to skip rocks, looked up into the sky where the night's stars had started shining, and said the first of her good-byes.

When Angela arrived at Rachel's house, she was shivering with exhaustion.

"Where's Rusty?" she asked as she came through the door.

"He's out in the tree house with Joe," Rachel muttered, shutting the door and switching on some lights.

"You been sitting here in the dark?"

"What's wrong with that?"

"Boy, oh boy. I can see I've got my work cut out for me."

"You think you're going to bring sweetness and light back into my life, talk me into moving up to that farm with you? Save your breath."

Angela sat down heavily in a big, mushy chair and pulled her knees up to her chest. "You got any brandy?" she asked.

When he came in through the back door, Rusty heard his mother and Rachel talking. He took off his jacket, meaning to join them, but then heard what Rachel was saying and stood where he was, listening.

"You all have too much faith in the man, and I can't for the life of me figure out why. You've known him for a couple of years only, and he's never done one single thing to prove he's capable of making this thing work."

"Come on, Rachel. You saw those houses. They're there. They exist. What kind of proof are you talking about?"

"Since when can a person like Joe—who's never had to work for a living, not really, or deal with the real world—in a single year build all those houses with all the proper permits, utilities, wells, you name it. One year. It's impossible. It'll be the middle of winter and some guy with a badge will show up on your doorstep and start asking you a lot of questions you just won't have the answers to. And who knows where Joe will be by then?"

Rusty listened for his mother to come to Joe's defense, but she did not.

"When I want to know something," he said, walking into the room, "I ask. Why can't you ask Joe about all this?"

When Rachel didn't answer, Rusty said, "I asked Joe what it was like, building those houses, having all that money and being able to say, 'I want you to build me a house here, and one over there, a bigger one, and a little cottage right in those birches there, and make them all beautiful.' I thought he must have felt like a king."

Rachel sat forward in her chair, opened her mouth to say something, but Rusty cut her off. "But he said, no, he didn't feel like a king. He felt good, but mostly lucky. He realized that he'd need all kinds of permits and probably wouldn't ever be able to get them, at least not in time to do what he wanted to do, as quickly as he wanted to do it. But when he called up some of the commissioners and told them what he wanted to do, as soon as he said, 'Belle Haven,' they jumped all over him trying to help. They made sure everything got done right. Imagine how happy they must have been when this strange guy with a zillion bucks walks in and says, 'Hi. I want to settle a bunch of people who are being burned out of their town.' So they helped him. Makes them look good, he figured. Makes Belle Haven an easier problem. Gets a few people out of town faster. That's what Joe figured, anyway. He didn't really care why they were so helpful, though. As long as they didn't try to stop him." Rusty sat down, looking pleased with himself, expecting the women to smile and fan themselves with their hands, relieved to hear that everything was taken care of all right. Rachel surprised him.

"He's not just an opportunist," she said quietly. "That was bad enough. Now he's a traitor, too. I feel sick."

"Oh, come on now, Rachel. I know you're angry with Joe," Angela said tiredly. "I know you want to hang on to this town as long as you can. But it's not Joe's fault we're in trouble. And you of all people ought to know he'd never do anything to hurt you."

Rachel smacked the top of her thigh. "But he has, hasn't he? You don't understand, Angela. He thinks he knows what's best for me. Goddamnit, I'm not a child. And he's not my father." Rusty remembered telling Joe the same thing. He felt awful.

Angela wanted to say, "If your father were here, he'd be on Joe's side." But she knew better than to say such a thing.

"I know what's best for me," Rachel said. "I always have." She walked off toward the kitchen.

Angela remembered how much Rachel had changed when her parents died. But in some ways she seemed exactly the same as she'd always been. For the first time, Angela wondered if Rachel was clinging to Belle Haven because it was a part of something else that she did not know how to give up.

If that was the case, no one, not even Joe, could loosen her grip until she was ready to let go.

Angela held her hand out to Rusty, who walked over to sit on the arm of her chair. "I don't think we'd better stay here too much longer," she said, running her hand slowly over the hair at the nape of his neck. "Everything's going wrong, and I don't think there's anything we can do to set it right."

"Will Joe come with us?" Rusty asked.

"I don't know," his mother replied. "But I don't think there's anything he can do, either."

Chapter 47

In the morning, Rachel drove her truck to Randall. Succinctly, she told Mr. Murdock to keep her money where it was.

"I've decided not to buy any land just now," she said, to his immense relief. "You were right. Owning a few acres here and there isn't going to change things." She had chosen to stand, had kept her coat. "I'm going to follow your advice, wait and see what happens, but perhaps for longer than you intended. The fire's coming faster and faster now. Who knows—maybe it won't hang around for very long. Or maybe it will change direction. The government's moving quickly now, too, buying up everything in sight. But maybe, when everyone who's going to leave has left, the government will start to wonder what it has gotten itself into. Maybe the fire will force them out, too, eat up all the coal they hope to mine, leave them holding the bag. It may take years, but when the fire and the government have both finished with Belle Haven, if there's anything left worth buying, I may well want to buy it."

"Fair enough," Mr. Murdock said. Once again, looking at her, he felt that what Rachel really needed was time. He was pleased that she had chosen to grant herself some.

On her way out of Randall, Rachel saw the road to Spence and took it. She wanted, unexpectedly, to see the government's development where some of the Belle Haven condemnees now lived. But as she approached the grid of cheap new houses, the sight of endless mud, the absence of even a single tree, the streets named by someone

who had never walked them, all of this sent her racing away in another direction, the radio turned up too high, the windows open to
the wind, an unwelcome memory of Joe's beautiful houses made more
alluring by the place she had just seen.

When she got home, she found Mendelson sitting on her front
porch.

"Good morning, Miss Hearn," he said, rising.

"Morning," she replied. "What can I do for you, Mendelson?"

"I know it's a long shot," he said, smiling. "But I just had to come
up here myself to see if maybe you'd decided to sell your house."

"Sell my house?"

"Uh-huh. I know you got a written offer, same as everyone else,
but I'd like to make an offer of my own, ten grand more than before, maybe move the house somewhere safer." He looked around
him, stomped his boot on the floorboards of the old porch. "It's a
good house."

Rachel stared at him. "This house is not for sale," she said. "Not
now or ever."

"Well, I know we're not talking about that much money here—
not by your standards anyway—but it's better than nothing, which is
what you're going to end up with if you keep this place."

Rachel waved him up out of the chair. "Why are you still here?"
she said. "I told you, it's not for sale. Didn't you hear me?"

"I did. I did. Can't blame a man for trying."

As he turned to go, Rachel said, "No one's ever blamed you for
that."

Mendelson stopped with his boot on the top step. "Now, what the
hell's *that* supposed to mean?"

"It means that all you've ever *tried* to do around here is screw
things up for the rest of us."

"*I've* screwed things up?"

"That's what I said."

In all the years since she had first laid eyes on Mendelson, Rachel
had known him to be rude, hard, disturbing, but she had never seen
him lose control.

"Why, you selfish, spoiled, stupid little bitch," he said, stepping
back up onto her porch and only now, incongruously, removing his
hat. "One of *you* started the goddamned fire in the first place, not me.
But let's not blame some old fool who's got cataracts and can't drive

out to the landfill no more so he dumps his shit in a mine pit and throws a match in after it. Or maybe it was some stupid little boys smoking butts. Whatever. All I know is, it wasn't me. But ever since I had the great misfortune to step foot in this miserable town, I've been blamed for every single thing that's gone wrong. I've done everything that anyone could have done, but nothing was ever good enough for you high and mighty, second-guessing, finger-pointing, armchair assholes. 'Dig here, dig there, do this, don't do that, hurry up, get out of our town.' " He was shouting now. Rachel could see his spit in the sunlight. "And none of it means anything at all because only two things are really true: *you* started the fire, and *I'm* the one who's spent nearly a third of my life trying to put it out." He jammed his hat back on his head. "Keep your goddamned house. It'll make fine kindling."

As she watched him drive away, Rachel realized that there was some truth in what Mendelson had said. But it was so very easy to dislike him, and from there it was only a small step to blaming him for the fire that had kept him in Belle Haven long after his welcome had worn out.

Rachel didn't really care. She was tired. It no longer mattered to her how the fire had made its way into town, only that it had. She had little energy to spare for Mendelson—not enough to condemn him or to absolve him, just barely enough to wish him away.

Chapter 48

After four days at Rachel's house, Angela was ready to head north. She was worn out with talking and with worrying, and she figured that Rusty would never feel he'd said good-bye properly, so why not go now. Lots of other people were on the verge of leaving. There were only about eighty people left in town, and the place was looking awful. It still amazed her that there were some people who had no intention of leaving town, now or ever. They were convinced that the fire would race on under the town and southward, away. They argued that the bulldozers had done all the damage, not the fire. Not counting Ross Caspar's place—which wasn't right in the town—only one motor home had gone down. No great loss. Not a single fire. Just some fumes, big deal.

Angela no longer cared whether the fire or Mendelson was to blame. The town was dying, by whichever hand.

"It's time we left," she said.

"If you say so, Angie. But you're welcome to stay here as long as you want." They were out in Rachel's front yard, giving the perennials their fall pruning. It was a lovely October day. "You sure you don't want to hang around until Halloween? For Rusty's sake?"

"You really think anyone's going to be trick-or-treating, Rachel?"

"If there are kids in Belle Haven, there will be trick-or-treating. You know there will. And jack-o'-lanterns, and all that stuff. Hell, I've already got my costume made and my candies bought."

"Well, I think maybe we'll have to miss Halloween this year, all the same. I don't want to push my luck."

"I understand," Rachel said, plunging her pruning shears into the ground, straightening up. "I'll even go up there with you when you're ready."

"You will?" Angela gasped, hoping.

"I didn't get a chance to give everyone a garden pot," she said, looking over the ones left in her yard. "They'll all fit in the back of the pickup, and there's plenty of room for the three of us up front. Save you a bus ticket."

"Oh." Angela turned away, looked down the hill toward the town. "For a minute I thought—" And then she stopped and abruptly turned her head, held up a hand to silence Rachel, opened her mouth so she could hear better, and suddenly began to run down the hill, her hair flying out behind her like a veil, just as Rachel, too, heard the sound of screaming from somewhere among the houses below.

Judy Sanderson had fallen into the habit of walking around barefoot as she packed up and prepared to move house. Her husband laughed about it—"Barefoot, pregnant, and in the kitchen," he said every night when he came home from work and found her cooking without her shoes on, her belly nice and big. She did not tell him why she no longer wore shoes in the house. He thought that her feet had begun to swell.

She was standing at the kitchen sink, washing potatoes, her feet on the cool linoleum, humming something unawares when she looked out into the backyard and wondered if maybe there was something going on between Mary Beth and Rusty. They were only thirteen, but that was plenty old. Then again, maybe they were just friends, as they had been for as long as she could remember. She watched them standing out there in the sunlight, throwing a baseball back and forth, back and forth, her daughter with a good arm, lean, tall for her age, going to be beautiful someday soon. Perhaps Rusty had seen that, too.

And she was watching carefully, through the window she'd washed that morning with vinegar and water (her husband had asked her, "Why you washing the windows when we're moving next Tuesday?"), when she saw Rusty throw Mary Beth a high one, saw her daughter backing up to catch it, laughing. Judy put down the potato in her hand, saying out loud in the kitchen, "Watch out for the tree, Mary Beth," and then saw her tall, sweet, lovely girl start to sink right down into the ground, her face changing, dust coming up in a cloud around her, dust and smoke, heard her screaming now, all of it happening so quickly, then racing out through the back door in her bare feet and feeling the heat coming up through the ground as Rusty grabbed at Mary Beth's hand, the hand all that was left showing, fingers stretched out taut like an exotic bloom, and then Rusty falling through the ground, the earth sinking away with him. And Judy stood there screaming, screaming while the soles of her feet began to scorch and the smoke coming up made it impossible for her to see if Rusty, too, had completely disappeared under the ground.

She lay down on solid earth where there was still grass showing, trying to lie flat on her big, hard belly, to reach her arms out and into the smoke, but she couldn't do it, she was shaking all over and so terrified that she could no longer hear herself screaming. But she was aware, suddenly, that her neighbor, Farley, was scrambling through the huckleberry bushes that grew up between the yards, pulling her to her feet and away from the smoke and the soft ground. Farley was fat and he was getting old and he hardly ever left his house these days, or even the old chair in front of his television, but he threw himself flat along the ground and plunged his arms into the hole where the smoke was billowing, began to yell and roll frantically, trying to scramble up onto his knees without letting go of whatever he had in his hands. And then, suddenly, Angela was there and Rachel right behind her, and they grabbed Farley's legs and pulled him away from the smoke as if he weighed nothing at all. And it seemed to Judy as if she were watching a birth, for as they pulled Farley away another figure slid up out of the ground as smoothly as a snake from its skin, covered with filth and spitting gobs from its mouth, and bawling and screaming, and choking there on the ground. And she could see that it was not her Mary Beth, that it was Rusty, that he was alive, and that he was alone.

"Get her out!" Judy screamed. "She's still down there! Mary Beth!" she screamed at the hole in the ground, at the smoke, as if her daughter might answer, "I'm coming, Mom. My foot's stuck, is all . . ." But although Farley plunged his arms back down into the ground until he, too, began to slide under and his arms came out bleeding, Mary Beth was gone. Rachel came running back then from the street where she'd gone for help, to fetch a bulldozer or some other almighty machine, but she was alone.

They took Judy inside and first called the fire department, then her husband, made sure the other children would stay wherever they were for a time. Then they tried to take her to the hospital, to make sure she was all right, but she would not go any farther from Mary Beth than her kitchen window.

Farley stayed with her, his sleeves in tatters, while Angela wrapped Rusty in a blanket, gently wiped the dirt from his eyes, and Rachel ran up the hill for her truck. She could hear the sirens as she ran.

Rusty fell asleep on the way to the hospital, but he never stopped crying even so.

"He'll be all right," the doctor in Randall said. "We're doing a few more tests, but there doesn't appear to be any real damage, although he must have breathed in an awful lot of carbon monoxide. But if he was only down there for a minute or two, well, I guess he was lucky."

"Lucky," Angela muttered, her face terrible, once the doctor had left. She began to pace back and forth along the hospital corridor, wringing her hands. "I almost lost my boy. I almost lost my boy." She looked at Rachel, who stood watching. "You hear me, Rachel? I almost lost my Rusty. That good enough for you? You gonna go now? God almighty. I'm taking Rusty away as soon as I get him out of here. The very minute."

"Of course you are," Rachel said. "Of course you are. I understand."

"Jesus Christ, Rachel, you don't understand a thing. I've tried to be patient and open-minded, but enough is enough. You're obsessed. I see you looking at what's happening, but you don't do a goddamned thing. You act like there's still something in Belle Haven worth staying for. But I can't for the life of me figure out what's got such a hold on you."

"I know," Rachel said, leaning her back against the wall. "I know I must seem crazy to you. Joe thinks I'm out of my mind. Sometimes I lose sight of everything, and I don't know what the hell I'm doing. Everything's all mixed up: things that happened years before the fire even started, things that happened hundreds of miles from here, things that happened this morning. But you've got to try to understand, Angela. Nothing seems important when I compare it to Belle Haven." She put her head into her hands. "What's so wrong with wanting to keep my home?"

"Nothing's wrong with that. I want to keep my home too. *But I can't*. It's not up to me anymore. And I do have things that are a lot more important than Belle Haven. One of them is lying on a table down the hall."

Rachel closed her eyes. "I'm so sorry this has happened," she said. "I never thought it would get so bad." She opened her eyes. "But I don't have a little boy like Rusty or a mother like Dolly. All I have is my home."

"Which you are clinging to like it's some kind of paradise. Jesus, Rachel. What do you think it will be like when we've left? I always thought you loved Belle Haven because of the people who lived there. Me included. And my mother. And Rusty. And Joe, for that matter. But you've made it clear that when we leave, you'll be staying on." She threw up her hands. "For what?"

Rachel closed her eyes. Tipped back her head. "For all kinds of reasons."

Angela took out a cigarette and held it in her trembling hand. "Name one."

But Rachel couldn't. Everything she loved about Belle Haven was changing. "I can't," she said. "I don't know why, but I can't imagine leaving. It seems wrong." She put her hands over her face again. They were filthy. There was powdery grime in her hair and on her clothes. "I can't explain it."

"I think I can," Angela said. The sight of Rachel so confused and unhappy made Angela sorry for what she was about to say. She was tempted to put her arms around her friend, but there were some things more important than comfort.

Rachel lowered her hands.

"I've been watching you for a long time now, Rachel. I used to worry about you when you were a kid. You were so . . . *selfless*. You never took a step out of line. I used to think you were going to explode. I remember hoping you would."

"Hoping I would explode."

"Yes." Angela shrugged. "Most people would say *bloom*, I guess. Come of age. But the way you tamped yourself down all the time, I figured you weren't likely to do anything so gradual. I figured it would come all at once. An explosion. But I was wrong."

Rachel waited. She knew there was more.

"You went off to college instead. Which I thought was a good thing at the time. I figured you'd grow out of your"—she searched for the right word—"your self-control. Throw out the script you'd written for yourself." She put the cigarette back in its pack.

"College was good for you, Rachel. Anybody could see that. You'd come home so relaxed. And confident. That's when we became friends, you know."

Rachel frowned. "I thought we'd always been friends."

"Uh-uh. You were always my friend, but I wasn't always yours. You were way too tense for me, like you might break if you weren't careful."

Rachel looked like she was going to cry. "Is there a point to all this, Angela? Because if there isn't, I think I'd like to stop talking for a while. The doctor should let us in to see Rusty soon."

Angela took out the cigarette again. She held it between her fingers. "The point is that it would have been better if you'd exploded. Being a later bloomer would have been okay, too, if you'd been able to finish what you'd started. But you had a couple of lousy experiences at school, right around when your parents got killed . . . and you stopped." She tapped the end of the cigarette against her wrist. "You'd opened up to the point where you started to take some chances and put yourself first. But you were only halfway there, Rachel. The place where you stopped wasn't where you were meant to end up. You went from being a mouse to a lion. If you'd kept going, I'm sure you would have found your place somewhere in between the two. Somewhere less deliberate. Less . . . calculated. Where you weren't always *reacting* to something, or someone. But you *stopped*."

"What are you talking about?" Rachel didn't know how much more of this she could take. "You sound like a goddamned shrink. I know I tried too hard when I was a kid. You think I don't know that? I know I was naïve. Jesus, Angela, I'm not stupid." She thought of Rusty somewhere down the hall, what it had done to him to lose his father. What surviving Mary Beth would do to him now. "Everybody reacts to everything," she said. "Everybody. Including me. Christ, look at Joe. How come you're not having this little talk with him?" Rachel waited for Angela to pick up this new thread. Follow this new road. But she didn't. So Rachel continued on down the one she knew best. "Everybody changes as they grow up. Which is all I did. What's wrong with that? Why try so hard to be . . . to live up to everyone's expectations when nothing around me came close to living up to mine? Except Belle Haven. That was the only thing that didn't let

me down. I don't know what I would have done if I hadn't been able
to come home after everything went so wrong."

"You would have gone on!" Angela cried, holding out her arms
and letting them fall at her sides. "You would have survived. That's
what people *do*." She almost said, "That's what *I* did." But this wasn't
about her.

"I did go on. I'm here, aren't I?"

"Yeah, you're here all right. But you're not telling the whole story,
Rachel. *Why* are you still here? That's what I don't understand."

Rachel felt like she was hearing an echo of herself asking Joe the
same question so many months earlier.

"Fine. Then you tell me where I should have gone. According to
you, I've still got a long way to go before I'm entitled to make up my
own mind about where and how I live. I've got to finish *blooming* first.
So tell me. Where should I have gone? Where should I go now?"

"Shit, Rachel, I don't know. I'm not saying you should do what I or
anyone else thinks you should do. That's what got you in this mess in
the first place." She pressed the heel of her hand against her forehead.
"I know this is going to sound terrible, and I'm not sure I ought to be
saying it, but even though your parents dying was a horrible thing,
and it wasn't something you would ever have asked for, it gave you a
freedom that you really *needed*. You—"

"Jesus God, Angela!" Rachel flinched as if she'd been singed. "My
parents were everything to me. You think their death was something
I should be thankful for?"

"No, Rachel, of course I don't. But I don't think it was something
you should feel guilty about either."

"I don't feel guilty about it!"

"Then why, when you were finally coming into your own, did you
quit school and come back home instead? Why haven't you ever
taken advantage of your freedom, whether you asked for it or not?
Why are you acting now like it's your duty to stay where you are,
even if it means risking everything else, including Joe, including
Rusty—" She bit her lip. Rachel had not asked them to stay in Belle
Haven. It wasn't her fault that Rusty had nearly died. "I'm sorry," she
said. "You weren't the one who risked Rusty by staying here. I was."

But Rachel knew she had played a part. She began to weep. Her
tears mixed with the ash on her face. Her hands left black smudges
across her cheeks. "I'm so confused, Angela. I miss them so much."

"I know, baby. I know." She stroked Rachel's hair away from her face. "You don't want to leave them, do you?"

Rachel pictured her parents' ashes dissolving in the water of the creek. She told Angela that she had not buried them in Belle Haven after all.

"Then what is it?"

"What is what?"

"What is so important that you can't leave it behind?"

Rachel grabbed her head in both hands. "I don't know. I wish I did, but I don't." She dropped her hands. There was a streak of dried blood on one of her palms. She closed her eyes. "Joe said something to me once. He said it wasn't the *place* that was important but what it meant to us. He said we should be able to take with us whatever mattered most about the places we loved." She opened her eyes. "And that makes sense to me. It really does. But if that's true, why am I so afraid to leave?"

Angela looked at Rachel and, for the first time since her son had gone nearly to his death, began to cry.

"Maybe because by staying here you've been honoring your parents, immortalizing them, insisting that your life here with them was always perfect. Somewhere along the way, you've convinced yourself that running away from Belle Haven means confessing to all the people you love, and who love you, and who have known you since you were a child that you might have been far happier somewhere else."

When the doctor called to her, Angela ran down the hall and into the room where they were dressing Rusty's burns. For the rest of her life, Rachel would wish that she had not followed. But she did, for staying alone in the too bright hallway that still rang with Angela's words seemed worse by far.

"It was so terrible. So terrible," Rusty was saying when Rachel walked into the room. Angela was leaning over the table where he lay, stroking the hair away from his face. "I was hanging on to some tree roots. There's a great big oak right there where we went through. I was hanging on to those roots with my face pressed into a hollow spot between them, and the dirt was coming down over my head and it was awfully hot and all I could hear was a sound like the wind howling down below me and there was screaming from up above.

And it all happened so fast that at first I didn't realize that something was hanging on to my leg, and then I could feel that it was Mary Beth. I could feel her hands slipping down my leg and grabbing at my shoe. And I was trying to pull us up out of the hole. And then somebody grabbed my wrist and I thought I was going to be torn in half." He stopped and opened his eyes, turned to look at his mother. "And then she let go of my foot and I started to come up out of the hole. I could feel the dirt sucking down under my feet as she let go and slipped away. Do you think she was dead already?"

Angela thought for a moment that he sounded like a much younger boy asking the kind of impossible question that little children always ask. Why is the sky blue? What am I going to be like when I grow up? Did you know that some people get old and die?

"I'm sure that she was, Rusty," was all she said, laying her fingers on his lips.

But Rachel was not so sure.

She was still thinking pretty clearly when she left the room, remembered to call Ed Zingham to come over to the hospital to drive Angela and Rusty home, her truck too small to give Rusty room to lie down. But as she pulled up alongside her house, she realized that she could not remember driving home, not at all. When she took her hands off the wheel, they began to shake, and her legs, when she put her feet down on the ground, nearly gave way.

The sight of her house in the evening sunlight sickened her, hurt her eyes, so she walked around it and through her backyard, straight into the woods and up the gently sloping hill toward the tree house.

Joe was sitting on the little deck, his legs hanging over the edge, carving a small nugget of wood, when Rachel came out of the trees into the clearing below with signs of fire on her face and hands.

She opened her mouth, and a croupy sound came out, as if she had swallowed acid. She tried again but managed only a louder sound, much the same, and Joe dropped the knife in his hand, let the half-done swallow fall into the leaves below, nearly falling out of the tree himself in his haste to reach her.

She could not climb to the tree house, so he gentled her down to the leaves and sat down beside her, cradling her in his arms, holding her head tight against the side of his neck. Her whole body was limp and cold, though he could feel her shake minutely with every breath, and her fingers sometimes jerked as if she had fallen into an unsettled sleep.

Something terrible had happened. When Rachel finally managed to say a word, it was "Rusty," and Joe's arms tightened around her so she could barely breathe. "He's all right," she managed, realizing she had to tell him now, as quickly as possible, what had happened.

When she had finished, Joe stood up and began to walk around the clearing, panting. Then he took her by her hands and pulled her to her feet.

"Do I have to say it?" he asked her.

"No," she said. "I'm leaving." She picked a leaf off her sleeve. "Maybe I'll be able to come back someday. Maybe they'll find an excuse to tear my house down, even if I don't sell it to them, since I won't. I won't do that. But it will be my land still, and maybe, up here on the hill, the house will be all right after all."

That she could be thinking about a house now, when Mary Beth Sanderson was somewhere down below their feet, made Joe sadder than nearly anything she'd ever done. But when he looked into her eyes, he realized that although she was talking about her house, saying the words that he was hearing, she was not thinking about what she would take with her or when she might return. She was thinking about the feel of a hand on her ankle and the feeling as that hand let go. She felt, in her mouth, in her nose, packed against the fragile globes of her opened eyes, the hot, gritty dirt that had claimed Mary Beth and carried her away.

"Say it," he said through his teeth, prodding her as if she had a boil that needed lancing.

"Say what?" she moaned.

"Say it!" he yelled.

She beat her hands against her hips. "All right!" she wailed. "Rusty wouldn't still be here, except for me. There's no other reason. Just that: because I'm still here. And if he hadn't been here, and been with Mary Beth . . . if he hadn't thrown a ball right to that exact spot, they might all have gotten out of here. And Mary Beth wouldn't be dead. But she's dead. She was only a little girl, and she's dead for no good reason."

Joe could barely understand her, but he knew better than anyone what she was saying.

"Everyone in this town is a part of your life," he said. "And in some way, even some very small way, you are involved when they die."

She looked up at him, remembering. "Maybe that's been true until now," she said. "But not anymore. Not like this. I can't live this way. Nobody ought to live this way."

When they got to Rachel's house, their arms full of whatever they thought Rusty would have wanted them to take from the tree house and the small wooden trunk that Joe could not bring himself to leave behind, they found Ed Zingham sitting on a stump in the backyard, waiting for them.

"Angela and Rusty are inside the house," he said. "I'm going to take them up to the farm as soon as Angela gets their stuff together. While I'm there I thought I might have a look at that spare house, if that's all right with you, Joe."

"Good," Joe said. "I was hoping you would. Here." He reached into his pocket and handed Ed a key ring. "It's yours if you want it. Let me know what you decide."

Ed looked at the key in his palm. "Mendelson was here a couple of minutes ago," he said. "Seems he arrived over at the Sandersons' just after you left there, Rachel. Took in that machine they use when they're probing. Turns out the hole goes down about three hundred feet, registered three hundred fifty degrees, eleven hundred parts per million carbon monoxide. He thought Rusty might want to know what he'd survived." He looked up. "But I wouldn't let him near the boy."

"That's good, Ed." Joe opened the back door. "Let's go inside, give Angela a hand."

When Joe saw Angela, he pulled her close to him and held her head against his shoulder. He wondered, not for the first time, why it was Rachel he loved so completely and not Angela. But then she stepped out of his arms and led him to the couch where Rusty lay wrapped in a clean sheet, his scorched face glazed with tears. And it was then that Joe realized for the first time, as he bent down and gently traced the perfect slope of Rusty's pale ear, that the boy was far more a brother to him than a son.

"Joe," Rusty croaked, struggling to open his eyes as if they'd been fused. "I was dreaming that I couldn't find you. You weren't anywhere I looked."

"I'm where you're looking now," Joe said. And in an instant Rusty was asleep again.

It didn't take long for them to get Angela and Rusty packed up and into Ed's car. Rusty lay on the backseat, wrapped carefully and propped like a newborn, his face turned against a pillow. Angela sat in the front with Ed looking straight ahead. Since the hospital she had not said a word to Rachel, but just as Ed was about to drive away, she thrust her arm out through the car window and grabbed Rachel's hand. "Don't you dare fuck around here anymore," she said fiercely. "Belle Haven's gone. Don't you go down with it."

And then she let go of Rachel's hand and Ed drove away, down the hill, and north.

Chapter 49

Even though she could no longer hear Ed's car, Rachel did not move. She felt completely unable to lift her feet, saw no reason to do anything but stand where she was, even if it began to rain, even if snakes began to slide up out of the dirt, the ground too hot even for them.

She expected Joe to put his arm around her, lead her inside, fix her something to eat, and perhaps, by and by, make another of his passionate speeches. She wondered what she would say to him in reply.

Instead, he said, "Let's go," tiredly, and began to walk down the hill.

She watched him for a moment and then said, not really caring if he heard her, "Where are you going?"

"I'm going down to Mary Beth's house. Would you rather stay here?"

She was appalled that he had thought to go there, that she had not. "Of course not," she said. "Of course I'm coming."

They walked down the hill together, across Maple Street, along a dirt-and-gravel lane that followed the course of the nearby creek, until they could see, up ahead, the house where Mary Beth had lived. There were several cars parked along the grassy edge of the lane. They heard the sound of a machine, tasted dust in the air.

Rachel grabbed Joe's sleeve. "I can't," she whispered, her hand at her mouth. She pulled him off the lane and into the shelter of the trees, and they stood there together, looking at the house. "I can't go in there. I just can't."

"Wait here, then," Joe said, taking her hand off his sleeve. "Or go on back home. It's all right. I'll tell them to call you if they need anything."

But when he started again toward the house, Rachel followed.

The front door was open, but no one answered their knock.

"Daniel?" Rachel called.

A man in jeans and a plaid shirt came down the hallway toward the door.

"Daniel," Rachel said through the screen. "We wanted to know if we could do anything."

"Hello, Rachel," Daniel said, opening the door, "Joe." He stepped out into the yard. "Judy's at the hospital." He did not stand still in one place, kept walking around, stopping, walking back to where he'd been. "She went into labor about an hour ago."

"Oh, God, Daniel."

"Yeah. She wants to die."

Rachel pictured her in a white room, white bed, somewhere close to where Rusty had been lying when they cleaned his filthy burns.

Joe said, "Do you want us to watch the kids so you can go be with her?"

"No, the kids are at my mother's in Randall. They don't even know what's happened yet. They think we're just moving a few days early." He looked around suddenly, as if startled to find himself standing in his own front yard, the light nearly gone now, the air cold. "We were going to leave on Tuesday," he said. He stopped and stared at them. Rachel had never seen such disbelief as she saw on his face.

"Judy's water broke right after we got to my mother's. I took her straight to the hospital, and I'm going straight back as soon as I get her things."

"She wasn't due for a while yet, was she?"

"Not for another three weeks, but the doctor says the baby'll be fine. Listen," he said, glancing back toward the door. "You really shouldn't be here. Mendelson told me to get going as soon as possible and to stay clear until they can take some more readings, see what's going on down"—he made a vague motion toward the ground. And then suddenly he closed his eyes, began to tremble all over. His suffering escalated quickly, violently, as if he had swallowed a lazy poison and was only now beginning, himself, to die.

"She was just a baby," he groaned, putting his hands over his face. "She was just my baby. Oh, God—" He wailed and ran away from them, into his house. And neither of them ever saw him again.

Chapter 50

As much as Joe wanted Rachel away from Belle Haven, as much as he was now eager to leave himself, even he could see that she would need a day or two, perhaps as much as a week, to make everything ready.

In some ways, he considered himself lucky to have lost his possessions and was glad that the things he valued fit easily into his pockets: a pocketknife, an opal, the key to the Schooner. But, given enough warning, he would have spent some time sorting through his meager belongings and putting the most important out of harm's way. His carving tools. His books. He would have saved everything in the Schooner if he could have. He would have saved Pal.

When he thought about it, which he often did, he admitted to himself that he'd had plenty of warning. He knew that he had made a choice: to stay a while longer with Rachel, at great risk. He was afraid that if she, too, ignored the warnings she'd been given—for another day, another hour—she might have more to regret than she already did.

But he was not so arrogant or so stupid as to condemn Rachel for her attachments. He knew that she would need some time to sort through her belongings and sever her ties. He thought that if he stayed with her, he could help her in some way. And so, when she asked him to stay with her, he did.

He was glad of the chance to use her shower, for the stream had made a cold, cold bath. He washed his sorry clothes, pared his fingernails, enjoyed the feel of a cushion at his back. He made her a good meal that first night after Angela and Rusty had left, but they ate it without exchanging a word. He had grown accustomed to the silence of solitude, of the woods, and she was far too preoccupied for talk.

Later, in her bed, they fell almost immediately to sleep, and it was only when they awoke in the early morning that they looked at each other and realized what they were facing.

"I'm going to miss you," she whispered, opening her arms.

And he suddenly found himself wishing, as Rachel always had, that somehow they could stay.

After that first night back in the house together, Joe slept on the couch and Rachel alone in her bed.

As she packed her belongings into boxes, took the pictures from her walls, dismantled the place she had built around herself and prepared to emerge undefended, she spoke less and less often, almost never smiled, and didn't laugh at all.

More than at any time since she'd emptied their ashes into the creek, Rachel was making peace with her parents and with herself, yet trying to understand why this was necessary when there had never been a single open battle between them.

Perhaps if there had been, things would have turned out better.

Since that horrible day in the hospital, she had been wondering if maybe Angela was right. She had always felt guilty about her parents' death, but she had never looked beyond the simple explanation that they had died while doing something for *her* sake.

Now she looked further.

She realized that whenever she thought about her parents' death, she also remembered sitting on a beach, immersed in disappointment, letting the wind and the spray scour her clean. She realized that if her parents had not been killed, she would have gotten over her small disappointments. Learned from her mistakes. Chosen a different course from the one she was on. She would have come to the conclusion that making decisions that were best for her did not mean defying her parents. She would have stopped putting herself in their shoes and found ones that fit her best.

But they *had* been killed.

She had been given complete control over her life, the freedom and the money to explore as she had made up her mind to do. Instead, she had quit school and returned to Belle Haven. It had never occurred to her to take advantage of her independence, as if it were a windfall.

Maybe Angela was right. Maybe all her choices were rooted in the guilt she felt: for wanting something different from what her parents could give her, and for surviving them.

Maybe not.

She was still too confused to be sure why she felt as she did. But looking honestly at herself had turned her attention from Belle Haven. It had loosened her hold on the town, and its on her. She was sorry to be going, and she knew she would miss it terribly, but she was finally ready to go. It felt right, in her belly, for the first time. For once, the arguments she fought inside her head ended with an admission that it was time to move on.

She would grit her teeth and say her prayers and go exploring. Maybe she would find a place where she could be happy.

The sight of Joe, lying in her hammock, made her wonder if such a place could exist without him in it.

Watching her, knowing that she was far away in a place of her own, Joe stayed nearby in case she needed him, but he did not approach her. He read a book from her library, napped in the cool sunshine, and stayed gratefully up on her hill.

When she was nearly through packing, had rolled her carpets, folded her drapes and quilts into bags, he drove with her to the lumberyard and brought back a stack of plywood for her windows.

"I guess there isn't much left to be done," she said as they carried the wood up onto her porch.

"Not much," he said.

"I've arranged for a moving van to come collect everything and put it into storage. I won't be taking all that much with me. I won't really need much, I guess."

She sat down on the porch steps and held out her hand to him, but when he sat down beside her she did not look at him. She said, "I have a favor to ask you." He waited, giving her time. Finally, he said, "You can ask me anything, Rachel. I won't be angry."

She looked at him. "It's a stupid thing, but it's what I want."

"What is it?" he asked.

"I want to stay until Halloween," she said. "That's just two days away. And then we'll need a third to board up the house. I can't live in it boarded up, so we'll have to wait until the day we're leaving. Three more days is what I'm asking."

There had been a time, before the fire had arrived, before people had begun to leave, when Rachel had held a strange sort of influence over her neighbors. Perhaps they looked at her, a young woman living alone, and thought that if she could stay and face the music, so could they. Or perhaps she reminded them of better days. Or perhaps they were so torn that they found it easier to follow her lead than to go their own ways. But these were the same people who had finally left or were now all set to go. The ones who were still determined to stay took no notice of Rachel. They, far more than she, had fought the fire—the idea of it, the threat of it—right from the start. Even when their monitors began to shriek and their basements to smoke, these people would fight. Some were fighting already, tooth and nail. But Rachel was no longer a part of that.

There was no one left in town who would be swayed, one way or the other, by the actions of a single young woman who kept, as much as she could, to herself.

"Fine," Joe said, longing to leave. "Three days is fine. As long as you promise me you'll be careful Halloween night. Stay up here and . . . hand out treats."

"Well, then I might as well go right now," she said, shaking her head. "No, I'm going down to the park and I'm going to sit in my tree, one more time. There aren't too many kids left in this town, but they'll be looking for me. I won't disappoint them."

"You mean you won't disappoint yourself." He snorted, partly amused, mostly weary. "I've said it before and I'll say it again, Rachel Hearn. You are the most stubborn woman I've ever met. But I'll stay here with you for three more days. I'll even be the goddamned troll, if you'll scare up a costume for me. And, come to think of it," he said, musing, "I'll like staying in the tree house for another night or two. The last night or two, at least for a good long while. And," he said slowly, "maybe I should board up the tree house, too, just in case."

She smiled at him, not too proud to accept these other small favors he had chosen to grant her.

"I don't know how I'm going to live without you," she said, leaning into him, forgetting for a moment the house at her back, the land under her feet, and everything, everything else but him.

"I don't know how you can live otherwise," he said, for he knew that instinct and wisdom sometimes met, sometimes made a place as unanchored as the horizon, as the junction of sea and sky, and that Rachel had found this place, as he had, one mild, invigorating season a million years ago.

Chapter 51

As Rachel walked through her last days in Belle Haven, her hands busy, dismantling her home, it was not only her parents who occupied her mind. It was also the constant, lethal image of Mary Beth Sanderson baking underground. Like the foreign, threadlike matter that sometimes swims a lazy course across the eye, a terrible image of the dead girl crept without warning across Rachel's vision, again and again, throughout those long, last days.

At night she dreamed about Mary Beth and Rusty sinking through the dirt. Awakened, she considered the course of events that might have been: if she, herself, had chosen to leave Belle Haven earlier; if Angela had not stayed on to try and make her leave; if Angela had taken Rusty north and Mary Beth, without him, had not stumbled onto the spot that killed her. *What if, what if, what if* sounded the nightly litany. Desperate for reprieve, she told herself again and again what she had once told Joe, about Holly, and what he had said to her, only days before: that she had been involved in Rusty's life and therefore, nearly, in his death. But the notion did not soothe her, for she remembered, too, what she had told him about the importance of his motives, how they absolved him of any guilt. Remembering this, she could not escape the fact that her own motives offered no such absolution. She had stayed in Belle Haven for her own sake. To postpone the hard task of taking back her life. And in part because of this, Mary Beth had lost hers.

Rachel waited, through those last days, for some sort of peace to descend. She waited for a pardon. When she sensed the image of Mary Beth fading a little, she thought that the beginning of forgiveness had come. But while the torment that spoiled her waking hours abated, it divided and multiplied in her dreams as if it had a life of its own.

As Mary Beth let go of Rusty's foot, the dirt parted beneath her and she slid down through it. It closed above her head as she passed. The hole was not like a tunnel, open, stable. It was simply a soft vein of earth. It was very, very hot in the hole, but Mary Beth could no longer feel the heat. There was only stale, exhausted air in her lungs. There was an impossible interval between the last beats of her stubborn heart. She was dying quickly.

Far below the surface of the earth, Mary Beth died, but her body kept moving. It slid faster and faster now, the earth slick and fire-hot. When she hit the deep bed of red coals, it consumed her. Her body moved the way a leaf turns and struggles as it burns. And then, as her body was reduced to its most resilient elements, it flared suddenly as if the fire had finally reached her volatile core and a blast of flame shot back upward. It split the dirt, erupted through the surface where Rachel stood, looking for signs of life, and caught her full in the face. It cauterized her eyes, bloodied her skin, consumed every hair on her head as if it were a fragile wick. But the fire did not knock her back. It spun her around and wrapped her up, drew her toward the hole and then down into it, down through the dirt, back down to the deep fire and the remnants of Mary Beth Sanderson. Only then did it let her go.

Rachel did not awaken herself from the dream. Her instinct for self-preservation was no longer any match for her regret. She permitted the dream to run its course. Then she crawled out of her bed and made her way from the house to the old apple tree where she had meant her parents to be interred. Finally, everything awful had come to pass. Finally, she said, "I am resigned."

Chapter 52

Rachel was cold. The huge willow had shed its leaves and gave her no protection. She sat in it and looked out through the thin branches that hung down all around her, nearly trailing on the ground. She felt like a bird in a cage.

Children were coming: ghosts, fairies, monsters. As they edged closer to the willow, she cackled and they jumped. "I'll eat you up, my little pretties," she said, showering them with licorice whips and sour balls.

She had thought this would be good for her, to sit in this tree and remember. She had hoped it would tie things off, heal her up, and send her away unencumbered. But, sitting in the tree, cold and very much alone, she realized that her departure had already begun and that she was impatient for its conclusion.

She climbed carefully out of the tree, snagging her witch's dress, and began to walk back through town toward her hill. She walked past all the empty lots, past the boreholes, past Angela's and Earl's, past the place where the Schooner had gone down and Pal had died, toward the bridge where Joe was patiently waiting for her to be done.

Chapter 53

Rachel Elizabeth Hearn, who had always wanted to be called Suzanne, after her mother, and who loved her own eyes, which were her father's, and who had made up her mind to save the money they'd left her so that she could someday, maybe, buy back some of the town she was leaving, looked down from her hill and knew that she would never come back here again.

"I want to leave now, quickly," she said to Joe, taking the hammer out of his hand and throwing it into the back of her truck. It was hard for her to climb into the cab without looking back at her house, but when they had nailed up the last board she had turned her back, walked away carefully, had not once looked at the house and would not look at it now.

"Would you go back and lock the front door for me?" she asked from behind the wheel, holding the key out through the window.

So Joe went back to lock the front door, then climbed into the truck with her. As she drove down the hill, faster than she should, tears dripping off her jaw, Joe put the key into her purse. Then he reached into his pocket and took out the opal he'd been carrying with him for more than three years now. He held it low in his palm, looking at it, turning it slowly so that it flickered, and then put it, too, into her small bag.

When they reached the farm, Rachel helped him carry his things through the woods to his cabin. He didn't have much. Only a few things that people had given him as they'd left town for good. Bits of wood for him to carve. Bits of Belle Haven.

"This is a wonderful cabin," Rachel said, standing just inside the door. He had furnished it with simple, comfortable things. The floor was bare, the walls plain.

"I only spent a couple of nights here," he said, "when I was up checking on how the houses were coming along." He put down the things he was holding. "It belonged to one of the horse trainers," he said, realizing suddenly that he'd told her this before. "The main farmhouse is on past where the lane turns off to come into these woods, over a rise and out of sight. The people who raised horses here still live there. They wanted to sell everything except the house and a couple of acres that it sits on. Didn't think they'd ever find a buyer who would agree to let them stay. But I didn't mind."

He realized that he was talking but not really saying anything, so he took the things out of her arms and put them aside. "Do you want to see the place I had chosen for you?" he asked.

They walked back through the woods to the lane and along it, around a bend to where it ended in grass, then beyond that and across a small meadow surrounded by trees. Along the far edge of the meadow there was a narrow stream. The trees were brilliant, the grass still very green.

"And if I came back here someday, would it still be here, just like this?"

He looked straight at her. "You ask a lot," he said.

"You seem to have a lot to give," she replied.

"It will still be here. But don't ever make me a promise you can't keep."

Afterward, they went to say good-bye to Angela and Rusty, Dolly, Earl, everyone she could find.

"Do you know where you're going?" he asked when they reached the truck.

"Well, west. That's all I know at the moment. Except that I made myself a promise once, right before my parents died, to go places. I don't know which ones. I suppose I'll know them when I get there."

"I understand, probably better than you think."

He handed her into the truck and kissed her through the window, not wanting to hold her, afraid if he did he would not be able to let her go.

San Francisco   *January 14*

Dear Kit,

Having you with me for Christmas was wonderful. Much nicer
than that August, really, when we were both in pretty bad shape.
I only wish you could have stayed longer. But, as it turns out, you
left just in time. Rachel arrived here the very next day.

   I didn't know she was coming. She just knocked on my door
that morning, explained who she was, and said she really just
wanted to meet me. She was on her way to Mendocino.

   I gave her some lunch and asked her to stay for a day or two.
She stayed for a week. We talked a lot about you, a lot about all
of us, really. She told me so many things about you that I didn't
know. I felt as if we were talking about two different people.

   I'm afraid I can't tell you what her plans are . . . and I will
let her be the one to tell you, when she's ready, about the turns her
life has taken. But I can assure you that she is all right, she is
taking good care of herself, and she is doing all the sorts of things
that I would be doing if I were her.

   She spent Thanksgiving in Albuquerque, Christmas on the
Baja, New Year's in Carmel. She doesn't know where she'll go
after Mendocino, but she probably won't go on to Alaska as she
had thought she might. She's afraid of bears, she said.

   I took her over to a shop in Sausalito to look at paintings and
pots and other artsy stuff. All very nice. We walked in, she looked
around, saw a shelf on the wall fifteen feet away and knew, immediately, that she was looking at your carvings. It really shook
her when she turned one over and found "Christopher Barrows" on
the bottom. After a while she turned to me and said, "A good way
to make a living."

   The next day, whenever we talked about you, she practiced
calling you Christopher, or Kit, as I still do. But I could tell that
she was having trouble, as if it was unnatural to call you anything but Joe. Of course it would be. At least for a while. I told
her that I thought she should just keep on thinking of you as Joe
and, for that matter, calling you Joe.

   "I don't plan on writing to him or calling him," she said, "so I
guess it's a moot point." She hates writing letters, as you do, and I

think she'd rather not call you because telephones can be such hideous, dangerous devices.

I wasn't going to tell you all this. I was afraid you'd just be miserable, knowing she was here but not knowing where she's gone. But I wanted you to know she is all right. Homesick, perhaps, but on the mend.

Let me know if you hear from her, will you?

Love,
Holly

In early March, Joe opened his door, expecting Rusty, and found a stranger on his doorstep.

"My name is Andrew Harriman," the man said, smiling, handing Joe a business card. "I'm here on behalf of my client, Miss Rachel Hearn. She seems to think that you have a lot for sale, and she would like to buy it."

"A lot? A lot of what?"

Mr. Harriman chuckled. "A lot. A piece of land. A meadow near a stream. She said you would know what I'm talking about." He made it sound like a question.

"Well, I suppose I do," Joe answered slowly. "How much is she offering?"

"That's what I asked her," the man said, passing his hat from one hand to the other. "But she said to name your price."

Joe smiled. Mr. Harriman smiled back. Like all real estate brokers, he worked on commission.

"Please come in, Mr. Harriman. Would you like some coffee? I just made some."

"Well, that would be nice."

Joe brought him a cup of coffee, a pot of sugar, one of cream.

"I'll take a dollar," Joe said, leaning against the wall.

"For the coffee?" Mr. Harriman said. He looked as if he thought he ought to be laughing but wasn't quite sure.

"For the land," Joe said, the hair on his arms standing on end, his chest swollen. "The coffee's on me."

Mr. Harriman wanted to believe that Joe was kidding, but in the end he saw how things were and agreed to handle the sale. "But I'll have to charge you for my time," he said. "You do understand that, don't you? I don't know if you've ever sold any land before, Mr. Barrows—"

"No, I haven't."

". . . but it is incumbent upon the vendor to pay the broker, to pay me."

"Miss Hearn will take care of your fee," Joe said.

"But I just explained—"

"Don't worry about it. She'll be glad to."

Mr. Harriman frowned at Joe. "If you don't have a lawyer, I can recommend one, but you'll have to discuss fees with him directly."

"I have one."

"Then perhaps I should contact Miss Hearn before we discuss this further. In the future, can I reach you by telephone?"

"Of course," Joe said, writing his number on the back of Mr. Harriman's business card. Mr. Harriman gave him a clean one and left.

Well, how do you like them apples? Joe said to himself as he shut the door. He felt as he had that summer night when he'd called Mrs. Corrigan, searching for his sister, thinking that perhaps she was alive after all. He stood in his cabin, on the verge of rejoicing, trying desperately to find a way back toward the calm and reasonable state in which he had been living. But when he suddenly found a way back it displeased him and made him wish that he were a simpler, rasher sort of man.

There was nothing left of Rachel's house when Joe got there. Nothing more than black timbers and the stones of the cellar walls.

"Didn't expect to see you back here again." Mendelson was walking up the drive. "Ever seen a house burned right down to the ground like that?"

"I never have," Joe replied, turning back toward the remains of Rachel's beautiful house. Even the porch steps had burned. There was nothing at all left.

"There have been other fires since you left," Mendelson said. "Down in the town. Nobody hurt, but a few shook up enough to leave, even though they swore they never would. Things would have been a sight worse if we hadn't razed the houses soon as they were abandoned."

"They weren't abandoned."

"Right," Mendelson said, shaking his head.

"So what are you doing up here?"

"I came up to see you, Joe. Actually, I wasn't sure who I'd find here. Didn't recognize the car. Figured I should have a look."

"And why is that?"

"Well, because this fire was set and I've got enough trouble without having a firebug around. Reminds me of the trees got burned out by my place that time."

"This was set?"

"Looks like it."

Joe stayed where he was for a long minute, staring at the last of Rachel's home, then started off toward the woods beyond it.

"So long," he said.

"Uh-huh." Mendelson watched him go, turned, and headed back down the hill.

The tree house was as Joe had left it, boarded up, sturdy and sound. He looked up into the branches of the tree, felt far removed from the charred wreckage of Rachel's house, and breathed the air in deeply. The town below the hill had looked terrible, all torn up, no one on the streets. But the trees here were greening with the spring. There were birds in the branches. He was very sorry that he had come back.

As he was leaving the woods, as he walked past a large pine that grew alongside the trail, Joe saw, in the deep moss beneath the tree, something shining. He knelt down and picked up a key. He held it in his hand for a while, his eyes vacant, and then put it back where he'd found it, but deep in the spongy moss where only someone who was looking for it would find it.

Chapter 54

By April Rachel owned the piece of meadowland that Joe had shown her before she had gone away. By May a small group of capable men had begun to build her a house. Joe often walked down the lane to watch them work, curious to see what she had instructed them to build for her. At first he thought it would be a house like the one she had left in Belle Haven, but this turned out to be a very different sort of house. She had chosen to build it at the top end of the meadow where the land sloped upward toward the sky. It clung to the slope and meandered down it, a low and spreading house, and Joe imagined that the rooms inside would be joined by stairs in couplets and crooked hallways. There were lots of windows, and, in the end, cedar shingles and places where gardens were meant to grow all around. The house reminded Joe of California houses, all wood, mated to the land.

By September the house was finished. Joe spent some time walking around it, picking up stray nails and litter. Then he went home and carried back, pot by pot, the small bits of Belle Haven garden that Rachel had left with him. "Give these last ones to your neighbors," she'd said. "Make sure Angela gets the lilac bush." But he'd done no such thing.

Early one morning he borrowed a shovel from Earl and planted the lilac, the roses, the huckleberries, and the columbine where he thought they'd do well, some of them nestled up alongside the house, some at the edge of the trees where they might strengthen and spread.

Then he walked along where the back of the house nudged the woods. When he found a good, sound tree stump, he laid out the tools he'd brought with him and set to work, left a chipmunk to keep watch.

It was dark by the time Joe finished, so he carried the empty pots home and put them in a shed behind the cabin. And then he waited.

He had, indeed, received no word from Rachel—not a single letter—and was, at first, hurt, angry, dismayed. But then he remembered that he himself had been the one to insist she make no promises she couldn't be sure to keep.

He was glad that he could not write to her. There were things that he wanted to tell her but knew should wait for her return. And there were things he was glad to be keeping from her: that Dolly had died in the spring, that Rusty still woke up screaming as many nights as not, that he himself had begun to feel the urge to start over, somewhere new.

He did not understand his discontent, although he knew how much he missed Rachel and the place where he'd found her. He thought that he had learned how to be alone, unencumbered, settled. He had imagined that leaving Belle Haven, Rachel leaving him, would simply make him stronger. Sadder, perhaps, but stronger. Why then, even in the company of people he loved, even when he was sitting at Angela's table, laughing, playing cards, Rusty learning how to play the guitar, Angela making soup and bread, the lamplight turning the dark windows to mirrors—why, then, did he feel the blood thinning in his veins?

It had become Joe's custom, on fair evenings, to sit in the clearing outside his cabin door and watch the day go down, listen to the dwindling noises of the birds and the crescendo of the sounds that belonged to the night: crickets in brisk chorus, awakening owls, small prowlers, and the like.

One evening, opening his door, Joe was met by the sight of such a glorious sky that he nearly dropped to his knees. The sun had set, but the sky was still light and the thin clouds that stretched out across it were pink, orange, and radiant. There were also thunderheads piled up to the south, and these were, in places, gray as smoke, in others a startling white, and the sky behind them was the deepest possible blue, a nameless color, so beautiful it made his heart ache.

Joe walked farther into the clearing with his head tipped back and looked at the sky, watched the clouds moving across it, and trembled with desire to see it whole, to see the sky unbordered by trees. He hurried along the path and out to the lane, slowed by tree roots, reluctant to lower his eyes, searching for a wider space between the trees. He nearly ran toward Rachel's meadow, but even this broader clearing was not enough. He ran in one direction, then another, but everywhere he turned the trees reached too high. He felt like a lion pacing in a cage. He felt a terrible longing to be lifted straight up into the sky. He heard the thread of a whistle and, turning, saw a formation of ducks flying just above the trees, out across the meadow, black against the sky. To be up there with them, to be unanchored, seemed the greatest thing he could imagine just then. Ian, he thought, must have felt this way: not just once, on a rare September evening, but for all of his life. And to have settled for a life along the land . . . even more, to have found a way to be happy there, seemed to Joe a nearly impossible accomplishment.

He realized, as he stood in the middle of Rachel's meadow, that he missed the hill where she had lived in Belle Haven. There, he had stood so much closer to the sky. But it was only now, having left it, that Joe realized fully what he'd had. What Rachel had had, and what she had relinquished.

He knew, as he walked slowly back through the early darkness, that he would wake up in the morning much as he had been before, loving the land, content with the anchors he himself had set. But he had begun to fear that these sudden bouts of discontent would continue to tug at him, to drag him from his mooring, until he foundered. He wondered if he would ever find, as Ian had, an anchor that he could truly embrace, that he had not only set but forged, and that would not give way.

Joe got his answer one mild October day when the breeze sounded like song and the ground smelled like the ages. He was outside in front of his cabin, sitting on a stump, working a piece of stubborn wood, when he heard someone driving down the lane. He heard the sound of one door slam, then, after a moment, a second. He began to breathe again. He turned back to the wood in his hands. And then there was the sound of footsteps on the path, disturbing the leaves, of someone laughing, and of someone crying.

When he looked up and saw Rachel coming toward him, her hair loose, he thought that he might die. He saw, as she came closer, that she wore the opal around her neck and carried in her arms, as she walked, laughing, a baby who was crying louder than thunder. It was waving its small arms up toward Rachel's face, its fisted hands like the buds of new leaves, miraculous.

He did not need to think about this, in truth had no chance to temper his immediate, organic reflex toward the two of them coming through the trees. His hands emptied themselves. His eyes shed their film and saw, as long before, all the colors of the world, undiluted. He tasted his own blood, inside his speechless tongue. Then, moving toward them, his muscles clumsy with impatience, he, too, began to laugh, and to holler, and to say, without a moment's consideration but with considerable surprise, "I always hoped it would be this way."

And in the timbre of her laughter, and in the character of his own, he suddenly heard the echo of his mother's lingering joy and in the air smelled a trace of oranges where there had been none before.

About the Author

LAUREN WOLK was born in Baltimore and has since lived in California, Rhode Island, Minnesota, Canada, and Ohio. She now lives with her husband and their sons, Ryland and Cameron, on Cape Cod, where she is at work on her second novel.

After graduating from Brown University in 1981, Wolk worked as a writer with the Battered Women's Project of the St. Paul American Indian Center. She later moved to Toronto, where she was a senior editor with Nelson Canada. Since the birth of her first son, Wolk has been a freelance writer and editor. She is also a contributing editor for *OWL*, an award-winning children's magazine.

About the Type

This book was set in Garamond, a typeface designed by the French printer Jean Jannon. It is styled after Garamond's original models. The face is dignified, and is light but without fragile lines. The italic is modeled after a font of Granjon, which was probably cut in the middle of the sixteenth century.

Printed in the United States
by Baker & Taylor Publisher Services